INTO AFRICA

By

William J. Millman

SB

Sunset Beach Press

SB

Sunset Beach Press

Copyright © 2014 by William J. Millman

Manufactured in the United States of America

Cover photos: Morguefile, Akurra/Pond5.com

ISBN: 978-0985791889

For My Friends in Nigeria
and All Around the World

CHAPTER ONE

The cry of a distant bird drifted on the cool night breeze as the door slid slowly open. From inside the old Union Pacific boxcar a cautious face surveyed the empty rail yard. The nervous young man had every reason to be cautious: a quarter moon threw off just enough light to cause him trouble. Despite what most people thought, getting out of a boxcar was nearly as dangerous as getting in. Hopping a moving train took guts, true enough, but getting out of a planted car, in the hovering silence of an abandoned siding, with track slime swarming on any sound, weighted nightsticks held tightly in their fists, steel-toed boots crushing the gravel underfoot, their cold grey eyes scanning the cars for any sign, any sound, ready to move...

"Damn it! I gotta knock that shit off," he mumbled to himself, crouched in the dim shadows of the freight car, shaking his head to drive the image from his brain. He'd hopped enough trains to know what he had to do. Dreaming up unseen demons wouldn't make it any easier. 'Don't die before they kill you,' some officer had told his worried recruits before some battle somewhere. That went for 'boes too. But after 36 hours on the bum it wasn't easy to keep a clear head. The click-clack rhythm of the rails still pounded all the way through to his toes, his heart pulsing with the same hypnotic resonance of steel wheels racing across the open prairie. He took a deep breath and hefted a stained green duffle bag to his shoulder. "Let's do it."

If there had been anyone there to see, they would have seen a tall, well-proportioned 'bo, not yet thirty, with his long brown hair pulled back tight into a ponytail and his denim jacket rolled up to the elbows, jump from the car and nearly stumble to his knees. His pointy-toed cowboy boots, worn rough at the heels and toe, dug into the gravel in the yard and nearly threw him down under the weight of his load. But he caught himself and, shifting the bag to his right shoulder, walked casually out from between the cars with just a passing glance at the lurking shadows that signified nothing and concealed no one.

An involuntary sigh escaped tight-pressed lips as he slid silently into the brush at the edge of the rail yard. Even though he'd been travelling for nearly four months he still couldn't move through a yard without painful memories of his first attempt, memories that grabbed at his throat and twisted the muscles in the back of his neck. It had been just south of Chicago, about this time of night. He had just bummed down from Ann Arbor, a free man setting off to discover America. Chicago was the gateway, the open door to the West and to an entire unexplored continent. Oh, he'd visited New York, Chicago, even Miami. But that wasn't America. That was post-modern high-density urbanized madness. He'd come in search of the real America, the unspoiled heartland and the golden coast, the green grass and amber waves that cut across the backbone of the country and bound sea to shining sea. Of honest men and chaste women, smiling carefree children and well-groomed pets. And most of all, he came in search of himself. Of an identity that had been torn from its moorings, set adrift in a place called here, a time called now.

He hadn't taken two steps when the frenzied bark of pursuing dogs echoed through the cave-empty cars. Against all logic he stopped, froze for just an instant in disbelief, until, convinced at last of the danger approaching, he forced his legs to action and sprinted numbly across the open rail yard. With the snarling sounds of pursuit reverberating in his ears he made straight for the nearest cover, a thick tangle of bushes not fifty feet ahead. But even that was too far. With each step the dogs closed the gap between them, bounding ever nearer until he could hear their hungry gasps just seconds behind. Just a few feet more...

The first dog reached him a scant yard from the bushes. He felt the jaws close on his ankle and kicked hard to shake free. In another instant he would have been clear, but a jagged tooth caught on his trouser leg and held tight. He whirled to counterattack but the second animal was already on him, leaping up at his chest with a blind fury that shocked him and a ferocious momentum that nearly knocked him down. He blocked the charge with his arm, but the dog took hold of his jacket sleeve and pulled as if to tear the arm from its socket. Entrapped in a pulsating web of fear and rage, the stunned traveler struggled to keep the dogs at bay. The attack seemed to stretch on interminably, each small ebb and flow magnified to absurdity. As if standing outside himself, he saw the struggle in a cool, detached vision and realized that he would soon go down under the determined attack. Strangely, the realization was somehow reassuring, almost as if the elimination of uncertainty was more important than survival. He closed his eyes and tried to brace for the final onslaught.

But even as he steeled himself a sharp whistle pierced the cool night air. Suddenly the maddened fury stopped, and in an instant there was quiet once more. Slowly, cautiously, he lowered his crossed arms from in front of his face.

The dogs turned away from him, their tails wagging obediently. It was as if he wasn't even there. For just a moment he thought he might yet escape. But the instant of optimism was shattered by the sight of an all-too-familiar figure waddling slowly into view: track slime. A fat, beer-belly shaking, flashlight toting, two-day-beard bull.

"You forgot to get your ticket stamped," the rail guard jibed sarcastically. "And that makes me mad."

"Hey, look, I don't want any trouble…" were the only words he could get out of his mouth before the first blow crashed down against his left arm. He wanted to argue, to explain the culture, the proud American tradition of riding the rails. He wanted to share his dream: discover yourself while discovering America. But he knew it was senseless. The track slime wouldn't listen, wouldn't understand. Probably couldn't. And so he pulled back inside himself and let the heavy four-cell Eveready crash down on him like waves breaking against the shore. One, two, three, four…the blows fell until he no longer felt the pain, just the click-clack rhythm of metal and plastic against skin and bone. As the blows began to slow, he started to think he might ride it out without more than just a few bumps and bruises to show for his troubles when the edge of the flashlight caught him flush on the side of his temple; he collapsed into unconsciousness.

When he awoke, he was alone with his pain. He performed a quick triage to see if anything was broken, but only his head hurt bad enough to cause real worry. He knew that with time the bruises would heal, the bones mend. It might take a few days, maybe even a couple of weeks, but he would survive. The edges of his dream might be tattered, but its heart remained strong. Setbacks were inevitable. He would persevere.

This night would not be so difficult. Once in the bushes it was almost easy. The knots in his neck and stomach slowly melted away as he wandered down a gentle slope into a natural bowl a few hundred feet from the rail yard. The charred remains of countless campfires identified the spot as a safe haven for railbirds. He scouted the perimeter of the bowl looking for firewood, or anything else that might come in handy during his brief stay. A few pieces of deadwood, an old coffee can, several broken wine bottles, their cheap dreams drained and smashed. It was a wanderers' camp all right.

He piled the few dried sticks in a rough teepee and pulled some matches out of his knapsack. The flame sputtered and flared, a brilliant grounded star in the pitch darkness of the cool autumn night. It took only seconds for the flames to glide across the surface of the wood, crackling pops echoing in the silent blackness. He opened a can of beans and positioned them carefully at the perimeter of the flames. Experience had taught him that slow cooking brought the best results, impatience only burnt offerings and an empty belly.

He laid out his sleeping bag and pulled a cigarette from the pack. It was funny, really. He seldom smoked back in the real world, but out here he couldn't resist. One before dinner and one after. Hardly a serious addiction, but an addiction nonetheless. Someday he'd have to examine why, but not here, not now.

The smell of the beans brought his stomach to life. Over the past few months he had learned the validity of the old truism: everything did taste better cooked outdoors. Of course, being seriously hungry didn't hurt either. And there was virtually never a night he didn't get to suppertime without the empty ache in his belly. He used a thin greenwood stick to maneuver the can out of the flames and plopped down on his sleeping bag to begin the slow savoring of his meager pickings.

But before the spoon ever reached his mouth the rustle of bushes nearby sent him scrambling to his feet, a long hunting knife grasped protectively in his right hand. The rustling stopped.

"All right, I know you're out there. If you're coming in, better do it now!" he shouted into the empty night.

For a long moment there was no response. Then, the rustling in the bushes resumed. He turned to the sound, straining to see beyond the dim circle of light. The sound grew closer, louder. Whoever was out there took no pains to conceal his movement. Finally, a pair of well-worn Reebok pumps, only half-laced, emerged into the light.

"Takes it easy now, brother. No need be flashin' that big ol' sticker."

An old black scarecrow waltzed into the firelight. At least that was the first impression he made. Little more than skin and bones dressed in oversized rags, his ebony black skin shone brightly in the flickering light. A receding hairline salted with grey edged a tight, almost pained expression. The younger man traced his line of sight to the blade held firmly in his hand.

"No offense," he said, holding up the knife, "but you never know who you're going to run into these days." He had already made up his mind that the old man was harmless. A sixth sense he'd developed in his months on the bum. "Come on in. I was just about to have some supper. Care to join me for some beans?"

The scarecrow stood his ground with no reaction.

"I said, do you want some food?" He took a step toward the stranger and the scarecrow skittered back a couple of feet. "I'm not going to hurt you," the young traveler said. "See - no worries." He put the knife away in its sheath. The black man still stood watching. "Are you hard of hearing? Is that it? You want eat?" he said loudly, motioning with his hand to his mouth as if eating. No reaction. "No, huh? Well, how about this. I haven't practiced in years, but I used to be able to make myself understood..." He began to diligently bend and shape his fingers into sign language. "Would...you...like...to...eat?" he mumbled aloud as he signed each word.

The black man shook his head. "You better knock that shit off before you gets cramps in your fingers," he said. "I hears you just fine."

"Then why didn't you answer me?!"

"Everythin' in good time," the old man said. "You never knows who you gonna run into these days."

The younger man smiled. Another of the crazy ones, maybe. "That's what I hear. So - you want some beans?"

"I guess I might be able to eat me some. You got any bread?" The old man dropped a small bundle and stepped toward the campfire. "Ain't nothin in there you'd be interested in," he added. His host quickly turned back toward the fire.

"As a matter of fact I do have some bread," he said. "But I'm afraid I don't have anything to drink except water."

"Water's good. Don't need nuthin' else."

"Fine. Then it looks like we're in good shape...You have a name?"

The old man shook his head in disgust. "Course I has a name. Every creature on this here planet got a name. You think I'm from some other planet or somethin'?"

A smile appeared under the ponytail. "Hard to say. I've never met anyone from another planet."

"Well I ain't."

"Okay then, I guess you've got a name. You going to let me know what it is?"

The old man eyed him suspiciously. "Malcolm," he finally said.

"Malcolm what?"

"Just Malcolm."

"Alright Just Malcolm, pleased to meet you. Some people call me Captain America. You can call me Wyatt." He held out his hand but the old man didn't budge.

"That your name?"

"It is for the time being."

The two men stared at each other for several long seconds, Wyatt's hand dangling between them, demanding attention. Finally Malcolm responded and gave the hand two quick shakes before dropping it like a used paper towel.

"Can't figures white people," he mumbled.

"I know what you mean, Malcolm. We're a confusing race. But we do make good beans. You have a plate?"

"Can's okay."

Wyatt nodded. "A fork?"

"Had a spoon, but lost it."

"Right." Wyatt went to the fire and pulled the can from its resting place at the edge of the flames. He located a plastic plate and camping fork in his knapsack and carefully turned to the task at hand. "Well then, I'll just pour myself a heaping pile of these delicious home cooked baked beans...and here, you can take the rest. Want some bread?"

Malcolm reached into the offered plastic bag and grabbed a fistful. "Helps sop up the sauce."

"I'm afraid you're going to be a little disappointed if you think there's going to be much sauce."

"Gots to be prepared."

"So I've heard. Malcolm, were you a Scout by any chance?"

The old man poured some beans onto a piece of bread, rolled it up into a makeshift soft taco and stuffed the whole thing into his mouth. "Never was in the military," he finally said after a titanic swallow. Followed by another.

Wyatt was mesmerized by the enthusiasm the old man showed for eating. Slice after slice of beans and bread disappeared in a voracious bite or two, until after just a couple of minutes the beans, and most of the bread, were history. The younger man looked down at the steaming pile that still occupied his plate.

"You want some more?"

The old man eyed the beans dispassionately. "You finished?"

Wyatt shrugged. "I might be able to eat a little more, but I'll never finish all this. I mean, I just had a few saltines and a banana not more than five hours ago."

"Eats what you can. I'll finish the rest for you."

"Yeh? Great. Thanks a lot. One thing I hate it's left-over beans. Nowhere to put'em, you know? And they can make a real mess if they get loose in your pack."

The old man nodded slowly. "Same with Spaghetti-o's."

"Exactly."

Wyatt went back to his beans and bread, eating slowly and trying not to stare obsessively at his visitor. Malcolm, on the other hand, stared off into the darkness as if Wyatt wasn't even there. Minutes passed with the only sounds the crackling fire and Wyatt's fork on the plastic plate. Wyatt was just about to start in with some questions when the old man beat him to it.

"What the hell you doin' out here?" he asked abruptly.

"How do you mean? I mean, I'm travelling, seeing the country..."

"I sees that. But why like this? Why bummin'?"

That was a question he'd asked himself more than once in the long months since that first painful encounter back in Chi-town. And he still didn't have a good answer.

"I don't know. Maybe because it's cheap, exciting, maybe because I never learned how to ride a motorcycle."

Malcolm snorted. "That bullshit."

"Excuse me?"

"I say, that bullshit."

"I heard you okay. I was just wondering what exactly you meant."

"Look at you: rich white boy, got yo'self a 'spensive gold watch..." Wyatt self-consciously adjusted his jacket sleeve. It had been a graduation present from his parents. "You can go anywhere, anyhow you choose. So why here? Why like this?"

"Why do I get the feeling you're going to tell me..."

"Get serious!" the old man spat with enough vehemence to make Wyatt start. "You lookin' for sumthin. Any fool can see that."

"Okay, I'll bite. What am I looking for?"

"You know."

"I do?"

"I shore as fuck hope so, 'cause if you don't, I don't know who does!"

"I thought *you* did." Wyatt was playing now. It was a game, without rules. But it was definitely a game.

"Oh, I do alright. Nobody travel much as I do and not learn a thing or two."

"I bet you have."

"Bet yo' ass. One look at you and I says to myself, I says 'Mal, that white boy, he lookin' fo' his dream. Ain't got one just yet, but at least he lookin.' And maybe, just maybe, if you real lucky, you gonna find it."

The smug smile froze on Wyatt's lips. Suddenly it got very quiet next to that dying fire, as if all the air had suddenly been sucked out of the campsite, out of his lungs. The game had turned. Or perhaps the game was over.

He wanted to come back with a sarcastic quip, to reassure himself of his control over the situation, to demonstrate his superior position, his superior intelligence. But the words quivered on his tongue and died. His stomach suddenly ached. Was this some kind of epiphany, or just bad beans?

"I'm heading west," he heard himself saying. "Going to try to find out what it's all about, what I'm all about. That's where the heartbeat of this country is, you know." He heard it, but he couldn't believe it; it was as if someone else was talking. He had become quite accomplished at conversing without saying anything over those past few months. Night after night of exchanging stories that never happened with travelers he'd never see again had honed his talents. Better to stay friendly strangers, connected only by circumstance. But there he was, telling a strange old fellow traveler the very essence of his dream. He hadn't even told Ellen before he left. He was afraid it would sound foolish, juvenile, the equivalent of jousting at windmills, albeit in L.A. But there was something about this guy...

The old man tilted his head judgmentally. "Huh," he said.

Wyatt squinted to try to see his face in the deepening dusk.

"What'd you say?"

"I say, 'huh'."

Wyatt waited for something more, but nothing was forthcoming. The fire flared briefly as it burned itself out; the glow seemed to linger in the old man's staring eyes.

"Any reason for saying 'huh', or did you just feel like it?" Wyatt asked. For the first time irritation crept into his voice.

Malcolm folded his hands across his knees and leaned back to stare into the glittering night sky.

"Africa," he finally said, his voice low and mystical. "That's where this heartbeat you talkin' about is. Not just for this here country, but for the whole damn world. The whole universe." He lowered his gaze to a steady bead on Wyatt. "California ain't nothin'. Bullshit. One of them false fronts with nothin behind it, just like them movie sets. That ain't no place for dreams to live; it's where dreams go to die."

The words surprised him, as did their effect. Wyatt could feel the muscles in his jaw tighten; he had to restrain himself. "You got a better place?"

The wide smile was visible even in the darkness. "You hear me: Africa, that where the pulse is. That where life began, the fuckin' cradle of civilization. Be the spir'tual center of this universe, the Homeland."

Now it was Wyatt's turn to smile. "Maybe for you, old man," he said, "but just in case you haven't noticed, I'm not black. For me it's just another place with too many people, not enough food, and all kinds of diseases I don't even want to hear about, let alone catch." He didn't want to hurt the old man's feelings, but enough was enough. He'd heard the same back-to-Africa bullshit a thousand times before, even from modestly hip brothers back at the university. It was always the same: back before colonization and slavery Africa had been this giant paradise, attuned to nature, with peace and prosperity for all, until the white man came and destroyed the native ways and brought ruin to the Garden of Eden. No matter what it was, if it was good it was African, if it was bad it came from the white man. He had never completely understood how otherwise intelligent people could swallow such nonsense uncritically.

"You ever see 2001?" Malcolm suddenly asked, disrupting his reverie.

"The movie?" He wasn't sure he'd heard him correctly.

"No, the anti-persprint deodrant. Yeh, the goddamn movie! You see it?"

"Yeh. What about it?"

"What that space guy got to at the end is what Africa is to here and now: the end and the beginning, the only place to find the answer."

Wyatt knew he shouldn't ask, but he couldn't help himself. He felt the question well up inside him and demand expression.

"The answer to what?"

Malcolm didn't answer immediately. Instead, he shifted his body until he was facing Wyatt more directly and leaned forward conspiratorially. His voice was low but his words insistent.

"The answer to the question that's been kickin' your butt all this time, the question every goddamn religious high holyman been sayin' they know the answer to for the past 5000 years, the question that we all lives to answer.... 'Why?' Why we all here, why us, why you, why me, why this, why now? Just plain fuckin' why."

"And you're trying to tell me the answer's in Africa?" Wyatt didn't even try to hide the skepticism in his voice.

"You bet your sweet white ass."

"Says who?"

"Don't matter who says. If you believe shit just 'cause some dim-witted sucker tell you it true, you ain't goin to never find nothin' anyhow. You gotta FIND it. Nobody can find it for you. And if you' lookin for somethin, you gotta start at the beginnin. Hell, lookin' for answers in California is like tryin to figure out how a motor works at the scene of a car crash. You gotta go to the source, whitebread, to the beginnin', to the absolute, positute fuckin' get-go. And that, if you ain't been payin' attention, is Africa."

There was a finality in his tone, a certainty that defied argument that momentarily stopped Wyatt dead in his philosophical tracks. But just for an instant.

"Malcolm, if that isn't the biggest load of bullshit I've ever heard, it's a damn close second."

The old man shook his head sadly. "Fuckin' white boy, wouldn't know the truth if it hit 'em in the face." He stood stiffly and walked toward the small bundle of belongings he'd left at the edge of the clearing.

"Hey, don't take it personally," Wyatt called after him. "I just don't buy all that Africa mumbo-jumbo."

The old man kept walking.

"Come on - come have a cup of coffee with me."

Malcolm bent down and picked up his belongings. "You too fuckin' stupid to drink coffee with," he said, and then, stepping out of the fading glow of the campfire, he disappeared into the darkness beyond.

Wyatt stood next to the fire for several long moments, staring out into the night in disbelief. He blinked unconsciously, as if trying to awaken from a dream, or shake a nightmare from his tired brain.

"Malcolm!" he called out. But the only answer was the chirping of insects and the rustling of the breeze through the trees.

CHAPTER TWO

With no food and no one to talk to, it wasn't long before the young man splashed some water on his face, scrubbed his teeth with a swollen index finger, and stretched out on the sleeping bag that now looked a little too new, a little too expensive. He closed his eyes and heard the distant rumblings of the city...

And then he was there. It was some kind of village or something, with thatched roof huts and smoking torches. He was moving quickly; maybe someone was leading him. He wasn't sure. It was dark, but in the flickering torch light he thought he saw figures hiding, lurking behind the huts and following them. Drums pounded, low and insistent, the rhythm fast and wild.

He came to a big hut, bigger than all the rest with a large ceramic figure guarding the doorway, and somehow he knew he was supposed to go inside. Something pushed him, pulled him, demanded that he respond. He didn't want to go, but he knew it was meant to be. The next thing he knew he was being swept along, his feet barely touching the ground, the drums pounding in his ears. He ducked down to squeeze through the low entrance, trying not to feel the fear that was welling up inside him. There was smoke inside, a thick churning cloud that swirled as though alive. He wanted to turn, to flee, but his feet wouldn't move, he couldn't tear himself free from the bonds of the throbbing beat, the grasp of the smoke. The drums roared louder, filling the hut, pressing against his chest, pushing him back toward the mud wall.

Suddenly he felt a presence just behind him. He spun instinctively, his heart pounding, sweat dripping down his neck.

A fearsome, brightly painted face rushed out of the smoke at him, images of demons and warriors dancing in the swirling mists. He felt the hut itself begin to spin, the ground falling away...

And then there was Malcolm, a sanctimonious smile on his lips, as calm as the eye of a hurricane. He reached out his hand, as if to save Wyatt from the maelstrom. If he could only reach it, if he could just stretch a little further...

"O-wee-bo!" a voice screamed.

Wyatt started awake, drenched in a cold sweat. He sat bolt upright, his eyes searching the campsite in the grey early morning light. For what? He closed his eyes, trying to remember, trying to bring back the images....

But they were gone. Only the click-clack rhythm of a passing train and the echo of its whistle disturbed the morning peace. He dragged himself out of bed, the dislocated feeling from his dream still reverberating in his stomach. Some cold water splashed on the face cut through the fog a bit, but nothing could shake the haunting images that echoed in his mind. He forced himself to eat some dried fruit and a banana that was on the verge of going bad. The birds were chirping now as the sun peered above the horizon. As he rolled his sleeping bag and tied it to his pack, he tried to reconstruct the dream, to pull all the pieces together and analyze them, but the harder he reached out for them the quicker they receded from his memory. It was like trying to grab smoke.

Yet even when the smoke had cleared, even when there was nothing left to reach for, still it nagged at the back of his brain, a stiletto thorn that would not go away. He looked around the campsite once more. There was nothing there for him. It was time to move on.

He knew that a freight would be coming through later in the day, heading west, final destination: California. But the camp was no place to wait. If the slime swept the area, that would be the first place they'd look. Besides, it was only at such breaks in his travels that he actually saw any real America. Otherwise it was all railside blur, rushing past at 40 - 50 miles per hour. A beautiful backdrop. But to what? It was the heartbeat he'd come to find, and that meant people and they were miles away.

He trudged up the incline at the far side of the hollow, picking his way through the brush at a slow but steady pace. Maybe he'd spend some time in this place, maybe even rent a room and do some day-work. Yeh, maybe that's what he'd do. California would still be there. No hurry.

He came out of the brush on a hillside overlooking Interstate 80. He'd learned long before that the highway system often paralleled the railway system. Something about rights of way and acceptable grades. In any case, he'd seen this roadway from the freight car as they'd come in. Now he had to get a ride.

Hitchhiking is a different experience than riding the trains. More social, intimate, perhaps more civilized. It requires a different mindset, and Wyatt worked to find the place within him that would attract a ride. It wasn't just a matter of standing there with thumb extended. It was body language, expression, and above all energy. Drivers could sense it when he was feeling down. He needed to feel great despite the ache in his head and the bruises on his arms, to convince himself so he could convince others. He walked down to the highway with a bounce in his step, whistling a happy tune.

He stepped over the steel guard rail, dropped his pack in the narrow breakdown lane, and took his stance: foot up on the rail, showing just enough boot, standing relaxed but conscientious, thumb extended crisply. Nothing lackadaisical. An 18 wheeler roared past, a single toot from its air horn the only recognition acknowledged. Wyatt settled in for a long siege. It was always better to expect a tough time. If you were wrong, so much the better. He stared into the distance, trying to make a vehicle materialize. Sometimes he thought he could do it. Not today.

The rustling of bushes behind him brought his hand to the knife he kept tucked inside his boot. He was just about to call out when a familiar face came into view. The old man walked slowly down the hillside, seemingly oblivious to everything around him. Wyatt let his hand drop casually away from the boot.

"Malcolm! I thought you were headed off to Africa!" he yelled.

Ignoring him, the old man walked up to the guard rail, carefully stepped over and sat on the steel beam, not three feet from where Wyatt was standing. He pulled a blue handkerchief from his pocket and wiped his brow.

"And I thought you was goin' to California," he said at last. "This highway be goin' East, Whitebread. California's the other direction."

"I know that. I'm going into town, see what life's like around here."

"Ain't no different than life in every other butt-ugly little town in this country: 100 per cent bleached whitebread. Might as well've stayed home as spend your time lookin' fo' yo' dream there."

"I've got plenty of time."

"Good thing. Yo' sho' is wastin' a helluva a lot of it."

"*I'm* wasting time?" Wyatt said. "What about you? In case you haven't noticed there aren't any lions and tigers running around out here. To hear this African heartbeat of yours from here you're gonna need one helluva big stethoscope!"

"Even a long journey starts with yo' first step," Malcolm said calmly.

"Great, 250 million people in this country and I gotta run into the black Confucius."

"I ain't confused. I know right where I is: I'm on the road home."

"Yeh, well I think you better consult a good road map: I don't think this highway goes to Africa."

"All roads goes to Africa."

Wyatt stopped and stared at the old man. "Do you just sit around and think of this stuff?"

"Listen, Whitebread..."

"The name's Wyatt, remember?"

"You done any more thinkin' about goin' to Africa?"

"I haven't done any thinking about going to Africa. I'm going to California, remember?"

"By headin' East. Yeh, I remember."

A car shot past before Wyatt could assume his position and get his thumb extended.

"Damn! Hey, look Mal, nothing personal, but if I'm going to get out of here before I'm as old as you are I've got to concentrate on the job at hand. So, if you'll excuse me..."

"Suit yo'self."

Wyatt waited for the old man to pick up and move, but he showed no inclination to do so. "So?"

"Just thought I'd hang fo' a minute or two, see a real pro-fessional in action."

"All right, fine. Suit yourself."

Wyatt turned back to the highway, propped his boot up on the guardrail, and tried to settle his thoughts. "Now I know what the Ancient Mariner had to deal with," he mumbled.

For several minutes they waited. Not a single car passed by.

"It shore is interestin', watchin' a real pro-fessional at work," Malcolm said after a time.

"You just keep watching," Wyatt shot back. "Maybe you'll learn something."

"I always learns something."

"I bet..."

The minutes dragged into a half hour, and then an hour. To pass the time Malcolm began whistling to himself.

"Don't you have something else to do?" Wyatt snapped.

"Patience be a virtue."

"And silence is golden!"

Malcolm shrugged and stopped his whistling. Wyatt turned back to his thumbing. Neither spoke as the time passed slowly. Two hours more passed before finally, in the far distance, the tell-tale hum of a car engine brought Wyatt to life.

"All right! Now, watch closely Mal."

"I's watchin'"

An aging Volkswagen Beetle, the front hood dented, one headlight smashed, emerged from heat waves rising off the highway and hummed toward them, its left wheels dangling precariously over the center line. Wyatt straightened to a lordly yet casual attention and dangled his thumb like a fly-caster angling for a trophy brookie. As the car crept closer he shook his wrist nervously, dancing the bait hypnotically in front of the approaching target.

The VW seemed to inch towards them, closing the distance with impossible sluggishness. It was as if the car itself was stationary, the road moving backwards beneath its tires giving the impression of movement. But then the perception changed, and as if fired from a slingshot the Beetle suddenly lurched forward and was upon them in an instant. Wyatt flexed, flashed a sly smile and flicked his thumb to full extension.

The car raced passed them as if they weren't even there. A full head of blonde hair flashed by in a blur. Wyatt's shoulders had just begun to slump, and Malcolm's tell-tale smile had just begun to spread ever-wider when the driver of the Beetle slammed on the brakes and slid, half-sidewards, to a 50-foot screeching halt. Dust and smoke drifted up from the shocked tires.

"Never fails," Wyatt gloated.

"Better hope the same 'bout them brakes," Malcolm answered.

The driver forced the gearshift into reverse with a grinding heave and started back in a hurry. It was only when the car slid to a stop directly in front of them that they could make out the features of a very bleached blonde young woman in the driver's seat, eyes hidden behind pale blue wrap-around sunglasses. In her left hand, which rested on the steering wheel, a half-smoked cigarette dangled languidly; in her right, a can of Coors.

"Where you headed?"

"Anywhere you are, beautiful," Wyatt said.

The blonde smiled. "My mama tells me I'm headed for damnation."

Malcolm sucked his teeth loudly as he shook his head in disgust. "That soun' 'bout right," he mumbled.

"He with you?" the blonde asked, suddenly aware of the old man's presence.

"Not exactly..."

"I's his bodyguard," Malcolm said, jumping up spryly and walking toward the car. "Don't go no place without me."

The blonde arched her eyebrows. Wyatt shrugged. "We all have our cross to bear," he said.

"Well, get in if you're comin'," she said. "I want to be in Greeley by noon."

"Got a hot date?" Wyatt asked as he threw his stuff into the back seat and pushed Malcolm in after it.

"I wish," the blonde said, stomping on the gas before Wyatt could even slam his door shut. "Dentist appointment."

"Ouch. Been eating too many sweets?"

She looked over at him with a leering smile, peering over the tops of her sunglasses. "Something like that. I do like to suck on hard candy. Especially candy canes."

"Yo gonna make damnation well befo' noon yo keep goin' at that rate," Malcolm piped up from the back seat.

"Hey, Malcolm, we're having a conversation here. Could you take a break? Maybe go for a walk or something..."

"Malcolm? Is that your name?" the driver asked eyeing the old black man in the rear view mirror.

"That's it."

She extended her hand back over her shoulder. "Pleased to meet you. I'm Sheila."

Wyatt found his eyes magnetized to the bulging front of her tee-shirt. Sheila found them there as well.

"You like?" she asked.

"Yeh, yeh, nice shirt," he stumbled, his cheeks blossoming telltale poppies as he turned away.

"I could tell. You looked like you couldn't wait to get your hands on it." Her laugh made his cheeks burn even brighter. "You got a name?"

"Wyatt"

She extended her hand. "Pleased to meet you too."

He gave it one half-hearted shake.

"Damn. I've seen better shakes in a men's room," she said. "Don't you like girls?"

"Not shaking their hands."

"Sorry, my foot's occupied just now."

A guffaw in the back seat was stifled by Wyatt's glaring look.

"Did anyone ever tell you you're kind of a smart ass?" he said.

"Nearly every day," she said."But most don't think I'm all that smart. I guess I should thank you for that. Why don't you reach in back and grab yourself a beer. Cool you down a little bit. You look like you just ran the two minute mile."

"Thanks. I could use one."

Wyatt reached into the back seat, opened the styrofoam cooler and pulled out a can. "Want one?" he asked Malcolm.

"I prefers wine," the old man said.

"Suit yourself."

Wyatt popped the beer and drank deeply, as much out of embarrassment as thirst. This Sheila was not your run of the mill shrinking violet. Even as he was drinking he could see her checking him out from the corner of her eye.

"So, where are you guys heading, really?" she asked.

"We 'guys' aren't heading anywhere," Wyatt corrected. "I'm heading out to California."

"You know we're heading east?"

"I tried to tell 'im," the old man chimed in.

"Yes, of course I know we're heading east! I just thought I'd take some time and check out the area. Maybe spend some time in Greeley."

"You ever been there before?"

"Greeley? Never. What's it like?"

"Small. Kind of pretty, I guess. I like the country better, myself."

"Oh yeh? Why's that?"

The blonde sucked up some more beer and tossed the empty can into the back seat, barely missing Malcolm.

"Hey, said I din't want no beer!" the old man groused.

"Sorry! I'm not used to having anyone back there," she said.

"No problem. Next time, tho, try throwin' some chicken and potato salad."

"Are you hungry, Malcolm? Why didn't you say so? I'll stop at the next place we pass. We can get something quick to go."

"Unless you've got money, it'll probably be very quick," Wyatt said.

"I've got enough for a hamburger," Sheila said. "Maybe even for two, if you play your cards right." Her smile made Wyatt feel uncomfortable.

The miles passed quickly behind a blizzard of small talk. Sheila did most of the talking, with Wyatt playing the game and Malcolm kibitzing. Seems she was 27 years old, divorced, without any kids. Her ex-husband drank, but that didn't bother her until he started hitting. Then, it was hasta la vista, baby. She could put up with just about anything, she said, but nobody was going to hit her and get away with it. She didn't know what he was doing now. "Don't give a damn." She loved Whitney Houston and Madonna, hated rap. She thought the Broncos should have won a championship by then, what with having Elway and all. Wyatt was afraid she was going to launch into a detailed discussion of her childhood when the pulsating sign of a roadside diner materialized in the distance.

"There you go, Malcolm!" Wyatt interrupted the blonde, "Food!"

"This might turn out to be a decen' day after all," the old man answered.

Sheila pulled off at the next exit, raced through the stop sign at the end of the ramp and slid to a stop in the dirt parking lot of The Chuck House Grille surrounded by a cloud of dust.

"You always drive like that?" Wyatt asked.

"Like what?" she answered with that same taunting smile. "Come on - I don't have all day. Let's get some food."

The Chuck House was like a lot of small diners just off the highway. It was small, the parking lot was dotted with pick-ups and a couple of Harley Davidsons, and the bar was nearly full even at ten in the morning. It smelled of beer and sweat.

When Sheila led the way inside conversation stopped. When Wyatt followed a few steps behind, a low buzz erupted. When Malcolm straggled in the buzz turned nasty.

"That nigger with you?" one of the good ol' boys at the bar shouted to Sheila.

"Don't go getting all riled up," the blonde said, not even looking back as she settled down into a booth, "we're just here to grab a bite, not to move into the neighborhood."

"I'd like to give you a bite!" another of the patrons yelled out. His friends whooped and hollered.

"I'll have to take a rain check on that one," Sheila said calmly, "I haven't had a rabies shot lately." The whooping was mixed with groans.

Wyatt sat down slowly, trying not to look as nervous as he felt. From all his travels he'd learned that most often rednecks just liked to poke fun at strangers to demonstrate their manliness. But he had had his share of trouble with fellows just like this bunch, and he hoped that things would stay friendly. Malcolm just ignored the whole episode.

"You like to stir things up, don't you?" Wyatt asked Sheila softly as things started to settle down.

"Girls just wanna have fun," she said, the smile saying it all.

"Let's get our food and get the hell outta this redneck roach motel," Malcolm groused, trying unsuccessfully to find a distance at which he could read the menu.

"You need some help with that thing, Malcolm?" Sheila asked.

He threw it down on the table. "They got chicken and fries?"

"I think we can probably dig some up. Wyatt, how about you?"

"I'll stick to a hamburger."

"Probably a good choice. Waitress?"

A young girl, probably 17 or so, wearing a Rockies tee-shirt with no bra, her hair piled on top of her head, saddled up next to Wyatt, a smile spread ear to ear.

"Is there something I can get you?" she cooed, her attention riveted on Wyatt.

Sheila took one look and snapped her fingers insistently. "Hey, Cinderella, we're in kind of a hurry. Do you think you could take our orders first and then come back to play goo-goo eyes with Prince Charming here?"

"Hey, come on Sheila. Give the girl a break," Wyatt said, returning the smile with flirting eyes.

"I'll give her a compound fracture if that's what it takes to get some service here."

The waitress got the message, though if looks could kill Sheila would be pushin' up daisies. "Yes ma'am. What'll it be?"

"This gentleman will have chicken and fries, and I'll have a hamburger and a coke. To go. You want something to drink, Malcolm?"

"Coke'd be fine, thank you."

"Make it two cokes. Put all that on one bill."

"Hey, what about me?" Wyatt asked.

Sheila lit a cigarette and sucked down nearly half of it in one venomous puff. "You got your foot stuffed so far in your mouth I didn't think you'd be eating anything else," she said, smoke roiling from her lips.

"Okay, all right," he said, rolling his eyes at the waitress. "Make mine a hamburger, fries and a coke."

"How would you like that done, sir?" the waitress said, tilting her head to peek at him out of the corner of her eyes.

"I don't care if you press it between your legs, just make it snappy!" Sheila bellowed.

The waitress jumped a foot in the air and ran for the kitchen. Customers nearby chuckled.

"That time of the month?" Wyatt asked solicitously.

The blonde's anger faded into a smile. "Are all men in your family such sons of bitches, or have you been taking lessons?"

"Got a hell of a teacher."

The two of them exchanged tit for tat smiles. Malcolm shook his head.

"White peoples..." he mumbled. "Got to be genetical."

While they waited for the food Sheila and Wyatt continued to joust verbally, studiously ignoring the stares and comments from the other customers. Malcolm, on the other hand, stared at everyone and everything as though a visitor at a zoo, seemingly transfixed by his close proximity to the rare species Redneck Americanus. None of the three noticed the waitress reappear until she plopped a brown paper bag down next to Sheila and set a plate daintily in front of Wyatt.

"Hope you like 'em hot and juicy," she panted.

"Honey, I'm sure the juices are just running down your leg, but unless you expect him to mail that plate back to you I suggest you go get him a bag 'to go' too," Sheila interrupted.

The young lady looked like she'd been bitten. She blushed three shades of purple and scurried off to the kitchen wordlessly.

"How about you?" Wyatt asked when she had gone.

"How about me?" Sheila snapped.

"How are *your* juices?"

The blonde hesitated maybe half a heartbeat. "Oh, I figure I'm just about a quart low, but I'm very particular about where I top off." Smile.

"I bet you are," Wyatt said. "Very particular."

Just then the waitress returned with the other hamburger safely bagged. "That'll be $9.44 for yours," she told Sheila, "and $4.35 for the man with the big blue eyes."

Sheila reached for the two checks. "I'll take care of them," she said. "Ol' blue eyes' too."

"I got mine," Wyatt said, snatching the bill away from her. He forced his hand into the front pocket of his jeans and pulled out a small wad of bills.

"Damn!" Malcolm moaned enviously.

"I thought you were busted!" Sheila said.

"Nope." He peeled off a five and handed it to the waitress. "Keep the change."

"Woa - high roller," Sheila muttered as she dug in her purse for a ten and tossed it to the teenager. "Bring me the change."

"A penny scrimped is a penny earned," Wyatt said.

"Someone's gotta pay for gas."

"Here. A contribution." Wyatt tossed her a ten.

She held the bill up in front of her, seeming to examine it closely, until dropping it in her purse. "What the hell are you doing hitching if you got money like that?"

Wyatt shrugged. "I like the people you meet." Smile.

"I used to think the same thing, until recently."

"Sumthin to be said for ridin' the rails," Malcolm mumbled.

Before either of his companions could respond, the waitress brought back the change. "Thanks for comin' and come again real soon," she said earnestly, all the while eyeing Wyatt.

"I don't think it's us who are coming," Sheila said, grabbing all the change except a nickel and one penny. "Come on, let's get out of this joint."

The waitress looked down at the change plate. "Thanks for nothing," she said.

Sheila reached back across the plate and grabbed the change. "As you like," she said.

Walking to the door she scanned the surroundings appraisingly. She knew every eye was on them. "Nice place you got here!" she called out to the bartender as they reached the front door, "if you don't mind the food and the clientele!"

She slipped out the door to laughter and catcalls, with Wyatt close behind. Malcolm was just a little slow on his feet and got hit in the back with a lump of mashed potatoes. He immediately picked up the pace.

"What are you trying to do, get us killed?" Wyatt bellowed as they hopped into the VW.

"Sorry, not today. I've got a dentist's appointment!" she laughed. They pulled out of the parking lot in a whirl of spinning tires and flying gravel.

CHAPTER THREE

The sign on the bank said '11:47, 69 degrees' as they pulled into Greeley.

"You two got anywhere in particular you want to be dropped off at?" Sheila asked her two riders.

"Is there a decent hotel around here that doesn't cost a hundred bucks a night?" Wyatt asked.

"Well, if you don't mind sharing a bathroom, there's a real nice guest house not too far from here. Only run you $35."

"Sounds good to me," Wyatt said.

"How about you Malcolm? Sound okay to you?"

"Don't like sleepin' indoor," the old man said. "Had a friend get burnt up that way."

"Okay...I guess you're on your own then. I'm afraid I don't know a whole lot of outdoors sleeping spots."

"I'll find me a place. Always do." Sheila didn't doubt him for a moment.

Just as described, the guest house was only a few blocks away. It was a small, two-story building, maybe a hundred years old. From the looks of it, it had probably belonged to a wealthy businessman back in the gold rush days.

When the Beetle pulled up in front of the house, Sheila didn't just drop them off as she'd suggested. She started to get out of the car almost before it screeched to a stop.

"I thought you had a dentist's appointment," Wyatt said.

"It's only about two minutes from here. Come on!"

She was inside the house before he could pull his pack out of the back seat.

"Gonna come inside?" Wyatt asked the old man.

He eyed the place discerningly. "Nah. Nothin' in there fo' me." He climbed out of the back slowly, unfurling himself like a tightly wound flag on a windless day.

Wyatt extended his hand. "Well, I guess I'll be seeing you then."

Malcolm nodded. "Guess so."

He turned and shuffled off without shaking hands.

Wyatt stood for just a moment watching the old man. The number of certified, A-1 characters that passed through his life when he was traveling never ceased to amaze him. Who knew where the old man would be off to now. Africa? Doubtful, but then again, who could say?

"Hey, you coming?" Sheila called from the front doorway.

He gave her a quick wave of acknowledgement and tossed his pack over his shoulder. As he walked up the brick walk to the guest house he felt the strongest urge to turn around and wish the old man well. But when he did, Malcolm was gone. Wyatt stared after him for a few seconds, shrugged, and continued inside.

"This is him," Sheila was saying to an elderly woman, perhaps 65 or so, short, plump, with grey hair pulled back tight into a bun.

"Doesn't look like a scoundrel," the woman said.

"Looks can be deceiving. If I were you, I'd get my money up front." She started for the door. "Wyatt, this is Emmy. Emmy, don't say I didn't warn you. See y'all!"

"Hey!" Wyatt called after her. "Thanks for the lift."

"The high point of my week," the blonde said, and with a taunting, sarcastic smile she slipped out the door and sprinted for her car.

"That's one heck of a strange woman," Wyatt said aloud to himself.

"She's one heck of a good woman," Emmy said. "And she seems to think you're a nice enough young man. Is she right?"

Wyatt shrugged. "My mother thinks so."

"Good enough for me. So you need a room - for just the one night?"

"I don't know. Maybe, maybe longer."

"What's gonna make up your mind?"

"All depends what I run into out there," he said, indicating the town.

"Well then, let's give you 2B. Then whether you decide to stay or go, we can accommodate you."

"2B or not 2B, that is the question."

"To pay or not to stay, that is the answer," the elderly inn keeper said with a smile.

Wyatt dug into his pants for the cash. "2B," he said handing over $35.

"The key," she said, handing him a big old-fashioned long-stemmed model. "Top of the stairs, first door on your right. If you need anything, just yell."

"Thanks. I'll do that."

There was something reassuring about the old house. The wide oak bannister felt cool and solid beneath his hand as he climbed up to his room. Even the squeak of the straining wood as he shifted his weight from one stair to the next brought back memories of other places, other times. And the smell. There's a damp, warm, lived-in smell in old houses that brings back memories of grandparents and early childhood, when everything was mysterious and nothing was threatening.

Wyatt fumbled with the key in the lock, trying to remember how to seat the narrow sliver of metal in the oversized hole. When, at last, he mastered the task, he casually tossed open the door only to find himself lost in a memory so strong that he couldn't make himself step into the room. The wallpaper in the room was identical to that in his grandparents' guest room when they had still been alive, a room he had slept in so many times as a youngster. Flushed, with an eerie tingling in his arms and legs, he drifted into the room as if floating through déjà vu. Only when he dropped his pack on the bed and saw himself reflected in the bureau mirror, his mouth half-open, his eyes glazed with surprise, did he snap out of the daze and shake himself back into the reality of the moment. *'This is too weird,'* he thought as he pulled some fresh clothes out of the pack. *'But then, it's been a strange couple of days.'*

He grabbed the bath towel, face cloth and hand towel that were neatly folded on top of the bureau and made his way down the hallway to the bathroom. There were three other rooms on that floor, and a stairway that appeared to lead to the attic. There was a door at the top of the stairway. It was shut.

Wyatt closed the bathroom door behind him and slid the lock into place. The knickknacks on the shelves seemed out of place in a public house, but the sign on the back of the door did not. "Haste makes friends. Be considerate of your fellow housemates." He smiled as he turned on the hot water. It took the better part of five minutes before the water turned hot, but finally the steam that snaked out of the tub announced that it was ready. He stepped into the old porcelain tub, pulled the flowered shower curtain shut and settled into the simple luxury of the flowing water. He never appreciated a good shower as much as when he was on the road. The reinvigorating capacity of hot water was truly magical. He lathered from head to toe with the sweet smelling bar soap and was busy massaging the peach shampoo into his long locks when suddenly the water turned cold. "Damn!" he muttered, stepping back out of the tepid stream. Wiping the soap from his eyes, he tried to adjust the taps to improve the temperature once again, cranking the hot up and the cold down, but by the time he found an acceptable temperature the once powerful stream was just a gentle dribble. He rinsed the soap out of his hair as best he could, and, muttering, dried himself off. Nothing broke a spell of ecstasy faster than foiled expectations. With a petulant frown he stamped back to his room and flopped wearily onto the bed.

He had only meant to rest a bit, collect his thoughts and make some plans for the afternoon. But the soft coolness of the sheets lulled him into somnolence, and before he realized what had happened he had dropped off into a deep, deep sleep.

Immediately he was back in the village, only this time it was daytime and the gentle sounds of birds and insects replaced the pounding of drums. He walked more slowly now with a sense of complete assurance, surveying the huts as though he was completely familiar with them, and they with him. Off to his left a campfire burned, with a black pot balanced precariously on flat stones at its center. A dog suddenly appeared at his feet; it eyed him suspiciously, sniffing from a distance. But when he reached down to pet it, it licked his hand. He felt like he was expected somewhere, but try as he would he couldn't remember where. He peeked into hut after hut, hoping to find someone who could direct him, but finding only small color TVs and a microwave or two. He thought it odd, but decided it was just his Western prejudice: why shouldn't they have modern conveniences? We do.

Wandering through the tightly-packed huts he wondered where all the people had gone. He would've liked to have met them, talked to them about their village, asked them about the masks, and the drums. But there was not a single face to be seen; the village was deserted. Up ahead the dog stopped in front of a hut. It barked to catch his attention.

"What's the matter pup? Want to show me something?"

He started in the direction of the dog, as calm and at ease as if he was walking through his parents' home. Looking up he noticed that the sky had turned suddenly dark; the sun was nearly set. The dog continued to bark, more urgently now. He tried to walk faster, but somehow the distance to the hut didn't diminish. The dog's barking turned to a deep-throated growl, and then a pained, gasping howl. Wyatt began to run. He felt the wind in his face, his hair bouncing on his shoulders. A lightning bolt rent the night sky, and the dog yelped and bolted into the hut.

Now the wind howled in his face, threatening to push him back. Thunder crashed all around him. He drove himself forward, leaning nearly perpendicular to the ground. Finally, just ahead, the opening to the hut loomed even blacker than the blackness of sky and storm. Pushing himself harder he turned the corner and stumbled into the doorway.

At once the wind fell silent, the thunder stopped. He struggled to catch his breath, slow the pounding of his heart.

But the quiet lasted for just an instant. In its place came the drums, the rhythmic, pounding drums from the night before. Wyatt turned, trying to decide whether to flee, but the doorway was gone. The drums roared louder, assaulting him, suffocating him. He covered his ears, collapsed to his knees. The room began to spin. He couldn't breathe!

He was just about to pass out when the drums stopped abruptly. As he lifted his head timidly to look around him, a fearsome medicine man, wearing the same terrifying mask as the night before, leaped out at him from the shadows, a human thigh bone in one hand, a Ken doll in the other. He shook both in Wyatt's face.

"O-wee-bo!" the holy man screamed. "O-wee-bo!"

Wyatt knew that voice! It was...it was....

The pounding on his door shattered the dream.

"Oh dream boy!" a familiar voice called out. "Dream boy! Open your sleepy little eyes!"

Wyatt stumbled to his feet and opened the door. There stood Sheila, her mocking grin in full flower.

"Rise and shine morning glory," she said, sweeping past him into the room. "Nap time's over. I'm starving. You?"

Wyatt rubbed his eyes, trying to meld with the reality that confronted him in place of the dreamworld that still lingered in his brain. "Should I be?" he asked.

"Well, I don't know. Maybe you operate on a European timetable, but I usually like to eat around 6-6:30."

"Six? What are you talking about?" He stumbled to the window, raised the shade and stared out into the blue grey twilight. Still disbelieving, he retrieved his watch from the bed stand. Sheila watched, bemused.

"Lose something?" she asked.

"Yeh...like half the day," Wyatt said.

"You must've been one tired little puppy. What's the matter, didn't sleep too well last night?"

"As a matter of fact, I didn't. I keep having this weird dream...."

"Lots of leather, whips?"

Wyatt smiled. "Wishful thinking. No, I keep finding myself in this deserted African village, and I keep going into the same hut, with drums beating, and this fierce looking medicine man wearing this big red and black mask leaps out at me..."

"Whoa! Sounds like Chaka Zulu time. You been eating too much spicy food or something?"

"I don't know what the hell's going on. But the strange thing is, this all started when Malcolm started talking about how I needed to blow off California and go to the 'spiritual center of the universe'."

"Disney World?"

"Africa. He seems to think you can find all the answers there."

"To what questions?"

"The biggie: Why?"

"Why what?"

"Why everything. Why us, why here, why you, why me? Just plain why."

Sheila plopped down on his bed, her skepticism blunted. "Malcolm didn't strike me as the heavy duty philosopher type."

"Huh. Just get him going on this Africa thing and you'll see a whole different side of him. It's like a religious thing for him."

"Seventh Day Africanist?"

"Exactly. And now he's got me dreaming about it."

"Yeh, well I'm dreaming about eggplant parmesan, Caesar salad and a nice bottle of wine."

"Your treat?"

"Actually, after seeing that wad you're carrying I thought maybe you'd do the honors."

"All right. Fair enough. Give me two seconds to get dressed and we'll hit it."

She fell back on the bed and closed her eyes. "Wake me when you're through."

Wyatt smiled and shook his head. He quickly pulled on some clean clothes and dragged a comb through his hair. He snapped a rubber band around his pony tail and presented himself for inspection.

"You still awake?" he asked.

"You still buying dinner?" she asked without opening her eyes.

"I'm buying."

She popped up, wide awake. "Then we're outta here! Come on - I know a great little place, no atmosphere, no class, but good food and cold beer at decent prices."

"You've said the magic words. Lead on."

Emmy was waiting by the front door as they came down the stairs.

"You kids have a good time," she chirped.

"Okay Mom, don't wait up," Sheila said, kissing the old lady on the cheek as they swept by.

"I know you better than that!" Emmy called out after them.

Without the warmth of the sun it was a cool Fall night, and Sheila pulled her sweater tight around her as they walked.

"Cold?"

"Not really. I like it cool. Makes me feel alive."

"Ha! I can't imagine you any other way."

"Is that a complaint?"

"No, no! I think it's great."

Sheila accepted the compliment with a quiet nod and a smile. "Sometimes I come on a little strong."

"Hey, I like it. You know who you are and you're obviously very happy with that."

"Pretty much. How about you? Got it all figured out?"

Wyatt sighed. "It's funny. When I was fifteen I knew everything: who I was, where I was going, what I wanted to do - the whole package. Now, here I am almost 15 years later, and I feel like I don't know anything. I'd say I had a bad case of mid-life crisis, only that would mean I'm only going to live to be 58 and I plan to hit triple digits."

"What happened? I mean, if it's not too personal or anything."

"I grew up. Realized that all those blacks and whites I saw out there were really shades of grey. You know, information is a dangerous thing. The more you get, the more you discover you don't know. It's the Catch 22 of education. It's why I didn't continue on for my doctorate. I woke up one morning and realized that I knew less about philosophy than I did when I started my master's program. Oh, I had a lot more information at my fingertips, but a lot less certainty, a lot fewer answers to the questions that matter."

"And so you hit the road to find the answers?"

"The ultimate post-graduate course," Wyatt explained. "Your classroom is all around you, your teachers everyone you meet, and the answers you find form your own ultimate truths, based on experience, not hypothesis."

"So what does that make you, some kind of guru or something?"

Wyatt couldn't tell if she was mocking him. "No. In fact, just the opposite," he said. "I don't believe in gurus. I believe in what I see, touch, smell. The rest is dreams."

Sheila was quiet for a while, the only sounds their own footsteps and the occasional passing car.

"Sorry," Wyatt said. "Sometimes I come on a little heavy too. But I'm working on that."

"I like it," Sheila said, looking up at him. "I like people who see more than just the everyday crap we all slog thru to survive."

"I see plenty of that, too."

Her smile suddenly beamed. "But not tonight!" she announced, grabbing him by the elbow and pulling him forward. "We've got steak to eat and beer to chug!"

With Sheila leading the way they half-jogged the block and a half to the restaurant. Just as she'd described it, it was a tiny place, just this side of seedy. From the outside it appeared to be nothing more than another storefront, with only the letters "Angelo's" stenciled on the glass door to distinguish it from the hardware store, dry cleaners and locksmith that rounded-out the neighborhood businesses. Even the interior - eight tables with cheap checked tablecloths and sawdust on the floor - gave no indication that the place was anything special.

On the other hand, the aromas that caressed Wyatt as soon as he walked through the door spoke volumes of the quality of the food within. As did the packed house.

"Whoa. If the food tastes anything like it smells, I'm in heaven," he said as they stood just inside the door, with Sheila scanning the small room for who knew what.

Suddenly, what appeared. "Sheila!" a white-aproned cook called out. He casually deposited a basket of bread on a nearby table as he dashed past to greet her; a middle-aged guy held up his hand as if to ask a question, but the cook was long gone. "Where have you been?" he asked, kissing her on both cheeks with the zeal only a true Italian could muster.

"Tony! It's true, I've been away too long," she said, feigning kisses in just the proper continental style. "Tony, I brought someone to see what real Italian food is all about. Wyatt, this is the best assistant chef in all Colorado, Tony Gribaldi. Tony, Wyatt."

Wyatt tried not to grimace. Tony had the kind of handshake that cracked knuckles.

"Anybody that can get Sheila back here is a friend of mine," he said. "Come on, come on, let's get you two seated."

As the chef led them to a table for two, Sheila was hailed by a young couple who were nearly as excited to see her as Tony.

"Jesus, what are you, a part-owner of this place, or what?" Wyatt asked when they finally made it to their table.

"Why? Because I know a few people?"

"That's like saying Amelda Marcos owned a few pairs of shoes. You know half the people in here."

Sheila laughed. "I used to be more or less a regular here...when I was married."

"What happened - stop eating when you broke up with your ex?"

"No, just tried to avoid places where unavoidable meetings might happen. He wasn't exactly at the top of my must-see list."

"Ah. A no-good, lying, cheating low-life bum?"

"Something like that. Actually, no. A halfway decent guy who drank too much and became a no-good, lying low-life bum when he was bombed. Which was just about all the time at the end."

"How long ago you two split up, if you don't mind me asking?"

"Oh, almost three years now."

"And this is your first time back here?"

"Yep."

Wyatt bowed his head. "I'm honored."

"You should be."

They exchanged the kind of silly, all-knowing smiles that only people on their first date can carry off.

"Want some wine?"

"I thought you'd never ask. White or red?"

"Well, let me go out on a limb and guess that a place called Angelo's has some culinary connection to Italy. I'd guess red."

"Good guess. How about some chianti?"

"Enchantied."

For almost two hours they drank, dined and talked about everything from their own checkered pasts to the chances of Colorado landing a big league baseball team. They were sipping cappuccinos, trading stories of dream vacations, when suddenly Tony scurried over and whispered something in Sheila's ear. Wyatt thought he was discussing the bill.

"I'll take it. Just bring me the bill," he said.

But the sudden pallor in Sheila's face told him that it was something more than just the bill.

"What's wrong?"

"You're in for a great treat. Tony just saw my ex drive up outside."

"You okay? Want to go?"

Sheila picked up her cappuccino and sipped slowly. "Can't run forever," she said coolly.

She was still sipping her coffee when the door to the restaurant swung open. Sheila didn't flinch. Wyatt couldn't resist sneaking a peek.

There's a moment, just before something dramatic is about to happen, when time seems to slow, the air becomes charged, and even bystanders sometimes forget to breathe. Probably a sensation most familiar to gang members. That was the sensation Wyatt experienced just at that moment.

The man who stepped into the restaurant was dark-haired, swarthy (possibly Italian, Wyatt thought), maybe a little over 6 feet tall, trim, with a bushy black moustache.

"Hey, Tony!" the man called out upon seeing his friend. "How's the veal tonight?"

Wyatt didn't see if Tony's gaze betrayed their position, or if they just came up in the newcomer's routine visual sweep of the room. Whatever the case, the nervousness in Tony's voice certainly would have made anyone suspicious.

"Gino! How are you? What a...surprise!"

"Surprise? It hasn't been that long, has it...?"

Wyatt saw the smile on his face suddenly freeze, then fall flat.

"Uh oh. Here he comes," he whispered through clenched teeth.

Sheila nonchalantly put her cup down on the table and dabbed at her lips with her napkin.

"Well, well, well - long time no see," Gino said, sidling up to her chair. Wyatt could smell the alcohol all the way across the table.

Sheila looked up at him as though shocked and surprised. "Why, Gino, how are you?!"

He bent down and tried to kiss her on the lips. She casually turned her head and he pecked at her cheek.

"Okay. As well as can be expected. You?"

"Great! Guess life's been giving me a break lately."

"Yeh? Terrific, terrific...You're looking good."

"Thanks. You too."

Wyatt reached for his water glass and the movement caught Sheila's attention.

"Oh, excuse me! Gino, this is Wyatt. Wyatt, my ex-husband Gino."

Her ex turned an unsmiling, evaluative look at Wyatt.

"How ya doing?"

"Fine, thanks. You?"

"Okay." He turned immediately back to Sheila. "So, you move back to town, or just visiting the old stomping grounds?"

"I just wanted to take Wyatt to the best restaurant in Colorado, so here we are." She flashed a surprisingly relaxed smile at Tony, whose own smile wobbled precariously.

"Yeh, right. That's good. You know, you really are looking hot. Better than I remember." He chuckled. Sheila's smile turned razor sharp.

"Your memory might be a little hazy," she said.

His smile disappeared. "I beat that little problem. I've been more or less dry for over a year."

"Really? Then I guess Seagram must be making an aftershave these days, huh?"

He blinked once before realization struck.

"No, it's not like that. I just had one. Stopped by Eddie's on the way over here. You know: just take the edge off."

"Yeh, I know," she said with a sigh.

"Right. So....can I join you?"

"Actually, we were just getting ready to leave," Sheila said. "You got our check ready yet, Tony?"

The flustered assistant chef jumped as if slapped. "Coming right up! Have it for you in just one second!"

"Too bad. Would've been fun to chew the fat, talk about old times."

"Yeh, a pity." Perhaps Sheila was a bit too sarcastic. Perhaps something just connected in her ex's booze soaked brain. Whatever the case, he wasn't happy.

"You know, you still got one hell of a mouth on you," he spat.

"It comes with the package, Gino. You know that."

"Hey, why so you have to be such a fucking bitch after all this time? Here I am, trying to be a nice guy..."

"Yeh, you're a prince. Tony, you got that bill yet?" she called out.

Gino grabbed her by the shoulder. "I'm talking to you!" he snapped.

Wyatt stood and pulled his arm away from her.

"Hey, buddy, why don't you have a seat and order, and we'll be on our way, okay?"

"Fuck you, you...long-haired hippy fairy!"

Gino wound up to punch him with the slow, methodical precision of a sauced redneck. Unfortunately for him, Wyatt was not about to wait around cooperatively for the blow to land. Instead, he stepped to the side and, with the same basic move fried chicken aficionados use to dislocate a drumstick from a chicken breast, gave Gino's arm a crisp twist and pinned it to his back. The woozy Italian howled in pain.

"Can we pay for our dinner and get the hell out of here now, or do you want to continue this discussion?" Wyatt asked.

"You mother-fuckin..."

Wyatt twisted his arm tighter and bent him forward against the edge of the table. "How's that?"

Gino's bulbous face had turned such a bright red that it appeared his head might explode. Sheila shook her head dispiritedly as she called over to her friend, who stood transfixed by the bar.

"Is that bill ready yet, Tony?"

"Coming, coming," he said, scurrying toward their table even while scribbling on his pad.

He thrust the bill into her hand. She dug into her purse and pulled out a twenty dollar bill. "Here. Keep the change," she said. "Nice seeing you again. Food's still the best." She stood and looked over at her ex-husband, who continued to struggle ineffectually against Wyatt. "Unfortunately, clientele still stinks. Wyatt, what do you say we get out of here?"

"I could get into that."

The blonde walked over to her ex and in a quiet, subdued voice explained the facts of life to him. "Gino, we're leaving now. You hassle us, give us any trouble whatsoever, and I'll call the cops. That restraining order's never been lifted - you just remember that."

"Okay?" Wyatt asked no one in particular.

"Let him go," Sheila said.

Gino collapsed onto the table top and rolled off into a chair. He rubbed his shoulder in obvious pain.

"You fuckin bitches are all the same," he mumbled.

"It's those crazy x chromosomes," Sheila said. She waved to Tony as she and Wyatt strolled out into the Greeley night.

"Nice guy," Wyatt said after they'd walked a few moments in silence.

"He's mellowed. Should have seen him a few years ago."

"Sorry I missed it."

Sheila stopped and put her hand on Wyatt's arm. "Actually, I'm sorry you got caught up in our little ongoing war. But thanks for the friendly persuasion. I know all too well what he can do when no one's around to stop him."

"My pleasure. I'm not real fond of guys who beat on women."

"Must be a flaw in your upbringing."

"Must be."

For a moment they just stood and looked at each other, the silly smiles fading to even more telling blank looks. Then, Sheila stretched up on her toes and gently kissed him. He feigned surprise.

"I'm shocked. Kissing a long-haired hippy fairy on a public street? Must be a flaw in your upbringing."

"Must be," she whispered.

He leaned down, took her in his arms and kissed her with passion that even surprised him. When they finally separated, neither could find the words.

"Well, what do you know?" Wyatt finally said.

"Yeh. Who would'a thunk?"

"So, what now? Is there some favorite club you'd like to go to - my treat this time?"

"Actually, it's been a real long day. Bed sounds pretty good right now."

"Do you have a place to stay here in town?"

Sheila dropped her eyes to the ground. "Well, I was kind of planning on staying at Emma's, but it turns out she doesn't have any free rooms. Available, but not free."

Wyatt nodded his head understandingly. "I guess that pretty much means you'll have to sleep in your car tonight...unless, of course, you wouldn't mind sharing a room with a long-haired..."

She kissed him quickly. "I thought I was going to have to draw you a picture," she said. "Come on." She grabbed him by the hand and half-dragged him down the sidewalk.

"I thought you were tired!" he protested.

"Just because I want to go to bed doesn't mean I want to sleep," she jibed.

Wyatt began to jog, pulling her along in his wake.

CHAPTER FOUR

Sheila awoke with a start.

It was pitch dark and for a moment she couldn't remember where she was. The images had been so real, so visceral! Then, through her sleep-muddled brain she heard the mumbling from the body lying next to her. 'What the...?' Finally the whole scene settled into place in her mind and she realized that it was Wyatt, talking in his sleep. She focused on his ramblings, thinking to tease him about it the next morning. But she quickly realized it was more than just a simple conversation. He seemed disturbed, as though caught-up in a nightmare.

Should she wake him? She hesitated: their first night together and she had to decide whether to intervene in this most personal of moments. 'At least the most personal outside the bathroom,' she thought with a smile. 'Oh, what the hell. I'd want him to do it for me.'

She shook him by the shoulder and said softly, "Wyatt - wake up...you're having a nightmare."

The frightful mask shattered like a mirror struck by a hammer. Wyatt awoke, drenched in sweat.

He sat up as though burned, looking left and right in complete disorientation. "Wha....?"

Sheila put her arm around his shoulder and stroked his matted hair. "Shh...it's okay. It was just a dream. You're okay now."

He turned to her and even in the darkened room she could see his eyes opened wide. "Sheila?"

"Yeh, Wyatt, it's me," she said softly, absently brushing the hair off his forehead. "You were out there in dreamland somewhere and it sounded like you needed someone to bring you back."

She could feel him shudder. "This is weird. This is fucking strange," he muttered.

"What? What's strange - your dream?"

"It's the same one. Remember what I was telling you - about the African village and the mask and all that?"

"Hmm. Yeh, I remember all right."

Something in the way she said it made him stop. "What?"

"This particular dream seems to be catching."

His eyes opened wide again. "You too?"

"I think that's what woke me up. At least that's the last thing I remember."

"What!? What do you remember?" He grabbed her by the shoulders, anxious, excited, verging on obsession.

"Drums, pounding rhythmic drums..."

"How? I mean, what did they sound like? Can you tap it?"

She slapped her hands against his shoulder in a rhythm she couldn't possibly forget.

"Jesus. What else?"

"There was a village, with thatched roofs, like you said."

"Anything stand out? Anything specific you can remember?"□

She closed her eyes, trying to draw the images back into her mind's eye. To her surprise, the images rushed back of their own accord.

"Yeh, yeh....I remember this one big...bowl-like thing, all painted..."

"What color?"

"Not one color - red, and blue..."

"And yellow? With a zig-zag pattern, sort of like a sine wave?" His excitement was infectious.

"I don't know about sine waves," she said, "but it was up and down like this..." She traced the wave pattern on the sheet.

Wyatt shook his head and sighed, looking off into the indefinite distance. "Wow."

"Same place?"

"I-fucking-dentical. This is really strange."

"That's an understatement. Maybe it was the antipasto?"

"Maybe in the Twilight Zone, but not here in Greeley. To put it in philosophical terms, this is heavy shit."

"Is that the technical term?"

For the first time they both smiled. "Yeh, that's the technical term," he said. "At least the only one I know of."

"And you say this whole thing with the village came up..."

Sheila thought he was going to jump right out of the bed. "With Malcolm! Goddamn it, of course! This all started with his back to Africa bullshit."

"You don't think this is some kind of voodoo or something, do you?" Her voice sounded small, even to her.

Wyatt didn't laugh. "I don't know. I don't know what it is, but I'll tell you what - first thing tomorrow morning, I'm going to go find that guy and have a word or two with him."

"Not without me, you're not."

"No?"

"No way. It's not everyday someone gets me mixed up in someone else's dream. I want to hear the explanation."

"If he has one." There was doubt in his voice.

"You know a better place to start?"

"No, not really. This doesn't make much sense, does it?," he said, thinking aloud. In mid thought he drifted off, shaking his head numbly. "So, I guess we'd better get some sleep."

She looked at him with eyebrows raised. "You've got to be kidding - right? You look like you just stuck your finger in an electric outlet and my heart's beating so fast it feels like it's going to jump out of my throat. Sleep?"

"You've got a better idea?"

That smile spread slowly across her face. "Well, as a matter of fact..." She gently pushed him down onto the bed.

"Good idea."

The next morning Wyatt was awakened by a ray of sunshine streaming through a thin crack between the drapes, directly into his eyes.

"Well, it's about time," Sheila groused when his eyelids finally popped open.

"Are you awake already? Don't you ever sleep?"

"I sleep all right. But not with voodoo floating around."

"Listen to you! We don't know that it has anything to do with voodoo!"

"Whatever it is, it's not conducive to sleep. Come on - get dressed. Let's go find Malcolm."

"All right, all right, take it easy. You've got to give me a couple of seconds to wake up here."

"Okay: one...two."

"Anybody ever tell you, you can be a big pain in the ass?"

"On a daily basis. Will you come on?!"

Grumbling all the way, Wyatt pulled on his clothes, splashed some water on his face and pulled his hair back into the pony tail. With Sheila nearly literally tugging him by the arm, they headed downstairs to begin their search.

"And what do you suggest we do if we find him?" Wyatt asked as they crossed the entry room. "Accuse him of dream manipulation?"

"We don't have to accuse him of anything. I was thinking more of talking - like 'what the hell's going on here?'"

"Oh, I can see this is going to be one congenial conversation."

"Congenial or not, I'm going to find out."

She stopped in mid-sentence as she opened the front door to the guest house.

"What? What's the matter?" Wyatt asked as she stared outside.

"This is truly bizarre," she whispered. "Look."

There, sitting calmly beneath a tree directly across the street, was Malcolm.

"Jesus H. Christopher....That *is* bizarre."

"But it's definitely not voodoo, right?"

"I didn't say that. All I'm saying is that it's definitely not definite that it's voodoo."

Sheila snorted. "I love a man who takes a stand."

"I prefer to know what I'm talking about before I do my talking. Let's go check this out, and take it easy, okay? Lay off the voodoo stuff."

Trying to act as casual as possible, they casually strolled out of the building, casually descended the front steps, and then casually sprinted across the street.

"Malcolm! What are you doing here?" Wyatt asked.

"And what's with these voodoo dreams?" Sheila joined in.

"Great control," Wyatt muttered.

"Never my strong suit." Sheila casually lit a cigarette and casually inhaled half of it in one drag.

Malcolm looked at them as if they had just stepped out of a UFO. "What you talkin' 'bout? What voodoo dreams?"

"Don't mind her, Malcolm. She had a bad night."

"You bet I had a bad night! And I want to know..."

Wyatt cut in front of her, pushing her none too gently away from the bewildered old man.

"She wants to know what you've been up to," he said. "She was worried about you." He turned around and glared at her.

"Worried? No sense bein' worried 'bout me. I takes care of myself."

"Oh, we know that, Malcolm. It's just...well, it's just..."

Sheila stepped in to help. "It's just that we know what a big bad world it is out there and we were concerned about you."

"Right. Greeley, crime capital of the western hemisphere," Wyatt whispered. He turned to Malcolm. "Basically, we just wondered how you were doing."

The old man looked from one awkwardly smiling face to the other. "Well, I guess I'm doin' all right. No complaints."

"Good. Good," Wyatt said. "Have you had breakfast?"

"Yeh, that's a good idea!" Sheila blurted. "I mean, yeh, I'm hungry too. What about you, Mal?"

"I ain't ate yet."

"Want to go grab something?"

"Grab something? Like what?"

Sheila could see him envisioning petty theft. "He means go to a restaurant and get some food - our treat. Interested?"

The old man got to his feet spryly. "Sho. I'm interested."

"All right! Sheila - know a good place? Maybe one a little less popular with your old friends..."

She smiled. "I think I know just the joint. Come on."

As they walked, both Sheila and Wyatt tried to subtly grill the old man for any insight he might have as to the cause of their stereoscopic nocturnal escapade. But try as they would he showed no knowledge of their situation. After ten minutes of hinting, they exchanged a secretive glance of desperate surrender and walked the rest of the way in sullen, plotting silence.After a short while they arrived at their destination: Jack's - a classic 50's-style diner, complete with Windstream stainless steel exterior and tabletop juke box consoles.

"All right!" Malcolm said.

"I hope the culinary fare is to your liking," Wyatt joked as they settled down in a booth with traditional red vinyl upholstery patched with green electrical tape.

"I don' know 'bout that, but dis is my kind'a place!"

Sheila winked. "Speaking of your favorite places, with all you know about Africa, you must've met a lot of people who've been there, or maybe were from there?"

"A few." The old man grabbed a handful of sugar packets and unselfconsciously stuffed them in his pocket.

"For a rainy day?" Wyatt asked.

"Fo' coffee," Malcolm answered.

Sheila glared at Wyatt. "About those friends of yours, from Africa, were they...businessmen..."

"Or merchant marines..?"

"Or witchdoctors?"

Wyatt glared at her. "She means traditional medicine practitioners," Wyatt explained.

"Did you ever think of going into politics?" Sheila asked.

"Witchdoctors?" Mal said, looking at them out of the corner of his eyes. "You mean like voodoo?"

Sheila nearly spit out the mouthful of water she was drinking. "Voodoo! Why did you say that? I didn't say anything about voodoo!"

Malcolm looked even more confused than ever. "Well, if you don't means voodoo, what do you mean?"

"Of course I mean voodoo!" Sheila half shouted. A young mother sitting in the booth next to them grabbed her daughter and scurried out of the diner.

Wyatt looked around the restaurant with a frozen smile, meeting a dozen hostile glares in the process. "Take it easy Sheila," he whispered through clenched teeth.

"Funny you say that," Mal said slowly. "There was this one man, come from...Benny, some place like that, and he..."

He was interrupted by the waitress, a hefty middle-aged woman with dyed orange-ish purple hair. Actually, although her hair was indeed somewhat orange, upon closer examination it was her purple hairnet that created the unique color combination.

"Menus?" she asked, offering three egg yolk-splattered plastic-coated menu cards.

"No!" Sheila barked, pushing them back at the woman with such ferocity that she fell back a step. "We'll have three 'bacon and eggs'. Coffee all around. Got it? Now go on Malcolm."

The woman scribbled in her tiny notepad as the old man began.

"Ma-shood. Called hisself, Ma-shood, sumthin' like that. He was a big ol' boy, must'a been 6 foot five, maybe six, and..."

"How would you like those cooked?" the waitress interrupted.

Sheila was about to explode all over the poor unsuspecting woman when Wyatt rested his hand on her shoulder to restrain her. "One scrambled, one over easy, one poached," Sheila said slowly, the strain evident in her voice. "Cream and sugar for the coffees, ketchup and jam on the side. Toast, no muffins, no grits, no juice, no nothin. See you again real soon. Malcolm?"

The waitress retreated dazedly to the safety of the kitchen. The old man looked at Sheila with narrowed eyes.

"I likes orange juice..." the old man complained plaintively.

"Next life," she said. "Go on with your story."

Malcolm looked to Wyatt, who shrugged helplessly. "Well, like I was sayin', he was a big man, and he had all these scars on his face, looked like some kind of fuckin' big black cat..."

"I'm sure he was real imposing," Sheila said. "But what about the voodoo?"

"He come from a real African village..."

"What about the VOODOOO?!"

Malcolm tried to back up through the seatback. Heads turned. Wyatt hung his head, trying to hide.

"You got a valium or something in that purse of yours?" he whispered urgently.

Sheila stared at him with pursed lips and flaming eyes. But she got the message.

"Okay, all right. I just got a little excited, that's all. I'm okay now. It's just that I'm very interested in all this Africa stuff, just like you," she told Malcolm. "Now, go on..."

"Yeh, okay, but now I knows why I never hung with no white bitches. Too weird," the old man said, looking to Wyatt for confirmation. The younger man rubbed his eyes, trying not to smile. Malcolm waited a moment before continuing, his voice dropping to a conspiratorial whisper. "This Ma-shood, he come here by boat. Jump off in New Or-leens. Stayed illegal. Travel a lot. But he knowed all this Africa stuff..."

"Incantations?" Sheila pressed.

"Don' know 'bout that, but he tol' me lots of stories; say he's a magic man, and sometime, late at night, I catch him 'round the campfire mumbling some powerful African words. One time I even seen him kill a chicken and drink its blood!"

"I knew it!" Sheila said. "That's where our dream came from!"

"What dream?"

"As if you don't know." She smiled at the old man, who stared back with a blank look. "The dream with the African village and the mask?"

A look of realization came over the old man. "Did you hears drums? African drums?"

"Of course!"

"You heard the heartbeat!"

"Here we go again," Wyatt said with a sigh.

"What heartbeat? Have you known about this all along?" she asked Wyatt.

"It's more of this cosmic, back to Africa stuff."

"You heard it. It's in you. Now you're part of it," Malcolm said, suddenly enlivened.

"What's in me? Are we still talking voodoo?"

"It ain't voodoo, woman, it's magic! It's Fuckin'-A, number 1, back to the beginnin' black magic!"

"Oh, that's reassuring," Sheila said.

"Don't tell me you's scared too?" the old man asked.

"What do you mean, too?" Wyatt asked indignantly. "I'm not scared of some weird African dream."

"That's not what your eyes said back there when we was hitchin' and you was tellin' me 'bout it."

"That's ridiculous..."

"Methinks the gentleman doth protest too much," Sheila said softly, one eyebrow cocked appraisingly.

"Oh come on, not you too!"

"Don't matter, don't matter," Malcolm said, trying to calm the situation. "All that's 'portant is the heartbeat. You heard it, you feels it, it's in you."

"Terrific. So exactly how do we get it out?" Sheila asked.

"Get it out? I's had that same dream for seven years now! Tried everythin'. Only one way lef' I can think of to get it out, and that's go to the source, the cradle of civilization, the spirit'shul center of the universe, the Homeland." He sat and looked at them with a contented, self-assured smile.

"Jesus, this is where I came in," Wyatt mumbled.

"Africa? You mean, go to Africa?" Sheila wailed. "I can't go to Africa, I've got responsibilities!"

"Like what?" Malcolm asked. "What's more 'portant than findin' out who you is, where you come from, where we all goin'?"

Sheila looked momentarily nonplussed. "Well, I'm supposed to have the carpets cleaned next week."

"You gots to have yo' *soul* cleaned!" Malcolm said. This time it was Sheila's turn to flinch.

"Malcolm, get off it, okay," Wyatt said. "If you want to go to Africa, bon voyage. Africa's not our homeland."

"Where is our homeland?" Sheila asked.

"I don't know, probably France or Germany or someplace."

"Ain't no heartbeat in no France or Germany," the old man said resolutely.

"We don't care, Malcolm! The point is, Africa has no attraction for us."

"I wouldn't say that exactly," Sheila explained. "I mean, I'd kind of like to visit Kenya, see the elephants, maybe a lion or two."

Malcolm shook his head. "You fuckin' whitebread turkeys wouldn't know shit if you stepped in it. You been brainwashed by all them mouthwash and pussy spray salesman."

Sheila grimaced. "Malcolm..."

Just then the waitress returned carrying their food. She was cautious, standing a few feet away from the table until she was recognized.

"You all ready to eat?" she asked in a tiny voice.

"Yes!" Sheila and Wyatt barked in unison.

Malcolm nodded listlessly.

The waitress quickly dealt their plates and just as quickly retreated. Malcolm plowed into his food without a word, without even raising his head. Sheila and Wyatt exchanged glances, deciding with a shrug here, a nod there, that they should do the same - eat and move on.

Breakfast passed in a blur of flashing forks and knives, with the only sounds the subdued crunching of slightly burnt toast and the occasional grunt by Malcolm, signifying exactly what, no one knew.

"Good food, huh?" Sheila asked at one point, trying to discern if the grunts were a sign of satisfaction or emotional distress. Malcolm grunted. Wyatt shrugged and all three went back to their food without further conversation.

Malcolm finished first, wiping the last vestige of yolk from his plate with a crust of toast and draining his coffee with a slurp that Sheila interpreted as a slap at she and Wyatt.

"Did 'ya have enough?" she asked, knowing that the question bore the risk of hostile response.

"Umm," the old man said.

"I think that's an affirmative," Wyatt joked.

Malcolm looked up at him and grimaced.

"Hey, just kidding Malcolm. No offense intended."

The old man started to collect his bundle as he prepared to leave.

"Where are you going?" Wyatt asked.

Malcolm stared for a moment before answering. "Out."

"If you wait for a few minutes until we finish we'll walk you back," Sheila said.

"I can finds my own way."

"I'm sure you can," she said. "I just thought you might want some company."

He shook his head slowly. "You two's hopeless."

Without even a glance back at them he slipped out of the booth and straight to the door.

"Nice seeing you again," Wyatt muttered under his breath.

"Any chance we can chip in and get him a personality transplant?" Sheila asked.

"Hey - all we've got to do is find the right witch doctor and he can voodoo him up a new persona. Jesus. Where do they come from?"

"Witch doctors?"

"No - people like Malcolm. I mean, he really believes this African heartbeat bullshit."

"You gotta admit, that dream is a pretty strong argument."

"It's a dream, goddamn it! Haven't you ever had a bad dream before? I mean, everybody has them. Hell, Freud made his whole reputation on bad dreams."

"But not shared bad dreams. Have you ever shared someone else's dream before? And a mighty darn weird one at that, if I may say so."

Wyatt shrugged with his palms turned skyward. "Okay. I admit it's a little weird. But that doesn't mean it's supernatural. Probably just the power of suggestion. You know, Malcolm told me late at night, just before going to bed, and I told you, and so we dreamed what we dreamed."

"But you didn't tell me any details, and I dreamed the same damn village! How do you explain that?"

Wyatt tilted his head thoughtfully. "Thought projection?"

Sheila laughed out loud. "Are you kidding me?! You think voodoo is bullshit but believe in thought projection? That's like saying you don't believe in Santa but still put your tooth under your pillow for the Tooth Fairy!"

Wyatt looked crestfallen. "You mean there's no Tooth Fairy?"

"You *are* hopeless!" Sheila said. "Come on - let's get out of here and see if we can forget this voodoo crap."

They paid the bill, Sheila tipping the waitress overly generously out of guilt, and went outside. Malcolm was nowhere to be seen.

"He's not here," Wyatt said, scanning the street.

"Malcolm? Yeh, I sort of thought he might be waiting for us too."

"Think we finally pissed him off?"

"Does that mean the dream goes with him?"

"God, I sure hope so. This whole episode is starting to get just a little bit irritating."

"Just a little bit?"

"All right, real fucking irritating. I was starting to wish I'd never met the old man."

"Well...what do you say we do our own disappearing act? There's a place I know, not more than an hour from here, quiet, peaceful, just the place to forget all about Africa and its heartbeat."

"Can we pack a picnic?"

"You can pack a fucking piano if you want, but the last mile or so is on foot. Might be a bit of a bitch."

"I was thinking more of a sandwich or two, some chips, a six-pack..."

"A bottle of white wine?"

"I'm open to negotiation," he said.

"Good. Come on, let's go before he shows up again."

The drive out of the city was a pleasant one, the cool morning mists having burned off to a crisp blue dotted with dramatic billowing white northern Colorado clouds.

"Jesus, this is fucking breathtaking!" Wyatt said as they cruised the two-lane highway out through the dry high plateau scenery.

"You didn't think we all lived out here just to root for the Broncos, did you?"

"I sure as hell hope not. That'd be grounds for institutionalization in some parts."

The miles rolled past, filled with huge angular rock formations, glimpses of the Platte off in the distance, and increasingly stands and then forests of evergreens. They began to climb steadily and soon the air temperature began to drop. By the time Sheila finally pulled over they had made their way over a thousand feet above Greeley, and the bright sunlight was a welcomed source of warmth on a cool fall day.

"This is where we get out," she announced, pulling over into a dirt turn-out on the side of the road.

Wyatt climbed out and stretched, drawing in a lung-full of the sweet mountain air. "I take it we walk from here?"

"That's right - take a deep breath, it may be the last one you get for a while. It's all uphill from here."

"You didn't tell me we were mountain climbing."

"Afraid of heights?"

"No, but I didn't bring my pitons..." Wyatt said.

"No problem, we're not making a salad here."

Wyatt groaned. They went around to unload their things from the trunk, but it was easier said than done.

"Jesus!" Wyatt said, hefting his bulging pack. "What did you put in here, that piano you were talking about?"

"You wanna eat? Then keep quiet. You'll survive."

"That's easy for you to say. What are you carrying?"

Sheila smiled. "I have to keep my hands empty - just in case I have to carry you back down."

"Is that a challenge?"

"Just a prediction."

Sheila wasn't far wrong. Even for someone used to hiking, as Wyatt most certainly was, the path was steep and exhausting. In the thin mountain air he found himself straining to suck in enough air to fill his lungs, even while trying to maintain a calm, cool exterior. After just 30 minutes his face was red, sweat was running down his neck and his legs began to vulcanize.

"How you doin'?" Sheila called out, stopping to turn back from her lead position.

"Fine," he wheezed, his voice so thin his vocal cords barely resonated.

"Want to take a little breather?"

"You?"

"I'm okay."

She stared at him until a thin smile tugged at the corners of her mouth.

"You look like a big red balloon about to burst."

"No problem," he panted. "Let's go."

She patted him on the shoulder. "Maybe I could use a little break. Let's take five - could I have a sip of water?"

Wyatt virtually collapsed on the spot, rolling out of the straps of his pack like a giant beached jellyfish. He fished the canteen out of the pack, unscrewed the top and, tempted, hesitated for just an instant before passing it.

"Go ahead, you can have the first sip," Sheila said, offering it back to him.

"No, no, go ahead," he croaked. "Ladies first."

"Well, I don't see no ladies, but I appreciate the thought," she said, drinking deeply of the cool water.

Wyatt eyed the canteen longingly; his hand reached out autonomously as soon as she lowered it.

"Ahhhhh. When you're really thirsty there's nothing like a nice cool drink of water," she said, holding the canteen evaluatively in front of her, seemingly oblivious of his need.

His hand crept out slowly, but she wasn't done torturing him.

"You know, I don't think there's anything that quenches a thirst quite like it. So cool, clean..."

His hand darted out and grabbed the canteen out of her hand. Water dribbled out of the corners of his mouth as he chugged it greedily. "And wet..." he finally said as he lowered the container.

"And wet," she echoed. "All ready now? We're just a few hundred yards from where we're headed."

"Is this where we break out the pitons?" he asked.

She laughed. "Not quite yet - I'll let you know," she said, bouncing to her feet. "Come on! You're gonna love it!"

"If I live that long," he mumbled, pushing himself slowly to the vertical. He stumbled along behind her lead, soon trailing a good distance behind. Beneficently, she stopped every few minutes to let him close the gap. Finally, after what seemed like an hour to Wyatt but actually was closer to fifteen minutes, they heard a low rumbling in the near distance. He was about to yell "rockslide!" and high-tail it back down the slope, but Sheila's studied indifference kept him where he was. He knew she could hear it, and yet she kept moving forward as if it posed no danger.

Stepping around a sharp bend in the path, Wyatt had to pull up quickly to avoid bumping into her.

"What the...?"

As he looked up he saw first her wide, beaming smile, and then following her gaze found himself staring into the roaring whitewater of a mountain waterfall. He followed the cascading waters down the sheer rock cliffs to a large, crystal clear pool about fifty feet below where they stood.

"Did I lie?" she asked, raising her voice to be heard over the rushing water.

"I love it!" he said.

She danced forward and kissed him lightly on the lips. "Come on - there's a perfect place for a picnic down below."

Before he could say a word she was off again. He took a deep breath, shifted the pack to relieve the strain to his shoulders, and set off after her.

The path down to the pool ran parallel to the falls and was slick from the fine spray that exploded off the rocks on either side. Sheila navigated the path without any apparent problem, but Wyatt had to brace himself repeatedly to keep from sliding butt first into the deep blue water below. With a few minor slips and spills they eventually navigated the path down to the pool and then around a large free-standing rock to a smaller pool, complete with a small series of rapids. The roar of the falls was diminished to a dull hum behind the natural rock wall.

"Well, what do you think?" Sheila asked when Wyatt finally straggled into the serene hideaway.

He stopped to look around slowly, a small smile of satisfaction on his lips. "I don't know what you charge for this, but it's worth it," he said.

"You'll get the bill later. For now, how about some of that wine."

She spread a blanket next to the pool and unpacked the food and drink while Wyatt sat on a rock overlooking the running water and marveling at the sight.

"This is just amazing to me," he said.

"What's that?"

"This, the whole scene. All this water in such dry country. You, me - us..."

"Are we an us?" she asked provocatively as she carried a tin cup of wine to the rock where he was sitting. He glanced over and saw that same taunting smile.

"Well, yeh, I mean, it depends how you define it I suppose, but..."

"You really are an artist with words," she teased.

He grabbed her by the waist and pulled her next to him.

"Hey - look out! You almost spilled the wine," she said.

"You're such an incurable romantic," he said, taking the two cups from her hands and putting them down on the rock next to him.

"I can be romantic enough, given the right circumstances."

"Like what?"

"Well...like this."

He gently pulled her down to him and they kissed. As they separated their eyes met, saying more than they would have admitted, even to themselves. Stroking her hair, he kissed her softly on the forehead. She rested her head on his shoulder and they sat there together, drinking in the beauty of the moment with the only sound the hum of the falls behind them.

The afternoon passed quickly as they sipped their wine, kept icy cold in the swirling pool, and talked of regrets from the past and hopes for the future. Both recognized the moment for what it was: that special time when two people realize for the first time that they share something beyond simple humanity, something important enough that each is willing to let down the barrier s/he maintains to fend off the ravages of the everyday world and reveal something of the fragile person within. Long before they were ready to surrender the moment, the shadows began to grow long and the fragile warmth of the sun dissipated.

"I hate to be the one to say it," Sheila said as she felt a cool breeze send a shiver through Wyatt, "but we'd better be on our way if we want to get back to town before dark."

"I don't suppose we could just pitch a lean-to and spend the next few years right here," he said.

"Not unless you want to freeze your ass off and end up a quick snack for the local bear population."

Wyatt shrugged. "Ah, a true romantic. Okay, let's go."

"Don't be mad: we'll have other waterfalls. Who knows, maybe even in Africa."

"Don't even joke about that," he said, eyeing her with a grim expression. "I don't want to joke about Africa, I don't want to dream about Africa, I don't even want to think about Africa."

"Malcolm will be disappointed."

"Fuck Malcolm! That heartbeat crap is his dream, not ours! Let him keep it to himself."

"Okay, okay," she soothed. "From now on we only talk about...Hoboken, New Jersey."

His frown dissolved. "Let's not get carried away," he said, kissing her quickly. "There are worse places than Africa."

"A shocking revelation," she joked. "Come on, let's get packed up and head back."

The hike back to the car was only slightly less treacherous than the hike up. Although they were walking downhill for the most part, and the pack was a good deal lighter, the wine and tired muscles made maneuvering on the slippery path all the more difficult. At one point just a few hundred yards down from the falls, Wyatt lost his balance and slid down the trail on his backside for twenty feet or so, coming to rest against a rotten tree stump.

"Are you okay?!" Sheila asked, half running and half sliding to his side.

One look at his smiling, embarrassed face gave her her answer. "I haven't had this much fun since third grade at St. Anthony's," he said.

"Some boys never grow up," she said, reaching out her hand to help him up. He took hold of it and pulled her down on top of him. She fell with a whoop.

"The thing is, some girls don't want us to," he said, rolling over on top of her.

"This is not a good time, or place," Sheila said with a straight face. They both burst into laughter.

By the time they got back to the car the sun was just starting to disappear behind the hilltops and the temperature was falling quickly. They piled inside, cranking the heat up to full, and with the radio blaring made their way uneventfully back to Greeley.

They marched up the front steps to the guest house lost in laughter and conversation. No sooner did they step foot inside, however, than they realized that they were no longer alone. Emmy took one look at the mud smeared duo and shook her head.

"Whatever happened to you two?"

"We went on a picnic," Wyatt said.

"Where - Hedley's pig farm? You two are a mess!"

"We slipped," Sheila said, exchanging a smiling glance with Wyatt.

"So I see. All right. Upstairs - and don't touch anything. We'll have to see if we can wash those clothes, or whether it'd be better to just burn 'em."

"Yes, mom," Wyatt said. He and Sheila ran up the stairs laughing as Emmy stood at the bottom and watched them with a broad smile.

CHAPTER FIVE

The smoke swirled eerily in the small enclosure. The drums were distant, echoing, as though communicating across a great expanse. Wyatt experienced a strong sense of dislocation, a feeling as though he were drifting through the smoke, his feet not even touching the ground. He didn't know why he was there, or where he would go if he left, but felt a powerful urge to turn and run. The drums began to beat louder, more urgently, their message pounding nearer and nearer. The urge to flee intensified; he could feel his heart throb, synchronized to the drumbeat, as if it lived inside him. He looked for an exit, somewhere to run, somewhere to escape, but the smoke grew more dense, a grey moving blanket that clung to him, blinding his eyes and burning his throat.

The drums came closer, the pounding rhythm surrounding him, engulfing him, the vibrations beating against his chest as if he were the drum head itself. He felt himself falling, slowly, almost imperceptibly, the smoke swirling around him like a giant whirlpool. The drums thundered into his head, overpowering all his senses; in that moment there was only the drums and him.

Suddenly a terrifying yell rent the darkness. Wyatt forced open his eyes only to confront a strangely familiar red and black mask, dancing just inches from his face. He wanted to run, to escape, but the mask held him in place, froze him to the spot. He struggled to break free, but his feet wouldn't budge. Finally, his strength failing, his nerves frayed, he reached out with his last ounce of strength and grabbed the mask, pulling it free and throwing it with all his might into the smoky surround.

The drums stopped abruptly. The smoke vanished. He looked back and there, staring him straight in the face, was the same red and black mask.

"Noooo!" he screamed, covering his eyes with his arms.

Sheila threw her arms around his shoulders and held him tight. "It's okay Wyatt, it's just a dream," she soothed. She rocked back and forth on the bed, cradling his head in her arms.

"I was there...again...the drums...the mask..."

"I know, I know," she said, kissing him on the forehead.

"In the smoke...I was trapped...the drums..."

"I know. I was there."

Wyatt stopped rocking and looked up at her, his eyes wide, the sweat-drenched hair at his temples plastered back against his head.

"You were there? You saw him?"

"Our witchdoctor friend? Yeh, I saw him."

For an instant Wyatt was lost, his head shaking back and forth of its own accord. But then he found himself.

"Goddamn it! What is going on here?!" he demanded. "What does he want from us!?"

"It's okay, Wyatt. It was just a dream..." Sheila tried to pull him close, to comfort him. But he would have no part of it.

"No way! This is something weird, something....I don't know!" He pulled away from her and jumped up, pacing as he raved. "It's that crazy Africa heartbeat bullshit! That's what it is - something like that....something weird.... something....I don't want anything to do with."

"Okay - let's say you're right. Let's say this is all Malcolm's doing. What do you suggest we do about it?"

Wyatt stopped pacing. "I'll tell you what we do about it - we get some sleep, get up first thing in the morning, find that old son of a bitch and make him turn us free! I mean, this is his dream, not ours - right?"

"Are we back to voodoo again?"

"Voodoo, black magic, subconscious suggestion, call it whatever you like. The point is, this all started with him and it damn well is going to end with him."

"And if he refuses? Or, more likely, thinks you're a lunatic for believing he's making you dream about Africa. What then? Are you going to sacrifice a chicken and drink its blood?"

Her point struck home. Wyatt sat quietly on the edge of the bed. "I've never been a big fan of chicken blood," he admitted.

"I'm glad to hear that. Got any less dramatic ideas?"

"Well, I suppose we could just talk to him."

"Not quite as colorful, but I think a lot more useful."□

"Yeh. I guess it would sound a little crazy if we accused him of practicing black magic on us."

"Just a little."

Wyatt smiled sheepishly. "I guess I got a little carried away."

"Just a little."

He nodded. "So, you tired?"

She snuggled up next to him and kissed his neck. "Just a little," she whispered.

It was some time before they finally fell asleep.

By the time they awoke the next morning the sun was already well up in the sky.

"Jesus! What time is it?" Wyatt asked, jumping out of bed and pulling on his jeans.

"Wha..? What's the difference?" Sheila asked, half awake.

"The difference is, if Malcolm's still around here somewhere - and that's a big *if* knowing the kind of railman he is - then he's probably planning on moving along real soon. If he hasn't left already, we have our best chance of finding him before the 10:40 comes through town."

"You have the train schedule memorized?"

"When you spend a day or two camping next to the tracks you can't help but notice when the trains come through. Now if you're coming, let's go!"

"All right, all right, keep your shirt on," she mumbled as she struggled out of bed. Despite his impatience, Wyatt couldn't resist watching her dress out of the corner of his eye. He stared with well-deserved lust and a surprising feeling of intimacy. The smooth white skin, the small but full breasts, thin hips running into long, dancer's legs...he turned away and exhaled heavily.

"All right, let's go find this dangerous witchdoctor," she said, pulling on a sweater and giving her hair a quick shake.

When they got downstairs Emmy was waiting for them. A pile of clean clothes sat on the reception counter.

"I won't say they're good as new, but pretty darn close," she said proudly.

"You washed them?" Sheila asked.

"You shouldn't have," Wyatt added. "It's not in the contract."

"An old mom never dies, she just cleans away," Emmy said with a smile. "Besides, what else am I going to do: Oprah doesn't come on til ten, and I try not to have my first drink until lunchtime."

Sheila kissed her on the cheek. "Thanks, Emmy. We owe you one."

"Don't mention it - the other guests will want the same!"

They all laughed. "Well, we'll see you back here in a few hours," Wyatt said, eager to get on with the search.

"Where are you off to now? I hope it's someplace cleaner than yesterday."

"Actually, we're going to go look for a friend of ours," Sheila explained.

"An old black man, about so tall?" Emmy asked.

Wyatt and Sheila exchanged a look of puzzlement.

"Yeh. How'd you know that?"

"He's sitting right outside, just across the street. Same as yesterday. Been there all morning."

They dashed to the front door and peered out the window. Sure enough, there was Malcolm, lazing comfortably under the same tree.

"Goddamn," Wyatt muttered to himself. He threw open the door and rushed down the stairs.

"Excuse us, Emmy," Sheila said. "We need to talk with our friend."

"I can see that. What's the problem - money?"

"Not exactly. Dreams."

The old lady showed her confusion but didn't ask.

"I'll explain later," Sheila said, kissing her on the cheek. Receiving a silent nod in response, Sheila ran after Wyatt, leaving Emmy to watch, fascinated, from the front parlor window.

As she crossed the street, hurrying as quickly as she could without showing it, she hoped Wyatt hadn't been too tough on the old man. After all, it really wasn't his fault they were having those dreams, was it? Wyatt and Malcolm were already deep in conversation when she sidled up next to them.

"So, how's it going?" she asked with too much good cheer.

"I was just asking how he'd spent the night, and he was telling me about a camp he'd found just a few miles from here," Wyatt said.

"Oh? Nice place?" she asked.

"Not so bad," Malcolm answered noncommittally.

"Actually, we were kind of surprised to see you still hanging around here," Wyatt continued. "Thought you might have decided to hit the road."

"Nope."

"How come?" Wyatt asked. Sheila elbowed him in the side. "I mean," he corrected, "Why Greeley? Do you have friends here?"

"Nope."

"So how come you're still here?" Wyatt pressed, his impatience overpowering Sheila's glare.

"It's a free country," the old man said.

"That's true. That's very true," Wyatt said, backing off a bit.

"We thought you might have...gone off to Africa," Sheila said with an awkward smile.

"Nope."

"Why haven't you - gone to Africa, I mean," Wyatt asked. "You're always talking about it..."

The old man cocked his head and sighed. "Ain't got the money."

"Oh, I'm sure you could find a way. I mean, there's always cargo ships - you could probably hire on as a hand..."

"Don't like ships. You ever been on one?"

"No," Wyatt admitted. "Can't say as I have."

"Well I has, and it ain't no fun. It's like bein' in the middle of the desert durin' an earthquake - everythin's movin', you can see fo'ever, and there ain't no place to get away. It be all aroun' you. And it's fuckin' hard work, too."

"There must be other ways..." Sheila prodded.

"Tell me one."

"Well..."

"I tried bein' a stowedaway - it ain't so easy as jumpin' a train. Caught me befo' we even left port."

"Okay...how about..." Sheila looked to Wyatt for support. He shrugged.

"Why you so interested in me goin' to Africa? Thought it was bullshit."

"Well, we just thought..."

"That you should live your dream," Sheila chimed in. "Everyone should live their dream."

"That's right!" Wyatt said. "You should live your dream."

The old man stared at his feet as he fiddled with a shoelace. "You din't have the dream las' night?" he asked suddenly.

Wyatt and Sheila exchanged a look usually exchanged only by caged rabbits.

"Well, actually, we did sort of have the dream again," Wyatt stumbled.

"Of the village?"

"Well, yeh, of the village, and the hut, and the smoke and the mask, and the whole goddamn thing!" Wyatt exploded. "And I'm pretty darn sick of it! What I want to know is what you have to do with it?"

Sheila grabbed him by the elbow but didn't interfere.

Malcolm looked up, his eyes screwed into a knotty question mark. "What I has to do with it? Like how?"

"Like how'd you do this to us!" the younger man raged. "How'd you get inside our heads to make us dream your dream?"

"More to the point, how do we get out?" Sheila added.

A sad smile spread the old man's lips. "Ain't no way out 'cept go to the source."

"You mean go to Africa?!" Wyatt shouted. "You got to be crazy!"

"Maybe. Maybe not. But like I say, I been havin' the same dream fo' mo' than seven year, and I ain't found no other way out."

Wyatt stared at him with wide, bulging eyes. "You mean we could be stuck with this nightmare for seven years?! Every night?"

"Every goddamn, motha' fuckin' night."

Wyatt leaned his head against the tree. He was speechless. It was even worse than he'd thought.

"You okay?" Sheila asked, gently rubbing his back.

"No, I'm not okay. And neither are you, or Malcolm for that matter."

"There's got to be some way to get rid of it. Maybe a shrink..."

"Hell, they can't help you lose weight, let alone lose a nightmare. We'd have a better chance going to a plumber."

"There's got to be a way," she pressed.

"Only one way," the old man said softly.

Wyatt looked down at him. "Go to Africa."

Malcolm nodded.

The younger man dropped his head into his hands.

CHAPTER SIX

Wyatt stared at the brake lights and shook his head in disbelief. "I gotta be crazy."

After driving for three days straight, taking breaks only for food and pit stops, none of the three was in any mood for the miles of bumper to bumper traffic that greeted them at the approach to the Lincoln Tunnel.

Sheila looked over wearily at the car next to them, and was greeted by a broad smile from a young Latino.

"Hey, bay-bee!" he yelled, pursing his lips with mock kisses. "Hey, I wanna' do dis wit' you!" he shouted, as his car began to buck up and down on hydraulic shocks.

"Very impressive," she said with a weak smile, turning back to Wyatt who was trying not to fall asleep at the wheel. "These New Yorkers sure are sophisticated."

"They aren't New Yorkers," Wyatt growled. "They're from Jersey. Those are the New Yorkers." He pointed over at the adjoining side of the tunnel, where equal numbers of drivers were fleeing the city. "It happens every Friday night: all the New Yorkers take off for the 'burbs, and all the turkeys from Jersey come into the city."

"Is that why the New Yorkers leave?"

Wyatt smiled. "That's a real possibility."

He reached down and turned on the radio. A rap song exploded over the speakers. He punched the channel selector:

another rap song. Then another, and a fourth. He changed the channel with increasing animosity. "I hate that shit!" he finally shouted.

"Great place. Two hundred stations and they all play the same song," Sheila said. "Here - let me try."

She rubbed her finger on her shoulder for luck and touched the seek button. U2 popped onto the airwaves.

"How's that?"

"How'd you do that?" he asked.

"You gotta have the touch. And you, quite obviously, don't have it."

"Quite obviously," he said, sighing deeply.

"I'm gettin' hungry," Malcolm piped up from the back seat.

Sheila dug into a crumpled MacDonalds bag and pulled out a half-eaten apple pie.

"Told you it'd come in handy," she said, handing it back to the old man. He accepted it, and devoured it, in silence.

"So do you have a place in mind to crash for the night, or do we just play it by ear?" she asked Wyatt.

"Like I said, I spent some time back here just a few weeks ago. I know a place that's not half bad, and it's cheap."

"Trump Tower?"

Wyatt shrugged. "Something like that."

Two hours later they had inched their way through the tunnel and across town to the Bronx. They passed a burned-out building and several stripped, abandoned cars.

"Nice neighborhood," Sheila said. "I take it we're passing on the Plaza."

"Keep your panties dry. It gets better."

They bumped and lurched through pot-holed streets, dodging gaping chasms that could swallow Greyhound buses whole and kamikaze pedestrians who seemed to delight in timing their headlong rushes across the street to coincide as closely as possible to passing vehicles.

"What is wrong with these people!" Sheila finally screamed when the third jaywalker in less than five minutes darted out of the darkness just in front of their bumper.

"They're New Yorkers," Wyatt said simply.

"So what does that mean? They all have some kind of congenital defect - a complete and total lack of common sense and an urge for self-destruction?"

"Yeh. That's a New Yorker, all right."

Around a corner and down two blocks Wyatt brought the car to a sudden stop, darting into a parking place just vacated.

"Why are we stopping?" Sheila asked, eying the seedy neighborhood with skepticism.

"This is it. The Hotel Paradiso. Home sweet home."

"This is it?"

"Relax. It's not as bad as it looks," Wyatt comforted.

"Couldn' be," Malcolm piped up from the back seat.

"Just grab your things. I wouldn't advise leaving anything in the car."

"Wouldn' 'vise leavin' the car," Malcolm mumbled as he struggled to fight his way out of the back seat.

He didn't have to make the point twice. Sheila stayed close to the car as they unpacked, looking up and down the street at the unsavory characters that hung out there. In the dim yellow street light they all looked like potential muggers.

"All set?" Wyatt asked when they'd hefted their measly luggage and locked the car.

"As set as we're gonna be," Sheila said.

"All right. Let's check in."

They crossed the street under the watchful gaze of three young ladies of dubious moral character. One wore electric pink hot pants that seemed to glow in the dark, another a leather mini-skirt that barely covered the curve of her backside, and the last a shimmering gold-glitter outfit that could have been spray painted on her deliciously curvaceous body.

"Local welcoming committee?" Sheila asked.

"The neighborhood watch. They're undercover," Wyatt said.

"Hey, Wyatt, you came back!" the mini-skirted black beauty yelled to them as they strolled up to the entrance to the hotel.

"A friend of yours?" Sheila asked.

"She must have mistaken me for someone else," he said, hurrying her inside the reinforced glass door.

To Sheila the hotel lobby resembled the vault area at the National Bank of Greeley. One small stained and cigarette-burned lime green couch sat off to the side, with a tottering three-legged coffee table just in front of it. The front desk was surrounded by two-inch bomb-proof Plexiglas, with only a tiny slot for cash transactions.

"Hey, Wyatt, good to see you again," the young clerk said over a small, tinny speaker when he saw them come in. "Looks like someone's going to have a party," he added, eyeing the three of them with a leering grin.

"How impressive: a legend in his own dive," Sheila mumbled. Wyatt ignored her.

"We just want a room," he said.

"What?" the clerk asked, straining to hear through the thick Plexiglas.

"A room!" he shouted. "We need a room!"

The clerk nodded. "By the hour or for the night?" he asked straight-faced.

"For the night!" Wyatt shouted. "Maybe two!"

"Two rooms?"

"Two nights!"

The clerk scanned a coffee-stained register. "Looks like you can have 203 again," he said, his voice buzzing annoyingly through the cheap speaker.

"Two-o-three," Sheila said. "Is that your usual party pad?"

"Cute," Wyatt said. "We'll take it!" he shouted through the Plexiglas.

"There a rail yard anywhere 'round here?" Malcolm asked.

"There's Penn Station over in Manhattan. But I wouldn't advise it."

"Yeh. It's probably kind of rough," Sheila said. "Not cozy like this place."

"Hey, it's cheap, the air-conditioning and hot water work, and I've never been hassled here."

"Great. Sounds like the Hilton," Sheila said.

"That'll be thirty five - fifty," the voice announced over the speaker.

"I's a little short," Malcolm said.

"No shit," Wyatt said, digging into his pocket and sliding the wadded bills through the narrow slot. A key quickly came sliding back.

"I'll sign you in," the clerk said. "Have a good time."

"No doubt," Sheila said with a smile. "So, should we wait for the bellboys or carry the stuff ourselves?"

Wyatt threw his pack over his shoulder. "You'll be waiting a long time," he said, making for the stairs.

"Somehow I knew that," she said. She and Malcolm followed close behind.

Except for the dim lighting and the areas of water damaged carpet, the inside of the hotel wasn't all that depressing. Or perhaps it was just difficult to see.

"Do you think they could've splurged a little on the light bulbs?" Sheila asked as they trudged down the darkened corridor to their room.

"Maybe 15-watt bulbs are expensive in New York," Wyatt said.

"These couldn't be more than ten-watt."

"Probably part of their environmental movement - you know, saving on electricity."

"Right."

Room 203 was halfway down the hallway on the right. Wyatt put the key in the lock, pulled mightily on the door handle, turned the key, and then shoved against the balky door with his shoulder.

"Part of the security system?" Sheila asked.

"Feel safer?" Wyatt said. "Come on in. Make yourself at home."

The room was slightly brighter than the corridor, but Sheila quickly realized that was because the pale green neon Hotel Paradiso sign hung just outside their window. An overpowering smell of stale cigarette smoke nearly gagged her. She thought she saw a small creature scurry behind the dresser, but decided she's rather remain ignorant and declined to mention it.

"I like the room freshener. What's it called - Ashtray Bouquet?"

"It's not so bad with the air conditioner on," Wyatt said, strolling over to a window-mount model with the decorative walnut grain cover sitting shattered beneath it on the floor. He flipped the dial and the machine roared to life, sounding surprisingly like an old man clearing his lungs first thing in the morning.

"There. How's that?" Wyatt asked, raising his voice slightly to be heard over the ruckus.

"Great. Masks the street noise too. Did we have to pay extra?"

"All inclusive price. That's why I love this place."

Malcolm had flopped down in a lime green armchair that looked like it had been borrowed from the set down in the lobby. He was shaking his head.

"What's the matter Malcolm. Disappointed there's no jacuzzi?"

"You sho' there ain't no rail yard near here?"

"Sorry, this is the best we can do for tonight. You wanna crash on the floor?"

The old man slowly scanned the room. He pulled himself painfully to his feet and shuffled into the bathroom. Sheila looked to Wyatt with a perplexed expression.

"When nature calls, you gotta answer," Wyatt said.

But the old man came back out of the bathroom almost immediately.

"Must have been the wrong number on that call," Sheila said.

"Find something?" Wyatt asked.

Malcolm grunted and shuffled over to the green armchair. He lifted the two cushions out of the chair and beat them together with surprising vehemence, raising a cloud of dust that nearly obscured the yellowish mood lighting. Without any explanation he made his way back to the bathroom. Both Sheila and Wyatt crowded into the doorway to watch the old man plop the cushions down into the bathtub. Then he crawled in on top of them, put his small bundle of personal property under his head, and curled up.

"Dis'll do," he said.

"You want a pillow?" Sheila offered.

"Got one," he said without deigning to open his eyes.

"Okay then. I guess we'll just wash up and hit the sack."

When no answer was forthcoming they turned and went back out into the bedroom. Sheila flopped down on the bed.

"I don't know about you, but I'm beat to shit," Wyatt said. "I could sleep on a rock."

"Good thing," Sheila said, pounding the horsehair mattress with her fist.

"Yeh, I know. Not exactly Sealy posturepedic. But, you get used to it."

"I really hope we're not here that long."

"With any luck, we'll be gone tomorrow, day after at worst."

"Good. Now bring that beautiful beat body over here."

"I thought you were tired."

"I will be, in another twenty minutes or so."

And in another twenty minutes she was.

The next morning Wyatt was awakened by Sheila literally leaping from the bed and streaking to the bathroom door. She knocked lightly and, without waiting for an answer, threw open the door.

"Are you okay?" he asked.

"Fine. Go back to sleep," she said before disappearing into canary yellow tile.

Of course sleep was out of the question. He sat up, angling his pillow behind his back for support. In just a few minutes she came out, her sense of urgency greatly diminished.

"What was that all about?" he asked.

"Couldn't hold it anymore."

"So why didn't you go earlier?"

"With him in there? I could just see him peeking out from under those half-closed lids."

"Come on. Besides, wasn't he in there just now?"

"Nope."

"No? Then where the hell is he?"

"Don't ask me. He doesn't keep me informed about his whereabouts or movements."

Just then the door opened and Malcolm crept quietly into the room.

"You don't have to sneak," Sheila said. "We're up."

"Wasn't sneakin'," he said. "Jus' bein' quiet."

"Thanks for the consideration," Wyatt said. "But where the heck did you go?"

"Out."

"I guessed that. Anywhere in particular?"

"Jus' for a walk. Don't much like bein' cooped up inside."

"Used to the freedom of living outside, huh?" Sheila asked.

"Don' like crappin' in them fancy white toilets. Give me a good steamin' shit outside any day."

"A pretty picture indeed," Wyatt said, hopping out of bed and slipping into his jeans. "But enough with the highbrow chit-chat. Who's hungry?"

"I guess I could eat something," Sheila said.

"Bacon and egg, over easy, toast an' coffee," the old man answered rapid-fire.

"Sounds good, Mal, but you're gonna have to save it till we get to a diner. There's no room service in this place."

"Or any other kind of service either. I was going to take a shower. Freshen up a little," Sheila said, eyeing Wyatt with raised eyebrows.

"Good idea. Keep the flies down at the restaurant."

"What!?" she shouted, tossing a pillow at his head. She followed the toss by immediately jumping on the bed and was quickly pinned beneath him.

"I love it when you're pissed," he said.

She thumped him in the chest, knocking him back off her.

"You're just lucky I didn't have my knife with me," she said as she stood and straightened her nightshirt.

"Why's that?"

"You know how some people like to carve their initials in a tree trunk?"

"Yeh."

"I prefer a warmer, softer, pinker medium."

Wyatt's hand drifted down to his crotch.

"You sho' got you a mean woman!" the old man said, shaking his head as he flopped down in the green easy chair, the cushions miraculously returned to their place.

"He ain't got shit," Sheila said, strutting her way to the bathroom.

"Need help lathering up?" Wyatt asked.

"I think I can handle it, thank you," she said, slamming the door behind her. The sound of the slide bolt could be heard snapping into place.

"You got you a hand-full," Malcolm said.

"Two hands." He started buttoning his shirt.

Malcolm stared out the open blinds. "You have the dream last night?" he asked.

Wyatt hesitated for just a second. "Yeh, I had it. Kind of different though - didn't wake me up. Like it wasn't so threatening, or something."

"The Homeland know you's comin'."

"I don't know about that, but we aren't coming anywhere if we don't get some plane tickets. You see a phone book in here anywhere?"

The old man glanced around. "Nope."

"There must be one here somewhere," Wyatt said, pulling open the drawer to the night stand. "Here we go." He pulled out a battered yellow pages, its cover torn and crumpled. "Now let's see what we can find around here." He flipped through the pages until he came to Travel, finding a section with more pages torn out than still remained. He ran his finger down the list of remaining agencies until he came across a name that seemed promising. "Talking Drum Agency," he read out loud. "African specialists. Sounds right up our alley, huh?"

"Sound okay to me."

"All right then, let's give 'em a call." He picked up the receiver to dial, but the ear piece fell out and dangled by thin multi-colored wires. "Too bad we don't have talking drums, maybe we could get through to them," he groused. "No problem. From the address they're just a few blocks from here. We'll walk over on our way to breakfast." He tore out the page and stuffed it in his shirt pocket.

As soon as Sheila got out of the bathroom Wyatt told her about the travel agency and she agreed to walk over and check it out.

"Will our things be safe if we leave them here?" she asked.

"Safer than if we left them in the car," he said.

They left everything where it was and set off for the travel agency. It was a cool overcast morning in the Bronx and the streets were bustling with pedestrians of every description.

"I don't see your friends in the hot pants," Sheila said. "What's the matter, doesn't that day-glow lipstick look good in daylight?"

"They're probably on their way to classes," Wyatt said.

"Blow jobs 101?"

"Whoa, a little nasty this morning, aren't we? As a matter of fact, at least two of those girls are working their way through college."

"Have they never heard of waitressing? Temp work?"

"You can't go to school full time and take care of your kids in the evenings, and still make enough money to feed and clothe them working for tips at some greasy spoon."

"Sounds like you've heard some life stories."

"I bought 'em a cup of coffee every once in a while," Wyatt said.

"Is that all you bought?"

"Writing a book?"

"Just want to know if I need to start IV penicillin immediately."

"I think you can wait until after breakfast."

Just as Wyatt had thought, it was only a few blocks to their destination. Malcolm saw it first.

"There the place!" he said, pointing to a sign in the shape of Africa hanging in front of a small, street-front agency.

"Are we sure we want to go through with this?" Sheila asked.

"We've already come two thousand miles," Wyatt said. "Another twenty feet won't hurt us. Let's go check it out."

Malcolm wasn't waiting. He led the way across the street with Wyatt and Sheila trailing close behind. As they entered the agency the lone employee was on the phone, arguing loudly in some foreign language. He was a hefty black man, wearing a flowing pale blue native costume and a pillbox cap. The conversation was so loud he didn't recognize their presence at first, despite the gentle tinkling of bells when the door opened. When he finally looked up and noticed them, he barked something into the receiver and hung up.

"Ek-a-ro!" he said with a big smile, rushing out to greet the three customers with his hand extended. "You are welcome!"

"Thanks. We were interested in checking out the airfare."

"To the Homeland!" Malcolm cut in.

"Yes?" the agent said.

"Africa," Wyatt clarified. "What's your cheapest ticket, round trip?"

"Well, that depends," the agent said, picking up a large dog-eared volume from his desk. "Where you wanna go in Africa?"

"I tol' you, to the fuckin' Homeland!" Malcolm insisted.

"Does this Homeland have another name - perhaps a country name?"

"I think we want to visit West Africa. Where the slaves came from."

The agent looked up from the book with a smile. "West Africa? Have you ever visited?" His accent sounded British, but earthier. The only sound Wyatt had ever heard that was similar was in the Caribbean.

"Never," he said. "Are you from Africa?"

"I am. From the greatest black nation on earth, the motherland of all blacks in diaspora, the leader of the emerging African continent: Nigeria!"

He stood tall and thrust out his chest proudly.

"Is dis Nigeria in West Africa?" Malcolm asked.

The agent looked at him as if he had farted. "Of course it is in West Africa," he said. "Here - look."

He directed their attention to an old, torn, ink-marked map of Africa taped to the wall. As Wyatt looked closer he saw that many of the country names had been crossed off and new ones written in.

"Looks like you've been busy keeping up with some changes," he said.

The agent nodded. "The era of colonialism has ended. The African peoples are finally able to name their homelands themselves. See - here is Nigeria." He pointed to a relatively large country just inside the bulge on the Western coast of Africa.

"When did your country gain its freedom?" Sheila asked, ignoring Wyatt's frown.

"In 1960. October first. A great day for all Nigerians."

"So what was it called before then?"

"What was what called?"

"Nigeria. Before the native people named it Nigeria, what was it called?"

The agent looked casually at the map, as if expecting to find the answer there.

"My country has had many names," he finally answered. "In fact, it is comprised of many nations."

"Was there slaves there in the olden days?" Malcolm asked.

"Sorry to say, there were. The old fort at Badagry was known as one of the most notorious slave trade centers on the coast."

"Is there anything to see there? I mean, any tourist type places?"

"In Nigeria? You might as well ask if there's anything to see in the U.S.! First of all there's Lagos, the New York City of Africa. They call it the Black Apple. Ten million people, skyscrapers, anything you want, you can get."

"Great. More of this," Sheila bemoaned.

"You don't like the city? How about animals? You like animals?" He showed her an old poster, the colors nearly completely faded from exposure to the sun. It featured a classic "Out Of Africa" photo of an elephant silhouetted against a red sunset. "In Yankari we have elephants, all kinds of antelopes, hippo, monkeys, lions even!"

"Giraffe? Zebras?"

"I am sure! It is a fabulous game park. Just like Kenya."

"Isn't that amazing. I never heard that about Nigeria," Wyatt said.

"The western press does not tell the truth about Nigeria," the agent said.

"Why's that?" Sheila asked.

The man moved closer to her and lowered his voice. "We are the largest black nation on earth. They fear us."

"I know'd it!" Malcolm said, slapping his hands together for emphasis.

"Yeh, well be that as it may," Wyatt said, "there's a more pertinent question that we haven't asked."

"Ask, ask!" the agent urged.

"Do you still have native drummers in Nigeria?"

The man's eyes opened wide and nearly bulged out of their sockets. "Drummers? Are you serious?! Nigeria is home to the finest drummers in all of Africa! Have you ever heard of Fela?"

"No, can't say as I have," Wyatt said.

"One of the greatest musicians in the world."

"And he's a Nigerian?" Sheila asked.

"Of course! And there are thousands more. They play the native drums in every village throughout the country. They dance to the drums, communicate with the drums, talk to their gods, talk to their neighbors..."

"It IS the Homeland!" Malcolm shouted, dancing an odd limping jig around the travel agency.

"What's he say?" the travel agent asked, watching the old man jump around from a safe distance.

"He says he thinks Nigeria is the Homeland. It's a theory he's working on," Wyatt explained.

"I am sure it is a good one."

"I'm glad someone's sure," Sheila said.

"How much is a roundtrip ticket to Lagos?" the younger man asked.

"That depends."

"On what?"

"Well, on whether you wish to fly through Europe or direct, whether you want to fly first, business or economy class, things like that."

"What's the cheapest ticket you've got?"

"We have a very special fare on the Nigerian national carrier. A direct flight. No stops, no changes."

"What kind of plane? I'm not flying all the way to Africa in some little puddle-jumper," Sheila said.

"Air Nigeria does not fly puddle jumpers!" the agent said with some indignation. "They fly only the most modern, best-equipped 747's from Boeing."

"How much?" Wyatt asked again.

"The meals are delicious, the service incomparable..."

"How much is the goddamn ticket?!" Wyatt exploded.

The agent scarcely blinked. "One thousand three hundred and twenty four dollars, economy class, roundtrip, not including tax and airport security charge."

"Whoa. That's some heavy money," Wyatt said, shaking his head.

"Of course, we have the special excursion fare..." the agent quickly added.

"What's that?"

"Seven days advance purchase, stay a minimum of 14 days a maximum of 21, there's no changing your departure flight, a few other small details..."

"Unfortunately we wanted to leave immediately."

The agent put his arm around Wyatt's shoulders. "Perhaps we can make an...accommodation." He looked around furtively as if there might be someone eavesdropping on their conversation.

"What kind of...accommodation?"

"If you are really serious, I mean, if you truly would like to visit my country..."

"We does!" Malcolm chimed in.

"Then it is my patriotic duty to see that you are able to do so. If you can buy the tickets right away, right now, perhaps I could make a small mistake on the date..."

"But won't the Air Nigeria booking center know that the ticket wasn't purchased seven days ago?" Sheila asked. "Don't they have computers?"

"Of course they have computers! The most modern available! But, as it turns out, I have a close friend, actually my brother's wife's cousin, who works for the airline, and in a special case such as this, if we were able to give him a small dash...of say, fifty dollars..."

"A bribe? Isn't that illegal?"

"Not a bribe, not a bribe," the agent said, motioning with his hands for them to keep their voices down. "It is merely a dash - a tip for services rendered."

"I don't think I want to spend fifty dollars," Wyatt began.

"Okay then, twenty, how about twenty dollars?" When he saw them hesitate, he continued undaunted. "Ten, okay? Ten dollars and you get the special excursion fare, your chance to visit the real Africa, see wild animals, visit the Black Apple..."

"Go to the Homeland!" Malcolm added.

"That's right, you can visit the Homeland. What do you say? Do we have a deal?"

Wyatt looked to Sheila, who shrugged. "Last chance to back out of this wacky idea," she said.

Wyatt hesitated.

"It be the only way to get rid of the dream," Malcolm whispered.

"Do you take plastic?" the pony-tailed traveler asked.

"M.C., Visa, Amex, Diner's, Barclay's, Discovery, you name it."

Wyatt dug into his pocket and pulled out a gold American Express card. "What the hell. Let's go.

The agent smiled broadly. "I knew you were a man of great taste. You will never regret visiting my great nation."

"I hope you won't be offended," Sheila said, "but if Nigeria's so great, what are you doing here in New York?"

"I am earning dollars so that I can return to Nigeria and start my own business," the agent said as he tried to find the credit card forms in an unruly pile of paper.

"How long have you been here?" she asked.

The agent never even looked up. "Twenty two years," he said.

Sheila rolled her eyes.

CHAPTER SEVEN

The sky was grey, a cold drizzle fell intermittently, and the air stank of bus fumes.

"Jesus I hate JFK," Wyatt groused as they trekked from the bus stop to the international terminal.

"I told you we should have taken the shuttle," Sheila said, shifting her backpack from her numb left hand to her cold and wet right.

"The guy said it was quicker to walk."

"Quicker. Not easier."

They walked on in silence, their bent shoulders and grudging gate speaking plainly of battered spirits. Malcolm shuffled along at the rear of their little parade, seemingly oblivious to, or at least unmoved by the inclement weather. Finally, through the grey mist, they saw the green and white Air Nigeria sign. With a grunt of satisfaction Wyatt picked up the pace, lurching forward so quickly he left his two companions struggling in his wake.

"Wyatt!" Sheila called after him, but his head was down and he wasn't listening.

As soon as he stepped through the automatic door and the warm musty air swept the worst of the chill away, he dropped his pack and sighed with relief. The terminal wasn't particularly crowded. Of course, by ten o'clock at night most people were at home fast asleep, or well on their way. He scanned the counters looking for Air Nigeria.

"Thanks for waiting," Sheila said as she dragged her pack in through the door. "I hope we're not slowing you down too much."

Surprised, he turned and instinctively took the pack from her. "Sorry. I just couldn't take that drizzle anymore." He put his arm around her shoulder and pointed to the green and white sign. "There it is! Our gateway to the dark continent."

"Sounds like a tourist ad written by Stephen King."

"Come on!" he said hugging her with his one free arm. "Aren't you feeling at least a little excited?"

"Course I 'cited," Malcolm said, coming up from behind them. "We gonna fly!"

His enthusiasm made Sheila curious. "Have you flown before, Malcolm?" she asked.

"Not 'xactly."

"Exactly what have you done?"

"Was up in that Empire State Buildin' once. Same thing as flyin'."

"Close enough," Wyatt said. "Come on, let's check in."

"You know, it's still not too late to change our minds," Sheila said, hurrying to keep up with Wyatt. "We could cash in the tickets, drive back out to Colorado..."

"In what? You gonna buy back your car?"

"I could."

Wyatt stopped in the middle of the terminal, turning back toward her with a look of utter disbelief. "Look, we've been through all this," he said holding her gently by the shoulders. "This'll be fun! Maybe."

"No need to be worryin'," the old man added. "I be yo' guide."

"You?! You've never even been there!"

"Don't need to. I goin' to Africa! Goin' home!"

Wyatt turned back to Sheila without comment. "Look, it's only three weeks," he explained with little conviction; was he trying to convince her, or himself? "We see the sights, have some fun, dump the dream and we're back here no worse for wear. Right?"

He bent down to look straight into her eyes. She tried to hold her pout, but it melted under his smile.

"What the hell. Look out Nigeria - here we come!"

"That's more like it! Let's go get 'em."

They marched up to the check-in counter and Wyatt presented their tickets and passports.

"You are welcome," the young woman behind the counter said with little inflection. She flipped through their passports and opened their ticket folders.

"I think we've discovered the national greeting," Sheila whispered to her two companions.

"You are going to Nigeria?" the young woman asked.

Wyatt immediately supposed the worst. "Is there anything wrong with the tickets?"

The woman scrutinized them closely. "No. Why would think that?"

"Well, you asked if we were going to Nigeria..."

"You are, aren't you?"

"Yes..."

"But I see you have no visa."

"We were told we didn't need one. We can get it at the Lagos airport."

"Who told you that?"

"The travel agent who sold us the tickets."

"His name was Shagoon something. From the Talking Drum Agency."

"Ah yes, I see. Fine."

"Then it's true we can get our visa in Lagos?"

"I'm sure."

Sheila looked to Wyatt with a frown.

"Have you sent other people to Nigeria without a visa?" he asked.

"Of course."

"Americans?" Sheila asked.

"I'm sure."

"Well, she should know," Wyatt said.

"I suppose."

The woman tore one coupon out of each ticket, stapled it to another piece of paper, stamped the ticket, wrote out their seat assignments on their boarding passes, put one boarding pass with each ticket and then looked up.

"There is an international airport tax and a security charge," she said.

"Yes, we know," Wyatt said, handing over the cash

The woman counted the money twice and then tore small tax stamps from a book and stuck them on the tickets.

"Do you have luggage to check?"

"Just this one," Wyatt said, passing Sheila's pack through to the scale. "That one will have to be checked also," the woman said, indicating Wyatt's knapsack.

"Are you sure? I think it'll fit under the seat."

"It needs to go in an overhead compartment and it won't fit."

"Okay..." He put the pack on the scale.

The woman tagged both bags, stapled the receipts onto their tickets, and passed the tickets and passports back to them.

"Your plane will begin boarding at 11:30 at gate 23. Have a pleasant trip," the woman said.

"Thank you. I'm sure we will."

The trio started the long walk toward their gate, but Wyatt stopped them before they had gone more than a few hundred feet.

"This may be our last chance to get a burger for a while," he said, pulling up in front of a Wendy's counter. "What do you say?"

"You can get a goddamn burger in Nigeria!" Malcolm protested. "Didn' you hear the man? Lagos be just like New York!"

"And I'm sure we'll get a meal on the plane," Sheila said.

Wyatt snapped his fingers. "We should have asked them."

"It's a nine hour flight! They've got to serve something!"

"Right. Then how about a chocolate chip cookie - for after dinner?"

"You're not hungry, are you?"

"Why would you say that?" Wyatt said

Twelve cookies later, they walked down the endless corridor that led to gate 23. After what seemed like an eternity they finally reached the security check-in area. Malcolm dropped his puny bundle on the x-ray conveyer, and Sheila added her purse. They were just about to file through the metal detector when Sheila nudged Wyatt and pointed to a sign sitting on top of the x-ray machine. "WARNING" it read. "PASSENGERS TRAVELLING TO NIGERIA ARE WARNED THAT MURTALA MUHAMMED AIRPORT HAS BEEN DECLARED DANGEROUS BY THE F.A.A. SECURITY PROCEDURES DO NOT MEET INTERNATIONAL STANDARDS."

"They probably say the same thing about dozens of airports all around the world," Wyatt said, shrugging it off. "Isn't that right sir?" He looked to the x-ray machine operator.

"How's that?" the man asked.

"This sign - the F.A.A. probably says the same thing about a lot of airports, right?"

"Not that I know of."

"But there are other signs like this around the airport, talking about other countries, right?"

"I've never seen one."

"God, this is right out of some horror movie," Sheila said.

"Now don't go blowing this out of proportion," Wyatt said. "I'm sure it's just a technicality. Their x-ray machine probably broke down."

"Right. Or maybe they don't have one."

"Don' pay no 'tention to that crap," Malcolm suddenly piped up. "Americans is always tryin' to put Africa down. They's jealous."

"Ah, is that it?" Sheila asked, clearly less than convinced. "Maybe we should see if there's some other airport..."

Just then a man dressed in the same long, flowing robes as the travel agent swept into the security area, appearing to be in quite a hurry.

"Maybe this guy knows something," Wyatt said to Sheila. He walked over to where the man was pulling off a half dozen rings, watches, chains and other assorted jewelry before passing through the metal detector.

"I bet that stuff would really start the bells ringing," Wyatt joked.

"It has happened too many times. I know better than to try to go through," the man said with the same sing-song accent as their travel agent.

"You're not from Africa by any chance, are you?

The man looked up, eyeing Wyatt suspiciously. "I am. Why do you ask?"

"Well, we're on our way to Nigeria, but we saw this sign..."

The African followed his stare to the offending sign. "Oh, that?" the man said with a shake of his head and a smile. "Just one more attempt by the American government to discredit Nigerians in the eyes of the international community. The airport there is as modern as this one. It has all the amenities. That sign is ridiculous!"

"Why would the American government want to do that?" Sheila asked

The man turned, taking notice of her for the first time.

"We are the largest, most powerful country in black Africa," the man said. "The U.S. already competes with us for influence in Africa. They know that one day we will compete with them on the world stage. Like all great powers, they are not eager for the lesser powers to challenge them."

The man swept through the metal detector. It beeped loudly. The man looked shocked, but then reached into a pocket buried deep within his robes and pulled out a tiny portable telephone. "I forget that I am carrying it," he said sheepishly, handing it to the security person who examined it closely. He stepped back through the detector and the security person handed it back to him. "Don't let that propaganda dissuade you," he said as he slipped his jewelry back on. "You will enjoy Nigeria."

"Thanks. I'm sure we will," Wyatt said. The man was gone in a rush of white robes. "Well, that was reassuring."

"I guess. If he's not some kind of lunatic," Sheila said.

"He's an African!" Malcolm said, as if that very fact automatically discounted the possibility.

"At least he's been there," Wyatt defended.

"Are any of you folks coming through, or what?" the security person asked, staring pointedly at the trio bunched in front of the metal detector.

"Sorry," Sheila said, stepping quickly through the gate. Wyatt tried to follow immediately, but the guard sent him back claiming he'd moved too quickly. Malcolm followed next, and the moment he stepped into the electronic scanning gate lights flashed and buzzers buzzed.

"Hold it right there!" the guard ordered brusquely, his hand resting on his revolver. The old man looked utterly confused, not sure whether to run or collapse on the spot. "Empty your pockets," the guard said, passing him a small tray.

Malcolm did as he was told, shakily reaching into each pocket and emptying its contents on the tray. At first nothing more interesting than a few coins, some matches and a balled-up handkerchief emerged. Then, he pulled out a small pocket knife.

"Ah-ha. That's probably your problem," the guard said. "Try it again."

Malcolm took a deep breath and stepped into the gate. His feet actually left the ground when the alarm sounded a second time.

"What's going on here?" the guard asked, looking to Sheila and Wyatt for some kind of explanation.

"Malcolm, do you have anything else in your pockets?" Wyatt asked, a note of desperation in his voice

The old man patted his pants pocket, his front shirt pocket, and then his coat pockets. A look of realization dawned as he felt the inside breast pocket on the left side.

"I bet dis could be it," he said.

He pulled out a battered linoleum knife

The guard took it from him daintily. "Yeh, this could be the problem. Try again." He nodded at the gate.

Malcolm hesitated just an instant, rocking back on his heels as if trying to urge himself onward. Then he jumped into the gate. No alarm sounded.

"Good. Looks like we got the entire arsenal," the guard said. "You know, it's illegal to bring this stuff on board a plane."

"I din't know," the old man said.

"He doesn't fly much," Sheila explained.

The guard eyed Malcolm head to toe. "I can believe that," he said. "Here," he continued, passing the old man a pad of forms. "Fill this out and your... possessions will be returned to you upon landing in Nigeria."

"I can't takes my knives?"

"Sorry. Not allowed. You can check them with your luggage, or you can leave them here with us."

"I don't let nobody touch my knives," the old man said to Wyatt.

"I understand; Billy the Kid probably felt the same about his guns," the younger man said. "Okay...Sheila, why don't you go down to the gate. We'll meet you there. I'll go back with Malcolm and check his 'arsenal'."

"You sure you don't want me to come with you?" she asked.

"We'll meet you."

"Okay, see you there. Just remember - flight leaves in just over an hour."

"I think we can make it. Save us a seat."

So as Sheila waved and continued onward, the other two reversed direction and headed back to the check-in counter. Sheila moved quickly down the narrow corridor, past a number of boarding gates, all the while wondering what she had gotten herself into. Not that she was unfamiliar with spur of the moment decisions and half-baked vacation ideas. She'd had her share. Maybe more. But usually she had at least known the guy she was travelling with for more than a few days. This had all the makings for a real goat fuck, as her ex-used to say.

Then again, maybe Wyatt was right. Maybe it'd be fun

She looked up from her reverie and saw the sign directly in front of her at the end of the corridor: 23.

"Why is it that every time I fly, my boarding gate is the last one in the terminal?" she asked herself as she strode into the waiting area

She had walked to the center of a large hemispheric room when she first noticed that many of the seats were filled with bodies stretched out horizontally. There were only 20 or so passengers waiting for the flight, but at least 15 of them were asleep.

"I wonder if they know something I don't," she thought as she found a seat under a moderately bright ceiling light and pulled out a paperback book to help pass the time. She had only progressed midway through the second chapter when the sound of familiar footsteps, or, more accurately, familiar footsteps and unmistakable shuffling, sounded on the bare floor. She looked up to see Wyatt and Malcolm.

"Get it all squared away?" she asked.

"No problem. Public enemy number one has been disarmed," Wyatt said.

"You feeling kind of naked, Malcolm?"

The old man looked puzzled. He checked his zipper.

"No, no. I mean, naked without your knives."

"Fuckin' cops. I don' never go nowhere without my knives."

"No need for them on this trip," Sheila said. "After all, this is Africa we're going to."

For a moment the old man pondered her words. Then, a small smile appeared. "That right!" he said, nodding energetically. "We don' need no fuckin' blade - this is the Homeland!"

"You tell her, Malcolm," Wyatt said. "We're headed for the land of milk and honey."

Just then a loud argument broke out a short distance from where they were seated. They couldn't understand the words, but from the tone it must've been serious.

"I just hope that neither of them has a knife," Sheila said.

"Or a gun," Wyatt added.

The argument continued at the top of their lungs for over five minutes, until finally it came to a sudden, inconclusive conclusion. Sheila expected to see one of the two men storm off to another portion of the waiting room, but instead they sat right back where they'd been. Within minutes they were chatting amicably and laughing.

"I'd hate to see them if they were really mad," Sheila said.

"Typical New Yorkers," Wyatt said. But they didn't look like New Yorkers. One wore traditional African garb, and the other bore scars on his cheeks that looked intentional. Sheila watched them surreptitiously for a few minutes, expecting another outbreak. But when quiet prevailed she went back to her book.

It was quite a while later when an announcement came over the loudspeaker. "The departure time for Air Nigeria Flight 293 to Lagos has been changed. The new departure time is 12:05." The message was repeated.

Sheila looked up at the clock and saw that it was already nearly 11:30. The room was much fuller than it had been earlier, with fully two-thirds of the seats now occupied.

"Nice of them to let us know about the delay, huh?" Wyatt said hopefully.

"I guess," Sheila said. She went back to her reading. A chapter and a half later another announcement came over the public address. "Attention passengers for Air Nigeria Flight 293 to Lagos. Attention." People began to grab their luggage and assorted boxes and bags in preparation. "The new departure time for Flight 293 is 12:30. Repeat, 12:30." A low groan passed through the crowd.

"It's still nice of them to let us know," Wyatt said.

"They keep being this nice and we'll never get off the ground," Sheila said.

A long chapter later the crowd began to stir, with a number of people grabbing their luggage and standing in front of the boarding gate. Sheila looked up. It was 12:35.

"Think it's worth getting in line yet?" she asked.

"May as well wait for the announcement," Wyatt said. "No sense standing for a half hour waiting." He looked over at Malcolm, who was out cold in his seat. "Beside, Malcolm can use the rest."

Emulating his fellow traveler, Wyatt leaned back and closed his eyes. Sheila returned to her reading. At the next chapter break she closed the book and shut her eyes for just a moment to rest them. The next thing she knew someone was shaking her by the shoulder.

"Sheila, come on, let's go! Everybody's gone!"

She opened her eyes to see Wyatt's anxious face just inches from her own. Suddenly the meaning of his words penetrated the fog of sleep. She jerked herself upright and scanned the waiting area. No one was there!

"What's going on?" she asked.

"Everyone's boarded the goddamn plane! Let's go!"

He grabbed her hand and jerked her to her feet. "Get your pocketbook!" he ordered and she numbly obeyed. As if in a dream he dragged her toward the gate, with Malcolm trailing just behind. A lone attendant stood counting the boarding passes.

"Don't let the plane leave yet!" Wyatt called out

The woman looked up, annoyance clearly etched in the corners of her eyes.

"You are late," she said simply while ignoring the boarding passes Wyatt held out for her to take.

"There wasn't any boarding announcement!" Wyatt protested.

"We announced 12:30."

"But the plane wasn't ready at 12:30!"

"You should have been ready. Everyone else was." The woman went back to counting her boarding passes.

"Well we're ready now," Sheila said. "Can we board?"

"They are preparing to leave."

"I'm sure they are, but they haven't left yet."

"I am not sure. Perhaps they have."

Sheila looked out the floor-to-ceiling glass wall. The Boeing 747 was clearly still parked at the end of the boarding ramp.

"From here I'd say they definitely haven't left. Now, are you going to take our boarding passes, or do we have to speak to your supervisor?"

A spark of interest flashed briefly across the woman's face.

"He is not here," she said.

"Then, goddamn it, we'll talk to the pilot!" Sheila pushed past the woman and started down the boarding ramp.

"That is not permitted!" the woman yelled after her. She looked to Wyatt and Malcolm, and then to Sheila, who was rapidly disappearing down the narrow tunnel. "You wait here!" she ordered, and took off at a fast jog after Sheila.

"Oh, you bet we will," Wyatt said, and as soon as the woman left he and Malcolm followed.

As they came around the last bend in the ramp, there was Sheila standing in the open door of the 747, arguing with the boarding agent, two attendants and another man decked out in a three-piece business suit. Wyatt didn't know what had been said, but he knew what he was going to say.

"Who's in charge here?!" he demanded in his most forceful voice. Even Sheila's head jerked around to see who had spoken

The man in the suit answered. "I am, sir."

"Well I want to know what you're going to do about this. I have never been treated so poorly by an airline in my entire life!" he said, waving his arms for emphasis. "We've been waiting in that lounge for three hours, while your departure times have changed, and changed, and changed again. And now this woman," he said, glaring at the boarding agent, "is trying to keep us from boarding, despite the fact that no final boarding announcement was made. This is an outrage!"

The boarding agent looked to the man in the suit with pleading eyes, but the man held up a hand to stop her from speaking.

"I'm sure this is all just a mistake that we can work out," he said, and Sheila recognized the tone of an experienced p.r. man. "We're all friends here, aren't we?"

"I don' know you from Adam," Malcolm said.

"Yes, well I'm pleased to make your acquaintance. Ogoke is my name. And you?" He held out his hand.

"We would like to get on board and go to Nigeria," Wyatt said, ignoring the offered handshake.

"Yes, of course." He took the three boarding passes and handed them to an attendant. "Taiwo, won't you show these three nice people to their seats? And make sure they're comfortable."

"Of course, this way please," the attendant said.

"I hope you have a pleasant flight," Mr. Ogoke said.

"Thank you. I'm sure we will," Wyatt answered.

Even as they stepped onboard they heard the boarding agent whispering intensely to Ogoke. His answer, unintelligible to them, stopped her dead in her tracks.

"That was quite a performance," Sheila said softly to Wyatt as they started down the aisle. "I was impressed."

"Like my Human Relations prof used to say, 'when in doubt, shout'."

"Catchy. I'll try to remember that."

The business section of the Air Nigerian jet was actually quite spacious. Also, nearly empty.

"Looks like we'll have some empty seats. Maybe we can stretch out and get some sleep."

"I sho' as fuck hope so," Malcolm grumbled

As they walked down the aisle Sheila couldn't shake the feeling that everyone was watching them. Perhaps it was her imagination. Perhaps people always look at whoever is walking toward them in a plane. Perhaps they were something of a curiosity, the only two white people on the 747. Whatever the reason, all she could see as she walked past were dozens of unblinking eyes following her every move. As they passed into the economy section the dozens of eyes became hundreds; the back of the plane was nearly full. And every one of them was waiting for her. It was so disconcerting that she didn't notice the smell until they arrived at their seats. A potent, crisp, mind-clearing smell of body odor far beyond anything she had ever experienced before. Self-consciously she snuck a quick sniff under her own pits, making believe she was turning to look at something to disguise the maneuver. The odor in the plane was so strong she couldn't smell anything else.

"Do you smell that?" she finally whispered to Wyatt as he struggled to put their one carry-on bag in the miniscule overhead compartment.

"What?" he said. "I can't hear you - the stench is too strong."

"Maybe we can move to another seat," she suggested.

"I don't know, it's pretty crowded back here," he said, finally shoe-horning the bag into the compartment and flopping down into his seat. He tried to get comfortable, but his knees were jammed up against the back of the seat in front of him. "How long did you say this flight is?"

"Nine hours," she said. "I'm going to ask." She reached up and pushed the assistance button. The button lit up and an annoying electronic bell sounded. In seconds an attendant was by their side. She turned off the alarm.

"What seems to be the problem?" she asked, sounding slightly indignant.

"My husband doesn't fit in this seat. Could we possibly switch to another with more legroom?"

"You should have bought business class," the attendant said.

"Yes, of course you're right. But we only had enough money for economy. And since we're here, and since there are at least a few empty seats, could we switch?"

"The plane is about to move," the attendant said.

"We'll take our chances," Wyatt said. "If I have to sit here for nine hours you'll have to take me off the plane in a wheelchair."

"We don't have a wheelchair."

"I could've guessed that," he muttered. "The question really is, do you have a seat available with more legroom? Like, at an exit or a bulkhead?"

The woman stared at him for several seconds, her arms crossed. "Once the captain turns off the seatbelt sign, you can move to any empty seat in this cabin."

"All right. It's a deal. Thank you."

The woman nodded and went back to her position somewhere behind them. "Isn't that what I asked?" Sheila whispered as soon as she left.

"It's that weird Colorado accent. People can't understand you."

"That's absurd!"

"Where?" he said, looking intently out the plane window.

"Where what?"

"Where's the herd?"

"What herd?"

"Didn't you just say, 'that's a herd?'"

Sheila punched him in the arm. "I said you're a nerd!"

He laughed and took her hand in his. "Herd or no herd, here we are: on our way to Africa!"

"Of course you may never walk again..."

"A small sacrifice to pay."

The plane began to taxi. He looked at his watch. It was 1:37. "Right on time," he said.

"Must be African Standard Time," Sheila said. Out of the corner of her eye she saw Malcolm sneer.

The plane began the long taxi out to the runway as Sheila settled in for take-off and Wyatt tried to minimize the pain in his knees. As the flight attendants began their pre-departure safety lecture, the plane hit a pothole the size of a small car and one of the oxygen masks in a compartment above the seat in front of them dropped down onto the passenger below. She screamed as if a giant spider had suddenly landed on her head. Taking their cue from her, several small children began to wail.

"I just love a relaxed take-off," Sheila said, her eyes closed and hands gripped tightly in front of her.

Wyatt looked over with a smile and saw that next to her Malcolm was nearly rigid in his seat, his hands locked in a death grip on the ends of the armrests.

"You're not the only one," he said. "Hey Malcolm, if you don't ease up on your grip they're going to charge you for that armrest."

The old man looked at Wyatt with an expression that mixed terror and confusion.

"If this damn thing's goin' up in the air, I gonna be holdin' on to sumthin'!"

Just then the pilot turned onto the runway, revved the engines, and a loud buzzing erupted somewhere in the back of the plane.

"Wha's that?" Malcolm asked, his knuckles whiter than the whites of his eyes.

"Probably just lost an engine," Wyatt said easily, laying back in his chair. Sheila glanced over at him with an expletive deleted stare. "Only one," he said with a smile.

Malcolm stared out the window, trying to see the back end of the jet to locate the missing engine, but just then the pilot released the brake and the plane shot forward. As the 747 picked up speed, Malcolm's expression became more and more tortured, until, finally, the nose tilted skyward and they left the ground.

"Whoa!" he yelled, his eyes pinched shut.

"Open your eyes, Mal. You're missing the best part!" Wyatt said. The old man obeyed tentatively, opening first one, then the other. At first he stared straight ahead, into the back of the seat in front of him. Then, with obvious trepidation, he snuck a peak out the window.

"Holy shit!" he said, loud enough for people sitting nearby to turn anxiously.

"I told you, it's the best part."

"We're flyin'!" he said.

"We'd better be, or else we're about to taxi right through downtown Manhattan."

With relatively little additional disturbance the plane climbed steadily for several minutes, until, finally, the fasten seatbelts sign went off with a reassuring ding.

"Thank god," Wyatt said, throwing back the belt and standing immediately. "Want to come look for a better seat?" he asked Sheila.

"Sure. Malcolm?"

"No way. I'm gonna stay right here. I don' wanna be walkin' aroun' in nuthin' that be flyin' through the air."

"Okay. I guess I can see the logic in that. We're going to look for a little more legroom."

They walked back toward the wing exits, hoping to find the elusive legroom there. All the seats on their side of the plane were occupied, but looking across to the opposite side they saw two open seats with seemingly acres of open space in front of them. They made their way across as quickly as possible, cutting through the galley where two attendants were busy loading a soft drink cart. When they got to the other side they went straight to the seats but hesitated sitting down.

"Excuse me," Wyatt asked the woman sitting in the middle row directly adjacent to the empty seats. "Are these seats available?"

The woman leaned forward in her seat, looked over at the seats with great care, and looked up at Wyatt. "There's nobody there," she said.

"I can see that," Wyatt said. "Was there?"

"Anyone there?"

"Yes."

"I really don't know."

"Do any of you?" he asked the other people sitting in the general area. One man shrugged, the others all made believe he was talking to someone else.

"What the hell," he said to Sheila. "Let's take a chance."

They plopped down in the seats with great anticipation. Wyatt wiggled his knees to demonstrate all the room he had available for them.

"Very impressive," Sheila said. "But can you do that with your ears?"

"And other parts of my body," Wyatt said with a vague W.C. Fields accent.

"I can't wait to see. Perhaps we can meet back in the restroom a little later and you can demonstrate."

"It's a date," he said. But just then a gentleman wearing a long powder blue robe, with a very attractive younger woman in tow, came rushing up to the seat in a huff.

"You are in our seats!" he announced loudly. Before Wyatt could speak he looked down the aisle and spotted an attendant. He waved rabidly for her to come.

"I'm very sorry," Wyatt began.

"You are in our seats. These are our seats!" the man repeated somewhat robotically. He pulled out two boarding pass stubs.

"I'm sure they are," Wyatt said. "But we thought..."

The attendant arrived at this point and the gentleman turned his attention immediately to her.

"They are in our seats. Here!" he said, shoving the boarding stubs into her face

She examined them closely, then stared at the seat numbers above the windows.

"You see, it's all a mistake," Wyatt began, but she cut him off with a wave of her hand.

"May I see your boarding passes please?"

"These are their seats," Wyatt said, jumping up from the seat. "We sat here by mistake."

"Do you know where your seats are?"

"Yes, of course, but we were looking for more legroom - remember?"

"I told you to sit in any seat that was *not* occupied. These seats are occupied." Wyatt had flashes of his third grade teacher.

"Yes. We didn't know. I'm sorry. We'll move." He looked down to Sheila. "Come on, before they call out the militia."

She got up with a weak smile and followed Wyatt.

"Damn owebos. Think they can get away with anything," they heard the man in the robes say as they skulked away.

"Owebos?" Sheila whispered.

"Probably means seat-stealing colonialist whities," Wyatt said.

"That's us, all right," she said

They looked for another seat with legroom, but they were too late. At one point they approached the business section, but the same attendant came scurrying over to block their path. "Any empty seat in your section!" she said.

"Just wanted to see how the rich folk live," Wyatt said, throwing his hands up in mock surrender.

"Looks like you're stuck," Sheila said.

"Yeh. Let's go back."

By the time they got back to their seats, Malcolm had stretched out across all three and was asleep. Rather than wake him, they found two aisle seats directly across from each other.

"At least I'll be able to use the one leg," Wyatt said, extending his left foot down the aisle.

"Is it time yet to demonstrate the wiggling appendage?" Sheila asked.

"Patience," he said. "It's a long flight."

By pushing his hips flat against the back of the seat and cocking his right knee at an obtuse angle, Wyatt was able to make himself more or less comfortable. Unfortunately, in that position his neck extended over the top of the headrest so he was unable to lean back.

"Comfy?" Sheila asked, looking over at him with a smile.

"Great," Wyatt growled.

Just then the ten-year-old in front of him leaned her seat back as far as it would go and virtually bent his right knee back double.

"Excuse me," he said leaning forward, his face turning red from the pain, "I don't have much leg space back here. Would you mind putting your seat up, at least a little?"

The young girl looked back at him at the same time her father sat up and peered over the back of his seat.

"A little tight back there?" he said.

"More than a little," Wyatt answered.

"Bene, could you bring your seat forward a little bit so the man behind you has some room for his legs?" he asked his daughter.

"I want to lean back," the daughter announced defiantly.

"I know, and you can lean back, but just a little less," the father coached.

"Do I have to?"

"Please..."

"Yes, father," the child conceded grudgingly. She adjusted the seat, giving Wyatt just enough room to move the knee minutely.

"Thanks," Wyatt said to the little girl

She nodded silently.

"The freighter option is looking better and better, isn't it?" Sheila asked.

"Walking is looking pretty good, right about now."

"I'd advise waiting nine hours or so. That first step is a big one."

"I'm almost ready to take my chances."

Sheila reached over and patted him on the arm.

☐ "Excuse me!" a voice announced from just behind her.

She yanked her arm out of the aisle just as the drink cart rattled past. An attendant carrying a basket of strange looking baked goods rushed past seconds later.

"You'll feel better after you get something to eat and drink," Sheila said.

"I certainly hope so."

They waited patiently as the lady with the basket moved slowly down the aisle dispensing her goodies. As she served the row in front of theirs they studied the snacks more closely. There was a choice of two: one looked like a large baked ravioli, or perhaps a small enchilada without the sauce. The other resembled a muffin, but with the texture of a doughnut.

"Feeling brave?" Sheila asked.

"Feeling hungry," Wyatt said.

"May I serve you something?" the attendant asked.

"What exactly do you have there?" he asked.

"Meat pie and muffin."

"Okay...I'll try a meat pie."

"And make mine a muffin," Sheila spoke up. The attendant looked over at her as if she'd cut in line, but served them nonetheless. "This way we can try both," Sheila explained.

Wyatt examined the meat pie closely, turning it over as if examining a newly discovered life form. Then he held it up to his nose and inhaled.

"Well?" Sheila asked.

"Smells great."

She smelled the muffin. "Smells like a doughnut."

"Well, here goes nothing," he said, taking a big bite.

Sheila watched closely as he began to chew. At first his eyebrows shot up as if he were pleasantly surprised. But then, confronted by a less-than-tender morsel, his eyes pinched shut a bit as his jaws attacked the unidentifiable substance mercilessly. Finally, straining to crush through the offending scrap, his face contorted as though chewing vulcanized taffy.

"How is it?" she asked.

He tried to answer but was unable. His napkin made a quick trip to his mouth and the problem was solved.

"Tastes pretty good," he said, massaging his jaw with his fingers. "But some of the meat is a bit chewy. How's yours?

She shrugged. "Here goes nothing, part two." She bit into the muffin, her eyes shut in anticipation. Moments later they flew open and she smiled. "Great! Tastes just like a doughnut."

"Just remember - half of that is mine."

"Do you have that in writing?" she asked, biting provocatively into the muffin.

"I'll let you wiggle the appendage."

She stopped chewing. "You drive a hard bargain." She passed him the rest of the muffin. He passed her the meat pie.

"No thanks. I just had two hundred dollars' worth of dental work last month. I'll pass."

"You don't know what you're missing."

"I can live with that."

"Coward."

As the clinking and clanging of the service carts finally faded into the roaring hum of the engines, both Wyatt and Sheila settled back for a restful flight. Or at least a flight. Of course, the loud voices emanating from virtually every corner of the plane made actual sleep impossible for everyone except small children and Malcolm, who continued to impersonate a log with surprising success. It was just as well they didn't fall asleep, however, for less than 30 minutes later the omnipresent carts returned again, this time fully laden with a more traditional airplane dinner: small, tough slices of overdone beef smothered in a thick, gooey sauce that tasted like axle grease, surrounded by what appeared to be dehydrated peas that had only been partially rehydrated, thin, soupy, instant mashed potatoes, a large thimble-full of salad, stale roll, frozen pat of butter, and a truly bizarre dessert that looked and tasted like it was made from a recipe found on the back of a jello box. For true connoisseurs who preferred a non-meat substitute, there was rubbery chicken on a bed of bb-hard rice.

"Wow, mom. This is great!" one child of about 15 said from the row in front of Wyatt.

"This does not bode well for fine dining in Nigeria," Wyatt thought, choking down the dinner roll with half a glass of coke.

When everyone had managed to ingest as much culinary excellence as their systems could stand, the gleaming stainless carts, wheels wobbling, sides dented, returned for one final strafing run. Wyatt could envision the stewardesses taking aim at stray legs and unsuspecting elbows, eyes gleaming, spittle dripping from sneering smiles.

"A crash survivor?" Wyatt asked the attendant nursing the most battered of the carts up the aisle. She sneered at him.

Long moments later, the carts back in their hangers, their mission complete, a voice came on the intercom and in two totally incomprehensible languages, one of which they later realized to be English, announced what turned out to be the movie presentation.

Wyatt contemplated paying the minimal surcharge to purchase the luxurious mock-stethoscope headphones, but when the picture appeared it was immediately obvious from the blurry multi-colored rainbow effect that the projector beam alignment left something to be desired.

"Do you get 3-D glasses with this flick?" he asked. The attendant's sneer was more of a snarl

With the majority of passengers engrossed in trying to decipher the jigsaw puzzle effect on the screen, others fiddling with the channel selector trying to get anything other than Wayne Newton Live in Las Vegas on the headphones, and the remainder nodding off from sheer exhaustion or four double brandies, Wyatt decided to give sleep one more try. He slipped his leg down the aisle next to the seat in front of him, tucking his foot under the seat to avoid having it severed by a runaway cart in the middle of the night. His other leg he artfully tucked into a half-lotus position, allowing him to slide down far enough in his seat so that his head just caught the top of the headrest. Feeling somewhat guilty at even considering leaning his seat back, he inched it to an ever-so-slightly-less-than-fully-upright position, reached over and squeezed Sheila's hand, and closed his eyes

The hum of the engines and the heavy, bloated feeling of indigestible food oozing through his innards soon carried him away to another place

At first it was ill-defined, nearly as hazy as the projected movie. But then, slowly, it came into focus. He found himself in a dense jungle, surrounded by towering ferns, vivid colors, and the exotic calls of strange unseen animals that shattered the stillness only to be absorbed into the heavy twilight air.

"Was that a monkey?" a familiar voice asked from just behind him.

He spun around instinctively and found himself face to face with Sheila.

"What are you doing here?"
"Same as you, I suppose."
"But this is a dream."
"Is it?"
"Of course it is! We're in a plane right now, flying to Nigeria."
"Are we?"

"Why are you doing that?"

"Doing what?"

"That! Asking inane two word questions that you already know the answer to."

"Am I?"

Wyatt was about to explode when a throaty, low rumble shook the jungle all around them.

"Was that a lion?" Sheila asked. Wyatt thought she sounded afraid.

"Finally, a real question. I was beginning to think this was one of those Alice in Wonderland dreams where everything happens to no end."

"Was it?!" Her question was more insistent.

"An Alice in Wonderland dream?"

"A lion!"

Wyatt stopped and listened. All that could be heard were the soft calls of undoubtedly rare unseen birds.

"It might have been," he said.

"And you're not afraid?"

"This is a dream! What's to be afraid of?"

"Have you ever heard the old wives' tale that says if you die in your dream you'll die in real life as well?"

Wyatt stared at her. "Why did you have to bring that up?"

Just then another roar shook the jungle, this time closer and more imminent.

*"**That** is a lion," Wyatt said.*

"Maybe we should continue this conversation elsewhere."

"Where would you suggest? I'm at a loss."

The roar sounded again, closer and louder still.

"I don't really care. Let's just get out of here!" Sheila yelled, setting off at a quick march in the opposite direction from the roar. Pushing through the leafy surroundings, they passed through the jungle like a fan-boat through the Everglades. At any moment they expected to collide with

beast or tree, but the foliage fell away before them effortlessly; in fact, it almost seemed to move before they touched it and then closed in behind them as soon as they passed. Despite their panicky gallop, however, the lion kept pace. The faster they ran, the closer the roar approached. Suddenly they burst through a curtain of interwoven greenery to stumble into a small clearing devoid of undergrowth, with only one discernible feature: a familiar face smiled at them.

"Malcolm! What the hell are you doing here?!" Wyatt yelled.

The lion answered, now scant yards behind them.

"This way!" the old man shouted, and with uncharacteristic nimbleness he sped off into the bush.

Wyatt looked to Sheila.

"I'm ready to wake up now," she said.

He pinched her on the arm.

"Owww!" she yelled. But the jungle remained. Just beyond the clearing the sounds of breaking branches came closer.

"Now! Run!" Malcolm yelled, sticking his head through the curtain of green that surrounded the clearing.

There was no time to debate. They followed at full speed.☐ No sooner did they break through the green barrier that encircled them than an all-too-familiar drum beat began to pound somewhere deep in the jungle. Sheila didn't know the meaning of the drums, but she had a strong feeling that they spoke of her and Wyatt and the reason for their presence. A thunderous roar momentarily drowned-out the drums; the drums grew louder in response.

Malcolm sped through the jungle without hesitation. Wyatt didn't know where they were or where they were going, but he inexplicably believed Malcolm did and that the old man would lead them to safety. He followed blindly, the effort of pushing through the dense undergrowth more like swimming than running. Despite the thick bush they ran at full speed, the rhythm of the drums sweeping them along like a rip tide, pushing and pulling at the same time so that their feet barely touched the jungle floor.

And then, suddenly, unexpectedly yet not surprisingly, the jungle ended and they found themselves running through the village, the thatched roof huts stretching out endlessly in front of them as they always had. Wyatt wanted to yell to Malcolm, to warn him about the hut with the masked stranger inside, but his voice was overwhelmed by the drums, swamped by it, drowned by it. By this time Wyatt knew what was coming, what would happen next, and next after that. It became more like watching a movie from inside the drama, an inevitability so strong that fear and excitement faded and then disappeared. Once again they saw the brightly colored bowl, the flickering torches. They turned into the open doorway, as they always did; the smoke enveloped them, as it always did. The drums pounded faster and faster, louder and louder. The lion's roar shuddered through their bodies, a living entity that demanded recognition.

The smoke began to swirl, enveloping Sheila and Malcolm, sweeping them away, spinning them round and round like some massive whirlpool, dragging them down, sucking them under. Wyatt struggled to break free, to find the door, to escape. He knew he should help his friends, but it was too late, they were gone. In seconds he'd be swept away too. He turned and ran, the drums thundering in his ears, the smoke swirling in ever-widening circles, the roar of the lion now just steps behind...

"O-wee bo!" a voice screamed out at him as the red and black carved mask rushed out of the smoke. A hand reached out and grabbed him by the shoulder.

"No!" he called out. "Let me go!" The roar enveloped him.

"Wyatt! Wyatt wake up!" a familiar voice called out.

Wyatt jerked awake, the blood pounding in his temples, sweat dripping from his hair, the roar of the jet engines shaking his seat. He looked around dazedly, lost between dream and reality.

"Wyatt, we're landing. Fasten your seatbelt!" Sheila said as she stopped shaking him by the shoulder.

He grabbed both armrests to anchor himself and sucked in a deep breath. His eyes focused on Sheila's face, then on the faces of the passengers seated around him, all staring with a mixture of concern and distaste. He shook the cobwebs from his head and did as he was told.

As he did he felt a sharp bounce, then a second. The engines roared loudly and the plane began to brake.

"Ladies and gentlemen, welcome to Murtala Muhammed International Airport in Lagos, Nigeria," a voice came over the intercom. "You are welcome." The passengers cheered and clapped.

"Well, looks like we made it," Sheila said.

Wyatt just nodded, the drums echoing in his ears.

CHAPTER EIGHT

Wyatt was pleasantly surprised when the plane door swung open revealing the familiar sight of a moveable elevated jetway.

"What do you know - a modern airport," he mumbled to no one in particular.

"What you 'spect?" Malcolm asked defiantly. "This here's Africa."

"I'm surprised you forgot that already," Sheila said straight-faced to a visibly pained Wyatt.

"I think I'm going to get very sick of that revelation very quickly," he said. "Come on."

Swept along by the riptide of returning nationals, the threesome moved through the modern, glass-walled terminal without a snag. Wyatt did notice that none of the arrival or departure monitors were working, the air-conditioning seemed overworked at best, and the only visible clock was frozen at 8:03, but none of that impacted upon the trio's movement with the exception of the tepid air, which had already begun to produce telltale rings of dampness under Sheila's arms.

"Kind of warm in here, don't you think?" she finally said, hoping to justify her un-lady-like perspiration before anyone else had the chance to comment on it.

"This is Africa," Malcolm said.

"I see what you mean," Sheila whispered to Wyatt. He smiled with a self-satisfied arching of the eyebrows that screamed 'told you so'.

Through the endless miles of connecting passageways, past duty free shops with the highest prices in town ("Should be conscience-free shops" Wyatt suggested), past a swarm of departing visitors (whose scrambling gait and wide-eyed expressions did not bode well to Sheila), they trekked expectantly toward an unknown reception hoping hopelessly that all would go smoothly

It did not.

They had just tramped down a long staircase and were about to 'cue up' in front of a half-dozen uniformed officials who seemed to be stamping passports, when a lone official, outfitted in what appeared to be the standard all-black uniform worn by security forces throughout the building, appeared out of nowhere and asked to see their passports.

Actually, all he said was, "Passports," and held out his hand.

Sheila looked to Wyatt, who shrugged. When he handed the blue-jacketed document to the officer, Malcolm and Sheila did the same

The officer flipped through the passports with the relaxed ease of someone who had done so many times before. His facility reassured Wyatt, for just an instant. Until he stopped and began to stare at one page with a perplexed look that told of trouble.

"Is there a problem, officer?" Wyatt asked politely.

The official raised his hand silently and perused the other two passports with the same concerned ardor. When he folded the three up and stuffed them in his tunic pocket, the rings under Sheila's arms instantly became bracelets.

"Come with me," he said, turning at once toward a doorway at the right side of the corridor.

"What's the problem?" Wyatt called after him, his voice a bit shaky from his own nerves and from Sheila's nails digging into the inside of his biceps where she hung on in disbelief

The official didn't explain. "This way," he called back, holding the door open in anticipation.

"Hell, probably jus' some confusion," Malcolm said confidently. He marched through the door without hesitation.

"Well?" Sheila asked.

"He's got our damn passports," Wyatt said

She sighed. "Right.

They followed Malcolm through the door and into a dark, musty corridor. Barely visible in the shadows ahead, the black uniformed official moved determinedly in front of them; Wyatt and Sheila quickly overtook Malcolm as they hurried to keep their passports in sight.

"Nice of this fellow to help us out," the old man said as his companions swept past him.

"Help us out?! Can't you see what's happening here?" Wyatt asked.

"African hos'tality."

"The man's gonna shake us down, Malcolm!"

The old man shook his head in disgust. "You jus' don' get it, do you?"

"Oh, we're going to get it all right."

Without waiting for any more of the old man's hopeful musings, Wyatt and Sheila pushed ahead to keep pace with the official. He led them through turn after turn in the gloomy dankness until neither of them had any idea in what direction they were headed or where they had entered. Finally, after what seemed like a half hour, they turned a corner and found themselves facing a short, empty hallway. It ended in a solid concrete block wall. On either side of the hall stood unlit, seemingly empty offices.

"Damn it! I knew this was a con!"

Sheila put her hand on Wyatt's arm. "There was nothing you could do. We're in his country and he had the uniform. Check, and mate."

Wyatt stood there for a moment staring intently at the block wall. "Well I'm not just going to let this guy get away with this. Let's go find a phone and call the Embassy."

"What you gonna call the ambassador fo'?" Malcolm asked, straggling in just as Wyatt finished.

"Our friend has disappeared."

"Disappeared where?"

Sheila gripped Wyatt's arm more tightly. He hesitated before answering. "I don't know where, Malcolm. That's what disappeared means. But the main point is that our passports have disappeared too."

Malcolm looked up at him with a puzzled scowl. "Don' make no sense. No African gonna pull no stunt like this."

Sheila grabbed Wyatt's arm with both hands. "Maybe he wasn't African, Malcolm. Maybe he was Finnish."

The old man nodded. "Could be. I don' know nothin' 'bout them Finnish. Probably can' trust 'em."

"Malcolm..." Wyatt began, but before he could finish his admonishment the battered door to their left swung open, revealing the black-clad official standing impatiently in the doorway. Behind him stood another black shirted official, and at a desk behind them both sat a man in a long white robe and white pillbox hat.

"Come in," the official insisted.

Wyatt wondered how much of his conversation they had heard. His cheeks burned.

"We thought we'd lost you," he explained.

"So I understand," the official said bluntly. "You were wrong."

"An increasingly common occurrence," Sheila mumbled as she pushed Wyatt past the official into the office. Malcolm brought up the rear

For several long moments no one spoke. Wyatt had no idea what they were supposed to do, and none of the men in the tiny cluttered office offered any assistance. But when he spied the three passports sitting on the desk he reflexively gravitated in that direction. Malcolm finally broke the ice.

"My friends is worried that there's a problem," he said. "But I tol' 'em you was probably jus' helpin' us out.

The man in white smiled. "That's very perceptive of you," he said. "You are welcome, brother."

"Then there isn't a problem?" Wyatt asked.

"I didn't say that," the man in white said. His smile disappeared.

"Well, is there or isn't there?" Wyatt insisted, his irritation poorly disguised. Sheila gripped his arm tightly

The man in white stared at him, his eyes narrowed. Then he turned toward Malcolm. "It seems you don't have visas in your passports for entering Nigeria," he said, so matter-of-factly that Sheila thought for just an instant that the problem could be resolved amicably.

"Our travel agent in New York told us we could get them here at the airport," Wyatt interrupted

The official in white didn't even look up at him. Instead he kept his eyes fixed on Malcolm. "Do you have any explanation as to why you would come to our country without visas?" he asked the old man.

Malcolm shrugged. "Travel agent say we could get 'em here."

Wyatt rolled his eyes and looked up at the ceiling.

"Yes, that would explain it," the official said softly, flipping through the passports. "The only problem is, he was wrong."

Wyatt's face fell. "But how could that be? He sends people here to Africa all the time!"

The man in white glanced up at him. "Perhaps he made a mistake."

Only the points of Sheila's nails digging into his arm kept Wyatt from exploding. "Right, right," he finally muttered, nodding absently. "So, what now?"

The official lifted his hands with a shrug. "Unfortunately, illegally entering Nigeria is punishable by a prison term of five years."

"Five years!" Wyatt yelled.

"That's ridiculous!" Sheila added. "We want to call the U.S. Embassy."

A quick glance passed between the three Nigerians.

"Perhaps after processing..." the man in white began.

"Don't give us that baloney," Wyatt said. "We're U.S. citizens. We want to call our Embassy now!"

The man in white stood abruptly. "You are not in the U.S. anymore!" he bellowed. "And you will do as you're told!" His words reverberated in the small office and the corridor outside.

"Why do I keep having visions of the Wizard of Oz?" Sheila whispered.

"Better than Midnight Express," Wyatt whispered back.

"You have something to say?" the official in white demanded.

Malcolm responded. "Now let's not everybody go gettin' all riled up. Ain't there some way we can work this out?"

The smile returned to the official's lips. "My brother. You bear the wisdom of your years."

"Jesus," Wyatt muttered under his breath.

"It is unfortunate that your friends don't share that wisdom." He stared at Wyatt and received an equally cool gaze in response

Malcolm saw the interplay and spoke up again. "Now come on now. All we interested in is settlin' this matter. You say there's a way?"

"Perhaps," the official said. "There is the alternative of a fine..."

"What a surprise," Wyatt said softly.

"You would prefer the jail sentence?"

"No, no. He was just...thinking out loud," Sheila said as she stepped in front of Wyatt. "A fine would be fine."

"How much?" Wyatt growled.

"Well, this is a very serious offense, and there is the matter of your attitude."

"How much?"

"One hundred American dollars," he said. "Each."

"One hundred dollars! That's highway robbery!" Wyatt said.

"This is an airport."

"Then this is airport robbery! I want to speak to the Embassy."

"Fine. As soon as processing is complete, you will be permitted a call. Sola, take the two men to Badagry and the woman to city jail."

"Woa! Just hold on a second," Sheila said. "Give us a moment to discuss your offer."

"Fine. It is a fine, not an offer."

"And a fine fine it is," she said. "Just give us a second..." She grabbed Malcolm by the arm and pushed Wyatt bodily to a corner. "Hey look, legit or not, these guys aren't kidding around. Do you really want to spend a day or two in a Nigerian jail? I don't think so."

"Listen to the woman," Malcolm said. "The brothers be offering you a way out."

"They're crooks, Malcolm. Plain, run of the mill fuckin' crooks!"

"They Africans," the old man said. "Ain't nothin' run of the mill over here."

"Listen to him, Wyatt."

"Three hundred bucks! That's almost half of all the money we brought!"

"I'd rather be spending three hundred bucks in a Hilton tonight than holding six hundred in some stinking hell-hole."

Wyatt sighed. "Yeh, well I suppose you've got a point there. Okay. Let's do it and get the hell out here."

"You wan' me to handle it?" Malcolm asked.

Wyatt patted the old man on the shoulder. "Thanks, Mal, but I think I can take it from here." He turned his back to the three officials and unzipped his belly pouch. He counted, and recounted three hundred dollars. "All right. Here's the money," he said, dropping it on the desk. "Can I get a receipt for that?"

"A receipt?" the man in white asked even as he continued to count the money.

"Yeh, you know, a piece of paper that says why I paid you three hundred bucks."

The official finished counting and looked up with a smile. "Yes, I know what a receipt is." He turned to his associate. "Give the man a receipt." The man stared at him with undisguised confusion. "A receipt?" The head man said something in a foreign language and the other man nodded. In seconds Wyatt had his receipt. *'Fine for entering Nigeria without a visa - $300 for three Americans'* it read.

"This is it?" Wyatt asked. "Don't we get visas?"

"Immigration will give you the visas. This is just the fine. Sola, show our friends back to the main hall so they can pass thru Immigration and get their luggage."

"That's it. We're free?"

"Enjoy your stay in Nigeria," he said, offering his hand. Sheila shoved Wyatt forward and they shook hands. Malcolm insisted on an intricate inner-city handshake, fist-bump and forearm slam - which the official followed only with great difficulty and irritation. Sheila started to offer her hand but was cut off by a curt nod of the official's head. She improvised a brush of her hair with the slighted hand.

"A pleasure," she said as she followed the black-clad official out of the office.

Wyatt hesitated. "I didn't catch your name," he said to the man in white.☐

"That's right," the official said. He made no effort to correct the oversight.

"Right. Maybe next time," Wyatt said. He followed the others out into the corridor

The way back was just as confusing but a bit quicker. Before they knew it they were back inside the main terminal hall at the bottom of the stairs. All of the other passengers were gone and the immigration booths were empty.

"You will find your luggage up there," the official said, pointing straight ahead. He handed them their passports. "But I'd be more respectful of local laws, if I were you," he said.

"No problem, brother," Malcolm said.

"Good. Enjoy your stay."

Before Wyatt could say anything further, the man disappeared through the side doorway.

"Thank God!" Sheila sighed. "I could just imagine what the local jails must be like."

"I doubt it. Let's get our stuff and get out of here before they get any other ideas," Wyatt said.

Unable to find anyone in the Immigration area, they walked up the short stairway behind the booths into the luggage claim area. By this time most everyone on the flight had already claimed their bags and the area was nearly deserted. Except, or course, for a handful of uniformed customs officials standing at the far exits, chatting boisterously.

"Great. More of our uniformed friends," Wyatt said as soon as he spotted them.

"I wonder what it'll cost to get our bags past them," Sheila asked.

"Cross your fingers that our bags are still here," Wyatt said to the other two as he struck off across the room to a pile of suitcases and boxes stacked next to an unmoving conveyer belt. Sheila and Malcolm hurried to follow

To their great relief they found the bags immediately. By the time they pulled them free from the pile and carried them to the exit, however, they were the only travelers left in the room. All five customs officials converged on them instantaneously.

"Why do I feel like a naked skin-diver at a shark convention?" Wyatt whispered.

"Let's hope they don't smell blood," Sheila answered through a clinched tooth grin.

"Hey, how ya doin'" Wyatt said gamely. The five officials stared through narrowed eyes.

"Where have you three been?" the lead man asked.

"Us? Oh, we had a little problem with some of your immigration boys," Wyatt said. "Had to pay the fine for arriving without a visa."

The customs officials exchanged glances. "Fine?" the lead official asked. "What fine?"

"The hundred bucks a piece," Wyatt said. "You know, for entering without a valid visa..."

"You can purchase a visa here at the airport upon arrival," another official said. "For five dollars U.S."☐

Wyatt's smile dropped to the floor. "What? You mean those SOBs ripped us off totally?!"

"Why don't you tell us what happened," the official said. As Wyatt explained, Sheila and Malcolm chimed in with comments and observations. When they'd finished they just stood there, shaking their heads in disgust.

"That cannot happen here," the head official finally said.

"It just did!" Wyatt said.

"But, there is no fine. I explained..."

"I know what you explained. What we're telling you is that somebody here at the airport is saying they're Immigration and ripping visitors off for a hundred bucks apiece."

"Couldn't happen," the chief official said. "Our Immigration people are professionals."

"I don't doubt that. The only question is professional what?" Wyatt asked. Sheila reached for his arm.

"What are you suggesting?" one of the customs officials asked, his tone anything but friendly.

"I'm not suggesting anything! I'm just telling you we got ripped off, five minutes ago, right back there in some dingy office somewhere! Are you going to do anything about it?"

"May I see your passports, please?" The lead official sounded pissed.

"Sure, fine - no problem," Sheila said, preempting Wyatt. She collected the three passports and handed them to the Customs man.

"You still don't have visas," he announced after a cursory examination.

"That's what I'm trying to tell you," Wyatt said. "We just got ripped off."

"Okay. I think you'd better talk to an Immigration official."

"Great! Exactly what we were hoping for."

The official said something to an underling in a local language and the man set off hesitantly, a scowl on his face.

"Now, while he is looking for someone who can help you with your visas, let's settle your customs situation," the lead man said. "Do you have anything to declare?"

"No," Sheila said

The man turned first to Wyatt, then Malcolm. "You?"

They both said no.

"Purpose of your visit?"

"I thought Immigration asked that one," Wyatt said.

"Perhaps in the U.S." the official said.

"We come to find the heartbeat of life, the golden essence of 'xistence," Malcolm said.

"You looking for drugs?" a secondary official asked. Wyatt couldn't tell if he was asking or offering.

"Peace of mind," he said. The officials mumbled amongst themselves.

"And you have nothing to declare?"

"Still." Wyatt said.

"I hope you don't mind if we take a look," the lead official said. He indicated the bags to his fellow officers.□

"I would have been disappointed if you didn't," Wyatt mumbled.

The officials quickly ripped into the three bags, rummaging around with rough expertise. After only moments, one customs man came up with the battered linoleum knife Malcolm had stashed inside his bag.

"What's this?"

"New Gillette razor - shaves real close," Wyatt said.

The official nodded and examined the knife more closely.

"Don' listen to him," Malcolm interrupted. "That my proteck-shun. A man need to take care of hisself."

"Well which is it?" the lead officer asked.

"My blade," Malcolm said.

"I've seen him shave with it," Wyatt insisted.

The lead officer looked at him coolly. "Do you think you are funny?"

Wyatt pursed his lips. "Occasionally. Usually when I'm not trying."

"Then stop trying."

Just then, Sheila spoke up angrily. "Hey, leave those alone!" she yelled at two officials who were gawking at a miniscule teddy they'd liberated from her luggage. One official held it up in front of him with a leering grin. At her outburst he stuffed it back into the bag embarrassedly.

"Nice. Don't think I've seen that before," Wyatt said.

"It's for special occasions."

"Would getting out of this airport qualify?"

"If you play your cards right."

The arrival of the Immigration man cut short their reverie. A few words in the same native language from the Customs man, a quick look at their passports, and the newcomer was up to speed on their predicament.

"You need a visa?" he asked.

Wyatt wanted to be sure the man understood the situation fully. "Did he tell you what happened to us?"

"Some strange men made you pay three hundred dollars as a fine. Is that right?"

"Not just strange men - men dressed in the same black uniforms as those guys over there," Wyatt said, indicating two security personnel who were watching from a distance. "And another guy in long white robes."

The Customs guy whispered something in their language and the Immigration guy nodded. "That is most unfortunate. But now you need a visa, correct?"

"Aren't you going to do anything about those guys that ripped us off?" Wyatt half-shouted.

Sheila stepped in front of him. "Yes, we do need visas."

"That will be five dollars American each," the man said. "Do you still have your disembarkation forms?"

"They took them from us," Wyatt said.

"The strange men?"

"Yes, the strange men."

He pulled out a small stack of forms. Sheila dug into her purse and handed him $15.

"Thank you," he said, handing one form to each of them. "Please fill these out and return them to me when you're done."

Wyatt grumbled audibly as he wrote, prompting Sheila to sing softly: "Mumble while you work, But please don't be a jerk, Hold your tongue, until we're done, And mumble while you work..."

"*Tongue* and *done* don't rhyme," Wyatt said without looking up.

"Neither do Wyatt and asshole, and that was my fallback position."

"I guess *tongue* and *done* rhyme okay after all."

"Thank you."

As soon as they finished, Wyatt and Sheila handed their forms to the Immigration man who initialed, stamped, re-initialed and re-stamped the forms. Meanwhile, Malcolm pondered his answers.

"Malcolm, what's the problem?" Wyatt finally asked. "They're not looking for a statement of your personal philosophy of life."

"I was wonderin' if I should use my slave name or my free name," the old man responded.

"Huh?"

"Should I use my slave name - Malcolm Green, or my free name, Kwazara?"

"Malcolm, I know you're pretty old, but I don't believe you were ever a slave."

"It the name that some slave owner gave my great-granddaddy long time ago."

Wyatt was taken aback. Once again he'd underestimated his travelling companion.

"Does the name Malcolm Green bother you that much?" he asked.

"It just a name," Malcolm said. "It what it stand for that bother me."

"I would suggest you use the same name as on your passport," the Immigration man intervened. "If you want a visa."

"My own brother tellin' me to ignore my roots," the old man mumbled as he completed the form. "What chance we got in dis world?"

"Once more, let me point out that this isn't your world," the Immigration man said. "This is *our* world, and here you will play by our rules."

"But I am a black African man!" Malcolm said, his head raised high.

"You're a black American," the man said.

"African-American."

"American-African," the official corrected.

"You say it the way you want, and I'll say it mine," the old man said with finality.

"Why is it that black Americans are always trying to be African, when here in Africa so many of our people would give anything to be American? I don't understand," a Customs official asked.□

"You know who you are," Malcolm said, passing the form to the Immigration man.

"You know who you are too. But you all want to be who you were. Why?"

"It be our roots!"

The official smiled. "We have a saying in my tribe: 'The roots nurture and support, but a wise man picks the fruit.'"

"I don't know nuthin' 'bout fruit. But we got a sayin' where I'm from too: 'Black is beautiful. Be proud of who you is.'"

"'The proud man lives in the past.'"

"And a stitch in time saves nine," Wyatt said. "I hate to interrupt, but if you're just about finished we really should be getting along before it gets dark outside."

Sheila glanced out the glass doors and was surprised to see that, sure enough, darkness was falling on Lagos. The Immigration man finished his stamping and signing and passed the passports back to them.

"There you go. Enjoy your stay in Nigeria. You are welcome."

"Why do I get butterflies whenever I hear that saying?" Wyatt asked Sheila.

"Even an old dog can learn new tricks," she said.

"Good one," Wyatt said. "You win the $10,000 Cliché Challenge. Your prize? A lovely night in beautiful downtown Lagos! Second prize, of course, is a full week."

"Wyatt!" Sheila cautioned with her omnipresent arm squeeze.

"Right...So, can any of you gentlemen suggest a hotel for the night?" he asked the assembled officialdom.

"The Sheraton is the finest Hotel in Lagos," the Customs man said. "Five Stars."

"Is that Michelin or Marquis de Sade?"

Sheila grabbed him by the arm and dragged him toward the exit. "Thank you very much," she called back. "We appreciate your help."

"Let us know when you catch those crooks!" Wyatt added.

Malcolm struggled to keep up.

CHAPTER NINE

It wasn't until they stepped out of the tepid air-conditioning that they realized just how warm it was outside. Even with the sun about to set, all three began to sweat as if caught in a spring downpour.

"Nice weather," Wyatt said to Malcolm.

"The warm weather reflects the warmth of the Nigerian people," Sheila said.

Wyatt stopped and stared at her. "Where did you get that?"

Sheila smiled. "The brochure from the travel agency in New York."

"I feel better already."

They hadn't taken two steps when several young men arose from seeming suspended animation to rush in their direction.

"Master! Master!" they shouted, pushing and shoving each other for position. The three travelers braced for the onslaught, but still were barely prepared for the hands that grabbed for their bags and tugged to pull them free.

"I will help you!" "No, I will help!"

Wyatt tried to remain cool, answering calmly, "No, that's okay - we've got them."

But it was like trying to douse a forest fire with a squirt gun. The young men ignored his refusal and pulled at the bags with increasing ferocity, arguing among themselves as though the three Americans weren't even there. "I saw them first." "It is my turn."

Wyatt's patience was already worn thin. But when the young Nigerians ignored his words, his pent-up aggravation boiled over.

"Leave the goddamn bags alone!" he finally bellowed. The young men backed up as though slapped.

"We only wish to help you," one of the would-be porters said, his tone more accusatory than chastised.

"And we thank you for that," Sheila said, intervening before Wyatt could speak. "But we can handle our bags ourselves."

The men hesitated a moment as if to leave. But then one of their number spoke up. "What do you have for us?" he asked.

"Have for you?" Wyatt asked.

"Something for the weekend."

"Hey, if you'd let me know ahead of time maybe I could have gotten you tickets to the Knicks at the Garden."

"Now hol' on a secon'," Malcolm said, digging into his pants pocket. "I don' have much, but what I have I'll share with my brutha's."

"Thank you brother," the young man said with dripping sincerity.

Malcolm pulled out a handful of change, perhaps a dollar in all. But as he reached out to hand it to the young man the others all grabbed for it as well, knocking the coins to the ground. When they looked down and saw how little it was, they turned back to the old black man without even bothering to pick it up.

"This is all?" one said. "This is what you offer us?! You shame us with your puny gift!"

"How can you be so greedy when you have so much and we have so little!" another said.

"Sorry," their shaken benefactor apologized. "That all I got."

"You expect us to believe that?! All you Americans is rich - you just don't want to share!" a particularly tall and angry looking man said. By this time a small crowd had gathered and they murmured their agreement.

Wyatt had had enough. "Hey look - you haven't done anything for us. We don't owe you anything."

"All whites owe us for slavery! Reparations are our right!" the young men interrupted.

"My relatives come from Minnesota," Wyatt said. "They never had any slaves. Now if you'll excuse us..."

He started to walk past the group, and the dozen others who had nearly encircled them, when the angry looking young man reached out to grab him. Wyatt was just about to slap his hand away when another man, slightly older than the others, jumped in between them and stood face to face with Wyatt.

"You folks need a taxi?" he asked.

"Yes, yes we do," Sheila said.

"Fine. Right this way..." he reached down to take Sheila's bag, but she pulled it close to her.

"That's okay - I've got it."

"You see?!" the angry young man shouted. "Damn Owebos!"

The taxi driver turned to him and angrily shouted something in the local tongue. The young man shouted back, joined by several of the others in the group. But the taxi driver wasn't having any of it. He counterattacked with a torrent of furious phrases, gestures and threats until finally the group edged aside to let the Americans pass.

"Come!" he ordered. "They won't bother you."

Like children, the three followed close behind, afraid to even look back at the young men who stood at the curb, staring icily at their backs. It wasn't until they were all safely in the cab that the three travelers spoke.

"Thank you for that back there," Sheila said. "It looked like it might get ugly."

"Might have," the cab driver said. "More often than not their bark is worse than their bite. Oh, they might have stolen a bag or two, or picked your pocket, but probably nothing worse. So, where would you like to go?"

"We've heard the Sheraton is the best place in town."

"True, if you have $200 a night to spend."

"Two hundred dollars!" Wyatt exploded. "Are you telling me there are people who spend that kind of money for a room in Lagos?"

"All the time," the driver said. "They are usually sold out."

"Isn't there anything decent at a more reasonable price?" Sheila asked, taking over for Wyatt who was nearly choking on his tongue.

"Might be," the driver said. "Depends on what you're looking for. We've got traditional African hotels, such as Nigerian visitors from out of town might use when they're here in Lagos, but I believe they would be a bit...basic for most Americans."

"Hell, we used to basic," Malcolm said. "Ain't that right, Wyatt?"

"But I'm not," Sheila interrupted before Wyatt could answer. "And I think we'd be more interested in something just a hair more..."

"Civilized?" the driver said.

"Well, yes, I guess you could put it that way."

"What she means is, you got anything with a heated indoor pool, Jacuzzis in the rooms and costs less than $10 a day?" Wyatt said.

Sheila slapped his shoulder playfully. "I'm not that bad!" she said. "Heck, I'm here with you two aren't I?"

"Just because you demonstrate terrible judgment in friends doesn't mean you don't know a good hotel when you see it."

"He's just kidding," she explained to the driver. "What I'm really looking for is something clean, safe and not too expensive."

The man nodded. "I think I know the kind of place you mean. I'll take you there - you decide."

With a lurch the taxi screeched away from the curb, sending the three travelers bouncing against each other in the back.

"Maybe we should just go to the Sheraton for one night, until we get a better idea of what's out there," Sheila said softly to her companions once she righted herself in the seat.

"Dis man gonna bring us to a good place," Malcolm said. "Who know better'n a cabbie?"

"Let's take a look. If it's terrible we can always leave," Wyatt said.

"Beside, how bad could it be?" Malcolm added.

'Famous last words,' Sheila thought, but she kept silent as the cab hurried through the deepening Nigerian night.

Wyatt was impressed by the modern highway that led from the airport to the city. Two lanes in each direction, not too many cars. Suddenly a car pulled out of a small side street and cut right in front of their cab. The driver swerved, nearly hitting another driver in the lane next to them who only avoided the accident by stomping on his brakes.

"Jesus! Have a lot of drivers like that one here in Nigeria?" Wyatt asked, his heart pounding.

"The drivers here are very aggressive but not always so safe," the cab driver said with a smile, turning completely around in his seat to face them as he spoke. "You must watch them always."

"I can believe that," Wyatt said, motioning for him to turn back to the task at hand

As they drove further the traffic gradually became heavier until, just in front of a modern multi-story building on the left, they came to a complete stop.

"That's a nice building," Sheila said. "What is it?"

"That? That is the Sheraton," the driver said.

"And the place you are taking us is almost that nice?" she asked, a note of incredulity in her voice.

"Almost."

Sheila was about to pursue her inquiry, when a tapping on the window distracted her. When she looked out she saw a young man carrying two handfuls of watches.

"You want watch?" he shouted through the partially open window.

"Oh look, Wyatt," Sheila said, "he's selling watches right here in the traffic jam."

"Go slow," the driver said.

"Why? Are they no good?" Wyatt asked.

"We call it 'go slow', not traffic jam."

"How about the watches?

The driver shrugged. "Probably go slow too."

Sheila tried to wave off the hawker.

"Which one you like?" the young man persisted. "The Rolex? How much you pay?"

"We're really not interested..."

"How much? Make you good deal. How much?"

"We don't want any, thanks," Wyatt tried.

"Okay, only 2000 naira for you. What you say?"

"How much is 2000 Naira in dollars?" Sheila asked the driver.

"A little over fifty," he answered immediately.

"Fifty dollars? For a Rolex?" Wyatt said.

"Okay, okay, 1500 Naira," the trader countered

Just then the traffic began to move. The trader trotted alongside of them.

"Sorry - we're not interested," Wyatt shouted.

"What's your last price? Tell me!"

It was as if he hadn't heard a word they'd said.

"No thanks! Not interested. Hasta luego!"

"That pretty cheap fo' a Rolex, ain' it?" Malcolm asked.

"Malcolm, it's a fake," Wyatt explained. "Either that or it's very hot."

"It ain't the only thing that hot," he said, wiping his brow with his hand.

"Okay, 1000 Naira! That good price - ask anyone! One thousand Naira," the young man persisted at a trot

They ignored him. As they moved further along the street the hawker finally fell back and attached himself to another vehicle.

"Thank god. I didn't think we'd ever get rid of him," Wyatt said, looking back to watch the young man set up shop with a new client.

"Don't look now, but I think we've got new friends," Sheila said.

As Wyatt swung back around he saw an entire army of young people lining the road on either side, their hands filled with merchandise of every stripe. There were youngsters not more than seven or eight scurrying about with golden brown loaves of bread, the dough sculpted with a twist here, a swirl there to identify the individual bakers. There were Jimi Hendrix wall clocks and Mickey Mouse alarm clocks and designer perfumes and shoes and paintings and garden hoses and briefcases and pens and cordless phones and radios and towels and clothing and belts and strange, confusing foods and seemingly at least one of just about everything else imaginable. Even small plastic bags filled with a clear liquid.

"What's that?" Sheila asked, her eyes wide with amazement.

"Water," the driver said.

"Is it safe?"

The driver chuckled to himself. "It's clean."

"There's something to be said for water you can see through," Wyatt said. "And that there - what's that?

The driver craned his neck to see a young boy selling small pyramid shaped containers. "That? That's yogurt," he said.

"Jesus. New Age poverty," Wyatt said.

"Why aren't these children in school?" Sheila asked, already knowing the answer.

"They must work to eat, and to feed their families - those that have families," the driver said. "Prices are very high here. It is not easy to live."

A man with half his arm burned off suddenly stuck his stump into the open window. As Sheila recoiled in shock he pivoted quickly and stuck his good hand in front of her face. "Something for me?"

She struggled to reach into her pocket book; he trotted alongside the car as it rolled slowly through the maelstrom of people and vehicles. When she finally handed him a dollar his face lit up in a huge smile. As he fell back into the crowd four more cripples suddenly appeared out of nowhere and struggled to catch up to the car window. Just then the traffic began to move, however, and they quickly left them - and the hawkers - behind.

"There are so many," Sheila said.

"You should be careful," the driver said. "You should not give so much. It is dangerous."

"Oh? How's that?"

"If people know that you have money, they will try to get it from you."

"Point taken."

As the twilight deepened into night the cab sped along a major highway at breakneck speeds, passing through block after block, mile after mile of shabby, often dilapidated homes and businesses that contrasted starkly with the serviceable quality of the major roads. Looking out through the open windows the three travelers watched in silence as the urban sprawl of concrete block buildings crowned with rusting tin roofs seemed to stretch endlessly. At one juncture they saw a massive community of unpainted, impersonal concrete buildings, each an identical three stories tall.

"What is that - an army barracks?" Wyatt asked.

"Government housing - the bureaucrats get everything," the driver complained.

After twenty minutes they realized they were no longer driving through the city but riding over an inky black expanse of open water; the highway had been transformed into a long, elegant bridge leading to towering high-rise buildings in the distance.

"Where are we now?" Sheila asked.

"Third Mainland Bridge," the driver said. "Leads to Lagos Island."

For ten minutes they cruised across the bridge, the buildings in the distance slowly coming closer and into focus. Suddenly the water ended and they found themselves once more in the city, in an even more densely populated, more congested, intensely dilapidated and polluted urban landscape.

"Looks like a cross between *Mad Max* and *Blade Runner*," Wyatt said.

"On a good day," Sheila said. Malcolm remained silent.

They exited off the highway and found themselves on a narrow, winding roadway that snaked through open markets and crowded bus stops, weaving its way past the high-rises and into a seemingly deserted business section of the island.

It was only close-up that they could see the real poverty of the city. The filthy, untended children scurrying through the streets, the stripped, abandoned cars, broken windows, accumulated garbage hosting rats the size of large cats. And above all, the smell, the smell of unwashed bodies, rotting garbage, burning trash, and the acrid smell of open sewers that lined the roadways.

"If you don't mind I think we'll skip the tour through the poorer sections of town," Wyatt said.

"Do not worry. We are just passing through," their driver said. "A short cut. We can avoid some of the traffic."

At one intersection a dozen young men stood idly on a corner, their silhouettes etched in the glow of a fire burning in a 50-gallon drum.

"Rotary Club meeting?" Wyatt asked.

"Many men without work. They have nothing to do."

"Shouldn' be like this," Malcolm said, his voice strangely choked. "Not here. Not in Africa."

"Sorry Mal. Looks like there are some things that transcend borders," Wyatt said.

"Don't get too upset," Sheila consoled. "This is just one city. And all big cities are the same. Wait till we get out into the countryside."

"Yeh, that right," the old man said, reinvigorated. "The countryside. That where we find the real Africa."

"Can't get much more real than Lagos," the driver said. "This is the capital of West Africa."

"Something to be proud of, I'm sure," Wyatt said, collapsing back into the seat with a sigh. He shook his head and turned to Sheila. "Man, I hope you're right," he said. "If this is all there is, we've come a long way for nothing."

"What was that you said, 'don't die before they shoot you'?"

"Trouble is, I can feel the bullets whizzing all around us..."

It was now completely dark, and on the unlighted streets only the dim yellow lights from homes and businesses revealed their surroundings. The driver obviously knew his way as they drove quickly through the narrow streets, turning first this way and then that, cutting across the center of the island without ever crossing a major street. Slowly the buildings changed, and they found themselves moving into what looked to be a more middle class residential area. Tall, poorly painted walls appeared, some with guards half asleep at the gates. More people, somewhat better dressed, lined the streets, frequenting dozens of tiny one-man stands selling food, drink, odds and ends. The piles of garbage became smaller and further apart. The stench of poverty faded

Without warning, the driver turned sharply into a broad driveway that curved around to the entrance of a white six story building. A well-dressed doorman opened the cab doors for them.

"Is this it?" Sheila asked.

"Le Matin," the driver said. "Almost as good as the Sheraton for fifty dollars a night."

"Looks pretty nice."

"A pleasant surprise indeed," Wyatt said. "How much do we owe you?"

"Two hundred fifty naira."

"What's that American?"

"Seven dollars, more or less."

"Why do I get the impression it's more less than more," Wyatt said, peeling off the cash.

"What's the difference?" Sheila said. "He just saved us a couple hundred dollars."

"Good point." Wyatt gave the guy a ten. "Keep it."

The driver beamed. He said something to the doorman in the local tongue, Yoruba they called it, and as soon as the doorman had unloaded their bags and slammed the trunk, drove off with a wave.

"You are welcome. This way please," the doorman said, leading them into the hotel.

Feeling upbeat for the first time since they had landed, the threesome strolled into the lobby. A ceiling fan turned lazily high overhead. Potted palms dotted the floor, and a spear and shield hung just behind the front desk.

"Now dis is Africa," Malcolm said.

"This is designer Africa," Wyatt said. "Wild Kingdom by Gucci."

"You are welcome," the young man behind the desk said with the grating mock sincerity that was already wearing very thin.

"Thank you. I think our driver spoke to your doorman - two rooms - a double and a single?"

The clerk skimmed through his list. "You are very lucky. We have two rooms - if that is, you do not mind bungalows."

"Not at all," Wyatt said. "In fact, I like them better than high-rises."

"Good. Then if you will just fill out these forms and give me your passports..."

With only a moment's pause they did as they were told, providing all the standard information about citizenship, home address, entrance and exit points and dates, visa number. But when Malcolm got to 'Reason for your Visit' he looked to Wyatt.

"What you put down?"

"In search of the source of the Nile," he said. Malcolm started writing. "Just kidding!" he said. "Put tourism - that should be safe."

The clerk watched with scarcely a raised eyebrow. When the old man finally finished with his form the clerk slapped a bell on the counter and everyone waited for the bellboy. Two slaps and a variety of mumbled expletives later, a tall, thin young man appeared from a back room, his uniform disheveled, the tail of his shirt untucked, and near-overpowering sleep weighing his eyes.

"Hope we didn't wake you," Wyatt said.

"No problem," the bellboy mumbled.

The clerk was less forgiving. "Where have you been?" he demanded.

"I was helping the maids fold the sheets." He barely stifled a yawn.

"Remind me not to send any clothes to the laundry," Wyatt whispered.

"Well next time you pay more attention to your responsibilities and less to theirs - do you understand?"

"No problem."

"Okay. Take these people out to the bungalows - A and B. Do you understand?"

"No problem," he said, grabbing the bags and starting off in a single movement.

"Extensive vocabulary," Wyatt said.

"Very reassuring."

Despite, or because of their uneasiness they followed close behind the young man as he led the way through empty corridors to the thatched roof huts behind the main lobby.

"Now this here's more like it!" Malcolm said as he flopped down on the king-size bed. "They even got air-conditioning that works!"

"I hope you brought your ear plugs," Sheila said, just barely loud enough to be heard over the clinking roar of the unit.

"Why you always knockin' Africa?" the old man asked.

Sheila turned with a quizzical smile. "Malcolm, the air-conditioner is probably made in the U.S. or England."

"Well, it here now."

"Okay, sorry. It's a wonderful air conditioner and we are lucky to have it."

"That what I think too."

"Good. Then we're all on the same page. I just hope that the wonderful hot water heater works, 'cause I'm looking forward to the longest, hottest, most enjoyable shower in history - followed by a short nap."

"God, sounds great," Wyatt said, handing the bellboy a small tip. "Want company?"

"I might be persuaded..."

"Well, dis is where I leave the scene," the old man said, turning to the bellboy. "Can you show me where's my room?"

"No problem."

"How did I know that would be his answer," Wyatt said.

"What do you say we all get cleaned up and rested and get back together for lunch?" Sheila said.

"Sound good to me," Malcolm said. "Especially that part 'bout rest." He stretched and yawned. "I'm gettin' too old for this shit."

"Oh, come on Malcolm. You'll still be traveling around when we're in rocking chairs," Sheila said.

"Only travelin' I be doin' then is six feet down. And I ain't lookin' forward to that trip just yet."

He waved as he left. "See you fo' lunch."

"Around noontime!" Sheila called after him

The moment the door shut Wyatt collapsed on the bed. "Well, we made it," he said, staring up at the slowly turning fan. "You know, I can't believe we're actually here."

"It *is* kind of amazing," Sheila said pulling aside the curtains to look outside. Her view was obstructed by thick wrought-iron bars. "Well, at least we should be safe enough."

Wyatt glanced over and nodded. "I never understood how people adjusted to those things. It makes me feel like being in jail."

"At least it's a co-ed jail," Sheila said lasciviously, gliding over to the bed to sit by Wyatt's side.

"You've got a point there. Actually, two of them," he said, running his hand across the front of her blouse. "Why don't you go get that shower all warmed up and I'll see if I can come up with a surprise for you."

"A BIG surprise?" Sheila teased.

"I don't think there'll be any complaints," he said, pulling her down to him and kissing her eagerly.

"Now I think YOU have a point," she said, running her hand across his lap. "Yup. A rather sizeable point at that."

"Go get that water running!" he ordered, and she scampered away from the bed with a laugh.

Sheila dug through her bag to find some clean clothes and then went into the bathroom with a promising wave. "Don't take too long."

"Coming!" he said, unbuttoning his shirt as he spoke.

"Not yet!" she said, poking her head back out.

"I don't hear that water running..."

The door closed and Wyatt continued undressing. He was just slipping out of his slacks when a blood-curdling scream erupted from the bathroom. With one leg still in his pants, he stumbled over to the bathroom door as quickly as he could, nearly colliding with an ashen Sheila.

"What's the matter?!" he asked as she hugged him tightly, her face buried in his chest.

"There's some kind of animal in there!" she said. "In the shower!"

Summoning his full quota of courage, Wyatt grabbed a towel and went into the bathroom. Slowly, cautiously, he went to the half-closed shower curtain. Stretching as far as his arm would reach, he pulled back the curtain almost imperceptibly. There, sure enough, was a large orange and black lizard, sitting on the wall near the ceiling, looking for all the world like it was asleep.

"Is this the vicious animal?" he called out to Sheila, who stood just outside the door.

"What is it?!"

"Well, from this angle I can't be sure, but I think it's either Godzilla or a lizard."

"You asshole," Sheila said, throwing her towel at him.

"Hell - the damn thing's asleep."

"Well then, bwana, why don't you just grab him and throw him outside so I can get your hot water running."

"Well," Wyatt said, throwing his hands into the air, "let's not be hasty. I mean, I suppose there's a chance it could be poisonous."

"I don't remember Godzilla being poisonous."

"Maybe it was son of Godzilla."

"If you're not going to get it out of here, I'm going to call room service."

"That sounds like a good idea. They're probably used to these critters."

"Let's hope so." Sheila picked up the phone, tapped several times looking for a dial tone, and finally punched 'o'. "Hello," Wyatt heard her say. "This is Ms. Wolter in Bungalow 2. Thank you - we feel welcome. But we've got a major league lizard in our shower. Do you think you could get someone over here to get it out of here?" She listened for a moment. "Yes, now would be good. I was thinking of taking a shower. Okay? Fine." She hung up. "No problem. Just like at the Ritz."

"Promises are cheap. Let's see what materializes."

While they waited for the arrival of the hotel lizard catcher they plopped down on a moderately uncomfortable, oddly stuffed sofa and flipped on the TV. They found that they only could receive two channels, though receive was really a misnomer. After staring through nearly impenetrable snow and thick, roiling waves of distortion that reminded them of the weather at JFK, they decided they were better off not being able to see things clearly. On one channel a modestly dignified military officer - at least he seemed to be wearing a uniform - droned on endlessly about how the country was not ready for civilian rule and how the military was thus volunteering to lead the country to great new heights. He made George Bush look like a scintillating speaker. On the other channel a man swathed head to toe in peach-colored cloth was chanting something catchy in one of what seemed to be the innumerable local languages.

"Something religious," Wyatt said, his attention glued to the screen. "It shares the rhythmic repetitions common to most participatory liturgies."

"Ooh, I love it when you talk philosophical," Sheila cooed, rubbing her hands across his chest.

Developments probably would have spiraled out of control at that point, if a loud knock hadn't just then shattered the near-mood that was evolving.

"There's someone at the door," Wyatt said tentatively, torn between stoking the spiral and getting some hot water.

"Either that or it's some of Godzilla's friends coming by to share the shower. Will you do the honors?"

"My pleasure," he said getting up to answer the door

It was, in fact, their old friend the bellboy who had carried their bags to the room.

"You have lizard?" he said.

"Actually, he has us. But yes, there is one in here. Can you catch it?"

"No problem." The young man reached down behind him and picked up a big steaming bucket of water.

"What are you going to do, boil him?"

"No," the bellboy said, walking past Wyatt toward the bathroom.

Wyatt and Sheila followed close behind, eager to see how this young African hunter, generations of stalkers reflected in his genes, would dispatch the threatening and possibly dangerous animal ensconced in their bathroom. The bellboy dropped the bucket of steaming water heavily on the floor and grabbed a small cloth sack that he had tucked under his belt. Wyatt and Sheila exchanged glances, edging nearly imperceptibly toward the open door. Reaching up, the bellboy grabbed the lizard by the tail, tossed it into the bag with a flick of his wrist, and tied the top of the bag into a knot.

"Is that it?" Sheila asked, a note of disappointment creeping into her tone.

"There are other animals?" the bellboy asked.

"No, no, that was it."

"Then that was it. No problem." He turned to leave.

"Wait a second, wait a second. You forgot your bucket," Wyatt said. Grabbing the pail, he struggled to carry it to the great black hunter.

"You do not wish to wash?" the bellboy asked.

"We are going to take a shower," Sheila said.

"No hot water."

"No hot water!" Wyatt said. "Since when?"

"Last month. They fix soon. No problem." He turned to leave again.

"No problem! What do you mean, no problem?!" Wyatt asked. Instead of responding, the young man ignored him completely and walked out of the bungalow. "What is a problem, nuclear holocaust?" Wyatt yelled after him. But the door closed in his face and he turned back to face a disappointed Sheila.

"Just like the Sheraton - right," she said, dropping down onto the bed.

"I'm calling the front desk," Wyatt said, marching resolutely to the phone. "This is outrageous." He tapped the receiver a couple of times trying to get a dial tone, and finally slammed it down in disgust.

"This is a joke!"

"Strange sense of humor," she said as she watched him pace next to the bed.

"I'm going to go back there and get us a new room," he decided suddenly.

"Don't be too hard on them," Sheila said as he rushed to the door.

He grabbed the doorknob and turned. To no avail. He pulled, and tugged, and tugged and twisted and pulled, but the door wouldn't open. In utter frustration he pounded on it with his fists. To no avail.

"What are you doing?" Sheila asked. "You look like you're having some kind of fit!"

"The goddamn door is stuck! I can't open it."

"Oh, come on, it's probably just a little swollen with all this humidity," she said, getting up and coming over to help.

"That I can believe," Wyatt said, wiping the sweat off his forehead. He stood aside as Sheila challenged the door.

But try as she would it wouldn't open.

"Now what?" Wyatt asked.

"We could call the front desk."

"If the phone worked."

"We could take a hot shower."

"If the shower worked."

"We could take a sponge bath."

Wyatt looked over at the steaming bucket. "We could, but from the looks of it we'd scald our butts off."

"Well, then what we need is something to do while the water cools."

"Any ideas?"

Sheila smiled and cozied up to him. "As a matter of fact, there is one..." She reached for his belt buckle.

"I hope that water's real hot," he said, taking her by the hand and leading her towards the bed, "'cause this may take a while."

"Don't rush on my account," she cooed.

CHAPTER TEN

He didn't

After a long interlude on the bed, and a much quicker lukewarm sponge bath, Wyatt and Sheila were awakened by the annoying buzz of their portable alarm clock. They got up, dressed for a late dinner, and tried once more to call the desk. To their amazement, the phone worked.☐

"Our door's stuck," Wyatt explained.

"Is it?" the clerk asked.

"Yes, it is."

"What exactly seems to be the problem?"

"The door is stuck. It won't open."

"Have you tried turning the key both ways?"

"Yes, yes we have. Actually, we've stayed in hotels before. Never one quite like this, of course."

"Thank you," the clerk said. "I'll send someone down right away."

"Thank you. We'll be here."

"Yes. Quite."

Wyatt hung up and shook his head.

"What's the matter?" Sheila asked.

"I can't quite figure out what language they speak. I mean, it sounds like English, but it couldn't be."

"What do you mean?"

"I say what I mean, they miss the meaning completely; I reply to what I think they've said, I'm wrong; they reply to what they think I've said, they're wrong. I don't know what it is, but it's not English as we know it."

"We'll get used to it. Probably just takes time."

"I'm not sure we'll be here that long. It might take years."

"You're right. We won't be here that long. We'll just have to fake it."

Just then a knock on their door brought a ray of hope to their faces.☐

Sheila ran to answer. "It's stuck!" she yelled through the heavy wood door. "We can't..."

She didn't finish her sentence. She heard a key turn in a lock and the door swung easily open. With a push from behind Malcolm stumbled into the room, followed by the mock Immigration gang from the airport. Other than the head man having changed from a white native costume to pale blue, they looked just as they had the day before. One of the black uniformed police types stood at the door, holding an automatic weapon across his chest.

"What is going on?!" Wyatt asked, jumping to his feet

One of the blackshirts pushed him back onto the bed. "Keep quiet," he ordered, with a tone and look that left little to argue.

The head man fluffed his robes and settled into a chair brought by one of his underlings to the middle of the room. Sheila took a head-bob direction from another of the blackshirts and went to sit next to Wyatt on the bed.

"Are you okay, Malcolm?" Sheila asked softly.

The old black man shrugged. "Guess so. But I can't make 'em understan' that I jus' wanna take a nap."

A blackshirt shoved him roughly onto the bed. "You were told to shut up!"

The head man raised a hand. "It's okay. They are probably a bit confused just now. Is that correct?"

"I think you'd be safe saying that," Wyatt said.

"Of course. You are far from home and this is all alien to you. We understand. Now, you are probably wondering why we are here this evening."

"To give us back the money you stole from us at the airport?" Wyatt asked

The man smiled. "You are direct. I like that. Of course, that is an American national trait, is it not?"

"Somehow I don't think you're here to discuss national traits."

"Quite right again. The simple fact is, we're here to collect another... installment of your tourist fees."

"We done paid at the airport!" Malcolm suddenly spoke up.

The man smiled. "Yes, you did. Twice in fact. However, due to an... administrative oversight, you haven't quite fulfilled your full obligation."

"What he sayin'?" Malcolm asked Wyatt.

"He's going to shake us down for more money."

"Direct. No question about it," the head man said. "And also correct."

"We ain't payin' nuthin mo'," the old man said, crossing his arms to add emphasis.

The head man raised his eyebrows. "Really? Perhaps you don't fully appreciate the alternative." He glanced at the three armed men around the room.

"What you gonna do, shoot us and dump us out in the jungle?" Malcolm said, the taunting sarcasm unusual for the old man.

"Actually, that's just about right," the head man said. "Of course, you left out what we'll do to try to persuade you to see things our way. You see, my men here are very persuasive, in a very unpleasant way."

Malcolm stared hard at the blue robed thief. "Why you no good..."

Wyatt restrained him. "Cool it, Mal. How much?" he asked the head man

The man pursed his lips, making the stylized scars on his cheeks swell into large, angry arrows. "Well, we do not wish to be unreasonable," he said. "I think...five thousand dollars should be sufficient."

"Five thousand!" the three Americans said in unison.

"There ain't no way..." Malcolm began, but Wyatt elbowed him hard in the ribs, sending the old man into a paroxysm of coughing.

"You don't think we have that kind of money on us?" Wyatt asked, trying to project just the right tone of incredulousness.

"I really don't know," the head man said. "Do you?"

"Do you think we would have been scraping to come up with your 'fine' at the airport if we had five thousand dollars sitting around?!" Sheila asked, her face turning an angry crimson reminiscent of boiled lobsters.

The man nodded. "Probably not. Perhaps we've made a mistake."

At that, Malcolm jumped up off the bed. "Ya see? I knowed these brothers was okay. They gonna let us go. It jus' a mistake, that's all."

The blackshirt standing next to him shoved him back down on the bed.

"Not you," the head man said, "just him." He indicated Wyatt. "You and the woman will stay here, for...insurance."

Malcolm's eyes bulged like two poached eggs. "WHAT!? What kind'a jiveass, motherfuckin' African bushman bullshit you tryin to pull here?!" the old man exploded.

Sheila put her hand on his shoulder. "Cool it Mal."

"I ain't coolin' nuthin' till these good fo' nuthin' black nazi stormtrooper mutherfuckers turn me loose!"

The head man signaled to the blackshirt nearest the old man. He cleared his automatic weapon and pressed the barrel against Malcolm's forehead.

Malcolm froze, only his eyes darting back and forth in terrified pursuit of a way out.

"I wish you would reconsider that decision," the head man said softly, all the while looking down at his fingernails.

Malcolm took a deep breath. "Well, hell. I s'pose I can dig that. I mean, when the man's got a point, he got a point." He turned to Wyatt. "Bring some take-out when you comes back - I'm hungry enuff to eat two week-old chitlins."

The blackshirt pulled the rifle barrel away from his head and Malcolm sank down on the bed mumbling to himself. "..floppy-lipped cannibal goat humpers..." Luckily, only Sheila could make out what he was saying.

Wyatt interrupted to break the tension. "So - what do we do now?"

The head man thought for a second. "It appears that we must take you somewhere you can get our money," he said with a smile.

"Good luck," Sheila whispered. Wyatt pinched her leg.

The jolt of pain caught her by surprise and before she could catch herself she cried out, slapping Wyatt on the shoulder and rubbing the offending thigh. When she looked up and noticed everyone staring at her, she improvised. "Bedbugs," she said.

"Vicious," Wyatt chimed in.

The head man eyed the two of them suspiciously. "That is unfortunate," he said. "I will have to discuss the situation with the manager. But for now, let's concentrate on the five thousand dollars. Get ready."

He stood.

"Get ready for what?" Wyatt asked.

"We will take you to the Sheraton. You can wire your bank - or a friend, I don't care whom - for the money. Come."

"And my two friends?" the young American asked.

"They will stay here, safe and sound. Until we return, at which time you are all free to go. Now come."

"I'll be back as soon as I can," Wyatt told the other two. "Hang in there."

"Don' forget the take-out," Malcolm said.

Wyatt smiled. "You got it." He kissed Sheila on the cheek. "Be back in a flash," he whispered. She squeezed his arm. "Okay, let's get this over with," he said to the head man.

"A good attitude." He gave an order to two of his men in Yoruba and stepped back to let Wyatt pass in front of him. "After you, my friend."

Wyatt took a deep breath and did as he was told. With a quick wave to Sheila and Mal, they were gone.

CHAPTER ELEVEN

They strolled through the hotel grounds as though nothing was amiss.

"So, what do you think of our country so far?" the man in blue asked jovially as they hurried past the lobby and out toward the parking lot.

Wyatt eyed him in disbelief. "Great. I particularly admire the high moral standards."

"Now don't judge the entire country by a few bad apples. Not everyone here is like us."

"No? What percentage - ninety?"

The man laughed loudly. "You Americans. Always quick with the quip. You know, Wyatt - do you mind if I call you that?"

"Not that it would do any good if I didn't. And you - what do I call you?"

"Me? You can call me...Oba." The man chuckled.

"Okay, Oba, what's on your mind?"

"I am very fascinated by you Americans. You are so very different than all the others that come here."

"Oh, in what way?" Small talk was the farthest thing from Wyatt's mind, but he thought it might break down this Oba's guard and give him a chance to get away and find help.

"Every way. The way you look, dress, your loud conversation, your instant friendliness to complete strangers just because they smile at you, your willingness to take chances, every way. But one thing I don't understand."

"And what might that be?"

"How can you know so much and understand so little?"

"Good question. What does it mean?"

"Well, you Americans travel all over the world. Millions of visitors from other countries visit yours. You have the top media in the world, the top universities, the top think-tanks, and yet you do not seem to understand how the world works any better than... a Nigerian farmer out in the bush. Why is that?"

Wyatt smiled. "Hubris."

"Again?"

"Hubris. It's a Greek term for pride, self-righteousness, arrogance. We are so confident that we've found the true path, that we are God's chosen people, we are blinded to reality. If something doesn't fit into our cosmology, we ignore it or warp it to fit." Wyatt thought how proud his doctoral committee would be.

"But isn't that extremely short-sighted?"

"Someone once said an American's vision only extends to their front door. They may have a point."

Oga laughed. "Ah, the delightful self-deprecation of you Americans. But, speaking of doors, this is ours." The blackshirt that was accompanying them opened the door to a grey Peugeot sedan that was parked off to one edge of the lot, out of direct view of the lobby. "After you."

Wyatt climbed in, followed by Oga. The blackshirt climbed into the front seat with a driver, who also wore the ubiquitous black military uniform. Oga said something in Yoruba and they pulled out of the lot.

They drove a few minutes in silence, the radio blaring a Yoruba talk program. Wyatt stared out the window at the now-familiar street people, their tiny stalls illuminated by candles or kerosene lamps. He commented to himself how sad and gloomy it all looked now, how different from just hours earlier when they'd arrived with such expectations. He sighed heavily.

Oga must have heard him. "Do you like the ride of this automobile?" he asked out of nowhere.

"I guess it's alright."

"It's a Peugeot - made in Nigeria for Nigerian roads," the proud Oga said.

"What do you know," Wyatt said, looking back out the window.

The affable Nigerian gangster wasn't about to let him be so easily. "It's the best car for this country you know, with the possible exception of the Land Rover, but they cost something like 20,000 pounds these days. For the average person, even someone like me, they are ideal. High clearance, will run on anything - even fermented palm wine in a pinch, and everyone can fix them. I can't of course, but everywhere you go you will find someone who can. And there are parts, and if you can't find them they will make them. Yes, a truly remarkable car."

Wyatt knew he should just sit and accept all this insight silently, but he couldn't restrain himself.

"If it's so remarkable, why do you see so many of them broken-down on the side of the road?"

"Ah, that is a very sad story," Oga began.

"Long sad, or short sad?" Wyatt asked.

"It is a long tale, but since I can see you are anxious, I shall tell it in an abbreviated version. You see, once upon a time, as recently as 1973 or so, Nigeria was - for Africa - a very successful place. We grew all our own food, exported some to our neighbors, made most of our necessities and imported just a very few luxuries. Then came the oil boom of the early Seventies. In one terrible decade we grew fat on the bounty of plentiful oil, and we grew lazy and greedy. If we wanted to shop, we flew to London or Paris. If we couldn't get the things we wanted at home, instead of producing them as we had in the past, we bought them from foreigners and imported them. We built roads and universities like there was no tomorrow, but we didn't have a water system, or drainage to match. 'We'll get to that one of these days' we said. But then, of course, the bubble burst. Prices dropped like a stone."

"Are the broken cars by the side of the road in here somewhere?" Wyatt interrupted.

"What? Yes, yes, just be patient. I'm getting to them. You see, when the bubble burst and the naira sank from two dollars for one naira to 40 naira for one dollar, people didn't know what to do. They weren't ready to give up their good lives. But the money wasn't there anymore. So what could they do?"

"Hijack tourists from the airport?"

The Oga smiled. "Some. The more creative. But most sank into an even deeper pit - that of corruption. A few naira to look the other way at first. Then hundreds, thousands, millions to circumvent the laws, gain access to the halls of power, eliminate the competition. But who were they really eliminating? The masses, our people. When I steal from a rich foreigner he loses an inch of cream from the top of a deep barrel. When these traitors steal from our people they steal the milk from their babies' mouths! They are scum!"

"Not benevolent benefactors like yourself?"

This time the Nigerian thief did not smile.

"It is the curse of my people," he said solemnly. "We would rather cheat than work, complain than act, steal than produce. Until the poorest of the poor cannot even afford fish, foo-foo, not even rice, for their dinner."

"And so you get the broken down cars on the side of the road," Wyatt said more dispassionately.

"Exactly."

In a strange way Wyatt would have liked to continue the conversation. This was not just some mindless thug. The young American felt he could learn a lot about Nigeria from this man. But the high-rise glass and concrete walls of the Sheraton loomed ahead of them. The time for conversation was over. It was time for him to act.

The driver parked in an open area of the lot, away from the main entrance and other cars.

"Here we are," Oga said as they rolled to a stop. "Now, if you will accompany me, we will go inside and you can contact a family member or friend who can send you the money via Western Union."

"And if no one is willing to send that kind of money?"

The Nigerian stared at him without emotion. "I think it would be better if you persuaded someone to do so," he said. "For you, for me, and certainly for your friends back in the hotel."

Wyatt didn't ask further. Oga gave orders in Yoruba to his driver and the blackshirt guard. The driver stayed with the car while the security man trailed behind, his weapon slung across his shoulder as if heading out on a five mile hike. And so they marched into the lobby of the Sheraton.

The Sheraton Lagos is not a five star hotel. Not even by African standards. Perhaps three. Guidebook writers tend to mark off for lazy, inept and nasty personnel, light bulbs that don't work (or worse, aren't even in the sockets), hot water that enlivens a shower with unpredictable fluctuations between boiling hot and freezing cold, a room layout that all too frequently features water-stained walls and ceilings as design features, food that varies between a three and four-Maalox rating. True, the lobby area is designed to lure the unsuspecting western traveler into parting with his credit card just long enough to process a somewhat astronomical room charge (many travelers seem to think they've misunderstood something in the exchange rate - they haven't). No matter if the actual preparation of the room (which doesn't seem to begin until guests are actually standing in the lobby - at least on busy evenings) is mind-numbingly slow, taking up to an hour for simple sheet-changing and towel fluffing. This is the Sheraton. THE BEST HOTEL IN LAGOS writ large. And so this is where a foreigner would likely go to try to get money wired from home. The crack staff has seen a million such down-on-their-luck Americans, and Brits, French, Germans, even a few Asians these days. No one thought anything of it when Wyatt and his retinue strolled into the glittery lobby. No one except, perhaps, those guards and staff members Oga knew personally and with whom he shared small crumbs from his various dealings in their 'five star hotel'.

The threesome made their way to a phone booth at one side of the lobby, back behind the elevators. Oga dug into the bottomless pockets of his native costume and pulled out a coin.

"Call collect," he said.

"And just who exactly am I calling?" Wyatt asked.

Oga shrugged. "Girlfriend, wife, mother, family, whoever has $5000 and will send it to you."

"And what am I supposed to say is the reason for this unexpected call?"

"You totaled your rental car, your traveling companion got mauled by a baboon, you want to buy trinkets - I don't care. Just make them believe."

Wyatt stood with the receiver in his hand, staring off into space as though thinking, tired, or both. Oga's patience was not extensive. "Call now," he said after only moments. His words were backed by the barrel of his associate's rifle.

Wyatt sighed and began to dial. "Okay..." he said. The phone rang several times before someone finally answered. "Hey, Chris, what's happening?" he asked. "Me? Oh, I'm over here in Africa just now. Yep, that's right. Nigeria. Uh-huh. Well, as a matter of fact, I was kind of hoping you might be able to help me out of a fix. You see, our rental car was mauled by a baboon and I need $5000 fast." Oga turned and shook his head, muttering. "Yeh - like a monkey, but nasty," Wyatt continued into the mouthpiece. "Yeh, sure, I understand. No, no problem. Hey, I understand. Just needed to try. Yeh, right, you too." He hung up. "He doesn't have it."

"Then keep dialing," Oga said. "And let's try to get the story straight."

Four calls later his parents committed to send the money right away.

"Good," the Nigerian said as he hung up. "For that you have earned some dinner. Come."

They made their way to the brightly lit, generic coffee shop where the two Nigerians ordered immediately and Wyatt agonized over a selection of unknown food groups. "Anything you'd recommend?" he finally asked.

"You must try our national dish," Oga said with great pomp and pride.

"And that is?"

"Foo-Foo." He indicated the selection on the menu.

"Sounds yummy."

When his order finally arrived it consisted of a softball-sized lump of some pasty concoction the color and texture of silly putty and a bowl of thick greenish liquid strewn with what appeared to be lawn cuttings and a small dark nugget of what might have been meat.

"What do you do with it?" he asked after closer inspection. "If I had my glove we could play a little game of catch."

"You eat it," Oga said, and by way of demonstrating reached over, tore off a chunk of the putty and dipped it into the green stew.

"Ummm," he hummed, licking his lips.

When the Nigerian was still upright and smiling after several seconds, Wyatt followed his lead. The lump was warm and soft, though slightly slimy. He dipped it into the green goo and - with Oga and the guard watching his every move with smiling anticipation - tried to subtly hold it under his nose to take a sniff. The only smell he could identify was a grass-like aroma that didn't seem particularly dangerous, so he popped the wad into his mouth and chewed enthusiastically.

The only thing he could compare it with was an undercooked matzo ball, but not quite so enticing. It was several seconds later, as the tender virgin taste buds on the back of his tongue began to report-in to his brain, that the impact of the peppery green stew overcame the texture of the putty and he realized he was sweating. His tongue felt like it was swelling. His eyes bulged. He reached for a glass of water and drained it in one gulp.

"Hahhhhhhhht!" he finally managed to moan.

"You like?"

"Hahhhhhhhht!"

"It is not so hot. You will get used to it."

"Why would anyone want to?" Wyatt gasped.

"We Nigerians like spicy food."

"We Americans like to be able to taste food."

The Nigerians didn't smile. "Eat," Oga said.

The American did as he was told, though with considerably more caution. Not long thereafter, after cramps developed in his jaws while attempting to chew the small nugget of meat stranded in the green goo, and as soon as he had choked down as much of the meal as he could tolerate, Wyatt threw down his napkin and leaned back in his chair, his bulging stomach feeling as though someone had implanted a small bowling ball in its midst. Oga nodded to his guard, who sidled over to the wall opposite the concierge's desk, a position from where he could see the action from desk to door.

With a nod from Oga they got up and started across the lobby. Oga stayed close to Wyatt, close enough that he could see and hear everything the American did and said at the Western Union desk. Of course, as is so often the case at five star hotels, there was no one behind the desk when they arrived.

"Now what?" Wyatt asked plaintively.

Oga reached out and slapped the desktop loudly. Heads turned halfway across the expansive lobby. Despite the commotion, no one came to their aid.

"You should have called ahead," Wyatt said.

"Patience is a virtue," the Nigerian said calmly, his smile just barely disguising smoldering eyes.

"Why don't we go get a beer?" Wyatt said, taking a step as if to do just that. "Maybe someone will show up by the time we get back."

Oga grabbed him by the arm. "We will wait," he said. As if to punctuate his order he pounded the desk three more times. The explosive concussions echoed throughout the ground floor of the hotel. A small child began to cry. No one came.

"I'm impressed. Good acoustics."

"Someone will be here shortly. They are probably dealing with other guests."

Wyatt looked up and down the reception area. They were the only people standing there. "I take it then that all business here is done in back rooms?"

"In Nigeria, business is done wherever business must be done," Oga said. Even his voice seemed threatening to Wyatt.

The young American was just about to press his Nigerian kidnapper further when a hotel clerk appeared from out of a door at the back of the reception area. One glance at Oga and Wyatt and he stuck his head back inside the door. Another man quickly appeared. He was tall, middle-aged with just a hint of grey at the temples, wore the omnipresent blue Sheraton blazer that Sheraton International clerks seem to wear in every corner of the globe, and possessed that unearthly combination of expressions common to so many of his profession that seemed to say "you're the most important person on earth to me, and yet I'm still bored out of my mind." His smile looked forced.

"Are you being helped?" he asked.

"This gentleman is expecting a money order," Oga said before Wyatt could respond. He spelled the name. The man looked at a computer screen. "I have no such order," he finally said after reviewing the three names a half-dozen times.

"Are you sure?" Oga asked

The clerk glared at him. "Very sure," he said.

"Perhaps it hasn't arrived here yet?"

"Perhaps."

"Perhaps we should come back in another hour or so."

"Perhaps."

"Then that is what we shall do. Come," he ordered Wyatt.

The young American was momentarily tempted to say something to the clerk, to call out for help, but the utter contempt in the man's eyes constrained him. Oga took him by the arm.

"We will have coffee," the berobed Nigerian said.

And so they probably would have, if not for the timely intervention of the British Royal Cockfinch Society whose members just then were coming down from their monthly convocation on the top floor. All three elevators opened virtually simultaneously and 26 chatting, guffawing, harrumphing Brits piled out into the lobby, just where Oga, Wyatt and the guard where crossing. Being good post-colonial Brits, they ignored the Nigerians and pushed ahead as if no one was there. In the ensuing confusion, Wyatt saw his chance and took it.

A large barrel-chested Brit, whose nose glowed with a ruddy hint of studied intoxication, slammed into Oga like a sturdy ice-breaker smashing through to the South Pole.

"Damn it man!" the Brit shouted reflexively, "Watch where you're going!"

Oga hesitated for the smallest part of an instant. Quiet acceptance is not a major component of the Nigerian character.

"It is you who should watch his step!" the Nigerian growled loudly. "You might have injured me!"

"And he still might!" another inebriated Brit yelled from the crowd that had congealed around the incident. Many laughed. Others simmered in righteous indignation that a local would dare challenge the unquestioned primacy of the British Empire and all its loyal servants.

"If you would pay attention to what you're doing instead of moving pell-mell here and there without any notice of what goes on around you, accidents such as this wouldn't happen." The Brit raised his chin in a gesture of utter contempt and total domination. Oga missed the gesture entirely.

"You are a very stupid man," he said. "A drunken stupid man."

"Go get'em Oga," Wyatt cheered.

The Brit's eyebrows shot up in amazement as his wife grasped his arm and a gasp of disbelief swept across the assembled multitude. It didn't take long before the gasp turned to muttering, and the mood turned ugly.

"I don't need some stinking wog telling me how to live me life," the Brit exploded.

Various compatriots mumbled their agreement. It sounded like a debate in the House of Commons.

"That is good, because you will not find a 'wog' hereabouts," Oga said.

"Funny, I could swear one was standing right in front of me this very moment."

The Nigerian's face contorted and his fists balled up under the flowing robes. "You go too far..."

"Too far for what!?" the Brit bellowed as he puffed up his chest and thrust it against Oga's shoulder.

"You have gone too far!" Oga yelled, raising his fist and shaking it in front of the Brit's face. Apparently several of the other monarchists thought the Nigerian had transgressed the line of proper behavior between a local and a member of civilized society, and they pushed forward to ensure he didn't follow through on his implied threat. One man grabbed his arms, while another duo restrained the guard, who had moved to help his boss.

Meanwhile, as soon as Wyatt realized that the Nigerians were incapacitated, he made his move. Without so much as a goodbye he turned and dashed out the front door, searching wildly for a getaway car. Luckily for him, a classic yellow 1978 Toyota cab sat idling at the curb.

"Take me to the American Embassy!" he yelled as he jumped into the back seat.

The driver turned around and eyed him suspiciously.

"Where did you say?" he asked.

"The Embassy! The U.S. Embassy!"

"That will be 150 Naira."

"Fine, great! Just drive!" Wyatt ordered

The man shrugged and started off slowly. Wyatt kept his eyes riveted on the front door of the hotel. For several long moments nothing happened. But then, just as they neared the guard house that straddled the entranceway, Oga and the guard burst through the glass doors, followed closely by a posse of the Brit's friends.

"I'll give you 200 Naira if you get me there in 15 minutes!" the young American said anxiously.

"Two Hundred? No problem."

The car lurched forward, gears grinding, exhaust billowing from a hole in the muffler. With a puff of smoke and a mighty hi-ho Toyota they slid into the boulevard, sliced through oncoming traffic as horns and tempers blared, and completed a u-turn over the center divider with practiced aplomb. No sooner did they pass by the entrance of the hotel, however, than Wyatt saw the familiar Peugeot come roaring out the hotel driveway hot on their tail.

Wyatt tried to keep one eye looking back to mark their pursuers' progress and the other focused on the road ahead as the cab driver careened through the tightly packed traffic like a pinball run amuck. Even in the inky blackness of late Nigerian night, the roadway running past the Sheraton was heavily travelled by all manner of trucks, taxis, personal cars and assorted converted school buses and mini-vans. Of course, unlike during the daytime, the traffic was at least moving.

From time to time Wyatt almost wished it weren't. The driver had taken seriously his admonition to get him across town to the Embassy in fifteen minutes. Only trouble was, Wyatt didn't know that even in the best of traffic, with the best of luck and the best of drivers, the Embassy was a good half-hour away. That was not going to stop the driver from earning his extra fifty naira.

Despite honking horns, shaking fists and screeching tires, the cab cut in and out between cars with total disregard for any traffic or safety laws. When a holdup loomed just ahead, the driver yanked the wheel angrily to the right to take evasive action; the cab leapt up on the sidewalk and continued on as though the thin concrete strip was marked 'Taxi Lane'. Of course, innumerable street hawkers and pedestrians were forced to dive every which way to avoid an intense episode of sudden cab syndrome, but the driver barely acknowledged their existence except to mutter to himself in Yoruba about their selfish lack of consideration for clogging the sidewalks.

With his heart lodged firmly in his throat, Wyatt glanced back to where he was sure their pursuers would be long outdistanced. The lump in his throat thickened dramatically when he saw the Peugeot following resolutely in their wake, re-churning the human flotsam and jetsam that had been cast adrift by their own wild passage. The Nigerians were still a good few hundred yards behind, but if anything they were closing the gap.

Wyatt was tempted to ask the driver if he could get any more speed out of his cab, but thought better of it. As if conscious of Wyatt's anxiety, the driver zipped down a service road that ran parallel to the major highway into the city. Traffic was heavy and at the first opportunity he jerked the wheel left and cut onto the larger highway. For about a hundred yards it seemed his move would bring dividends. But then they hit an absolute no-go, with four lanes of stalled traffic crammed into a three-lane thoroughfare.

"Damn it all!" the driver yelled as he slammed the cab into reverse.

"What are you doing?!" Wyatt yelled back, his voice rising as the car began to pick up speed.

"The road is blocked," the driver said. "We must go another way."

"But this way?"

"Do not worry. We'll not go far."

"That's what I was worrying about," Wyatt said

Although he tried to close his eyes, the hypnotic allure of impending doom forced him to stare out the rear window. With half the cab in the breakdown lane and half in the right traffic lane, the driver played a life and death game of chicken backing up at forty miles per hour into the oncoming traffic. Cars rushed at them with lights flashing, horns sounding, refusing to cede the half-lane necessary for their survival until the very last moment when they swerved aside, nearly colliding with the traffic in the center lane. The driver cursed at their stubborn lack of cooperation and from time to time inched out into the traffic lane a few feet further to chastise particularly uncooperative drivers. But despite all the potential for disaster they were making good time and Wyatt was just beginning to relax ever so slightly when suddenly a threatening grey presence loomed just ahead, the burnt-out hulk of a mini-bus filling the entire breakdown lane and a bit of the traffic lane as well.

"Now what?!" Wyatt asked, his fingers digging ever deeper into the back of the front seat.

"No problem," the driver said as nonchalantly as if they were cruising through Century City.

"No problem?!"

Before he could say more the cab darted out into the middle of the traffic lane, accelerated rapidly, and swept past the smoldering hulk. For just an instant it looked like they'd survive unscathed, until from off the access road came a frighteningly familiar Peugeot, hurtling forward at breakneck speed, as determined to move forward as they were to go back. Unfortunately, there was only room enough for one car in the lane, and the lane next to them was occupied by a steady stream of traffic. The driver of the Peugeot had no time to react, but he had no alternative. Slamming on his brakes, smoke roiling from all four tires, he yanked the car to his left, smashing his left front fender into the right rear panel of an unsuspecting by-passer. That car, caught completely off-guard, slid right and forward, clipping the car to its left and smashing into the back of the car ahead of it. The driver of the car behind the Peugeot's victim tried to stop in time to avoid the growing mess, but succeeded only in throwing his vehicle into a slide (on four glassy-slick bald tires), which tossed him into the slow-moving fast lane and buried his hood into the sliding side door of another mini-van passenger bus.

The cab driver, meanwhile, roared backwards up the off-ramp to the access road, screeched to a smoking stop at the top of the ramp (terrifying a lady driver on the access road who panicked at the sight of the yellow Toyota backing straight toward her at dizzying speed and drove her shiny new Volkswagen Passat across a divider, through a chain-link fence and into the side of a pounded yam stand), and took off full speed ahead on the access road.

All this did not escape Oga's attention. Screaming orders in Yoruba, he intimidated his driver into pulling a U-turn from the midst of the carnage they had just caused and driving back up the off-ramp in hot pursuit of the cab. Dozens of dazed drivers and passengers stood by the myriad smashed cars, front row observers, and occasional participants, in the ferocious arguments that ensued about who was to blame for what.

Wyatt caught just a glimpse of the Peugeot reappearing onto the access road before his cab dodged and dipped between cars, turning sharply off the access road onto a smaller side road lined by small candle-lit food stands.

"Where the hell are we going now!?" Wyatt asked.

"I thought you wanted to go to the Embassy."

"This is the way?"

"This is a way. You would like to go another way?"

"No! Just keep going - you're doing...great."

Reinforced by the American's praise, the cab driver prodded his old Toyota to run a little faster, screeching around a sharp corner that emptied them back onto a major thoroughfare.

"This is the way to the Third Mainland Bridge," the driver announced. "We will be there in no time."

Wyatt was afraid to comment further.

True to his announcement, it was only moments before they swept past the thinning traffic and onto the ten-mile bridge that linked the mainland with Lagos Island. Completed only a few short years earlier, the bridge already showed the corrosive impact of endemic corruption, hurried construction and abusive overuse: guard rails were missing on nearly one-half the length of the bridge, gaping pot holes revealed steel reinforcing bars and even the water sixty feet below, and worst of all - at the speeds they were travelling - large sections of the concrete had sunk to the point where even a strong, modern auto suspension could not cushion the passengers from a bumpy rock and roll rollercoaster ride. In the aging Toyota Wyatt slammed against the roof of the cab time and time again as the body bottomed out on the massive dips.

"You okay back there?" the driver asked after one particularly nasty bump.

"My organ donor card is attached to my driver's license," the young American said. The driver nodded and accelerated.

Like a surreal mirage, the skyline of the city seemed to rise up out of the sea at the end of the bridge. From a distance it looked surprisingly like Miami. As they drew closer the similarity ended. Once again Wyatt found himself in a Mad Max cityscape, the inner city's bare bones concrete block buildings, abandoned cars and mountains of rotting refuse replaced at the bay's edge by stick and tin shacks on stilts. The cab raced past all that, into the balmy Lagosian night

Just as the driver had said, it wasn't much farther to the Embassy. Around a couple of cloverleaf turns and across a short road bridge, they arrived at a residential area with little of the raw, angry intensity of the city.

"Victoria Island," the driver announced. "Not far now."

As they raced down a four lane boulevard lined by sidewalks, Wyatt kept his vigil at the rear window. Somewhere back there, somewhere in the boiling darkness, Oga and his driver were zeroing in on the cab, focusing all their energies on finding and stopping them. But they were almost at the Embassy. Almost safe.

The cab turned down a narrow side street and whizzed past big embassy homes hidden away behind tall vine-covered walls. For the first time in what seemed like an eternity Wyatt felt confidence returning, felt a little of the tension melting off his shoulders. He turned back toward the driver just in time to see the grey Peugeot pull out of a side street and block the entire roadway ahead.

They had gotten there ahead of them!

"Look out!" Wyatt yelled, but the driver was way ahead of him. He yanked the steering wheel hard to the right and the cab lurched up and over the dirt curb onto the narrow sandy strip that ran between the embassy row and the ocean channel. Dodging trees, boulders and animals, the cab bounced and lurched its way around the Peugeot, cutting back onto the roadway just a few meters further down the road. Instantly the Peugeot screamed into action, just seconds behind. The Toyota strained to keep the lead, but the Peugeot was closing fast. Wyatt could see Oga yelling orders to his driver and gesturing furiously. It would only be a matter of seconds before they overtook the cab...

Suddenly the cab screeched to a halt in front of a huge iron gate. Wyatt braced for shots, or at least Oga's attack, but the Peugeot swept on past without hesitating. A Nigerian guard walked out to greet them from inside the gate. Only then did Wyatt see the engraved sign plate on the ten foot wall: U.S. Embassy.

He quickly explained the situation to the guard, and then explained a second time when it was obvious that the guard had no idea what he was talking about. Then, when a second guard appeared, he explained a third time. Finally, the second guard nodded and walked back to a small concrete shack just inside the gate. Wyatt could see him talking on a walkie-talkie, even while the first guard chatted in Yoruba with the cab driver.

Moments later the protective grill that covered the glass front door of the embassy slid upwards and a young Marine came striding out to see what was happening at the gate. He ignored the two guards, who came to a close approximation of attention upon his arrival, and concentrated instead upon Wyatt.

"The guard tells me that you have a problem. Is that correct, sir?" the marine asked in a clipped, authoritative tone.

Wyatt cringed at being called sir by a man just a couple of years younger than he, but the urgency of the moment quickly dissolved his discomfort. He explained as succinctly as he could what had happened. The Marine nodded understandingly.

"So where is this Oga guy now?" he asked when Wyatt finished.

"I don't know. But I'm afraid he's headed back to the hotel. We've got to get there before he grabs Malcolm and Sheila!"

"All right, now calm down," the Marine said. "Let me call the RSO and we'll see if we can get someone down here to take you over there right away." Thankfully, the marine used his walkie-talkie to send the message.

"Big Bear, Big Bear, this is Lighthouse, over."

For a moment there was no response, just the crackling of radio interference. Then, just as Wyatt was going to ask the Marine to repeat the message, the reply came over the radio.

"Lighthouse, Lighthouse, this is Big Bear, over."

The Marine explained the situation and came straight to the point.

"The Amcit thinks they're headed back to the hotel to grab his two friends. He wants to know if we can send someone over there to keep an eye on them."

Once again, there was an awkward moment of silence. "Yeh, okay. Call the guard force; tell them to get the V.I. roving patrol over there pronto. Do you copy?"

"That's a Lima Charlie, Big Bear. I'll get them over there right away. And what about this Amcit?"

"I'll be down there in five minutes. Tell him to hang tight."

"That's a copy, Big Bear. Lighthouse out."

As soon as the Marine signed off he contacted the guard force control office and gave them their orders. It took him a few seconds to make them understand the urgency, but at last they seemed to understand.

"How long before they get there?" Wyatt asked.

"Oh, probably no more than five minutes or so. They're out in that area already, so it shouldn't take long."

"And we can be pretty sure they'll actually go there and do as they've been told?"

"Pretty sure." The Marine said straight-faced. "Don't worry, sir, they'll get there."

For the next few minutes Wyatt answered questions from the young Marine about their trip to Nigeria, judiciously avoiding a full explanation of the dream and the magic they hoped to find. It wasn't so much that he didn't believe, although he had his doubts, but that he didn't want the Marine to treat him like a nut case. This was no time for the full truth.

Sooner than he had hoped a big white Chevy Suburban came roaring down the street, its red and white diplomatic plates clearly visible even in the blackness of early morning. It pulled up next to the cab and a tall, balding, heavyset man wearing a bright Hawaiian shirt climbed out.

"You the guy they're trying to shake down?" he asked Wyatt without the niceties of introductions.

"You Big Bear?"

"Mr. Big Bear to you. Bill Wolf." He held out his hand and Wyatt shook it.

"Pleased to meet you. Can you take me to the hotel?"

"I suppose that could be arranged. But I have to warn you, I don't kiss on the first date."

Wyatt smiled despite himself. "I can live with that."

"Good. Then hop in and let's go get those two friends of yours so I can get back home and get a few more hours of sleep."

"I really do appreciate this," Wyatt began.

"Yeh, I know. I'm a saint," the Regional Security Officer said, waving him off as he walked toward the Suburban.

Wyatt began to follow, but the cab driver wasn't having any of it.

"Hey, you! Where's my 200 naira?" he yelled, moving angrily toward the Suburban.

"Oh, yeh - sorry man," Wyatt said. He bent down and reached into the elastic ribbing of his right sock.

"Two hundred naira! Is that what this sleazebag is trying to charge you for a ride in from the airport?" Wolf asked. "He'll take a hundred - won't you?" The tone of his voice said it all.

"No, no - that's okay," Wyatt said. "I promised him 200 if he got me here pronto, and he sure as hell did that. Here - I'm afraid I've only got American dollars, but that should cover it." He handed him a ten dollar bill.

"Cover it - you just smothered it," the RSO said. "You know that's almost twice what you promised him?"

"I'm a big tipper. Come on - let's get to the hotel."

"It's your money." Wolf hopped into the Chevy.

"Hey, thanks a lot - all of you," Wyatt said as he climbed into the passenger seat. The Marine snapped off a quick wave, the two Nigerian guards nodded and the cab driver smiled.

Before Wyatt even had time to think, the Suburban was squealing into reverse and rushing down the narrow roadway at breakneck speed.

"Don't worry, our react vehicle will be over there in no time," Wolf said, feeling the young American's unease. "Your friends will be okay. Speaking of which, how did you get involved with those Nigerian sleazebags anyway?"

Wyatt explained their arrival and how they had been whisked away to the back room shakedown. Wolf shook his head. "Don't feel too bad - you're not alone. This is about the tenth report of that kind of thing we've had in the past year or so. Actually, you got away cheap with just a couple of hundred dollars."

"Maybe compared to some of the others, but that was more than half our living money."

"Well, I wish I could promise you that you'll see your money again, but I don't think it's very likely."

"Yeh, I know. At this point, all I want is to see my two friends again and get the hell out of Lagos."

"I can understand that feeling."

"I bet you can."

"This is a tough city. I think you'll like the rest of the country a lot more."

"I don't think it'd be possible to like it a lot less."

Wolf laughed. "No, I suppose not."

Just then the radio crackled alive. "Big Bear, Big Bear, Rover 1."

The RSO picked up his radio mike. "Go ahead Rover 1."

"We're here at the motel. No sight of the two perpetrators."

"And the two Americans?" Wyatt cut in.

"What about the two Americans?" the RSO asked over the radio

There was a long pause at the other end.

"In what room are they again?"

Wyatt groaned.

"They're in one of the back bungalows. Get back there and make sure nobody goes in or out! Do you copy?"

"We copy. Rover 1 out."

"Sometimes I could just strangle every damn one of them," Wolf muttered.

"Do you think my friends will be okay?"

Wolf half-shrugged. "I'm sure they will be. But just to be sure, let's get there a little quicker." He reached under the seat and pulled out a blue police light that he placed on the hood. With a flick of a switch the light began to pulse and a siren wailed. "We're not actually authorized by the Nigerian government to use this," he explained with a broad smile, "but what the hell - we'll say we were testing new equipment." He stomped on the gas pedal and the scenery blurred.

Less than five minutes later they pulled into a familiar driveway.

"It's back there - behind the main building," Wyatt directed

They moved quickly through the hotel parking lot and pulled up in front of the bungalows with lights flashing and siren still screaming. Sheila and Malcolm came running out of the bungalow.

"I guess maybe I can turn this off now, huh?" Wolf asked with a smile. Lights were popping on throughout the hotel.

"Might be a good idea - I don't think we're making any friends," Wyatt said

Before he could even step out of the car Sheila was hugging him so hard he thought his ribs might break.

"Hey, hey, take it easy," he said, "don't crush the merchandise."

He bent down to give her a kiss and was surprised to see tears rolling down her cheeks. "Hey - what's this?"

"I'm sorry," she sobbed, "I was afraid I might not ever see you again."

He stroked her hair gently. "Not much chance of that. Probably be just the opposite - you'll be seeing too much of me," he joked

A smile broke through the tears. "That's a problem I'd like to have."

Meanwhile Wolf had finished talking with the Nigerian guard force and came over to fill them in on what had gone down. Malcolm, who had been hanging back while Wyatt and Sheila talked, came hurrying up to hear the story.

"It looks like we got lucky," the RSO explained after Wyatt had introduced him to his two companions. "You were right - your two friends headed over here after you gave them the slip at the Embassy. But our guards pulled up just after they did and they took off in a hurry with the other two when they saw our guys arrive - doesn't look like they're so tough after all."

"They plenty tough when they has the guns," Malcolm said.

"Yeh, I'm sure they are," Wolf said. "But I don't think you'll see any more of them tonight. We can leave a guard here with you just to be sure..."

"I'm not staying in this motel another minute," Sheila interrupted. "Guard or no guard."

"I really don't think you'll have any more problems with them," Wolf began, but Sheila cut him off again.

"Not this woman. I'm not staying anyplace that doesn't have a ten foot wall and a dozen armed guards around it."

"For instance?"

"How about the Embassy? Can we go back to the Embassy?"

Wolf tried to be diplomatic. "We really don't have facilities for sleep-overs."

"Then we won't sleep!" Sheila said. "I don't think I could sleep even if I wanted to."

Wolf turned to Wyatt. "You?"

"I could sleep. But if she doesn't want to stay here, then I guess we aren't staying."

"That make three of us," Malcolm chimed in.

The RSO shook his head. "My wife's going to kill me for this, but why don't all of you come over to my place - just for tonight. I've got beds and couches enough for the three of you."

Sheila threw her arms around his neck and half-strangled the man. "Oh, thank you, thank you!" she said.

"I guess that's a yes," Wyatt said.

"And you - are the accommodations okay for you too?" Wolf asked Malcolm.

"You ain't leavin' me here," the old man said.

"All right then - let's get back home while it's still dark out."

Wolf gave some instructions to the Embassy guards and explained the situation to a sleepy motel guard who had finally wandered out to see what all the commotion was about. Then they all piled into the Suburban and set off for the RSO's house - without the flashing light and siren.

CHAPTER TWELVE

"I gotta be crazy," Wolf mumbled as he drove through the empty early morning streets of Victoria Island.

"That might well be true," Sheila said from the back seat, "but we kind of like nut cases - don't we guys?"

Malcolm and Wyatt gave their enthusiastic approval.

"Well, that's nice, but I just hope the wife sees things the same way," the RSO grumbled as they sped past a Fellini-esque line-up of hookers bordering the wide boulevard. One seemingly attractive young woman pulled up her tank top to advertise her wares. Wolf honked and flashed his headlights.

The huge white Suburban, the omnipresent Moby Dick of the Embassy set, raced quickly across the island, until, with a quick leap across the bridge uniting Victoria with Ikoyi Island, they found themselves in an even more exclusive residential neighborhood. The walls were higher, the houses more stately, the trees and gardens more expertly trimmed.

"Now this is more like it," Wyatt said.

"This is the Africa I been dreamin' about," Malcolm echoed.

"But with any luck, that's a dream we won't have much longer," Sheila said.

"How's that - you thinking of going home?" Wolf asked.

"We wish," Sheila said. "But no such luck. Not until we're rid of the dream."

"And what dream is that?" Wolf asked.

Wyatt looked to Sheila who looked to Malcolm. He shrugged. There really wasn't any way to explain it without sounding as nuts as Wolf thought himself to be.

"It's hard to explain," Sheila said.

"Well, you got a few minutes before we get there - give it a try."

Wyatt and Malcolm deferred to her. She hesitated, trying to think of a way to put events in their best light. Finally she took a deep breath and launched into the whole story, with her two companions filling in the details she forgot or never knew. Wolf never said a word. When she finished the car was awkwardly silent.

"I told you it was hard to explain," she said defensively.

"You explained it all right," Wolf said. "It's what you explained that's a little hard to swallow."

"We've all had the same exact dream for over two weeks now," Wyatt said. "You tell me how you'd explain that."

"I don't know that I could. But I'm not sure I'd go to Nigeria to try to figure it out."

"We didn't say we were thrilled with the way things are working out," Sheila said, "but if there's a chance that we can lose the dream, I'd go to hell itself."

"You've made a good start," the RSO said.

"This ain't Africa," Malcolm said. "This jus another city. Once we gets to the real Africa, then we be okay."

"Now there's a man with a head on his shoulders," Wolf said. "Why don't the three of you get on a plane, or a bus, or whatever tomorrow morning and head to the real Africa - Ghana maybe."

"Ain't nec'ssary to leave this country," the old man said. "Jus got to get outta this damn city."

Wolf nodded. "Yeh, well I guess that's the next best thing. But I'd still consider Ghana if I were you."

"I'd turn back if I were you," Sheila whispered in her best Margaret Hamilton voice.

"And your little dog too!" Wyatt added.

"We don't have a dog," Wolf said.

"And it's a good thing.

Just then the big Chevy pulled up to a closed gate. Through the narrow steel bars they could see a half-dozen town houses huddled behind eight foot concrete walls.

"Well, here we are!" Wolf announced.

Moments later a sleepy looking Nigerian guard stumbled out of a tiny guardhouse inside the gate and, after a cursory look to make sure they weren't terrorists intent on overrunning the compound, he opened the gate and let them in.

Wolf waved to the guard, who more or less saluted. The compound wasn't big, perhaps 150 feet square, but there was a certain familiarity with the look of the buildings - despite the palm trees and other tropical foliage - that made Sheila feel instantly relieved.

"Who's your color coordinator at the Embassy, Liberace?" Wyatt asked as the pink and grey paint glowed under the nighttime security lighting.

"I guess GSO got a deal on some surplus paint," Wolf said. "Come on – I'll need you to defend me from a potentially violent woman."

"Your wife?" Sheila asked.

"Dr. Jekyll and Mrs. Wolf," he said. And then, turning back added: "Don't tell her I said that."

They walked through another metal door into a small patio that fronted one of the units. A few local plants struggled to survive in the heavily shaded red clay. Wolf opened the door gently and tip-toed into his house. His three charges followed. They hadn't taken three steps when a voice drifted down from upstairs.

"Bill - is that you?"

The RSO opened his eyes wide in mock horror. "Yes dear. With a few friends who've just met some of our friendly local thugs."

"Oh? I'll come right down."

"No, no, that's not necessary dear," he called up.

Footsteps padded across the hallway floor upstairs and then sounded on the stairs. "Don't be silly. Of course it is." Wyatt, Sheila and Malcolm waited anxiously as feet appeared through the bannisters, becoming a torso and finally the full figure of a plump middle-aged woman in a pink terry cloth robe and fuzzy slippers.

"Mrs. Wolf?" Wyatt said, echoing the disbelief of the other two.

"Why yes. What a pleasant surprise."

All three visitors looked to the RSO. "She must've taken her medication," he whispered out of the side of his mouth.

"I'm so glad you could stop by and visit us," she said sincerely. "Can I fix you all something - or get you something to drink?"

"No, no, we're fine, thanks," Wyatt said. Sheila tried to stifle a yawn, but the overpowering urge would not be denied. She slid her hand over her mouth trying to disguise it.

"Oh, you poor dears, you must be exhausted," Mrs. Wolf said. "Let's get you right upstairs to bed." She took

Sheila by the arm. "I'm afraid we only have two beds - a queen and a single. I hope that matches your needs."

"That'd be wonderful," Sheila said.

Wyatt and Sheila were quickly situated in a guest bedroom, while Malcolm was placed in the room of one of the Wolfs' daughters who was spending the night at a friend's.

"Now all of you shut your eyes and get some sleep. We'll probably be at work by the time you wake up, but just help yourself to whatever you'd like in the kitchen. Bisola will help you," Mrs. Wolf said as she dropped off towels to each. "Sweet dreams."

"Ay, there's the rub," Wyatt said softly.

"Maybe not," Sheila said. "Only one way to find out." She kissed him lightly and rolled over on her side.

Heavy breathing could be heard from both rooms before Wolf could even undress.

"Nice people. What's their story?" Mrs. Wolf asked her husband when he finally slipped beneath the sheets.

"It's a beaut," Wolf said. Although half-asleep, his wife had no problem staying awake as he explained.

The next morning Wyatt awoke to find Sheila already up, sitting by the window staring out at the lush greenery in the communal courtyard.

"You're up bright and early," he said, stretching languidly but making no move toward joining her.

"If you consider two o'clock in the afternoon early," she said. "I was about to call the embassy doctor to see if you'd slipped into a coma."

"Two o'clock!" Wyatt grabbed his watch off the nightstand in disbelief. Sure enough, it was two-eleven.

"So, do you think you're going to straggle out of bed anytime soon, or should I go down and get something to fill the great emptiness I'm feeling in my stomach?"

"Yes, and yes," he said throwing off the sheets and struggling to his feet. "Go down and see if you can find something. I'll be down as soon as I take a quick shower."

"I was hoping you'd say that."

"About breakfast?"

"About the shower."

He threw a pillow at her but she dodged out the door with a giggle.

Now that it was daylight, and she was a little more awake, Sheila could get a better sense of the RSO's house. It was an anomaly in these surroundings: in every way it looked exactly like what she'd expect to see back in the U.S. -- a medium sized townhouse with all the basic amenities of home. They had four bedrooms, two and a half baths, a living room filled to overflowing with art, carvings and hangings. At one end they'd pushed enough stuff aside to locate a massive big-screen projection TV. So despite the swaying palms outside and the small orange and black lizards that sunned themselves on the compound walls, she felt surprisingly at home. A twinge shot through her stomach as she thought of home, so very far away.

"Sleep okay?"

Sheila jumped at the voice. She looked up in time to see Malcolm stroll out of a small dining room that joined the kitchen and living room, a thin wooden skewer in his hand. "You got to eat som'a dis stuff," he said, some of the stuff still filling his mouth. "It be somethin' else."

"What kind of something else?" she asked.

"Dey calls it soo - yo or somethin' like that."

"And you cooked it?"

Malcolm shook his head in bemusement. "Not me. The woman in the kitchen. She be doin' all the cookin' round here."

"Oh?" Sheila quickly walked to the kitchen door and peeked in. A short, heavyset black woman with bright eyes and a big smile greeted her.

"Good morning, ma'am," the cook said. "I bet you're hungry by now."

"Starved." She held out her hand. "My name is Sheila."

The woman wiped her hand off on her multicolored apron before shaking Sheila's. "Bisola," she said. "It's good that you slept. The Madam told me all about your adventure last night. You needed it. What would you like to eat?"

"Oh, I don't know," Sheila said. "Malcolm seems awfully fond of those soo-yos."

"What's that? Oh, you mean suya. Would you like anything with it? Eggs? Toast? Coffee? Orange juice?"

"Maybe one slice of toast. And the eggs sound good. Maybe some o.j. And coffee would be great, thanks. I suppose it's pretty strong, huh?"

"Instant Maxwell House," she said. "We can make it as strong as you'd like."

Sheila smiled. "Start with one rounded teaspoon and we'll go from there."

The cook nodded and set about her work. Sheila watched her move efficiently around the kitchen, slicing meat, cracking eggs, in complete control of her environment. But then she began to rifle through a silverware drawer repeatedly, mumbling to herself as she did. Sheila didn't want to interfere where she was a stranger, but at last she could not bear to watch Bisola's frustration any longer.

"Is there something I can help you with?" she asked.

"I'm afraid I cannot find a rounded teaspoon," the cook said, holding up a standard old-fashioned teaspoon. "Could you make do with an everyday spoon?"

Sheila smiled. "Actually, I meant that I wanted a full teaspoon of coffee in my cup," she explained. "We call those rounded."

Bisola nodded, seemingly not the least bit embarrassed. "Oh, then I will use a normal spoon then." And she returned to her work.

Sheila was about to ask her more about herself, when a gentle tap on her arm distracted her. It was Malcolm.

"Did you have it - the dream, I means?"

She had become so accustomed to the same nightly visitation that she hadn't even thought about whether their arrival in Africa had caused any change. She thought for a second, trying to dredge up the faded shreds of memory. She never remembered her dreams for long. If she didn't really concentrate when she first awoke the images slowly faded to nothingness during the course of the day.

"Yes, yes I did," she said, the outlines of the brilliant red mask flooding back into consciousness.

"Anythin diff'rent?" The look on his face was expectant.

"Different?" She closed her eyes and tried to piece together the all too familiar course of the recurring vision. She saw once again the green, tangled jungle, heard the pounding of the drums. Then she and Wyatt were running through the underbrush, pushing and hacking their way as something - or someone - hurried after them in determined pursuit. She saw the outlines of the village huts, knew they were being drawn to their rendezvous with the masked man. But then.... "Wait," she said aloud. "He's outside the hut - he's waving us in!"

"The mask man," Malcolm said with a smug smile.

"Yes! You too?"

He nodded. "If I sees it, you all sees it too."

"Then it has changed! Something is affecting it."

"Africa," the old man said simply. "I tol you. Dis is the place. Dis is where we finds what we lookin fo'."

"Well I hope we find it soon. I don't know how much of this place I can take."

"Wait til we get outta dis city. Then we'll see changes."

She nodded without conviction. At first this whole trip had seemed like a wonderful, crazy, fun adventure. Now she wasn't so sure. There might be elemental good spirits here; she remained open to the possibility. But she knew perfectly well that evil cohabited; that much she had experienced herself.

"Something smells pretty damn good!" Wyatt said as he ambled down the stairs, his face bearing the bright glow of a recent shower. "What's for eats?"

Sheila described the possibilities and asked Malcolm to demonstrate suya. Wyatt was dutifully impressed and asked Bisola for the works; she smiled agreeably.

"No problem, Mastah," she said, setting to work.

"Thanks, but I'm nobody's master," he said, slightly embarrassed.

"Don' think nuthin' of it," Malcolm said. "To her everybody is a Mastah."

"Not me." His conviction sounded unshakeable. Unfortunately, Bisola wasn't listening.

Sheila decided to change the subject. She realized that their sensibilities were very different from the locals, and that that would not change quickly.

"How'd you sleep?" she asked, coming to a subject of more immediate interest.

"Pretty well. At least this version didn't wake me up."

"Was it different for you too?" she asked, suddenly energized.

"Our good friend in the mask was the doorman this time. You two?"

"Same dream, one hun'red percent," the old man said.

"So something is going on here. Maybe Mal is right - maybe we can find the answer here in Africa."

"'Course I right," the old man chimed in.

"I certainly hope so," Sheila said. "I could really get into a whole night without one drum beat, or one witch doctor, or one jungle."

"Just you, your lover boy and a gallon of whipped cream, huh?" Wyatt said.

Sheila quickly scanned the counter, and finding a grape, threw it at him. "You are truly a sick puppy," she said.

Wyatt ducked, laughing. "To each their own."

"I likes whip cream," Malcolm said to himself.

"So do I, Malcolm," Wyatt said. "So do I."

Sheila eyed him with a superior smirk. "Enough with the whipped cream. We've got more important subjects to discuss."

"Such as?"

"Such as, where do we go from here?"

"To the countryside, I guess. I mean, that's what we came here for."

"It gots to be better'n here," Malcolm said.

"That's not saying a whole lot. Bisola, you've been in other parts of the country, haven't you?"

The cook looked up from the task at hand and shook her head. "Not really. Been on the road from here to Benin. That's about all."

"You're not Nigerian?" Wyatt asked

The woman laughed heartily. "Not likely. I'm Ghanaian."

"Really? Then what are you doing in this god-forsaken city?"

The three travelers could hear her sigh across the kitchen. "Come here seven years ago when times was tough in Ghana. Economy was bad. If you wanted to make money you had to leave the country. Most of us come here."

"This is nicer than Ghana? Remind me never to visit that poor country."

"Not now!" Bisola protested. "Now Ghana is much better. Accra is clean, and the people are not so crazy. There are jobs. Food. Much better than before."

"Then why are you still here?" Wyatt asked, his real puzzlement showing clearly on his face

The cook shrugged. "Everything I have is here now. My parents are dead. My husband and children live here with me. He has a job driving for the Lowes. If we go back to Ghana, what is there for us? We will have no jobs, nowhere to go."

"What about your brothers or sisters? And your husband's family."

"They did not want him to marry me. It would not be comfortable. We could stay with one of my brothers, but I do not wish it."

"So you're trapped here then?" Sheila sounded apologetic.

"Not trapped. One day we'll go back, when the children are bigger. For now we save our money so that we can start our own business when we return."

"Good for you, Bisola," Wyatt said. "I bet you make it."

"And what odds are you giving on us?" Sheila interrupted.

"Don't know. Better'n even money, though."

"Ah, an optimist."

"I don't think so."

"Are you ready for your breakfast?" Bisola asked from the stove behind them.

The discussion ended in a dash for the table. While they ate they discussed their plans for getting out of the city and out to the countryside where they hoped to find....?

"Redemption," Wyatt said.

"Peace of mind," Sheila offered.

Malcolm was more metaphysical. "The heartbeat," he said. "The goddamn plain and simple heartbeat of humanity." The old man saw his two companions exchange jaded glances. "I dreamed it," he said. "Lon' time ago."

"You do have the damnedest dreams," Sheila said.

As soon as they'd finished and thanked Bisola, they called Wolf at the Embassy and told him of their plans.

"Hey, don't take me so seriously - no one else does," he said. "You don't have to run off so soon. Hang around for a few days. Talk to some of the people in the Embassy. Maybe Cotonou, or Accra might get you what you're looking for."

Malcolm wouldn't hear of it. "You all do whatever you wants. I knows this dream. I knows where I has to go. And it's right here - in Nigeria."

Sheila looked over to Wyatt, who nodded resignedly.

"Thanks for the offer, but I think we'll be heading north. Whatever it is we're looking for, it seems like that's the place."

There was a long moment of silence. "Well," Wolf finally said, "I wish you the best of luck. I gotta hand it to you, you're determined, if nothing else. So anyway, you take care of yourselves now, and if there's anything I can do..."

"Don't worry," Wyatt said. "I'll keep your phone number right next to my heart. You'll definitely hear from us if we run into trouble."

"Then I hope I don't hear from you, at least until you get back to town."

"Thanks. And thanks again for the help and hospitality."

"My pleasure. I hope you find what you're looking for."

"So do we, Bill. So do we."

When he hung up the phone Wyatt couldn't help but think that they'd cut their last link with civilization. Their last hope for backing out. It was the ultimate act of conviction, the final act of commitment. Or were they just friggin' nuts?

"Ready?" he asked the other two.

"Sho' am," Malcolm said.

Sheila smiled wanly. "Ready or not, here we go."

With hearts racing from nervous anticipation they bid Bisola goodbye, and stepped out of the compound and onto the streets of Lagos.

CHAPTER THIRTEEN

In the warm midday sunlight the city hardly looked as forbidding as it had the night before.

"Maybe we overreacted," Sheila said as they stood by a main roadway waiting for a mini-bus that would take them north.

"I don' think so," Malcolm said. "I don' feel no heartbeat t'all in this city."

"I'm afraid I have to agree with Malcolm," Wyatt said. "This place sucks morning, noon or night."

Sheila was in no mood to argue. She wasn't at all convinced that Lagos wasn't the most evil, despicable place on earth. She'd just thought to give it the benefit of the doubt and now was more than happy to go along with her partners' assessment.

As they waited, they experienced firsthand the midweek suburban rhythm of the island. In a way it was impressive. Houses were large, streets wide, and a stately demeanor graced the neighborhoods. Unfortunately, it was a demeanor diminished by omnipresent neglect and largely negated by the overwhelming poverty of many of the street people who moved within it. And there were many. Despite enough buses, trucks, vans and cars to create endless traffic jams (called go-slows locally), what was most remarkable to the trio was the number of pedestrians and street merchants that dotted every street and sidewalk. The small stands they'd seen in the rush of the night now revealed themselves in an endless array of food, dry goods, and god-knew-what commercial outposts. In the traffic circle where they now found themselves there must have been twenty such stands, selling everything from bananas to bread, water, soda, junk jewelry, stockings, cigarettes, sunglasses, imported whiskey and much, much more. It was as if an amoebic K-mart had been caught in mid-cell division and spewed its individual counters across the urban landscape. Of course, no blue police lights on raised metal stands were visible, but then, every day was savings time at the Lagosian markets

A constant flow of huge, battered Bluebird buses and dilapidated VW vans came and went, each one carrying a conductor/fare collector who yelled out the vehicle's destination upon arrival at an ad hoc bus stop. Neither Sheila nor Wyatt could discern anything in the din of the street market, though truth be told they would have had a good deal of trouble understanding many of the announcers even in a soundproof room. Good diction was evidently not a requirement for employment. Malcolm, on the other hand, after a few minutes adjusting to the strange lilt of the British/pidgin/tribal pronunciation, was able to make out virtually every destination as they were offered.

"Badanabadagraoboshogobo," the conductors would seem to cry.

"What'd they say?" Wyatt and Sheila would ask, and the old man would patiently explain what he'd heard, even if he couldn't identify any of the words as town names. Then they'd look the names up on the map and get some idea of where the ragged fleet was headed. And, in fact, they were headed everywhere. East to Benin City and even Port Harcourt, West to Badagry, north to Ibadan and Abeokuta.

And then, finally, the old man heard the word they'd been listening for: Oshugbo.

It seems this Oshugbo was some kind of holy place for the Yoruba tribe. A place where a goddess had come up out of a river. A place where a shrine had existed for as long as anyone could remember.

"I really don't know if you can find what you're looking for there, but it might be a good place to start looking," Wolf had told them. And since they didn't have a better idea, they decided to give it a try

The conductor who beckoned them was young, probably no more than 16 or 17, and hung halfway out of the open sliding side door so as to leave more room for paying customers. This seemed to be the approved stance for men and boys in his position (they hadn't yet seen a woman holding the job), since virtually every van featured this death-defying balancing act, half-in, half-out, clinging to the door frame much like the lizards Sheila had seen defy gravity on the sides of concrete walls

They approached as if to enter but were blocked by the young conductor at the door.

"Oshugbo?" he repeated, a look of surprise or doubt inscribed on his prematurely lined face.

"That's where we goin'," Malcolm said. "How much?

The youngster hesitated. Then he said something to the driver in Yoruba. The driver seemed to weigh his options before responding. "Three hundred naira," the youth finally said.

"Three hundred!" Sheila exploded. "We were told 150."

The conductor ignored her. "Three hundred," he said to Malcolm.

"One-fifty," Wyatt said. He looked to the old man.

"Tha's right," Malcolm said on cue. "One-fifty."

The conductor said something else in Yoruba. The driver shrugged and answered monosyllabically.

"One-fifty," the conductor said, holding out his hand. "Each."

"Pay him before it's 300 each!" Sheila urged.

Wyatt grimaced but paid him his money and they piled into the ramshackle van, joining two other travelers already inside.

"This isn't so bad," Sheila said as they got underway. "From what Wolf said I thought it was going to be much worse." The RSO had described virtual sardine cans on wheels.

"Maybe we got lucky," Wyatt said. "Maybe nobody's travelling to Oshugbo today."

The old VW chugged down the wide suburban boulevard and picked up speed as it merged into traffic on the highway that led to the bridges. For ten minutes the three travelers relaxed in the relative comfort of the van, for although the seats were badly worn and the underlying springs attacked the body in strange ways, the early morning temperature was mild and the breeze through the open door was refreshing. Then they stopped at another bus stop/market just across the first bridge

This market was much larger than the first. Actually, the market was located down below the bus stop, which was really nothing more than an overcrowded strip on the side of the highway at a railroad overpass. But from the looks of things the spot had been used as a de facto stop for a long time, since the detritus of hordes of people accumulated over many years was everywhere. Here throngs of people in every kind of garb jostled for position - from men in western style business suits to women wearing traditional multi-colored wrappings. Yet for all the crowd there on the roadside, down below the situation was impossibly worse. Through the smoke rising from huge mounds of burning garbage appeared a massive sprawling market that had grown up on both sides of the railroad tracks - and even in-between - stretching as far as Wyatt and the others could see. From a distance it appeared like a chaotic, multi-hued ant hill, with uncountable masses of humanity seemingly crowded in on top of each other, with no apparent order, no sense, no reason. It would take time to be able to discern the natural rhythm that sustained the place. □

But they didn't stay around that long. As he had before, the conductor yelled out their destinations as they approached the stop, and a mini-horde of fellow travelers pushed and elbowed and cursed their way through the uncooperative mass of sweating flesh to the van. With five passengers already aboard, only four more seats remained. And yet when the four had already been seated, three more made as if to climb aboard.

"Hey! We're already full-up!" Sheila yelled. "They'll have to catch the next one."

"Plenty more space," the young conductor said, pushing the last of the would-be passengers from the back to wedge her irrevocably into the VW bus.

"You can't be serious!" Wyatt said. When no reaction was forthcoming from the conductor, he leaned forward to address the driver. "This is dangerous," he said. "You can't drive like this."

"No problem," the driver said.

"No problem for you, but it's big problem for us!" Sheila said, trying to shift her weight so she could take a full breath.

"You want off?" the conductor asked.

"I don't suppose there's another bus coming along soon that's going to Oshugbo?" Sheila asked.

"Could be. But it gonna be full-full like this one."

Wyatt looked around at the 11 other passengers plus the driver and the conductor hanging out the door. They looked nonplussed at all the fuss being made by the two crazy white people. He realized that the current state of affairs was likely the normal state for bus transport in Nigeria. Wolf, once again, had been right.

"No, that's all right," Wyatt said. "Let's go."

And so the VW bus lumbered down the highway, struggling to pick up speed, while inside the 14 fellow-travelers got to know each other much better than they had ever wanted. At first Sheila didn't think she was going to be able to take it. The van was so claustrophobic that she had trouble making herself breathe. Then too, as the tropic sun flamed high into the sky and temperatures soared, the smell of unwashed bodies, unfamiliar with deodorant, made any inhalation painful. But as the minutes, and then hours passed, the heady mixture of body odor, gas fumes and foul breath, mixed liberally with the occasional uncontrolled release of excess intestinal gas, benumbed the senses and bemused the mind. The constant high-pitched pinging whine of the VW engine pushed to its limits droned on through the day, as temperatures soared and the miles fell away beneath them

It didn't take long to move beyond the city limits. What at first seemed to be an interminable urban sprawl of crumbling concrete block bunkers and omnipresent mountains of rotting garbage gave way almost miraculously, as if some psychotic urban planner had waved his pen and ended the senseless, degrading joke of a cityscape with a defining line of liberation. And then, almost literally in the blink of an eye, they were in an entirely different landscape, a sea of greens and browns, of dense tropical vegetation and wild mud-laden streams. Sheila stared out through unwashed windows as the countryside rushed past in a blur of intense verdancy.

"Beautiful, isn't it?" Wyatt said.

"Compared to Lagos, it's magnificent."

Of course they hadn't escaped the poverty of the land; it had just thinned out and found hiding places beyond the view from the highway. Every now and then the reality was impressed upon them as they came upon desperately poor farmers eking out a meager existence carving yams out of the hard earth or struggling to feed their children by harvesting and selling the banana and plantain bounty of the jungle. But the images didn't linger; the bus roared on toward its destination. Lives intersected but did not connect.

It was four hours later that the van finally made a stop at a small, seemingly abandoned gas station in the middle of the closest thing to nowhere Sheila had ever seen. As they pulled up to the pumps a stirring inside revealed two attendants half asleep in the sweltering midday heat. The driver beeped once and then got out and went about his business of filling the tank and checking the fluids. The horde inside the van unfolded out into the sunlight with a cumulative pained groan of release and reprimand. As if summoned, several merchants appeared with fruit, cola nuts, water, candy and tiny bags of delicious roasted peanuts (or ground nuts, as they called them).

Sheila and Wyatt made straight for the back of the concrete block garage, hoping against hope to find one small remnant of life as it had been back home. To their amazement, they found the two doors they sought, side by side, unmarked.

"What do you think?" Wyatt asked as they paused, momentarily nonplussed by the lack of any designation on the doors.

"What else could it be?" Sheila asked.

Wyatt pursed his lips. "Massage parlor?"

"Good choice. Wonder if they have a Jacuzzi?"

"Weight room?"

Just then one of their fellow passengers, a middle-aged woman enwrapped from head to toe in blue wax-dyed cloth, emerged from the door on the right, unthinkingly adjusting the waistband of whatever she wore beneath her robes as she exited.

Wyatt jumped back out of her way, embarrassed by their proximity

The woman glanced at him briefly, unwrapped the skirt portion of her robe and casually re-wrapped it as she strolled away.

"No false modesty here," he said, watching her disappear around the corner of the gas station.

"And no time to lose. Hope you don't mind," Sheila said, slipping quickly into the tiny room and closing the door behind her.

Wyatt waited for a few seconds, and then emboldened by need stepped up and knocked on the other door. When no one answered he followed Sheila's lead

The toilet was even tinier than it seemed from the outside, scarcely six by four. Where a toilet would normally be found a simple hole in the floor gaped, with two footprints - one on either side - set into the concrete. There was no toilet paper, the water in the scarred, cracked and impossibly discolored sink (appearing in the dim light like some three dimensional impressionistic creation) did not work, and the single bulb high overhead did not emit light. The smell grabbed instantaneously for his stomach, but he took a breath, did his business standing tall, and rushed out of the overheated concrete stall just as his lungs threatened to explode. Sheila was already out there, shaking her head in dismay.

"What a fucking hell-hole," she mumbled.

"Should have used my side - just like Texaco back home," he said, turning to walk away

She started to follow but then, her curiosity aroused, scurried back to peek into the darkened toilet on the left.

"You lying scumsucker!" she yelled, but Wyatt had wisely retreated back around the front of the station.

As soon as he turned the corner he saw Malcolm, gesticulating wildly, yelling something none too polite at the bus driver. Hoping that there wasn't a real problem, and realizing that Sheila would soon be coming around the corner, he rushed over to the confrontation to see what had happened

The old man was spitting profusely, the veins in his head bulging at the temples.

"You no good, lyin' son of a bitch!" he yelled. "What are you tryin' to do - poison me?"

Wyatt slid in between them, holding a hand up to restrain Malcolm.

"What's the problem, Mal?"

The old man sputtered and spit a few more times. "This no good lyin' mutherfucker gave me some bad shit!"

Wyatt turned to the driver. "Is that right? What kind of shit did you give him?"

"I don't give him no shit," the driver said righteously. "Give him cola and alligator peppah."

"Alligator peppah and a coke?"

"He din't give me no sodapop!" Malcolm protested. "Jus' a piece of some mangy ol' nut tha's bitter'n hell, and some pepper that jus' about tore my tongue out."

"Is that right?" Wyatt asked.

"Give him cola nut and alligator peppah."

"What's it supposed to do?"

"Make you awake. Wake you up."

"Does it taste as bad as he says?"

"What d'ya think - I'm making it up?" Malcolm asked.

"Everybody's got a different sense of taste," Wyatt said.

"My taster been burned out!"

"Taste good. Want to try?"

Just then a slight push jolted Wyatt from behind. "Taste what?" Sheila asked.

"Cola nut and alligator pepp-ah," Wyatt said, exaggerating the latter. "Some kind of natural up."

"You got some there?" she asked the driver, who had calmed considerably

The man opened his hand to reveal a small brown nut that resembled a cross between a brazil nut and a clove of garlic. It was nestled in what appeared to be a pile of tiny black seeds. "You want try?"

Both she and Wyatt examined the two offerings closely.

"Don' do it," Malcolm warned. "You be sorry."

"Oh come on, Malcolm. I eat Thai food twice a week. How bad can it be?" Sheila said

The driver smiled slightly and handed her a pinch of the black seeds and one section of the nut.

"How do you eat this stuff?" she asked.

"You chew it," the driver said.

"That would make sense," Wyatt said. "What were you thinking - suppository?"

Sheila punched him in the arm.

"Ow! Man, I hope that stuff improves your disposition."

Sheila eyed the two substances warily. "Only one way to find out," she said, and ignoring Malcolm's knowing shake of the head she took a few of the tiny black seeds and popped them into her mouth. For several seconds she sucked on the seeds but little flavor emerged.

"You have to chew," the driver said, and then mumbled something in Yoruba.

"He wonders how white people from the States eat if they don't know how to chew," Wyatt deadpanned.

"Very funny." She bit down on one of the seeds tentatively. A surge of peppery spice shot through her mouth.

"Whoa!" she said, her eyes opening wide. She manipulated the other seeds into position in her mouth and crushed them as well. The spice multiplied geometrically, tantalizing her tongue with electric intensity. A little bit of the free-flowing juices slipped back down her throat and she nearly choked. Wyatt slapped her on the back to help calm the coughing. When she straightened back up her cheeks were flushed and beads of sweat appeared at her temples.

"Good stuff," she croaked.

"I can see that. When you're done I think they've got a little spare battery acid in back, if you're still game," Wyatt jibed.

"Tol' you the stuff's evil shit," Malcolm said. "Wouldn't listen to me."

"No, really. I like it," Sheila explained. "I mean, I wouldn't make it part of my daily diet, but it has a good, strong taste."

"Should I have them uncork the battery acid?" Wyatt asked.

"She drink battery acid?" the driver asked.

"No! I don't drink battery acid. My...friend is just joking, in his usual perverse, depraved fashion." Sheila made a face at Wyatt. He smiled beatifically.

"How about the cola?" Wyatt prodded.

"I wouldn' if I was you," the old man said.

"Sure. Why not?" she said, unwilling to back down from a challenge, even if her tongue did feel as if she had chugged a fine Chateau Pep Boys battery acid. "Just bite off a piece?" she asked the driver.

He stared at her blankly. "You use your teeth," he said.

"Ah, there's where you would've gone wrong," Wyatt said.

"Watch it," she said. "My teeth are still plenty sharp and there are parts of you that are plenty soft."

"Not if you do your job correctly," he said

She tried to punch him again but he was ready and darted back out of the way. "You're right," she said, looking closely at the cola nut. "Your softest parts are between your ears."

"Are you going to eat that nut or just try to stare it down?" Wyatt said as she inspected it ever closer.

"You're mighty brave for someone who won't even give it a try."

"I don't kiss rattlesnakes either," he said. "But the way I see it, that makes me smart, not chicken."

"That's not the only thing you won't be kissing," she said, and having made her commitment she bit off a goodly sized chunk of the nut

She had already decided to hide her reaction to the cola, no matter what it might be. And it was only her stubbornness that kept her to her pledge. For the taste that stabbed through her tongue was as bitter as dandelion and twice as strong. She chewed stoically, not allowing any emotion to show on her face.

"What I tell you?" Malcolm said. "Damn nasty shit, right?"

She concentrated on moving her jaws up and down, fighting the urge to spit the crumbling mess out onto the ground.

"Not so bad," she said through clenched teeth.

Wyatt watched her closely, a tiny smile edging up at the corners of his mouth. "Not so bad, huh?" he said, nodding in seeming agreement. "Maybe I should suggest this to Ben & Jerry - I can see it now, Cola Nut Supreme."

"Probably be a big hit," she said, her words coming out slightly slurred as she tried to manipulate the waxy fragments in her mouth without swallowing.

"Yeh, sure thing. Can I get you a soda or something - to wash it down?"

She hesitated. "Yeh, okay. Thanks."

Wyatt pulled out a ten naira note and offered it to the driver. "Could you get the lady a soda?" he asked.

"She want a coke?"

Sheila nodded.

"I get her coke."

As the driver strolled off to find a coke, Wyatt and Malcolm stayed close to Sheila, their eyes glued to her puckered mouth. For several seconds no one spoke as they eyed her intensely. She tried to ignore them, but without success.

"What'ya waiting for - think I may explode?" she said at last.

"Getting a little touchy, aren't we?" Wyatt said. "Maybe feeling just a hint of caffeine overdose?"

"I'm feeling fine. It's you two that are ill."

"I'm feeling pretty good. How about you, Mal?" Wyatt asked.

"Feelin' okay."

"Good. Good. I'm kind of surprised about you though, Sheila. I mean, as I understand it those cola nuts have as much kick as ten cups of coffee. By now you should be feeling something. Not even a crawling sensation across your skin? A queasy sensation in the pit of your stomach?"

Sheila tried not to think about it, but hearing his words she did feel a bit sick to her stomach. And maybe there was just the faintest itch across the back of her shoulders...

"Your coke," the driver said, and Wyatt turned to find the Nigerian right behind him, a bottle of Coca Cola in his hand.

"Hey, great. Thanks," Wyatt said. He took the soda and handed it to Sheila. "There you go."

She grabbed the bottle and with a slightly pinched face gulped down more than half its contents in one extended swallow.

"It's a good thing you're not feeling anything from that cola," Wyatt said as soon as she lowered the bottle.

"What do you mean?" she asked.

"Well, with all the sugar and caffeine in that Coke, you'd be bouncing off the walls if you were sensitive to cola."

Suddenly Sheila felt her stomach turn a double axel as a column of army ants scurried down her legs.

"Yeh, good thing," she agreed. She struggled to refrain from swatting the backs of her thighs.

"No more time for break," the driver announced as he turned to go back to the van. "Many kilometers to go."

Floating several inches above the ground, her heartbeat beginning to elevate, Sheila made her way back to the van with her two companions just in time to see several of their follow travelers appropriate their seats.

Wyatt and Malcolm were willing to go with the flow, and in anything approaching a normal condition Sheila would likely have agreed, but she was in nothing close to her normal condition. With multiple stimulants coursing through her veins she was not about to take any crap from anyone.

"Excuse me," she said, struggling to keep an edge out of her voice and being only partly successful, "those are our seats."

The Nigerians stared at her as if they'd been hit by lightning.

"The seats," she explained, talking louder and slower. "They're ours."

"No special seat," the driver said bluntly.

"But we've been sitting in them for the past five hours!"

"No special seat," the driver repeated more determinedly, turning away from her.

"What kind of a van do you run here?!" Sheila half-shouted. Wyatt put his hand on her arm and smiled awkwardly at the other passengers.

"This a Volkswagen," the young conductor explained. "Get in."

"Good answer," Wyatt said. "What do you say we do as he says?"

"This is bullshit!" Sheila said much too loud.

"This Africa," Malcolm corrected.

"This is van - got to go," the driver said, revving the engine in warning

The other passengers all mumbled their agreement.

Sheila looked to Wyatt with anger and frustration. "Are you going to take this crap?"

"It appears to be a crap accompli," he said calmly. "Would you rather walk?" He looked around at the lush, empty countryside to lead Sheila's thoughts back to reality. Her eyes followed his and she got the message.

"I still think it's bullshit," she said, pushing none too politely into the over-packed bench seat.

"Thank you for sharing," Wyatt said.

As soon as everyone was sandwiched into their new spots, the conductor shouted something in Yoruba. Once again, they were off

If anything, the roads got worse. A few unseasonal downpours had mined dozens of sharp-edged potholes and the van driver seemed unwilling or incapable of missing any of them. On one particularly nasty bump Wyatt grabbed for something to keep from falling out the open van door and found only the fleshy thigh of the Nigerian woman sitting next to him. He apologized; she smiled seductively

The miles passed slowly. Sheila mumbled incessantly for the first two hours or so, but eventually she began to drift down off her induced high and the monologue concluded. As the shadows lengthened and the heat of midday began to abate, they came at last to the outskirts of a larger village. They wound their way through narrow dirt streets into the center of town. The three Americans were surprised, though pleased, to see paved streets and electric lights once again.

"Oshugbo!" the kid conductor shouted as the van slid to a stop in a particularly dusty lot at the side of the main street.

"Isn't this where we're going?" Sheila asked, staring out into a mass of street vendors and hangers-on that had immediately congregated.

"This is it," Wyatt said. "All ashore what's going ashore."

Not that they had much choice. As the last passengers in, they had to make way for the others who were de-vanning. And the others had no intention of waiting for them to make up their minds. The woman sitting next to Wyatt began trying to get out almost the instant the van came to a stop. She put her hand on his thigh to brace herself and squeezed appreciatively.

"Take it easy, take it easy," he said. "We're getting off here too."

The woman winked at him.

As soon as Wyatt regained his composure he joined his two companions in the swirl of activity. Peddlers were yelling unintelligibly, the conductor shouting louder still with the van's next destinations, and the roar of cars and trucks rumbling past nearly overwhelming both.

"Now what?" Sheila shouted as soon as they'd recovered their bags from the rooftop rack.

"A place to stay, a decent meal and maybe a cold beer," Wyatt shouted back.

"Any suggestions?"

Wyatt threw up his hands. But then, as the young conductor strolled past trying to round up new passengers, Wyatt grabbed him by the arm.

"Any decent hotels here?" he asked.

"No white man hotel."

"That's okay. How about black man hotel?"

The youngster thought for a second and then yelled something to the driver who was re-tying the baggage. The driver didn't hesitate, yelling what might have been a name.

"He say try Adiz Palace."

"Thanks. Anyplace el...?"

He stopped himself as the preoccupied conductor walked away from him, unhearing.

"You need a place to stay?" a woman suddenly asked from behind.

He turned to see the woman who'd been sitting next to him in the van, a come-hither smile spread across her face.

"Ah, I think we've got it handled," he said.

"We definitely have it handled," Sheila said, stepping between them.

"We definitely have it handled," Wyatt corrected himself.

"Too bad. Good man need good woman."

"He has a good woman," Sheila said, planting her hands defiantly on her hips.

"Maybe good man need two women."

"Now there's an original idea," Wyatt said.

Sheila planted one hand in the middle of his chest and shoved him backwards. "This man need just one woman," she announced, looking from the Nigerian woman to Wyatt.

"Yeh, right," Wyatt said on cue. "Just one woman suits me fine.

The woman shook her head sadly. She mumbled something in Yoruba and, tossing her bundle atop her head, walked off into the maelstrom.

"I wonder what she said," Wyatt asked aloud.

"She say, 'American man need bigger balls'," a Nigerian trader standing nearby said, his smile openly sarcastic.

"His balls are just perfect," Sheila said. "And I would know."

The man's eyes flew open wide in surprise and, mumbling in Yoruba, he beat a hasty retreat.

"Now I wonder what he said?" Sheila asked.

"Probably wondered where you got such big balls," Wyatt translated.

"Amen," Malcolm said.

Sheila smiled. "Another secret of the universe," she said. "Now where is this palace?"

A few questions of the townspeople and a host of explanations later, they were on their way across town in search of the recommended hotel. It seemed everyone had heard of the place, but they all had different directions how to get there. When they finally found a believable source they paid him ten naira to show them the way.

Oshugbo wasn't a big city, at least not in the sense of Lagos, but it had many of the same characteristics writ small. The streets were crowded, with pedestrians as much as vehicles, and chaos seemed to be the rule. As they trudged through the tightly packed crowds several young men tried to pry the luggage loose from the three travelers' vice grips, ostensibly to carry it to the hotel. But after their previous encounters the three were understandably reticent about turning their possessions over to strangers, particularly in this strange land. So they yelled "No thank you!" a hundred times, became adept at yanking their possessions out of over-eager hands without breaking stride, and learned to ignore dozens of small children crying "Oh-weee-bo!" as soon as they came into sight

After more "Oh-weee-bo"s than they cared to hear, Wyatt couldn't restrain his curiosity one moment longer. He grabbed their guide by the arm to interrupt his laser-intensity march.

"Hey! What's this Oh-weee-bo crap?" he asked.

The young man stared at him.

"It probably means 'ignorant foreigner who's about to be taken to a fleabag dump'," Sheila said, sidling up tightly against Wyatt to hear the response.

"Not foreigner - stranger," the man said. "White man."

"What that make me - 'Oh-neee-gro'?" Malcolm asked.

Wyatt turned around, a surprised look caught on a smile. "Mal - I didn't know you had a sense of humor."

The old man smiled. "Lot you don' know. But that ain' surprisin' - you jus' some po' dumb 'oh-weee-bo'."

A crowd of children had started to gather and the 'Oh-weee-bo's began to fill the air in a mystical, almost disbelieving chant.

"Let's get out of here before I deck one of the little twerps," Wyatt said.

"First you're having my dream, now you're reading my mind," Sheila said. "Let's go."

It was nearly a half-hour later when they arrived at the Palace. When they turned the corner off the main street onto a small roadway that was little more than an alley, Wyatt knew immediately which building was the Palace. It wasn't the sign, which was so badly faded as to be virtually invisible from a distance. Nor was it the gated entry, which resembled most of the others on the alley. No, it was the growing realization that in Nigeria, as if they had passed through the looking glass, everything was exactly what it was least likely to be. And so the dilapidated hulk of a three story building that teetered off to their left was unquestionably the Palace. No other building nearby looked quite so un-palatial. Though there was certainly competition.

"This is Palace," their guide announced authoritatively upon approaching the gate. He knocked boldly. A head appeared over the top of the wrought iron, a sleepy lack of concern framing bored eyes.

"Yes?"

The guide muttered something in Yoruba. The head disappeared and several long seconds later the gate swung slowly open.

"You are welcome," the gatekeeper said in a noncommittal monotone as the three travelers followed their guide into the hotel entranceway.

"Think he means it?" Wyatt asked sarcastically.

"Are you going to tip him?"

"For what?"

"Then he probably won't mean it."

Sure enough, the man positioned himself at the doorway, an eager puppy dog look in his eyes. When Wyatt passed by with just a perfunctory 'thanks', the man shuffled back to his post muttering evil sounding nothings that did not sound thankful.

But they were inside. The peeling paint, lone uncovered light bulb dangling from the ceiling and faint whiff of urine made their welcome all the more memorable.

"Just like home," Sheila said as they followed the guide straight to the front desk.

"If you happen to live in Alcatraz."

Not surprisingly, no one manned the desk. The guide pounded the weathered wood and yelled at the top of his lungs. Nothing happened.

"Maybe we should try the concierge," Wyatt said.

Sheila shook her head. "He's probably out cleaning the pool."

"Dis dump got a pool?" Malcolm asked in disbelief.

"A better question is whether they have beds."

"They have bed," the guide answered. He pounded the desk top a few more times and yelled with a vehemence that startled the three Americans. Finally, the heavy steps of someone padding down the stairway to the right of the desk brought him to an impatient stop. A middle-aged woman with thick fleshy arms strolled into view, adjusting her skirt in the never ending battle Nigerian women seem to have with their clothes.

Their guide spoke first, in Yoruba. She answered in kind, without much enthusiasm.

"No room at the inn?" Sheila asked.

"You are welcome," the woman answered with even less conviction than the gatekeeper.

"A noble sentiment - and so original," Wyatt said softly.

"Thank you. You want rent room?" the woman said.

"We would like two rooms. Do you have two rooms available?"

The woman looked down at a dog-eared ledger. "Yes. You want mini-suite?"

Sheila looked at Wyatt with an 'it doesn't matter to me' look.

"How much?" Wyatt asked. Sheila rolled her eyes and sighed. "Doesn't hurt to ask," he told her.

"Four hundred naira."

"And the regular room?

She paused as if calculating. "Three hundred fifty."

"Hell, there's less than two bucks difference between them - let's go wild with the suite," Wyatt said. Sheila nodded.

"Jus' get me a reg'lar room. I be okay," Malcolm said.

"You're a saint," Wyatt said, knowing that he'd be paying for whatever accommodations the old man required.

Wyatt paid their 750 naira and the woman recorded a vague approximation of their names before reaching down below the desk and ringing a bell. She looked around expectantly but no one appeared.

"Are we waiting for the bell boy?" Wyatt asked.

"No. For luggage boy."

Sheila giggled. "That makes sense. We really don't have all that many bells to carry," Wyatt said

They stood there for several minutes, the sweat from the oppressive heat and lack of any breeze staining their shirts and trickling down the small of their backs into the cracks of their backsides. Combined with the increasingly heady odor of urine, it made for a distinctly uncomfortable occasion. The desk clerk, however, seemed not to notice, but stood scanning the three entrances to the tiny room like some ancient mariner high up in the rigging, looking far into the distance for any sight of land. Just as Sheila felt herself wavering, her knees growing weak as a buzz began to swell in her ears, Wyatt spoke out.

"Hey - that's okay. We'll carry our own bags." He expected that the woman would concede easily. He was wrong.

"I carry. This is The Palace," the woman announced as she stepped out from behind the desk and grabbed for their three bags. Sheila gave hers up without a fight. Malcolm was caught by surprise. Wyatt, chivalrous to the end, hefted his himself.

"No problem. I can take this one," he said.

No sooner did he get the words out than the woman reached over and yanked the bag out of his hands.

"Come," she said as she started up the darkened stairs.

"Walk this way," Wyatt said in his best Bella Lugosi impersonation, throwing one shoulder out of whack and dragging his right foot. Sheila, a weak smile the best she could muster, struggled to keep upright while Malcolm brought up the rear.

Unwilling to set their luggage on the floor, the desk clerk fumbled interminably with the lock until she finally managed to open the door to their room.

"This room yours'" she said to Wyatt and Sheila. She dropped their luggage just inside the door and continued down the corridor to show Malcolm his room.

"Are you sure this is how Hilton does it?" Wyatt asked.

"Just like in the training films."

Grabbing their bags off the floor, they tumbled into the room, tired, thirsty, hungry and dirty. Yet despite all their immediate needs, they paused for just a second to fully appreciate the ambiance of their new digs. The wallpaper was peeling. Water stains blotched the ceiling and oozed down the walls. A bent clothes hanger served as antenna for a black and white TV set with no channel selector. The ceiling fan hummed loudly and wobbled precariously as it spun. The bed was more or less full-size, but when Wyatt plopped down to find the perfect position for viewing the water stains, he bounced back again as though on a trampoline. A table and chairs filled the tiny room to overflowing; there was barely room to breathe.

"I gotta pee," Sheila said numbly.

"Take one for me," Wyatt said, sitting on the bed more cautiously to avoid injury.

He was just starting to determine exactly what animals the water stains resembled when a scream from the bathroom brought him running.

"What is it?" he asked, throwing open the bathroom door to find Sheila, panties at her ankles, cowering off in one corner of the room.

"I'm not sure," she whispered, "I think it might have been a cockroach."

Wyatt frowned. "A cockroach? From the way you screamed I thought it was at least a rat!"

"It was nearly as big as a rat!"

He took a perfunctory look around the bathroom. "Well, the killer roach ain't here now. You can go on about your business. You probably scared the shit out of it."

"Likewise," she said.

"Want me to stay and make sure he doesn't come back?"

She allowed a small grin. "I think I can handle it from here."

"Okay. Don't get wet."

She threw a gooey miniature bar of soap at him as he scampered to safety and shut the door. After each took a lukewarm shower - a trying affair that began with trying to find a spot on the stall floor not covered by green slime, progressed to maneuvering under a dripping nozzle that barely kept them wet, and concluded with a futile attempt to dry off in the oppressive humidity using a towel so thin they could see through it - the two of them, slightly cleaner, laid down for a quick nap before dinner. Two hours later they awoke. One or both had rolled over toward the center of the bed, which sagged so badly they'd collided in mid-mattress and bumped heads.

"What time is it?" Sheila asked groggily, rubbing her head and trying to focus her eyes.

Wyatt held his watch up to the bright lance of light that shone through the not-quite-narrow gap between the two halves of the tattered drapes; he had tried to pull them tight, but if the two sides met, the ends pulled clear of the wall.

"Seven fifteen."

She rubbed her eyes and sat up. "Wow. We really conked out. Must've been more tired than we thought."

"Nothing like a nice relaxing trip with ten of your closest friends in a terminally ill VW to make you feel tip-top."

"I'm hungry."

Wyatt looked at her out of the side of his eyes. 'Do all women do that?' he wondered. 'Jump from one topic to another in the middle of a conversation without signaling?'

"Okay...I can go along with that," he said without further comment. "Do you think there's a Wendy's anywhere near here?"

She chuckled. "More like Shola's Suya Kitchen. I don't care, as long as it's edible."

"Always the one with unrealistic expectations," Wyatt said. "Well, only one way to find out - let's get out there and see."

Dragging themselves from the rift valley of their mattress, they dressed quickly. In a gentlemanly effort to give Sheila enough space to do her thing, Wyatt cracked his knee against the edge of the table and then nearly killed himself trying to sit in one of the two decrepit chairs as he awaited Sheila's reappearance from the bathroom

When she finally emerged he was in a testy mood.

"Goddamn it, what took you so long? I was attacked and nearly killed by this so-called furniture."

"Have you ever tried to put on make-up looking into a jagged shard of mirror about an inch and a half wide?"

He cocked his head as though in thought. "No, can't say as I have. But I can see the potential for disaster." A flicker of doubt flashed across her face and prompted quick backpedalling on his part. "Of course, now that I see the results I just might decide to break all the bathroom mirrors in our rooms. You look terrific." The look and peck on the cheek made him smile. *Funny how it's the little things that make us happy.'*

After a brief struggle to lock the warped door ("Why bother? A ten year old could kick it in in two seconds"), they meandered down the increasingly dark hallway to Malcolm's room. He answered the door almost before they knocked.

"You're not hungry, are you?" Sheila asked.

"Starved. I been sittin' here dreamin' of a thick, juicy steak."

"Dreaming is right. We'll be lucky to find chicken. Let's go see what's available."

While the old man went to get his key, Wyatt surveyed the room.

"You know something, this room looks bigger than ours."

Sheila stuck her head in the door. "You know, I think you're right! But I thought we got the suite."

"We did, we did. You know why it looks bigger?" he asked.

"Atmospheric conditions?"

"The table and chairs. He doesn't have that damn table and chairs taking up all his floor space. It's the exact same room without the killer furniture."

"Live and learn," Sheila said

With that profundity hanging heavily in the breeze-resistant hallway, Malcolm finally located his key and locked the door without a problem.

Sheila looked to Wyatt with a raised eyebrow.

"All the suites come with a warped door - costs a little extra, but it's worth it," he said.

Malcolm didn't get it, but he was too hungry to stop and ask. Moving slowly to avoid nasty spills in the deepening evening gloom on uneven steps, the three travelers made their way downstairs to the lobby where they intended to ask directions to the nearest decent restaurant. Only thing was, the desk clerk wasn't there. Someone else was.

They saw him when they first came into the tiny reception area, standing quietly off to the side near the entrance from the outside. He was wearing the full native regalia - long, flowing white robes with massive sleeves flipped up over his shoulders, and a white, pill-box hat that reminded Sheila of something Jacqueline Kennedy might have worn. It was hard to determine his age. Wyatt later thought him to be in his mid-forties. Sheila thought he was older. Malcolm shrugged.

His quiet presence caught the attention of each of the three travelers, but since they were looking for the desk clerk they tried to ignore him. Wyatt pounded on the desk-top as he'd seen their guide do, and yelled "Hello!" at the top of his lungs.

Sheila flinched involuntarily. "Could you yell just a little louder? I'm not sure they heard you back in Lagos," she said.

"When in Rome..."

"Dis ain't Rome," Malcolm said.

"My mistake."

They waited patiently, but no one answered their call.

"Maybe I should try 'fire!'" Wyatt suggested after a long wait, only half in jest.

"How 'bout 'free beer'?" Malcolm asked.

Wyatt smiled. "You know, Mal, I'm really starting to see that there's more to you than meets the eye."

They were trying to decide their next move when a voice from behind demanded their attention.

"Excuse me. Perhaps I can be of assistance." It was the white-robed stranger.

All three turned as though welded at the hip and shoulder.

"Excuse me?" Sheila managed to sputter.

"Perhaps I can be of help," he repeated. "I am Walli Mustafa Ogoke." He bowed his head ever so slightly in a nod of acknowledgement and introduction.

"Pleased to meet you, Wally," Wyatt said. "Do you work here?"

A tiny smile crossed the man's lips. "Not in the hotel. But here in the community, yes."

"Oh, you're a guide!" Sheila blurted

The man bent his head in the same gesture of acknowledgement. "You might say that."

"Just the man we're looking for!" Wyatt said. "Do you know where we can find a good restaurant around here, not too expensive."

"Is that all you are looking for? A good restaurant?" There was something in the way he spoke that sent a chill up Sheila's back.

Wyatt was immediately on the defensive. "What do you mean?"

The man shrugged. "I thought perhaps you sought something more... ethereal. Something...for the spirit."

"Ahhh - are you connected with that Shrine they have around here?" Sheila asked

The man breathed deeply. "In a way."

Wyatt was in no mood for cryptic discussions with mysterious strangers, not even if they were well-dressed. He was hungry. "Actually, all we really need right now is a good restaurant. Do you know of one nearby?"

The man paused for just an instant, as if mulling over the situation. Then he nodded slowly. "Yes...yes I do. If you will follow me."

He turned without waiting for an answer and swept out the door.

"What do you think? Should we go with him?" Wyatt asked the other two in a conspiratorial whisper.

"I don't know," Sheila said. "There's something weird about that guy."

"Sumthin' mighty po'erful too," Malcolm said in a soft, almost trancelike voice.

Wyatt looked at him with narrowed eyes. "You got a feeling about this guy?"

The old man nodded slowly. "He one po'erful sumbitch."

"You already said that!" the younger man snapped. "What the hell is that supposed to mean?"

Malcolm opened his mouth as if to speak and then stopped, his eyes fixed on the door. Wyatt and Sheila followed his gaze. The stranger had returned and was standing silently in the doorway.

"Are you coming?" he asked.

Wyatt looked to Sheila, who hesitated. But Malcolm was already in motion, walking toward the door in a slow, sleep-walking shuffle.

"Looks like we are," Sheila said. The quake in her voice did not escape Wyatt's attention. But Malcolm was already out the door. And he was hungry.

"Well, here goes nothing."

They followed into the darkness.

CHAPTER FOURTEEN

The stranger led them through darkened streets and narrow back alleys. From time to time they heard hushed voices, coming from the darkness of an un-illuminated doorway or from an open window high above their heads. But the voices were too soft to be understood and they didn't stop to listen more carefully. The stranger moved quickly, as sure of his destination as they were unsure of theirs.

But as their path twisted and turned through passageways only three feet wide, with dirt beneath their feet and the powerful, earthy smell of raw sewage wafting over them, Sheila began to get worried. What if this man did not know the way, or worse yet, what if he was a robber, or a murderer, and was luring them to their deaths? Their experience with strangers in Nigeria had not engendered much confidence, and now what little she had was fading fast.

"Wyatt - I don't know about this," she finally said, matching her gate with his so she could speak confidentially without stopping. "This place gives me the willies."

"And the tom, dick and harries," Wyatt said, his voice lacking the humor he tried to project.

"I'm serious!" she said. "This is too weird."

"Yeh, I know," he said, trying to decide the next course of action. "Let's just give him another couple of minutes. If we're not eating foie gras and sipping a fine chablis by then, we'll go our own way. Okay?"

"Two minutes," she said firmly. "And that's it."

They marched on in silence, hoping against hope that they'd glimpse a sign, a light, or something that spoke of an eatery. But the heavy concrete block and mud walls showed no sign of giving way. It seemed hopeless.

Just as Sheila was about to protest, to demand that the stranger take them back to the hotel or at least set them free of that oppressive maze, he stopped. Malcolm, who had never hesitated, pulled up next to him, waiting patiently.

In the dim light all Sheila could see was a ghostly white-garbed arm, pointing into the blackness. She tried to escape the image in her mind of the ghost of Christmas Future pointing down at Scrooge's headstone, but somehow it was all too real and all too familiar. Her knees trembled as she approached the silent specter.

Her eyes followed his pointing finger. She started as Wyatt put his hand on her shoulder.

"Well, it's not the Ritz, but sometimes these little dives are the best places," he said blithely.

Sheila stepped forward and found herself staring into a tiny, one-room inn. There were only four roughhewn tables and barely enough room to move about. Candles flickered on each table, a good thing since there were no electric lights to be found. Shadows danced on the walls and ceiling; the gloomy image did little to improve her mood.

"Ah, mood lighting. I hope they don't charge extra," Wyatt joked, but his voice did not disguise his unease.

"Well, we gonna eat o' jus' stand here?" Malcolm asked.

"I'm still hungry," Wyatt said.

But when he looked to Sheila she was not so quick to agree. "I don't know," she began, "maybe the food's great, but..."

Wyatt saw her eyes widen and turned quickly to see what had caught her attention. There, tucked away in one corner by the door to the kitchen, was a piece of African pottery, a water jug perhaps, or some sort of ornamental art. It was well made, simple with colored patterns similar to many they'd seen in stalls by the side of the road en route to Oshugbo and even there in the city. For most customers it would be nothing special. Just one of thousands. But Sheila recognized it in an instant. It was the exact same piece she'd seen by the entrance to that all too familiar hut that appeared every night in her dream. In their dream.

"It's the same pottery!" Wyatt gasped.

"I be damned," the old man said.

All three hurried into the inn to check more closely, to convince themselves that it was the same piece, or perhaps to try to prove the impossibility of its existence. But there was something about the piece, something that stopped them beyond arm's reach to inspect it from every angle, eyeing it suspiciously as if it might suddenly transform into the masked demon that bedeviled them nightly. But it did not. It sat there in the dim candlelight as still as the night. Finally Sheila leaned forward and reached out a shaking finger to touch it.

"It be real?" Malcolm asked in a hushed voice.

"It's real all right," she said, stepping up to feel its glazed surface more freely. "Real surreal."

"I wonder where it came from. Who made it?" Wyatt asked aloud.

"A good question," Sheila said. "Maybe our friend back there..."

They all turned to where they had left the stranger in white, but in his place there was only the blackness of the night.

"Don't you hate it when people do that?" Wyatt said, his joke falling heavily in the charged atmosphere.

"This is getting pretty weird," Sheila said. "Pretty damn weird."

Just then the door to the kitchen swung open. All three of the travelers jumped back, Malcolm with his hands up in self-defense. But it was only a young woman, just a girl really, carrying a single worn menu and a basket of bread.

Her look of confusion sparked Wyatt back to reality.

"Sorry. We were just looking for the man who brought us here but we couldn't find him. You don't know where he went my any chance, do you?"

"A big man, all in white," Sheila added. "Did you see him leave?"

"Never saw him at all," the girl said meekly, a tentativeness tingeing her voice and eyes.

"No, no I don't suppose you did," Wyatt said. "Well, I guess that's the menu, huh?"

The girl looked down at her hand as if just then remembering what she had come to do. "Yes. It's the menu. You did come to eat, didn't you?"

Wyatt looked to Sheila. She smiled wanly. "Yes. I suppose we did."

Wyatt pulled out a chair for her and they all sat silently as the girl left the bread and menu. Wyatt placed the menu in the center of the table where all three could see it, but Sheila kept sneaking a look out of the corner of her eye at the pottery, as if still convincing herself that it was really there.

"Decide what you want?" Wyatt asked after a time.

Sheila could only shake her head. "Order anything. I'll have some of yours."

Neither Malcolm nor Wyatt shared her lack of appetite, and soon they were eating a variety of traditional Nigerian fare with gusto. Avoiding the Nigerian Sleeping Pill and all variations of processed starch, they were pleasantly surprised when the fish, chicken and suya all satisfied their palates at prices that suited their meager pocketbook. Even Sheila, who started off just picking distractedly at Wyatt's plate, wound up eating her fill of the dishes, the shock of their arrival momentarily overwhelmed by an empty stomach.

But when they had finished their meal and paid the equivalent of a few dollars' worth of Naira, a sudden realization dawned on them - separately but virtually simultaneously - that their tribulations for the evening were not yet over.

"Anyone have an idea how we're going to find our way back to the hotel?" Wyatt asked

Both of his companions had been thinking the same thing but neither had come up with a solution.

"I suppose we could ask our waitress," Sheila suggested. "I'm sure she must have heard of the famous Palace hotel."

"I don't know about you, but I don't think I like the idea of roaming around this town late at night trying to follow directions to a place we're completely unfamiliar with," Wyatt said.

"I seconds that one," Malcolm said.

"Good point," Sheila conceded. "But maybe she'll show us the way. I mean, she doesn't seem too busy." She gestured at the three empty tables.

"I don't know. Maybe the fashionable dinner hour doesn't begin until nine around here," Wyatt said. "Maybe she's just waiting for the big rush."

"Right. I think we were the big rush for this week. Why don't we at least ask?"

"Okay, relax. Waitress!" Wyatt called out loudly.

"That won't be necessary," a familiar voice said.

Three heads turned as one to see the stranger in white standing exactly where they had last seen him, his frame nearly filling the doorway. "You are ready to return?"

"Where did you come from?" Sheila asked, apprehension coloring her voice.

"And how did you know we were ready?"

"When the yam is ready, the farmer appears," the stranger said slowly.

"Oh great, Kung Fu farmer," Sheila said under her breath.

"We are not vegetables," Wyatt said. "Although we may appear to be a bit uncultivated." He smiled nervously at his pun. Sheila shook her head and sighed. Neither Malcolm nor the guide reacted at all. "Just a little joke," Wyatt felt forced to add.

"We may need a microscope on this one," Sheila said.

"Are you ready?" the stranger asked again, neither impatient nor hurried, as if the previous thirty seconds had not transpired.

"Yeh, yeh I guess we are," Wyatt said, the smile gone from his lips.

"Good. Then follow me." The white robes moved off into the darkness at once. The three travelers hurried to catch up.

In the now near-total darkness none of them even bothered to try to commit their route to memory. The innumerable narrow alleyways, dirt paths and intricate multi-faceted switchbacks completely overwhelmed their sense of direction. Besides, all three were focused on the ceramic pot and the mysterious appearance and disappearance of their guide. The scenery was incidental; they needed answers.

Before they were ready, seemingly before it was possible, they came out from between two decrepit old buildings and found themselves once again standing in front of the Palace Hotel.

"Here you are then. I trust you found the food of acceptable quality?" their guide asked.

"Yes. It was very good," Sheila said, barely restraining her curiosity. "But we had a question about that piece of pottery..."

The man held up one hand. "No questions tonight. You may ask me in the morning."

"The morning? We didn't say anything about the morning," Wyatt said at once, his scam-radar highly sensitized.

"I can help you find what you seek," the guide said.

"How you know anythin' 'bout what we seeks?" Malcolm asked

A very slight smile crossed the stranger's face. "You might say it came to me in a dream: the yam is ready."

The three travelers turned to each other and pulled into a close huddle.

"I don' knows 'bout this yam shit," Malcolm said quietly. "But the man do have some heavy duty po'er."

"He kind of scares me," Sheila said. "He knows too much."

"Yeh that bothers me too," Wyatt said. "Maybe we should just pay him off now and go our own way."

Sheila nodded. "That's my vote."

Both turned to the old man. He shrugged. "I don' know. We might be missin' sumthin' big here."

"We can handle it ourselves," Wyatt said. "I mean, hell, we got here without any help didn't we?"

Malcolm stared at him. "That what I mean," he said. "We could use help. But if you two don' wants him, I can go along."

"Good," Wyatt said. He turned back to the stranger. "I'm sorry, Mr....?"

He stopped in mid-sentence. The stranger was gone.

"How the hell does he do that?" Sheila asked, her voice showing the strain.

"The man got po'er," Malcolm said once again.

"Enough with the power thing," Wyatt snapped. "He probably just heard us talking and slipped away. Or, maybe he decided that these three yams aren't ready after all."

"Or maybe he's already decided what he's going to do tomorrow and it didn't matter what we said," Sheila said.

"So you think we'll see the Yam Man again tomorrow?" Wyatt said, his bravado sounding hollow.

Sheila pursed her lips. "I wouldn't be surprised."

"Great," Wyatt said. "Pleasant dreams."

They went into the hotel and up to their rooms without further conversation, each lost in his own thoughts. For the first time they were glad for the exhaustion that overcame them. Otherwise, they might not have slept at all.

CHAPTER FIFTEEN

Morning came early.

Brilliant white tropical light streamed through the tattered curtains by six o'clock; the sounds of street life were already in full swing.

"Goddamn," Wyatt groused. "They're out in the streets until midnight, and by sun-up they're back out there again."

Sheila kissed him on the top of his head. "Somebody needs his coffee," she said. "Let's go see what we can find."

"If that guide of ours is so damn good, why isn't he here with some now?" Wyatt said, dragging himself out of the trough in the bed.

They showered as best they could under the lukewarm trickle and dressed quickly. A combination of excitement, worry and hunger motivated them, an unspoken need to see if the stranger had returned and to learn what he really knew about them - and the Dream.

They were almost ready to go out when a knock sounded on their door. Both Wyatt and Sheila froze.

"Is it him?" she asked. He understood immediately that she meant the guide.

"Only one way to tell," he said, going to the door. With no peephole to look through, he hesitated a second, took a deep breath, and then turned the knob slowly.

"You two looks like you seen a ghost," Malcolm said, looking as concerned as they felt.

"Malcolm! We thought it was that Wally guy," Sheila said.

"Nope. Jus' me."

"Have you been downstairs yet? Did you see him?" Sheila pressed.

"Ain't been nowhere but right here," the old man said. "But I wouldn' mind a cup 'a coffee."

"That makes three of us," Wyatt said. "Let's go see what we can find."

A bit less stressed but still not at ease, Sheila and Wyatt followed Malcolm downstairs. An uncontrollable knot crept into the pit of their stomachs as they tip-toed down the stairs and into the reception room. Even before looking to the hotel desk all eyes scanned the room for the guide. But, just as when they first arrived, there was no one there.

Without waiting, Wyatt grabbed the bell from behind the desk and rang it ferociously, yelling at the top of his lungs for the clerk.

"Feel better?" Sheila asked, the sounds of his summoning still echoing throughout the hotel.

Wyatt smiled. "As a matter of fact, yes. I'll feel even better if that clerk actually shows up while I'm still a young man."

"I'm coming as fast as I can," a familiar voice called out from the stairway. But the sounds of her shuffling step belied her words. Eventually the dim stairway light was completely blotted out as a massive form emerged into the room.

"All right, I'm here. What's so damn urgent?" the clerk said, taking her position behind the desk with some difficulty.

Her bubu had the look of having been wrapped on the move. Wyatt imagined that it would only be moments before she was re-adjusting it.

"Is there any place that serves coffee around here?" Sheila asked with the quiet sincerity of someone who realizes they may have overplayed the bell-ringing routine.

"We really need it," Wyatt said, trying to cover both his own belligerence and Sheila's sincerity

The woman looked from one, to the other, to the other.

"Yeh, I guess maybe you do," she said solemnly. "There is a little place, just a couple of streets from here." She gave directions that were, in fact, vague and confusing. But the three of them were so embarrassed they accepted the advice without comment. They fled the glaring looks of the clerk and soon found themselves in the midst of the usual hubbub on the streets of Oshogbo.

It took a couple of questions, the interfering cooperation of several passersby to translate both the question and the answer, and what they were beginning to identify as a typical Nigerian shouting match, but finally they found the place. It was, truly, small. But, just as the night before, there was an open table and they were quickly seated and eventually served.

Three steaming cups of brown liquid were placed before them, along with a pitcher of a white liquid and a bowl of a granular white powder.

"What do you think?" Sheila asked.☐

Malcolm bent down and took a deep whiff of the steam roiling up off his cup. He coughed vigorously for nearly ten seconds.

"Smell kind'a like coffee," the old man said as soon as he could catch his breath.

"Great. I can just see that as the new Maxwell House slogan: 'smells kind of like coffee,'" Wyatt said, eyeing his own cup suspiciously.

"What a bunch of babies we're becoming," Sheila said. Without further debate she grabbed the pitcher of milk and poured a liberal dash into her cup. Wyatt and Malcolm both leaned over to examine her experiment. Tiny flecks of solid white floated to the surface, but other than that the deep brown color barely paled.

"Looks like it's spoiled," Wyatt announced.

Malcolm stuck his finger into the pitcher and then licked it.

"Nope. Taste okay."

"Then why does it look like somebody threw up in it?" Wyatt asked.

"Oh really," Sheila said, grabbing the pitcher once again. "It's probably just the cream rising to the top." This time she poured as much as the cup would hold. The surface of the coffee was now nearly completely white with floaters, but when she stirred the coffee itself it was still distinctly brown.

"Kind of like trying to dilute 30-weight, huh?" Wyatt said.

Sheila ignored him. She dipped her spoon into the roughly granulated off-white sugar and dumped a heaping teaspoon into her coffee. A goodly amount spilled over the sides into the saucer.

"Must've been what Vesuvius looked like," Wyatt said, his eyes glued to the steaming concoction.

Sheila had come too far to back out now. As she sipped with cautious pursed lips, both her companions pulled back involuntarily, as if distancing themselves from any spray that might erupt.

"Woa!" she cried, her eyes popping open wide. "This stuff makes Bisola's java look like Ovaltine!"

Both Wyatt and Malcolm eyed her closely for several seconds.

"Well, she didn't keel over," Wyatt said to Malcolm.

"Not yet, anyways," the old man answered.

"What a bunch of sissies," Sheila said, sipping the now-stirred mixture with disdain. "Do you want me to taste your toast and jelly too?"

"If you live long enough for it to get here," Wyatt said.

But she did survive to see the rest of their breakfast delivered to the table, and both Wyatt and the old man joined her in their morning caffeine fix. With some decidedly pale sunnyside-up eggs ("they probably sell the yolks separately," Wyatt suggested), some thick, surprisingly satisfying toast and jelly, and a second cup of coffee ("I think I'm a pint low"), they finished their breakfast and paid the bill. Their waitress gave them directions to the Shrine, which were at once contradicted by the cook and then modified once more by a customer who jumped into the conversation uninvited. Eventually they felt fairly secure that they could find their way out to the Yorubas' holy temple without too many problems.

With money growing increasingly short, they decided to take a local bus out to the stop nearest the shrine. "How much worse than the VW van could it be?" they asked. They were about to find out

They found a bus stop close-by the coffee shop, another crowded meeting place surrounded by shouting vendors and hordes of people seemingly doing nothing except milling about. Just as with the van, it took Malcolm to decipher the yelled destinations. After three false alarms a battered yellow Bluebird tottered up to their stop and the young conductor yelled for the Shrine, amongst other locales.

They pushed and elbowed their way onboard, more in self-defense than from an overwhelming urge to join the horde already situated in the tattered green bench seats. Once inside, they realized that not only were there no seats available (those that were occupied looked sufficiently uncomfortable to make standing a very real option no matter what the occupancy), but the aisle was so crowded that every passenger was literally hip to hip with those immediately in front of and behind him. The day was warmer than the day before, and the number of bodies was multiplied by four. Although it was difficult to calculate accurately, Wyatt figured the body stench was multiplied by six.

No one collected a naira from them, but they had no doubt that the conductor would make his way to them sooner or later. Of course, with the driver slamming the balky transmission into gear every time they started up, and then pumping the brakes to a head-snapping halt every hundred yards or so, it was unlikely that anyone could keep on his feet long enough to make a collection unless wedged into an upright position between two other passengers. And where the gas fumes in the van were alleviated somewhat by the hurricane force breeze whipping through the vehicle when it rolled along the highway, the heavy diesel exhaust from the ironically named Bluebird just settled over the assembled multitude like a thick fog over San Francisco Bay.

"At least it cuts the body odor," Sheila gasped.

"I'm not sure I can tell which is which anymore," Wyatt said as his eyes glazed and his cheeks took on a pasty pallor

Luckily, it took only a half hour before they reached their destination. They had made such a point of letting everyone on the bus know where they were going that they were advised en masse when the Shrine stop was in sight. Sure enough, the smiling conductor waited for them outside the door, his hand extended expectantly.

Wyatt shoved three one naira coins into his hand. The smile fell with the teen's expectations.

"What - you expected a tip?" Wyatt asked, a little too loudly, a little too aggressively. "For what - allowing us the privilege to stand while we were gassed?"

Sheila put her hand on his chest to calm him.

"Hey, relax," she said. "You're starting to sound more like these folks than they do."

"Lucky I didn't demand to be paid for the inconvenience," Wyatt mumbled. As he stalked away Sheila slipped the teen another naira. The smile returned.

Oshogbo is laid-out (the term is unquestionably a misnomer; like most cities in Africa and elsewhere it just sort of grew, pell-mell, like an urban cancer) in much the same fashion as Lagos and the other major Nigerian cities: a central core of businesses and government buildings surrounded by residential areas that give way abruptly to thick green tropical growth. The Shrine bus stop was just at the edge of the residential area. Twenty steps down the dirt road toward the Temple and the houses virtually disappeared.

"I don't think we're in Kansas anymore," Wyatt said as they listened to the strange animal cries coming from the forest on either side of the road.

"'Course this ain't Kansas," Malcolm said, shaking his head. "I think you drank too much 'a that damn coffee."

Actually, they all had. How else to explain the pounding hearts and vivid, palpable energy that surrounded and permeated them.

"It the power," Malcolm said.

"What power?" Wyatt didn't even try to keep the sarcasm from his voice.

"The power of this here Shrine. The power of Africa.
You feels it, don't you?"

Wyatt was tempted to answer cynically, to joke about
Malcolm's susceptibility to his surroundings, but the words
died on his suddenly parched lips. True, there was a strange
sensation, something... almost tangible in the air. An energy,
perhaps. But surely it was the coffee.

"Do you feel anything?" he asked Sheila

Even before she answered he could see in her face that
she did. Her eyes were open wide, but she didn't appear
frightened. More like alert, concentrated, focused.

"There is...something," she said.

There was nothing more to say. They walked along the
dusty road in silence, the sounds of the forest animals whirling
about them like a windblown soundstorm. The effect - of the
heat, the coffee, the cries, the dust - the effect was
disorienting, an intense sensory assault in a pastoral green
surrounding. All three felt it, and the intensity grew with each
step closer to the Shrine entrance

It seemed like miles, but was probably much less,
when they finally approached the wrought iron gate to the
Shrine. A narrow worn path, more like the dry bed of a
stream, led from the road down into a broad, flat open space
that fronted the gate. In other circumstances Wyatt might
have said it looked like an overgrown parking lot. But there
were no cars, and Wyatt said nothing.

They stopped in front of the gate, scanning the area
for a guide, or ticket-taker. For anyone. But there was no one.
For the first time since they'd landed in Nigeria, they were
alone. This place was solitary, isolated, and quiet.

"What happened to the animals?" Sheila whispered
when she realized the forest cries had vanished.

"Don't ask," Wyatt said, forcing a small twisted smile that communicated quite the opposite of humor.

"Well, we goin' in?" Malcolm asked after they'd stood staring through the iron bars of the gate for an interminable time.

Wyatt and Sheila exchanged a look of quiet resignation.

"I guess that's what we came here for," Wyatt said. And then he whispered, more to himself than anyone, "Here goes nothing."

The iron gate swung open surprisingly easily. On the other side of the gate the dirt path curved down through sparse undergrowth to a walled structure fronted by strange, distorted figures and a huge, tangled baobob tree. From the entrance to the structure another, smaller path led down to a lazy green river just a few hundred yards below. With the sun now high in the sky the air was heating up quickly, and all three travelers sweated profusely as they edged down toward the temple.

Despite the heat and humidity, it was the silence that oppressed. After the tumult of the city, and the raucous cries of the forest, the utter absence of noise lay heavily upon them, a barrier that seemed to block out even the brilliance of the sunlight as they trudged onward. Excitement and expectation slid toward dread.

"Nice place," Wyatt said, his voice hoarse from tension and thirst.

"Where is everybody?" Sheila asked, glancing all around the abandoned compound.

"I wish I knew," Wyatt said.

Just where the path down to the river split off from the main approach, Sheila pulled up short.

"I don't like this place," she said. "The power here isn't what I'm looking for. It gives me the creeps. Why don't we get the hell out of here."

Wyatt would have agreed with her, but Malcolm wouldn't hear of it.

"Get out? We din't come 10,000 miles to run away first time we feels the power," he said. "Le's at least take a look inside."

Wyatt vacillated. On the one hand he didn't like the vibrations emanating from that place any better than Sheila. But on the other, they'd come a long way and been through a lot already to turn tail and run at their first confrontation with the unknown. It wasn't a philosopher's way.

"Let's just take a look inside. If there's anything weird, we leave. What do you say?"

Sheila took a deep breath. "You two go. I'm going back up there."

"Alone?" The question hung in the air with surprising vehemence, a marker to the need of each of the three for the other two in this strange place, this strange time.

She nodded at the realization. "Right. Okay then. But just a quick look. And if inside is even one bit weirder than this out here, you'll have to be running hard to catch me."

Wyatt put his arm around her shoulders. "We'll be running side by side."

With Malcolm leading the way, they moved cautiously up the path toward the walled temple. As they got closer they could see the unrecognizable glyphs that decorated the dried mud walls. The symbols were painted in a dull brown that blended in well with the dusty color of the ten-foot high barrier. A single doorway broke the continuous flow of the enclosure, a doorway without a door that revealed nothing of what lay inside.

Whether it was the coffee, their own imaginations or some inexplicable force emanating from the temple itself, they found it increasingly difficult to press forward. Wyatt didn't know if he was helping Sheila so much as supporting his own determination as he held her tight and followed Malcolm into the maw of the mud building.

Inside the thick earthen walls the light was faint, elusive, as it fled before them with each step they took. In the center of a small courtyard, surrounded by more sculpture and paintings, sat a hut of bamboo, its roof thatched with palm fronds, its floor the powdery red clay they'd seen in their travels of the past day. At first Sheila thought it must be the hut of their dreams.

"No. It's not the same," Wyatt said aloud, as if reading her thoughts.

"But it got the power," Malcolm said, his voice dreamy and distant.

"It's got something, that's for sure," Wyatt said. "And I think I've had just about enough of it."

He was about to turn and leave, with no objection from Sheila, when suddenly a massive shadow stepped out from behind the hut.

"The gods will be angry if you do not pay them homage," a voice proclaimed.

Sheila's first impulse was to run, but even if Wyatt's grip around her shoulders hadn't stiffened, her own legs showed no sign of responding to her terror.

It was Malcolm who first realized just who they were confronting.

"Goddamn, Wally! You got the worst habit of showin' up where you's not expected and scarin' the livin' shit outta peoples!"

The shadow stepped forward into the dim sunlight and the mysterious guide's features emerged from the darkness.

"My apologies. I meant only to inform, not frighten."

Sheila could feel the tension drain out of Wyatt's arm and her own nerves settled considerably. With a familiar face in front of her, even that face, the Shrine did not feel so unearthly, so isolated, so strange.

"What the hell are you doing here?" Wyatt asked as soon as he regained the use of his tongue

The young American's rough tone seemed to have no effect on the guide whatsoever. "This is a religious place," he said softly. "I come here to pray."

"So this is just a coincidence then? We just happen to bump into each other in a city of 500,000 people twice in 12 hours?"

"The world is a strange and wondrous place."

"And a bird in the hand can be messy," Wyatt snipped. "I don't buy it. You came here to pitch us or...I don't know what. So let's drop the charade and get on with it."

Sheila leaned close to his ear and whispered. "Did he even know we were going to be here? I don't think we told him."

The self-assured look on Wyatt's face dropped flat. "We must have," he said.

"Don't think so," Malcolm spoke up.

"So how'd you know?" Wyatt asked, turning toward the guide. "Did you ask the hotel clerk, or the waitress at the coffee shop?"

"I have not asked anyone anything about you. I already know what I need to know."

"And that is...?"

"You have come seeking an answer. And you have come to the right place at the right time."

"I tol' you..." the old man said.

"Come on, Malcolm. You don't believe this mumbo jumbo, do you?" Wyatt asked, a hint of exasperation - or was it desperation - in his voice.

"For a philosopher, you sure don't keep a very open mind," Sheila said.

"You too? Are you telling me you believe this crap too?"

"I'm not saying anything one way or the other. But I do remember when I didn't believe that three people could share the same dream."

"Oh great. Now you're going to tell me this guy has something to do with that?"

"I don't know!"

"Well I do. Here," Wyatt said, digging into his pocket and bringing out some crumpled naira notes. "This should cover your time and effort last night." He handed them to the guide without even counting the bills. "Now, could we just be on our way?"

"You have always been free to go where and when you please. You might even find what you are looking for. But I can save you time and effort. And I do not want your money." He handed the bills back to Wyatt.

"Well thank you very much for your offer, but I think we can handle this ourselves. Okay?" Wyatt reached out to give the bills back and smiled perfunctorily.

"Uh, jus' a secon' here," Malcolm interrupted. "I fo' one kind'a likes the idea of this man showin' us the way."

"The way to what?!" Wyatt exploded. "We don't even know what the hell we're looking for. How the hell does he?!

The guide held up his hand to calm the American. "I do not wish to cause trouble. I have made my offer. If you change your mind, I will be back."

"Good. Fine. Thanks for your time," Wyatt said.

"Good luck in your quest," the guide said, nodding to each of them. He started for the doorway. "And may the red mask of self-knowledge be yours in due course."

The three travelers exchanged looks of disbelief.

"What did you say?!" Wyatt asked, running to the guide and grabbing him lightly by the elbow. "About a red mask?"

"It is what you seek, is it not?"

Wyatt stared into the man's eyes. They did not blink.

"We have seen a red mask, all of us," Wyatt said.

"In the dream."

Sheila sucked in a tiny gasp of surprise. Wyatt's eyes narrowed involuntarily.

"What do you know about it?"

"Many of us have had the dream. It beckons us. It teaches us. And now it offers to teach you."

"But why us?" Sheila asked. She felt numb, as if her voice came from someone else.

"Because you have been chosen."□

"By whom?"

"For what?"

"I knowed it..."

They all had questions. The guide held up his hand.

"All will be answered in good time. For now, you must decide: will you allow me to lead you, or will you go off on your own?"

Wyatt looked to his partners and then back to Walli. "Could you give us just a couple of minutes to talk this over?" he said. "Just two or three minutes."

The man nodded. "Of course. I will be outside."

As soon as he was gone, the discussion began.

"Well, what do you think?" Wyatt asked.

"I don't know," Sheila said. "As a far as I'm concerned, the guy is spooky."

"So's dis dream of ours," Malcolm reminded. "Maybe what we need is somebody spooky to get rid of somethin' spooky."

"Malcolm's got a point," Wyatt agreed.

"Then you think we should go with this guy, to who knows where, for who knows what?"

"Hey, after all the scams we've seen here already, I'm not sure of anything. But he does seem to know a lot about us that nobody could know..."

"That's what's spooky!"

"What' you expect?" the old man asked, exasperation showing in his voice. "Did you think we was comin' all the way over here and there'd be some big flashy sign sayin' 'lose your dreams here', like MacDonald's or sumthin'?"

"No, of course not. But..."

"You got an alternative?"

Sheila stopped for an instant, trying to come up with something that was safer, more predictable, more...normal, but with no success.

"No, I suppose not."

"Well, then I guess he's our best option, at least for now," Wyatt said. "I mean, this whole trip is crazy. Why shouldn't he be too? And hell, I don't feel any worse about him than about most of the smiling slicksters we've already met."

"What's that about faint praise?" Sheila asked.

"Faint praise is better than strong condemnation."

"Who said that?"

"I did. Just now. You ready?"

"I was borned ready," Malcolm said.

"Somehow I believe that," Wyatt said. "You?"

"I guess so," Sheila said. "As ready as I'll ever be.

Without further discussion the three travelers left the temple and went out to meet their guide. He was seated on a fallen tree trunk, staring off into the distance toward the sacred river.

Sheila couldn't shake the feeling that he looked like a white-plumed vulture sitting there. She shuttered despite the heat.

CHAPTER SIXTEEN

They picked up their bags from the hotel, paid the bill, and set off with Walli in the lead. He had explained his plan to them as they'd walked back into the city, his voice a soothing, reassuring instrument that calmed as it informed. They were going to travel "a long way", to some high plateau in the center of the country. It was there, he proclaimed, that they would find the truth they looked for.

"But do not shut your eyes to discovery as we travel," he'd explained. "Truth often comes in small doses in unexpected places."

The man seemed smart, Sheila agreed grudgingly. Even educated. But there was something dangerous about him as well. Or was it, as Malcolm described, just his 'power.'

There was a moment, just after they'd paid their bill at the hotel, when Wyatt was shaken for a second, open once again to the doubts and skepticism he'd managed to repress.

They had just left the Palace, and the three of them were adjusting their packs (Walli carried nothing), when he turned to Wyatt and asked, "How much money do you have?"

Immediately Wyatt's warning alarms went off. "Hey look," he'd said, "if you're looking to make money on this deal you picked the wrong foreigners to shake down. We've just barely got enough for food."

Walli nodded. "Then we will walk."□

Sheila elbowed her companion. "I'm not walking five hundred miles!" she whispered. "Tell him we can afford to travel by van!"

The guide had already started walking down the dirt roadway, and Wyatt had to hurry to catch up.

"My companion reminded me that we might have enough money to take a van," he said, hoping the patent dishonesty of the statement wouldn't anger the guide.

"Good. It is a long way. It is better to save your strength," the guide said. He didn't wait for a response from Wyatt, but turned and continued walking.

"Well?" Sheila asked.

"He took it well, I think. I guess we'll be taking a van."

It soon became evident that Walli knew the area very well indeed. He took them directly to a busy market in a section of the city they had never seen before. Wyatt scanned the surroundings for any sign of a bus stop, but there was none. He waited patiently for several minutes, chatting with his two companions while their guide stood off to one side and surveyed the market. Then, without explanation, Walli disappeared into the hyper activity of the market, swept away like a single snowflake in a vibrant, multi-colored blizzard.

Wyatt watched with a scowl. "Now where the hell is he going?"

"You din't give'em any money yet, did you?" Malcolm asked.

"No, of course not," Wyatt said. "And if this is any indication of what we can expect, I'm not sure I should."

"Don't you think maybe we should give him a minute or two - the benefit of the doubt," Sheila said.

"I thought he gave you the creeps."

"Everything here gives me the creeps. At least he seems to know what he's doing."

"And if he's just jerking us around, trying to get the last few bucks we own?"

"That'd be very disappointing," Sheila said quietly. "But then again, if he really does know how to get rid of the dream, that'd be wonderful. I'm willing to take the chance."

"I second what she say," Malcolm said.

Wyatt shrugged. "It's not like we have much of a choice. I guess we just stand here looking pale, dazed and confused until he comes back."

"Speak fo' yo'self," Malcolm said. "Nobody never call me pale befo'."

Wyatt smiled. "I stand corrected."

It wasn't long before the familiar white robes reappeared from the midst of the marketplace. The guide was carrying two handmade bags, one made from old calendar pages and the other from what appeared to be an old fishnet.

"Find any bargains?" Wyatt asked as Walli rejoined them without a word.

"It is a long journey," the guide said. "We must be prepared.

With no further explanation he led the way through a small crowd of gawkers who had gathered to stare at the Owebos. One woman reached out to touch Sheila's long straight hair as she passed.

"Don't worry," Wyatt said when he saw her start from the unexpected contact. "She probably just wants some good luck - like rubbing the stomach of a Buddha."

"She better keep her hands off my stomach," Sheila said.

"Got any other lucky spots I should know about?" Wyatt asked, flexing his fingers like a surgeon preparing to operate.

"Keep your hands to yourself unless you want to get hurt," she said, elbowing past him to keep pace with the guide.

"Tough broad," Malcolm said as he moved past his momentarily nonplussed companion.

Wyatt smiled. "Sure is."

The guide took them a few hundred yards down the road to a turnout where small crews of young men were unloading brightly colored cargo trucks with names like 'Sweet Gloria' and 'Redemption Is Mine' hand-lettered on the back tailgate. The trio watched as yams, bananas, plantains and perfectly round watermelons were off-loaded. They stood there for several minutes, apparently just observing.

"Are we looking for something, or do you just have a thing for fruit?" Wyatt finally asked.

"Something must come out before something can go in," the guide said.

"Wasn't that Newton's fourth law of fruit trucks?" Sheila asked.

"It was either him or Kane on Kung Fu," Wyatt grumbled.

Despite the cryptic explanation they stood there for another ten minutes, until one of the trucks was completely empty. Sheila was busy calming Wyatt, trying to restrain him from verbally assaulting Walli, while the guide went over to a short, heavyset fellow who had also watched the proceedings.

"If this is another scam, I'm gonna lose it," Wyatt said.

"Relax. Count to ten. We don't have anything to complain about so far."

"Right," Wyatt said, but his jaws continued to grind.

Moments later, the guide returned.

"We have a ride. Come - let's go."

The three travelers looked to each other in momentary confusion. A ride? There was no bus, or van, or taxi or car in sight. Just the big, open-backed cargo truck...

"Woa, wait a second," Wyatt said. "You're not telling us we're riding in the back of that moving graffiti gallery, are you?"

"You do not have enough money to take the bus all the way to where we must go and back again. Unless you care to walk - or not eat for a week or so - we must go this way," the guide said.

"The man got a point," Malcolm said.

"Damn good one," Wyatt agreed.

"Last one in the back of the truck is a rotten yam," Sheila said, and they climbed up without further debate

There were no chairs, no cushions, just a few 50 pound bags of rice. They flopped down on the burlap bags and stared out the open back of the truck. Above them the hot mid-morning sun shone down without mercy. Already the metal floor was hot enough to penetrate their shoes.

"Just like Greyhound," Sheila said.

"Once again I'm reminded why I rode the rails," Wyatt mumbled.

Malcolm found a more or less comfortable spot while the guide stood off to one corner of the enclosure, seemingly content to stand for the time being. With a shaking roar and a huge cloud of noxious smoke, the engine fired up and the truck lurched into action.

If the van ride had been cramped and uncomfortable, the truck offered its own disadvantages. With only the four of them in an area twice that of the van, they were certainly not crowded. However even the rough, suspension-less ride of the van was nothing compared to the bone-crunching abuse of the cargo carrier.

"I think a filling just fell out," Sheila said after one notably intense pot-hole.

"Filling? I think I just lost my left eye," Wyatt groused.

Sheila reached over and pulled his floppy bush hat up from where it covered his eye.

"I can see again!" he shouted.

"I jus' hopes this contrapshun stop every hour or so," Malcolm said. "All this shakin' gonna drain the pee right down into my legs."

"Sounds like a hygiene problem to me," Wyatt said.

"Maybe we can find some Prevent shoe liners."

"Better find sumthin' or this rice gonna be mighty damp by the time it get to where it goin'"

"Yumm," Wyatt said. "A new flavor for Uncle Ben."

They would have liked to have complained some more, to share their frustrations and reassure each other that it could be worse - somehow - but the roar of the engine and the constant thud of the tires smashing into the wheel wells with each new bump or gaping hole in the roadway made it hard to communicate at anything less than a full yell. They settled back as best they could and girded for the long journey.

But it was only about forty minutes or so before the roar of the engine diminished to a tinny whine and the truck began to slow perceptibly.

"Now what?" Sheila asked, peering up over the wooden tailgate to see if she could somehow determine what was happening.

"Nothing to worry about," Wyatt reassured. "Probably just a broken driveshaft or a thrown piston."

As soon as the truck drifted to a bumpy stop, a low murmuring of voices began up front. Without explanation Walli jumped out and disappeared almost before the tires stopped turning. The three travelers listened closely to the discussion, even though they were unable to understand a word of the Yoruba language all the parties used, their imaginations playing out possible scenarios from engine trouble to highway robbers. The dialogue quickly dissolved into a loud argument, with male and female voices shouting emphatically.

"I'm not sure I like the sound of that," Sheila said after one particularly intense exchange.

"Probably just debating whether the tread design on the truck's tires is better for small ruts or big potholes," Wyatt said.

"As long as they're not debating whether to kill us or just rob us."

"A pleasant thought. Have you ever heard of valium?" Wyatt asked with a smile. But he was not feeling anywhere near as secure as he pretended.

Suddenly a man's voice ended the discussion with a loud, angry shout that echoed in the quiet of the surrounding jungle.

"Uh oh. What's going on now?"

Wyatt jumped up to confront whatever was coming, followed immediately by the other two. They heard a group of people coming back toward their location, their conversations once again soft and indecipherable.

"I don' like this," Malcolm said.

"Get ready to run if we have to," Wyatt directed.

The voices approached slowly from around the side of the truck, with each step the large number of voices becoming clearer. Suddenly, a hand reached up and unlatched the tailgate. It swung down and crashed against the metal bumper. Wyatt was about to grab Sheila's hand and make a dash for it when a familiar white robed guide came bounding up into the truck.

"Walli!" Sheila shouted reflexively.

"We will share our space," he said.

Before anyone could ask him what he meant, a little Nigerian boy climbed up over the back bumper, followed by two more young boys, a girl of about 12 and three women. The children stood huddled together in one corner, staring at Wyatt and Sheila as if they'd seen a ghost.

"They probably think they have," Wyatt said.

"Looks like we're not the only ones trying to get somewhere cheaply."

Sheila smiled at the new passengers and said hello. The women nodded shyly. The children continued to stare.

"Going far?" Wyatt asked, trying to break down the barrier between them.

No one spoke.

"Are...you...travelling...far?" he repeated, speaking more slowly and louder, as if that would somehow allow them to understand his language.

"I...don't...think...they....understand," Sheila said to him.

"They speak pidgin'," Walli said. "They do not understand English well."

"I used to speak pig Latin - think that would help?" Wyatt said.

"Can you say hi for us and ask them how far they're going?" Sheila asked Walli.

The guide nodded and then said something that sounded like a cross between a child's fractured language and a Jamaican reggae singer. One woman answered similarly.

"They are going to Omawashu. Six hours. They say, 'you are welcome,'" the guide explained.

"Why am I not surprised," Wyatt said. "Well, tell'em to fasten their seatbelts and get ready for a real lulu of a trip. Anyone who needs to go should do it now."

The guide passed the message and the women told their children. One little boy turned to the back of the truck, pulled down his shorts and peed off the tailgate.

"This is going to be very interesting," Wyatt said.

In fact, it was not. The road was seemingly endless, a constant barrage of the diesel engine's roar, the smell of the exhaust, the neck-snapping bumps and the ever-present, white-hot, dripping sweat, dust-dry sunlight. Wyatt found himself studying the light, comparing it to the sunshine back home. It was whiter, there was no question of that, a bleached bone white that branded their retinas and burned into their brains. But it also filled the air more completely, a luminous presence that surrounded, engulfed, devoured the truck and all it passed through.

"I think I know now what a potato feels like in a microwave," he said at one point.

Sheila smiled wanly, her lips too dry to peel back without cracking.

About two hours later the truck stopped again, and four more passengers got on board - one old man and three women. The women each carried a large bundle on top of their heads, wrapped in a colorful cloth that belied the heavy load within. At one point one of the women opened her bundle to rearrange its contents and Sheila saw long green plantains inside. *'Must be taking it to market,'* she thought, but it was too much effort to ask.

The hours melted away as the sun arced across the sky. As evening approached, the shadows lengthened in the dense jungle on both sides of the road, giving the living greens a deeper, denser, more mysterious appearance. The animal sounds, which had all but disappeared during the heat of the day, could be heard from time to time when the truck slowed to a crawl to negotiate a particularly difficult pothole: bird calls, what might have been monkey cries, the intertwining cacophony of the insect symphony

By this time the three American travelers were numb. They no longer cared how far they had come, or even how much further they had to go. The assault on their senses had finally overwhelmed them. So it was not surprising when they did not notice, or at least did not react to the sudden darkening of the sky, the stillness of the air, nor to their guide pulling his dusty white robes close around him. And it was a shock, a real, electrifying jolt to their systems when a sudden wave of water, much as if someone had emptied a huge 50 gallon drum of water over their heads, suddenly broke over them like a tsunami.

Sheila screamed out loud, first in fright but then in delight. She threw her mouth open and sucked in the cool reviving rain. Wyatt watched in amazement as the water pounded the truck bed, mesmerized by the rhythm and intensity. Malcolm watched the two of them with consternation, thinking that both had lost their senses.

Wyatt had never seen rain like this, so intense, so powerful that it truly seemed like a single giant wave. The sound of the water hitting the truck drowned out even the roar of the engine laboring to pull the heavy monster through the mud that churned up under its tires. The raindrops stung where they hit exposed skin; Sheila had to shade her eyes to be able to see through the curtain of water.

They struggled on like this for at least twenty minutes, until at last the driver conceded to Nature's supremacy and pulled off the road. As soon as the truck stopped the other passengers scrambled over the tail gate and disappeared into the hissing darkness. The guide stood at the gate, waiting for them to follow.

"Where are we going?!" Wyatt shouted from a distance of just a few inches, leaning into the guide's ear to try to overcome the roar of the rain.

"We must rest," he said.

No one was about to debate his decision. All three climbed down off the back of the truck with Walli's help. Their feet sank instantly into the red clay mud, a heavy, cakey goo that clung to their shoes so relentlessly that with each step they accumulated ever more weight and resistance. *'This must be what it'd be like to wander into the tar pits,'* Wyatt thought. He pictured a mastodon struggling to free itself from the clutching viscosity.

In the midst of nowhere, without so much as a streetlight or even a match, with the moon and stars blotted out by the rain, the darkness was total. All three stumbled over and into all manner of obstacles as they walked, an affliction that did not seem to bother their guide in the least. Finally, after several minutes of following blindly, their hopes were revived by a faint grouping of lights that appeared through the driving rain and undergrowth. As they came closer they realized that the lights emanated from inside a small grouping of thatched huts. As their guide led them to the center of the cluster, people suddenly appeared from virtually each and every hut. Wyatt watched without comment as the village representatives approached the guide with what seemed to be extreme deference - or was it fear? They exchanged brief pleasantries before Walli motioned for the three travelers to follow him.

He led them to a hut that was set off from the others, larger than those they could see, but still no bigger than a good-sized hotel room. For an instant Sheila thought that they had found their phantom village, but as soon as they stepped through the hanging cloth doorway she realized her mistake. There was no pottery, no masked native, just a plain dirt floor with three blankets stretched out around the remnants of a fire and a flickering oil lamp.

"You will sleep here tonight. We will go on at first light," the guide said.

"What about you?" Sheila asked.

"I have tasks at hand. Sleep well."

Without waiting for further conversation the guide disappeared through the doorway. For several seconds the three just stood there, water dripping into ever expanding puddles at their feet, eyeing the stark accommodations with dazed confusion.

Wyatt broke the reverie. "Think they have room service in this place?"

"I could sho' use a big, fat hamburger," Malcolm said.

Sheila allowed a tiny smile. "I could use about fifty gallons of lemonade and a king size bed."

As if summoned, a teenaged girl, wearing only a long cloth skirt and a necklace of beads, swept into the hut carrying a platter with a jar of what appeared to be some kind of juice, and a healthy load of bananas, avocados and guava.

"Wow. You should have wished for lobster tails and champagne," Wyatt said. "Do you accept tips?" he asked the girl. She looked at him and shook her head.

"No, you don't accept tips, or no, you don't understand what the hell I'm talking about?" he continued

She shook her head and smiled.

"Too bad. I wouldn't mind knowing where we are."

Sheila was examining the food. She held up the jar and smelled the contents.

"What *is* this?" she asked the girl. She pointed at the jar and raised her eyebrows in consternation.

"She doesn't speak English," Wyatt said.

The girl said something that sounded like she was clearing her throat. Sheila tried her best to duplicate the sound and pointed once again to the jar

The girl nodded and repeated the harsh sound.

"Doesn't smell like anything I've smelled before, but it's not too bad, either," Sheila said.

"Thank you," Wyatt said to the girl, speaking slowly and loudly.

"I think she'd get the idea better if you looked into her eyes instead of at her chest," Sheila said.

Wyatt straightened up with a chastened smile. "Sorry. Just browsing."

"I wouldn' mind browsin' that little cookie myself," Malcolm said.

"Malcolm! That girl's young enough to be your granddaughter!" Sheila said.

"She old enough to peel my banana."

"Malcolm, I'm shocked and appalled," Wyatt said, protectively hustling the girl out the door.

"Oh, right," Sheila said. "What you mean is, he'd have to fight you for her."

"Sheila, you slight me!" Wyatt said with a vaguely upper-tier British accent. "I would never stoop to physical combat. The flip of a coin, perhaps..."

A none-too-ladylike right cross was just barely blocked as he ducked and scampered out of her reach.

"Men!" she said as she turned to the fruit.

It was quite a while before Sheila would talk with her two companions. As it was, they spent most of that time gobbling up the fruit and draining the sweet greenish juice. As

Sheila had predicted, the unidentified nectar was actually quite tasty. In a show of remorse, Wyatt saved Sheila the last gulp.

"Hmmph," she mumbled as she took the offered jar.

"I suppose that's Yoruba for 'thank you'," Wyatt said. "You're welcome."

She smiled, despite her best efforts.

"You know, I can't believe we're sitting here, in the middle of Nigeria, in a thatched hut, soaking wet, looking for a dream," she said.

"Maybe we should sue our travel agent when we get back."

"Sue, Debby o' Janie, I be goin' to sleep," Malcolm said. "And I hope you don' minds, but I's takin' off these wet clothes."

He started to do just that.

"Uh, I think that's a good idea, Malcolm," Sheila said, making her way quickly to the lamp. "And I think we'll do the same. Good night." She blew out the flame. Instantly it was pitch black.

"Damn. It so dark in here I can' even sees my buttons."

"Just wait a few seconds. Your eyes will adjust."

But their eyes never really adjusted. In the total blackness they stumbled around undressing and spreading their wet clothes out to dry until finally they found their blankets and collapsed in exhaustion. Outside the rain had begun to let up a bit and the wind was coming up out of the south. Lulled by the swirling sounds of the gentle rain and gusting breeze, all three were asleep in moments. High above, the clouds began to clear and a brilliant crescent moon rose above the fluttering palms. Hours later, when the wind finally dissipated completely, the village was silent.

CHAPTER SEVENTEEN

Wyatt was the first to awaken.

Perhaps it was the sunshine streaming in through the innumerable cracks between the bamboo poles that formed the siding of the hut. Perhaps it was the strange sounds of the jungle, so near, so encompassing. Most likely it was the rock-hard ground and the arm that had gone numb beneath him. In any case, he awoke gently enough, as if awakening from a strange dream in a familiar bed. But it took only a few blinks of his eyes to realize that he was, indeed, in a native hut in the middle of nowhere. He sat upright and rubbed the circulation back into his arm as he tried to clear his head.

As he looked around the simple structure he was reminded how much he and all the people in more developed nations took for granted, how much they had, how much they wasted. Life there in Africa was so simple, so pure. Not that those villagers were any happier than he was, but then again, they might have been. *'If I'm so happy,'* he thought, *'why have I been I bumming all over the map searching for.... what? Even before this damn dream, what was I hoping to find?'*

He didn't have any answers. Before he could wring even the slimmest clue from his re-emerging consciousness, he noticed a tray sitting just inside the doorway. At first he thought it was left from the previous night. But upon closer examination he saw that the juice in the jar was bright orange and the fruit included two types of melon. It was enough to lure him out of bed. He pulled on his jeans - still damp and incredibly difficult to slide over his aching legs - but left his shirt splayed out on the ground to dry some more. Besides, there was something more native, more natural about going bare-chested to breakfast. He threw back the cloth from the doorway and stood leaning against the bamboo frame, examining the village like some exotic jewel.

He had only just begun to gulp the juice straight from the jar when Sheila began to stir, and moments later Malcolm. For an instant he battled a bout of irritation with his two companions. It was so quiet, so peaceful, with just the sounds of the animals in the surrounding trees and the muffled sounds of the villagers going about their day. He knew it was selfish, knew it was impossible to sustain a moment forever, but he didn't want to give it up, to share it with them. But the moment passed, and to his surprise he found that the irritation passed too.

"Up already?" Sheila said.

"Already? It's after nine o'clock - you've been sacked out for thirteen hours!" Wyatt said.

Sheila yawned and stretched lazily. "Seems about right."

"Can't be no thirteen hours," Malcolm mumbled, reaching for his watch. "I don' sleep no thirteen hours."

"That was in the States," Wyatt said. "This is Africa. Home of the ever-popular sleeping sickness."

The old man blanched. "Damn! It have been thirteen hours! You don' think I got that sleepy sickness, do you?"

"Who knows?" Wyatt teased. "Could be sleepy sickness. Then again, could be grumpy or dopey."

"What the hell you talkin' about?"

Wyatt smiled and waved the question off. "Just kidding. You were just tired from all the heat."

"And all the potholes," Sheila added.

"Still, I don' never remember sleepin' that long. Not even that damn dream woke me up."

Suddenly the air was charged; both Sheila and Wyatt turned to face their companion. "You had the dream?" Wyatt asked.

"Well, sort of. Not 'xactly the same..."

Sheila leaned forward, her eyes now open and alert. "No? What was different about it?"

The old man pursed his lips and glanced up at the thatched roof. "Well, ain't that funny. I mean, I remember havin' the dream, and I remember thinkin' it was different somehow, but I'll be damned if I can remember 'xactly why."

"That's just how I was feeling!" Sheila interrupted. "It's as if it started to evaporate the second I woke up."

Wyatt nodded. "That makes three of us. Maybe that's why I feel so calm and relaxed this morning. There's definitely something going on here."

Malcolm's worried frown turned to a smile. "I tol' yous! This here is Africa! We gonna find the heartbeat and the dream gonna be jus' a memory."

For the first time, his two companions didn't have a ready comeback. For several long moments they just stared off into the mid-distance, each lost in his own thoughts. It was their guide who broke the reverie. Without any warning he suddenly appeared at the doorway, his white robes looking clean and fresh as ever.

"Good morning! I trust you slept well?"

"Yes. Quite well," Wyatt said.

"This is a good place for sleep. Strong spirits here. The dreams are not so vivid."

"What do you know about our dreams, anyway?" Sheila asked.

The guide smiled. "I know," he said. "I know that the dreams bring you here. I know that you seek relief. And I know where you must go. Now get ready. We are already late. The truck must leave soon."

Without waiting for a response he turned and left the hut.

"You know, that guy could make big bucks in Vegas," Wyatt said.

No one laughed. "He has a gift," Sheila said. "A real gift."

"I don' know 'bout that, but he sho' give me the willies," Malcolm said.

"Well, willies or not, that truck isn't going to wait for us," Wyatt said. "Hurry up and get dressed so you can have a bite to eat before we have to get back in our limo."

Malcolm crawled out of his bedroll, his tee shirt and underwear a bright white against his dark skin.

"Only take me a second," he said, pulling on his pants and shirt. With that he sat down to pull on his socks and lace his shoes.

"Uh, Malcolm, if you wouldn't mind covering your eyes for just a second," Sheila said, poised behind her blanket.

"Huh? Oh, right." The old man did as he was asked and Sheila crawled out from under the blanket. Wyatt, who studiously ignored her request, appreciatively eyed the long shapely legs, the tight round bottom, her firm breasts, nipples erect.

"Hey Malcolm, I couldn't persuade you to take a little walk, could I?" Wyatt asked.

As he glanced over at the old man he saw the fingers of Malcolm's right hand slide shut over a watchful eye.

"Well, I s'pose I could..."

"No need for that," Sheila said, completely unmindful of the lust pounding through Wyatt's body. "I'll be ready here in just a second." She pulled on her shorts and quickly buttoned them up. "Okay. You can open your eyes now."

Malcolm took his hands down from in front of his eyes and got up. "Sorry," he said with a shrug toward his younger companion.

"No problem," Wyatt said, but the hangdog look seemed to say otherwise.

"Nothing to be sorry about," Sheila said slipping into her sneakers and sweeping across the hut to the fruit and juice tray.

"Easy for you to say," Wyatt mumbled.

Sheila and Malcolm quickly filled up on fruit, Sheila stashing a quantity in her backpack. Outside, the familiar air horn of the truck began to sound.

"We're out'a here!" Wyatt announced, and the three hurried to the back of the truck to join their fellow travelers. Walli stood at the tailgate, waiting patiently.

After the heavy rains of the night before it was a little bit cooler that morning, but the heavy humidity had scarcely decreased at all. As soon as most everyone was inside, the truck began a slow, careful retreat back out the way they'd come, the driver obviously familiar with the surroundings and the low points where water - and mud - had accumulated. With only a couple of small detours around questionable ground, the truck finally made its way out to the main road. By that time the last few stragglers had hurried out to intercept them and scrambled aboard the moving vehicle. It seemed to be a custom in Nigeria for transportation drivers to keep to their perceived schedule no matter what the needs or wants of their passengers. The three travelers had seen a number of instances where riders had had to jump on, or off, a moving vehicle that refused to stop. Admittedly, the passengers had never complained, and they seemed very adept at the stuntman-like maneuvers.

The trip was pretty much identical to that of the day before - bumpy, hot and uncomfortable - except that some of the other passengers began to sing tribal songs about a half hour into the ride. As far as Wyatt could tell there didn't seem to be any particular reason for the songs, other than perhaps to pass the time and keep spirits up, but on those counts they succeeded well.

The music had a seductive rhythmic quality that energized and soothed simultaneously. After a while he found himself humming along. Then, about forty minutes later, the singing stopped as suddenly as it had begun, without any apparent sign from any of the singers.

From then on, the trip evolved into a carbon copy of the day before. Explosive white clouds raced across the sky in the early morning, chased by the relentless onslaught of the blazing African sun. Cool morning breezes quickly gave way to the same blast furnace temperatures of the first day. The three travelers tried to find a scrap of shade in which to hide, but with the constant switchbacks in the road it was nearly impossible. Hour after hour they were held captive by the constant drone of the diesel, the hum of the tires, and the expected but unpredictable collisions with the omnipresent potholes, even as the lush green beauty of the countryside rushed by.

For most of that time there seemed little variation in the scenery. They passed through several small villages, each little more than a cluster of thatched huts and one-room concrete block houses with rusting tin roofs. Occasionally the truck collided with larger towns, each an oversized version of the villages without the thatch. In each they were met by a familiar cadre of entrepreneurs -- trays, pots and assorted dry-goods balanced precariously on their heads. At that point there was usually the trademark full-voiced bargaining session, in which small crowds of potential buyers and sellers yelled at each other in an assortment of languages as if they intended to kill each other. The discussions usually continued until a roar of the diesel engine and a huge puff of half-burned smoke announced that the driver - having got what he wanted - was bringing the episode to an end by simply moving on. No entreaty carried any weight with the man; once he was ready to leave, they left.

Sheila passed most of the time reading a paperback she'd brought with her - a no-minder about maidens with heaving bodices living and loving their way through full-tilt adventures. In retrospect, her own life made the book seem dull. Malcolm tried to write in a journal of some sort, though the innumerable potholes made the writing nearly indecipherable at times. Wyatt dug out his cassette player and headphones and turned the journey into the world's biggest Omnimax experience. He drank in the constant visual stimulation while songs by Hendrix, Clapton, Jackson Browne and other chroniclers of days gone by provided a familiar backdrop for the unfamiliar sights: endless golden-green savannahs dotted with strange bent trees that looked like they had grown upside down with their roots reaching for the sky; processions of three to ten women and young girls, walking slowly from what seemed to be literally nowhere to some equally undefined destination, carrying huge piles of firewood, or pots, or empty plastic bottles atop their heads, sometimes with little babies strapped to their backs; dusty unmarked crossroads, with only three or four buildings in sight, with hundreds of natives in their multi-colored finery, milling about, doing who knew what. He watched it all, the music providing a backdrop from which to observe, a familiar context. *'It would be easy to get lost in such a vast place,'* Wyatt thought. *'Very easy.'*

Once they stopped for fuel. A couple of times for food and water. Other than that, the wheels kept turning. Slowly, the landscape began to change: as the truck labored up long inclines the air grew cooler and drier, large outcroppings of boulders erupted from the red clay soil. Even the vegetation gave way to the demands of the higher altitude, with eucalyptus and unknown assiduous trees taking the place of some of the palms and the ferns in the dense tangle of jungle.

Finally, after seven hours under the fiery sun, the truck bounced to a halt, the ever-present cloud of thick, choking dust settling over them like a stifling blanket.

The guide stood at the back of the truck and lowered the tailgate. No one got out.

"We will ride no farther," he announced.

"Meaning exactly what?" Wyatt asked.

"Meaning we walk the rest of the way."

"I was afraid of that," Sheila said. All three Americans struggled to their feet, weaving and swaying as if disembarking from a sailing ship. Their fellow passengers, tired and dazed from the long, difficult journey, made no effort to move out of their way. They picked their steps carefully among them.

It was eerie: not a single Nigerian said a word. After two days and hundreds of miles in the back of that damn truck, not one person said a single word.

"Nice to see we had such a powerful impact on their lives," Wyatt said.

"What were you expecting, balloons and ice cream?"

"That would have been nice."

"They knows," Malcolm said.

"Know what?" Wyatt's voice carried a sharp edge of irritation.

"They knows 'bout our journey."

"Come on, Malcolm. How the hell do they know anything about us? Except maybe how often each of us has to pee."

"They know." This time the voice came from the guide. He wasn't even looking at them, staring off down the road at something visible only to himself. Wyatt wanted to challenge him too, to poke fun at the inane idea. But he didn't. He couldn't. Malcolm walked by, a broad smile on his face. Sheila shrugged and followed. There was nothing left for Wyatt except to fall in line. As the truck roared back into action, the four travelers shouldered their packs and began a silent procession down the narrow dirt path that veered off to the north. Walli led, his eyes focused on something in the far distance. No one else could see what it was he was looking at.

Wyatt wasn't sure any of them ever would.

CHAPTER EIGHTEEN

It soon became evident that they would not reach wherever they were headed by nightfall. But even as the sun nestled down into the tree tops, they pushed further and further into the dense foliage. The intertwined branches overhead created a massive canopy, through which the afternoon light shone only in a subdued green glow. It was as if they were moving through an endless living tunnel, though moving from what to where they were not sure.

For the guide seldom stopped and almost never spoke. At first the three travelers tried to keep up a light patter, joking at their circumstance and marveling at their surroundings. But as the hours wore on and the impossibly serried vegetation closed in around them, the easygoing attitude faded until the only sounds to be heard were the soft impact of their boots on the jungle floor and the myriad cries of invisible animal life.

The gentle breeze that had made the heat almost bearable faded as well, cut off from their greedy faces by the green tunnel that surrounded them. The stillness exaggerated the heaviness of the air and they began to drip perspiration from every pore. Shirts clung to the skin; hair melted against the temples. Breathing itself became difficult, more an amphibious act than simple respiration. But the guide seemed not to notice. His long white robes flowed out in undulating waves as he moved silently through the undergrowth. His steps were fluid, unhurried yet unburdened; he moved as though gliding along on a hidden current.

"Hey, how about a break?" Wyatt called out after nearly three hours of constant movement.

Walli stopped and surveyed the surrounding jungle, once again searching for something unseen by the others.

"It will serve," he said. "We will camp here tonight."

"Uh, not to throw water on your plans, but none of us has a tent. You didn't happen to bring one, did you?" Sheila asked.

"Maybe his robes convert into a condo," Wyatt whispered.

"Tent?" the guide said. "Why would you want a tent?"

"Oh, just to keep off the malaria-carrying mosquitoes, the tsetse flies, the scorpions, snakes and spiders, as well as protection from any more downpours like last night," Wyatt said.

Walli nodded thoughtfully. "It will not rain tonight," he said.

"Well, that's reassuring," Sheila said.

"Good. Then let me suggest we find firewood while it is still light."

"Think it's going to get cold tonight?" Wyatt asked. "Going to drop down to 95 or so?"

"The fire is for light. Unless you care to sleep as soon as the sun sets," the guide corrected.

"No, that's okay," Sheila said. "A little light wouldn't be so bad. We'll look for wood."

"Good. Be careful. Watch where you step. Only take the dead wood. We do not wish to offend the spirits of the jungle. And do not wander far."

Before Sheila could ask him for clarification, the guide moved off down the path. She was about to call after him when he turned into the jungle and disappeared without a sound.

"Sumthin' freaky 'bout that guide," Malcolm said, looking none too lively.

"There is something...unusual about him," Wyatt agreed. "But he's right about the wood. If we want a fire, we'd better get searching."

"I suggest the buddy system," Sheila said, grabbing ahold of Wyatt's sleeve.

"That leave me one buddy short," Malcolm said.

"That it does," Wyatt said. "How about the overlapping buddy system?"

"What the hell yo' talkin' 'bout?"

"Well, Sheila can be my buddy, you can be her buddy, and I'll be your buddy."

"Seem like kind'a a daisy chain buddy system to me."

"If you will. I just thought 'overlapping' had more.... panache."

"Panache or no panache, let's all three of us buddies go find some wood," Sheila said. "The way that sun's setting, we're going to find ourselves standing here arguing in the dark real quick."

Her two companions looked up at the huge orange ball and instantly saw her point. It was like some kind of fast-action movie, with the clouds blowing past and the sun sinking into the west at double speed.

"This more of your 'Africa' shit?" Wyatt asked the old man. Even he noticed a sour note of anger, or was it anxiety, in his question.

"Don' know," Malcolm said softly, his eyes locked on the incredible phenomenon. "But it kind'a freaky."

"I'm going to get wood, now. You coming?" Sheila interrupted.

They almost tripped over each other scrambling to her side.

"Where do you suggest we start?" Wyatt asked.

"You got me. I guess we just go with the vibe and hope the wood finds us," Sheila said.

"Now yo' startin' to sound like that freaky guide," Malcolm said.

"Let's just hope she can find her way around like him."

Packed so closely together they almost tripped over each other's feet, the trio made their way cautiously into the jungle. It was not easy going. The tangle of vegetation intertwined into an almost impenetrable net. They picked their way carefully past succulents with dagger-sized thorns, tough, wiry vines they couldn't break with their hands, and huge undulating ferns that stood taller than they did. They made their way slowly, inspecting the jungle floor meticulously, but no dead wood came into view.

"This is crazy," Wyatt finally said after fifteen or twenty minutes of fruitless investigation. "We're only going to get ourselves lost wandering around like this."

"Walli say get some fire woods."

"I heard him. But it doesn't look like we're having much luck."

"Maybe we should spread out a little bit. Like they do when they're searching for someone," Sheila said. "You know, keep in sight of the person next to you. We'd cover a lot more ground that way. If we keep on like this we'll all just see the same two-foot path."

"I don't know..."

"She got a good idea. If we don' finds nuthin' in ten minutes or so, we can go back."

And so it was decided. Sheila stayed in the middle ground, with Malcolm to her left and Wyatt to her right. Of course, not everything went smoothly. Wyatt first took up a position only about six feet from Sheila.

"When I said you should stay in sight I didn't mean close enough to read over my shoulder. Why don't you try another twenty feet or so?"

It was hard to tell if Wyatt was embarrassed or genuinely concerned. "Just trying to keep an eye on you."

Sheila took it in the best possible way. "Aren't you a sweetheart," she said. "You just earned yourself some extra goodies tonight."

"Great. Maybe Walli and Malcolm will take a ten mile hike to give me enough time to collect."

She smiled. "Now, now - patience. If not tonight, soon. For now let's get some wood and get back to camp."

This time Wyatt stuck to the plan and slowly worked his way through the undergrowth to a position some twenty feet to Sheila's right. Cautiously they began to move through the tangle, working their way into its midst until the living green curtain between them became an opaque barrier and only the sounds of breaking twigs and snapping branches signaled to each the location of the others. Even in the growing dusk the warm humidity lay heavily upon them, and it wasn't long before Sheila had to stop to let her pounding heart slow and to wipe the sweat from her forehead. It wasn't until she caught her breath that she noticed that even the sounds of her cohorts had been swallowed by the rapidly encroaching darkness.

"Wyatt? Malcolm?" She tried to call out to her companions but the words caught in her throat. The sounds of myriad unseen creatures seemed to swirl all around her, drowning her words in their elemental intensity. Sweat rushed down her cheeks as her heart began to thunder once again. The closeness of her surroundings edged toward claustrophobia. She could almost feel the vines and thorns creeping in to entwine her. Her stomach was squirming. She felt faint.

"Hey! Over here! I founds a hol' pile!"

Malcolm's voice shattered the illusion and set her free.

She struggled to control herself, to keep from running blindly through the jungle, screaming in relief. The best she could do was hold herself to a quick jog, stumbling every which way but desperate to rid herself of her vision of abandonment. She knew she was on the verge of panic, but she did not succumb.

"Where the hell are you guys?!" she called out after running for an inordinately long time and not finding them.

"We're over here!" Wyatt's voice called out from the darkness. They were close now and her breathing, and gait, slowed.

Finally she made her way to where her companions were breaking up the twigs and branches of a fallen tree. They scarcely looked up as she emerged from the shadows to join them.

"I was starting to think we'd lost you there," Wyatt said.

"Not quite. But I can tell you I wouldn't want to be out here by myself. It's a jungle out there." Her attempt at humor sounded hollow even to herself.

"Well if we don't get this wood all stacked and moved within fifteen minutes or so, it's going to be a pitch black jungle out there. And I, for one, don't intend to be around to see what it's like."

"I seconds that one," Malcolm said. "Come give us a hand."

Sheila took a deep breath and went over to help them. She became the designated stacker and loaded both men's arms with as much firewood as they could hold. Then she grabbed as much as she could carry and scurried after them. For a moment she thought they'd lost the way in the now nearly complete darkness. But Malcolm continued on, seemingly unaffected by the gloom and strange surroundings. And, despite her misgivings, Sheila followed close behind. It was with a sigh of relief, then, when they saw a glimmer of firelight through the dense foliage. Moments later they stepped into a small clearing where the guide hovered over a roaring campfire, like some massive fluorescent white moth, watching a small unidentifiable animal cooking on a spit.

"So there you are!" Walli said. "I was almost ready to send out a search party."

"Next time don't wait so long," Sheila said only half-jokingly, dumping her small pile of wood next to the fire and then collapsing from nervous exhaustion.

Wyatt dumped his armload and eyed the sizeable pile of wood that the guide had brought back himself.

"I don't want to seem petty about this," he said, "but why did you send us out to get wood if you were going to bring back enough for three or four fires?"

The guide did not acknowledge the question but continued to stare into the fire. "If I am not mistaken, you came to Africa to find something. How do you expect to find anything unless you look?"

"We came to find a way to rid ourselves of a shared dream," Wyatt said. "Not for firewood."

The guide smiled. "You came to find more than that, my friends. As of yet you still haven't found the reason for your search, let alone the thing you seek."

Wyatt stepped closer to the guide, looking him square in the face and drawing an equally intense look in return. "You know, I'm getting a little bit tired of all this veiled magical realism crap," he said. "If you know something, why don't you just come out and say so. And if you don't, why don't you just shut up."

"Wyatt!" Sheila said. "Don't take it personally, Walli. He's just tired."

"He can be a big assho' when he tire," Malcolm added.

"Thanks for the support," Wyatt said.

"It is all right. He deserves an explanation. You all do. But what I know, I can't explain. An even if I could, it would not satisfy you. You must learn the truths for yourselves."

"Goddamn!" Wyatt said, turning away from the guide and flopping down next to the fire. "There he goes again with that medicine man mumbo jumbo."

"Oh, I don't know," Sheila said. "It doesn't sound all that different than the philosophy treatises you had me reading back in the States."

Wyatt snorted derisively. "This guy is not Kant," he said. "Nothing personal, Walli."

"Well, maybe you thinks he can't, but I thinks he can," Malcolm said. "And I kind'a likes his mumbo jumbo."

"That's very reassuring," Wyatt said. "I feel better already."

In the hurt silence that followed Sheila looked to change the subject. "Is that your dinner?" she asked, looking to the unidentifiable animal on the spit. "Don't you think it's done?"

"It is dinner," the guide said. "But it needs more time."

He got up and moved the charred meat to a spot on the periphery of the fire where the heat was not so intense.

"Just what the hell is that?" Wyatt asked. "It looks like blackened New Orleans guinea pig."

"Grass cutter," the guide explained. "Very tasty."

Wyatt opened his pack and pulled out some bananas and guava. "I'll take your word for it."

But by the time they had sat there for another fifteen minutes or so, and had stared long and hard at the omnipresent fruit that was their only alternative to the grass cutter, smelling the hypnotically appetizing aroma, they changed their minds. Of course, watching the guide attack his portion with gluttonous zeal didn't help any.

"Think I could try a bite o' dat grass cutter?" Malcolm asked first, nearly drooling as he spoke.

"Help yourself," the guide said, barely looking up from his feast.

"I...I'd like to try a little bite myself," Sheila said humbly.

The guide motioned for her to follow the old man to the fire. Each cut a small tidbit of the seared flesh and with prissy timidity nibbled at it as though sampling sautéed puppy entrails stuffed with raw slugs.

"Dis shit is gooood!" Malcolm crowed almost immediately.

Sheila chewed till her jaws ached, a silent statement as to the tenderness of the meat, but her delayed reaction was nonetheless positive.

"It tastes just like...chicken!" she said to Wyatt. "Here - try some."

The angry itinerant philosopher tried to feign disinterest, but his stomach was grumbling and he found his mouth watering despite his intellectual disapproval.

"Oh, all right," he conceded, grabbing the proffered knife with its tiny nibble of grass cutter tagged to the point. "When in the jungle..."

He popped the meat into his mouth and chewed. He tried to maintain a stony visage of studied neutrality, but in seconds his eyes opened wide even as his jaws continued to labor. About a minute later he joined the consensus. "This stuff IS good. Could you spare a little more?" he asked the guide.

"Eat all you wish," the guide said between mouthfuls. "I bought it for all of us."

"Bought it?" Sheila asked. "You mean you didn't catch it here in the jungle?"

"I knew we would be travelling until nightfall," the guide explained. "And the man who hunts by the light of the moon shoots shadows. I bought it at the village this morning."

Wyatt, hearing more than the guide expressed, stood and dug into his pocket. "How much do we owe you?"

The guide smiled. "You do not owe me anything until you find what you seek. And I do not believe that is grass cutter."

"Who knows," Sheila said. "Maybe it is. Maybe we came all this way to eat grass cutter. Truth is, we don't know why we came, exactly."

"You will know when you find it."

"God, I wish I had your confidence," Wyatt said only half-sarcastically.

"Perhaps you will find it," the guide said.

"Perhaps."

They finished the meal quickly, since in truth the grass cutter was not all that large and once they overcame their reluctance it disappeared in a flash, or more accurately several gulps. There were no plates or silverware to clean up, no television to watch or radio to listen to, and the nearest coffee bar was probably a good couple thousand miles away. And so, once the darkness was complete, their stomachs full and the fire burned low, there was nothing better to do than sleep.

"We will be up at first light and we have far to go before we reach our destination," the guide explained as he rolled out his own sleeping blanket.

"You mean we will get there tomorrow?" Sheila asked, a note of excitement in her voice.

"If we travel quickly, yes."

"And exactly where is 'there'?" Wyatt asked.

"It is where you may find what you are looking for," the guide said matter-of-factly.

"What you means, 'may find'?" Malcolm asked. "You means to tell me we maybe ain't gonna find the answer for this dream of ours?"

"Everything you need to find the answer will be there. But you must find it. It will not find you. You must have the courage and the perseverance to see your journey through."

"Or else?"

The guide shrugged. "The world does not change easily," he said. "But it does not change at all unless we change it."

"Are you telling me we might go through all this mumbo-jumbo and hassle and still have the same damn dream?!" Wyatt exploded.

Sheila put a hand on his forearm to calm him. It did not have much effect.

"I cannot see the future," the guide said, easing himself down on his blanket. "But I do know that what will be, will be."

"Jesus. Now he sounds like Doris Day," Wyatt grumbled. Sheila increased her grip on his arm.

"Do not worry about tomorrow," the guide said, laying down and pulling the blanket up to his hips. "Just prepare for it."

"Easy for him to say," Wyatt said quietly.

Sheila stroked his hair and kissed him on the cheek. Despite his best efforts a smile broke through his pout.

"Will you go with me while I take a pee?" she asked sweetly.

"Sounds like something I wouldn't want to miss," Wyatt said.

"I comin' too," Malcolm said, jumping up to join them. "I gots to pee too."

"Hell, why not. We can make it a good ol' pee-a-thon with prizes for longest, loudest and most accurate," Wyatt said.

"I think I may be at a disadvantage there," Sheila said.

"Nobody ever said the world was fair."

The decision made, the three travelers tramped off to a spot where Sheila could have some privacy without venturing more than a foot or two into the jungle. Wyatt stood just a couple of feet away and Malcolm took up residence a few yards further downwind. With a symphony of insects and birds and animals all around them, they each made their contribution to the natural environment.

"Sounds like one of those tapes with music to meditate by," Wyatt said as soon as the waterworks ceased. "Titled 'Serene Jungle with Gentle Rain'."

"Sound more like 'three tired hikers takin' a pee in the woods' to me," Malcolm said.

Sheila started giggling and almost fell over as she struggled to pull up her shorts.

As soon as they were back at the fire all three unrolled their sleeping bags and stretched out under the incredible panorama of a sky alive with stars. A soft breeze kept the stillness from being oppressive and kept the bugs at bay. In just moments the heavy breathing of Malcolm joined that of their guide, creating a steady human backdrop to the hypnotizing surroundings of the jungle and its inhabitants.

"Isn't it wonderful?" Sheila whispered to Wyatt.

"Are you still awake?"

"I never thought I'd experience anything like this. The jungle, the sounds, the stars...you." The way she said the last made Wyatt sit straight up.

"You ARE awake."

"Every bit of me." She reached her left hand under his bedroll and rubbed his bare chest lovingly. "You?"

"Getting there..."

She lifted the edge of the bedroll and slid in next to him. He was surprised to feel her naked skin pressing against his. When had she slipped out of her shorts and 'Ski Breckenridge' t-shirt? On second thought, who cared?

She kissed him on his neck and nibbled at an earlobe.

"Here? Now?" He couldn't control the nervous bewilderment in his voice.

"You don't want to?" she teased, pulling her hand back languidly.

"I didn't say that," Wyatt said, grabbing her wrist and pulling it back to where it belonged.

In the nearby jungle a night bird let loose with a strange, nearly human cry of release. At least that is what anyone within hearing range would have thought.

CHAPTER NINETEEN

When they awoke in the first hours of morning Walli was already up, Malcolm was awake but enjoying the stillness of the early hour from his bedroll, the fire was throwing billowing clouds of pale grey smoke into the sky and the sun was a huge orange ball entwined in the treetops.

"Did you sleep well?" the guide asked as they stretched and yawned their way to consciousness.

Wyatt thought he detected a slight knowing smile. "Great. Best night's sleep I've had in ages."

"Not bad," Sheila said with a smirk. Wyatt frowned in her direction.

"No dreams?"

They hesitated for an instant. "Actually, there was a dream," Wyatt said.

"He ax you into the hut too?" Malcolm asked from the other side of the fire, where he was now perched on one elbow.

"He did!" Sheila said. "And did he offer you that gourd to drink?"

"Sounds like we're still all watching the same channel," Wyatt cut in.

"But I likes the show a whol' helluva lot better," the old man said. "I could almos' get use to dis."

"Almost," Wyatt said.

"The choice will be yours," the guide said.

"What choice is that?" Wyatt asked. He made no attempt to hide the cynicism.

"Whether you want to continue dreaming of life or continue living a dream."

Wyatt looked to Sheila with an expression of utter disdain. "Here we go again," he muttered through closed teeth.

"Give him a chance," she said. "He can't help it if he talks that way."

Malcolm's face, meanwhile, had twisted up into a contorted mask of confusion. "What you talkin' 'bout?" the old man asked.

"Thank you," Wyatt said. "I was starting to think I was the only one around here that didn't get it."

"You will understand, when the time is right," the guide intoned.

"I just hope I live that long."

"You? I's the one should be worryin' 'bout livin' long," Malcolm countered.

"Nobody needs to be worrying about such things!" Sheila ordered. "We're all doing just fine and I think everything will be all right if we just have patience. Hell, we came all the way over here to find something we can't even explain; I think we can wait another day or two to see how things turn out. Right?"

She turned to Wyatt, who maintained his look of misunderstood martyr. "Right?" she repeated, a bit more emphatically.

"Yes, dear." His sincerity was less than convincing. Sheila ignored it and turned to Malcolm.

"Right?"

The old man nodded. "What the hell."

"Then why don't we get some food in our stomachs, wash up a little, and get on our way? The sooner we hit the road, the sooner we'll find what's waiting for us at the other end."

"I'm not sure I want to know," Wyatt groused.

"Then you can stay here and keep the fire burning," Sheila declared. "We'll stop back for you after we've done what we came here to do." She turned away and began to pack up her bedroll.

Wyatt stared at her a bit wide-eyed. For just a moment he looked as though he was considering a snappy retort, but just as quickly he changed his mind. When she continued to studiously ignore him, he got up and went about his business as directed. They all did, and in no time they had eaten, dressed, washed up and broken camp. It was a quieter, more motivated group that started out that warm, blue morning.

The guide did not have to urge them on quite so often as he had the day before. In fact, it was he who called for the first break of the day.

"In this heat you need a great deal of water," he explained, passing an animal skin water bag that seemed unnaturally cool to his three charges. "Without it, you will soon find yourself quite uncomfortable, or perhaps worse."

They drank deeply, silently thankful that the guide had finally chosen to rest. They had walked at a steady pace for more than three hours, and in the damp heat of mid-morning the sweat was rolling down their sides. Yet not a one had said a word. Wyatt refused to surrender before Sheila; Sheila was buoyed by a newfound sense of motivation, expectation and confidence; Malcolm was nearly entranced by the very idea of their proximity to their goal - whatever that might prove to be. All three felt a new source of strength, a sudden surge of energy. They were going to make it to the end of their trek, come what may. And then? They'd face that challenge when they got there.

The break proved to be painfully short, just long enough to gulp some of the cool, sweet water carried by the guide. As soon as the water bag had made its rounds he settled the weight of his pack squarely on his shoulders and set off once more. The three travelers scurried to catch up.

If anything, the jungle that surrounded them grew even more dense and entangled as they travelled north and west. It overwhelmed everything except the narrow path they travelled, a passageway that seemed carved from the living green, more of a tunnel than a walkway. As the sun climbed directly overhead and the shadows shrank back to mere outlines like a melting glacier field of black ice, the guide raised his hand to call for a stop and quickly found himself a place to stretch out in the refuge of the protective shade. His three companions immediately followed suit.

After the ritualistic passing of the waterskin and a few moments of quiet rest, Wyatt was emboldened to ask questions that had been bothering him for days.

"Walli. You know, we've been following you pretty much on blind faith for these past couple of days. Just what is it that you think you can lead us to?"

The guide, who had been staring at his feet in restful contemplation, nodded slowly without looking up. "It is a good question, and long overdue," he said.

"Thank you," Wyatt answered. "I suppose you have an equally good answer."

"That is for you to determine."

"Okay. Let'er rip and we'll let you know."

"Very well..." A long pause became a very long pause and the three travelers began to fidget. Just as Wyatt was

about to remind the guide of his commitment, Walli took a
deep breath and began.

"You see, there are two worlds that all of us exist in,"
he said slowly, his voice a melodic instrument that
mesmerized. "The world of the living and the world of
dreams. We all recognize the first, yet many of us deny the
validity of the second. We journey through the land of dreams
nightly, and still we do not recognize that land as a reality in
our lives. We denigrate our dreams, making them mere
shadows of our reality. When in truth they are just as real as
our waking lives, just as important to our existence, just as
needful of our care and concern. And just as what happens in
our lives influences our dreams, our dreams can influence the
very essence of our lives - for good or bad."

"You believe this?" Wyatt asked.

"I know this. And you, of all people, know it too. But
although you know it to be true, you do not believe it. Like
many of your world, you find it difficult to accept with your
mind what your heart knows is true. You have been separated
from your inner self, divorced from the essential impulses that
speak to all of us every minute of every day. It is not your
fault. I do not blame you. Your world is centered in a material
plane. What you have is what you are. But here, as you have
seen, and will see, who you are is what you are, and what you
dream is what you can be.

"True, many of our people are being caught up in the
values and beliefs of your world. But the essence remains, the
truths remain self-evident."□

"Amen, brother!" Malcolm called out. "You done
heard the heartbeat!"

For the first time, a small smile crossed the guide's
lips. "That is good: The Heartbeat. Perhaps that is the best
way to describe what you seek. The Heartbeat of your

creation; The Heartbeat of your salvation; The Heartbeat of your emancipation."

"You are a priest," Sheila said, a note of wonder in her voice.

"Not as you use the term in your world," the guide said. "I do not draw my authority from a book. I do not demand adoration or sacrifice. Perhaps guide is a better title. I trace the path along which searchers find their own truths."

"And we are the searchers?"

"Are you not?"

"I don't know what the hell we are," Wyatt said. "All I want is to get rid of this damn shared dream."

"Why don't I believe you?" the guide asked.

"Will we ever finds The Heartbeat?" Malcolm interrupted.

"I can lead you to the path. I cannot make you take it."

The guide waited, as if anticipating a question from Sheila. She didn't speak at first, but finally surrendered to her curiosity and concern.

"You say we are molded by the realities of our world," she said tentatively. "So how can we rise above the limits of that world? Aren't we all bound by our traditions, our beliefs, our ignorance?"

"Truth cannot be ignored once it is confronted," the guide said. "It is my responsibility to allow you your confrontation. And now we should go. Your path is still long, and our time is short. Come."□

Without waiting for an answer he slipped his pack over his shoulders and started back down the path. Wyatt looked to Sheila.

"This is some weird shit," he said as he struggled to slip into his pack before the guide disappeared from view.

"Cool shit," she corrected.

"I seconds that."

All three scrambled to catch up.

"Who the hell is this guy?" Wyatt asked in a decidedly subdued voice as he sidled up to Sheila. "What is he?"

"You heard him. He's a guide," Sheila answered.

"From what planet?"

"Who knows? Who cares? I've got a good feeling about him."

"You're connecting with your inner self?" The sarcasm was intended but not half as pointed as before.

"You should try it," Sheila said. "It might do you some good." She unexpectedly picked up her pace and raced on ahead of him.

"Now what do you mean by that?" he called after her, but she was already out of earshot, or at least pretended to be. "Oh great, now he's got her believing it," he mumbled to himself before hurrying to catch up.

But now that the sun was full overhead and the early morning orange tint had faded to a blinding white, the tropical heat built quickly, held close by the green blanket of the jungle foliage. Even the short double-time surge to close the gap with the guide had both Sheila and Wyatt panting for breath and sweating heavily. Below the bottom of her pack, Wyatt could see the small of Sheila's back stained dark by the stream of perspiration running down the channel between her shoulder blades. Malcolm somehow stayed close to the guide without showing any sign of distress. *'Must be running on sheer adrenaline,'* Wyatt thought. He himself felt lightheaded and had to slow to catch his breath. Sheila stayed a step or two ahead, refusing to forgive his comment.

"Okay, all right, I apologize," he whispered to her bobbing backside. "Maybe he does have something to say."

"And...?" she asked without turning around.

"And...maybe we have something to learn."

She slowed her pace just enough so that he could fall into step beside her. "I always thought you were a fairly bright guy," she said. "But to ignore what we've experienced here is not what I would call bright."

"And just what is that?" he asked. "What have we experienced?"

"I don't know. It's like trying to identify an elephant by its tail, or like asking what I think of a movie when it's only half over. I need to see it to the end to know what it is and whether it has value. But as of now, I think it will. Can you at least open yourself to that possibility?"

He hesitated, falling a step behind. "Yeh, yeh I can do that." He surprised even himself. She let him catch up without comment.

The afternoon passed in a blur of greens and browns, the heat growing so oppressive that no amount of water could slake their thirst or cool their overheated systems. They stopped for a brief fruit lunch at midday, but then continued on at full speed for the entire afternoon, stopping only twice more for water and rest. By this time not even Malcolm's enthusiasm could carry him at the speeds demanded by the guide, and he dropped back into a slower gait with his two fellow travelers.

"How far up there is he?" Sheila asked when the old man fell back into their midst. There was a note of concern in her voice that neither of the other two missed.

"Can't say. Must be a ways - I ain't seen him for a while now."

"What the hell is he trying to prove?" Wyatt asked.

"I just hope he doesn't forget we're back here."

"A spiritual guide wouldn't do that, would he?" Wyatt asked skeptically. As soon as he said it he wished he hadn't.

"No, no I'm sure he wouldn't," Sheila said, but she didn't sound convinced. "Unless...he's hurt. Or worse!" Her words fell heavily on the three travelers as they looked around at the impenetrable jungle.

"I think we'd better get going," Wyatt said.

They picked up the tempo as best they could, but there wasn't much left to give. And still the guide did not come into sight. As the afternoon hours wore on, their stamina and determination were stretched to the breaking point. Malcolm, in particular, was having considerable trouble keeping up the pace.

"This isn't going to cut it," Wyatt finally announced when they had stopped for the third time that hour to give the old man, and themselves, a chance to rest. "I'm going to go find that guide and tell him to get back here and do what he was hired for."

"By yourself?" Sheila asked.

"I'll make better time that way. Of course, for all we know that SOB might be hiding just out of view and this whole thing is some kind of test or something."

"If it is, tell 'em we get an 'F' an' wants to start over," Malcolm said with a weak smile.

"I'll tell him a whole helluva lot more than that," Wyatt said. He kissed Sheila and gave Malcolm a mock salute. "See you in a few."

Without waiting for formal goodbyes he turned to start down the path.

"Wyatt, wait!" Sheila yelled after him. She told Malcolm she'd be right back and ran the few steps down to where Wyatt was waiting impatiently.

"Now look, this is the best way..." he started to explain. But rather than argue Sheila threw her arms around his neck and kissed him passionately.

"You take care of yourself," she whispered, just a trace of concern in her eyes.

"You too. Rest for a while and when you're both feeling up to it, come on down. You shouldn't have any trouble finding me. I'll be the white guy who looks like he's about to shit in his pants."

"I'll be there."

He kissed her quickly and tried to step away, but she held him tight.

"Have I told you lately that I love you?" she said.

He smiled. "Not lately, but then again you've had other things on your mind."

"That's not true. You're always there, no matter what."

"Good. Hold that thought."

They held each other close. "Don't worry," Wyatt said after a long moment. "In the immortal words of Dick Nixon, 'You ain't seen the last of this bad boy.'"

He didn't wait for an answer. He gently removed her arms from around his neck and turned back down the path. After just a few steps, however, he turned back to her.

"Ditto," he said. With a wink he was gone

She watched him until she could neither see nor hear him any longer. Then she turned back to the old man.

"You really think sumthin' might've happen to the guide?" Malcolm asked.

"I don't know," she said.

"'Cuz if he gone, we's fucked."

She nodded to herself. "Let's just get some rest," she said. "Maybe Wyatt will find him."

Then again, she thought, maybe he wouldn't.

CHAPTER TWENTY

For the first half hour or so, Wyatt's anger and anticipation fueled his movement. He marched down the jungle path without so much as a thought as to the task that faced him or the consequences if the guide couldn't be found. But then, as that initial energy faded under the onslaught of the wilting heat and humidity, he was forced to stop -- to rest and to ponder his circumstances.

The thought was not a pretty one. There he was, quite literally in the middle of nowhere, in an environment totally alien to him, with virtually no food, limited water, no sense of where he was going and with nothing in terms of defensive equipment, with only his own knowledge, courage and ingenuity to get him - and his two companions - to safety. Even after all his experience trekking around the U.S. he knew that he was unprepared for this. For the first time he knew what it was like to be truly alone, truly dependent on his own skills. And it was not a comfortable feeling.

But he had no choice. As soon as he felt sufficiently rested, he found himself a fairly straight and sturdy walking stick that could double as a bludgeon should push come to blow, and with a deep breath set off once again down the trail. The look, sounds and smells of the jungle rushed at him from all sides. He realized then how deadened his senses had become to the flora and fauna that surrounded him. Having allowed himself to become completely dependent on the guide he had tuned out much of what went on around him. In all honesty, for much of the walking leg of the trip he had been too tired and too caught up in his own thoughts to pay much attention. Now the situation was different. Now his very life, as well as that of Sheila and Malcolm, might depend on his acuity.

What had seemed just a solid green mash of verdant growth now became an intricate mosaic of trees, vines, ferns and an infinite variety of smaller plants. The sounds of the animal life, which had been condensed in his preoccupied mind into a backdrop curtain of buzzes, whistles and cries, now called out in a thousand different individual voices, from the chirping crickets all the way to unseen and unimaginable throaty rumblings from who knew what. The necessity now facing Wyatt was to perceive, analyze and act without slowing his pace. The pressure was enormous. For the first time in a long time, perhaps the first time in his adult life, he could say that he felt real fear.

He remembered a time back when he was a child, lost in the woods behind his house, wandering aimlessly as night began to fall. The trees took on anthropomorphic forms with hurtful, malignant qualities; arms reached out to grab him as long spindly feet snatched at his shoes, trying to throw him to the ground. He had tried to find his way back home, tried to remain calm and think it all through. But the spirit of those woods, the dark, brooding spirit of a forest at twilight, overwhelmed him and left him defeated, crying helplessly at the base of a huge old oak. And that was where they'd found him soon after, huddled in a small, defensive ball, crying his eyes out. Sometimes it seemed to him that he'd been trying to find his way home ever since, trying to obliterate the embarrassment, the sheer terror of that night. If only he'd been able to hold out for fifteen minutes more...

A sound off to his left dragged him back from his reverie. It was a deep, throaty rumble, the sound of some animal neither small nor shy. Wyatt pulled his walking stick up to shoulder level in a defensive posture, ready to strike back at any attacker, to make them pay for their meal. He could hear his heartbeat, feel it shake within his chest. He tried to control his breathing, without much success

Another roar from a short ways to his right. Was it a second predator? Two of a larger group - a hunting pack? He decided to move away from there as quickly as possible without drawing attention. Still holding the stick at chest level he backed slowly down the path, his feet barely seeming to move in an unthinking impersonation of a slow-motion moonwalk.

"All right now, I'm not really doing anything here," he tried to convince the unseen stalkers as he glided across the hard-packed soil. "It's just some very pale, sickly-looking creature kind of slip-slidin' away."

A rustling in the bushes just a few short feet away nearly froze his knee joints in place, but he forced himself to continue. What had been a constant trickle of sweat down his back became a gushing torrent. His senses seemed attuned to a higher level, as if he could see and feel every detail of the late afternoon shadows that surrounded him. If he could have heard more than the thunder of his heart pounding like a living drum he would have realized that an eerie silence had befallen the jungle. It was as if it was holding its breath, waiting.

*****

"You feeling up to walking some more?" Sheila asked her prone companion.

"Don' think we's gonna get too far sittin' here," Malcolm answered, struggling stiffly to his feet.

"No, I don't suppose we will. How are your legs holding out?"

"They been holdin' out pretty damn good for 68 years. Don' see no reason they gonna stop now."

"That's good. But just in case, you let me know if you start to feel a bit weary, okay?"

"I let you know. But I think right now what we needs to do is catch up to that boyfriend of yours. I been thinkin' he be needin' us more'n we needs him."

"You may have a point there," Sheila admitted ruefully. "Well, only one way to do that."

With a long sigh she shifted her pack to settle the weight evenly and led the way down the deepening green pathway.

*****

Gradually, painfully, the seconds turned to minutes. Wyatt stood perfectly still, as if by doing so he might somehow disappear from the field of interest of whatever was out there. As the minutes slipped by the pressure of the moment became diluted and ever so slowly his heart rate returned to normal; he could hear the sounds of the jungle close in around him once again. He listened intently, trying to hear through the background noise to the sounds that tormented him.

There! There it was again! Or was it? He held his breath until he could hold it no longer, but still he wasn't sure.

Was he hearing it, or was his mind playing tricks on him? There! No, that wasn't anything.

The minutes seemed to stretch interminably until finally, his patience worn thin, he relaxed from his frozen pose and nonchalantly scanned the bush around him. Nothing. He couldn't see anything threatening, couldn't hear anything dangerous. Perhaps the danger had passed. If it had existed at all.

He shook his head in disgust and jumped off to a near-jog to make up for lost time. From a short distance, invisible in the heavy undergrowth, a pair of jet black eyes watched his every move.

*****

The shadows were getting longer. Sheila knew it would only be a couple of hours before nightfall. For some reason even she couldn't fathom she wasn't terribly afraid of their predicament, but nonetheless hoped fervently that Wyatt would make his way back before darkness fell. Her feelings were partly inspired by the understanding that the three of them would likely fare much better as a team in any sort of confrontation that might come up, and partly by worry for Wyatt. Even though she had great confidence in his ability to take care of himself, in the past few days she'd found herself increasingly concerned for his welfare.

"He be okay," Malcolm said out of the blue, interrupting her reverie.

Sheila turned back to the old man. "How did you know?"

"Hell, you be swervin' all over the path with dis moony, don'-know-where-you-be look all over your face. I figures you gots to be thinkin' of him."

316 William J. Millman

"I guess I was."

"No doubt about it. You got feelin's for the guy."

Sheila thought about arguing. To minimize her worry. To hide her fear. But before she could second guess her feelings she blurted, "Yeh. I think I love him."

Malcolm nodded sagely, leaning against a thin tree by the edge of the pathway to catch a moment's rest. "You could do worst," he said. "He got a strange sense of humor, that true, but he got him some gumption. All tol', not too bad."

Sheila smiled. "I'm glad you approve. But for now I think we'd best get moving to see if we can catch up with him and the guide. Otherwise, this could be one long night."

"I got a feelin' it gonna be one long night anyway you look at it," the old man said softly. Sheila showed no sign of having heard and he didn't repeat himself.☐

*****

For the first time, Wyatt was getting seriously worried. He had been hiking as fast as he could to catch up to the guide, but after more than four hours hadn't seen even a sign of the man. The jungle shadows were beginning to merge into twilight and he knew he couldn't keep up the pace for long. If he didn't catch up to Walli soon, he'd have to go back to find Sheila and Malcolm. But where was the guide? At the worst he couldn't have gotten more than a half hour ahead of them. Unless he was trying to lose them. Unless he had decided to abandon them to their own fortunes.

Enough of that thinking. Maybe he was hurt. Maybe he'd been attacked, by an animal, or robbers. Maybe it was headhunters...

'I'm the one losing his head around here,' he thought wearily. *'I've got to pull it together. Another thirty minutes or so, and I'm heading back.'*

Just then he heard the pounding of a drum, distant but clearly defined. He stopped dead in his tracks. He recognized that rhythm. He'd heard it many times before. In fact, he'd heard it each night for many weeks. It was difficult to tell how close, or how far, it might be. Sounds carried unpredictably in the jungle. But one thing he did know. He had to go take a look. He knew the safe thing to do was to go back to find Sheila and the old man, but it was almost as if he couldn't help himself. The pounding rhythms drew him to them, pulled him along hypnotically. He knew what he was doing, but he couldn't stop. He didn't want to.

*****

Less than a mile away as the vulture flies, Sheila and Malcolm heard the same drumbeat.

"What the hell is that?" Sheila asked, her voice more than a bit shaky.

"That's what we been lookin' for," Malcolm said, his eyes focused somewhere in the far distance, his voice low and dreamlike.

Sheila heard the familiar rhythm and turned to follow his gaze. "It is, isn't it," she said, barely breathing as she listened. "Now what?"

But it was as if she knew the answer before she even asked the question. They would go there, and somehow she knew that they'd find Wyatt, and the guide. But it was what else they might find that scared her. A line from an old song kept bouncing around her brain: "It could be heaven, it could be hell."

CHAPTER TWENTY-ONE

Like moths drawn to the light, the three travelers pushed on into the deepening dusk, Wyatt a good half-hour ahead of the others, Sheila and Malcolm following at their own pace.

After keeping to the path for twenty minutes or so, Wyatt realized that he had come no closer to the drumbeats. The path apparently bypassed the spot where the drummer was summoning them, running nearby but never approaching close enough to see or communicate with the unknown shaman. Should he stay on the path and wait for Sheila and Malcolm, or go in search of the drums? In the moment he realized his predicament, he had already decided what he would do. Or perhaps decided wasn't the right word. It was decided for him. He had to go. Had to find those drums, find what they signified. Find how to rid them forever from his dreams and return to the world as he knew it

Without his customary lengthy internal debate he left the path and plunged into the vast shadowed unknown of the jungle. The sun was now nearly set and only a hint of red-orange glow tinted the horizon. Beneath the pulsating green canopy daylight was virtually nonexistent. It was dark, very dark. And yet Wyatt felt a confidence in his step, a sureness that belied the situation. Crashing through tangled undergrowth, throwing aside the innumerable branches and heavy-leaved stems that crowded the jungle floor, he pushed forward with a recklessness that would have surprised and frightened him only moments before. But at that moment, in that place, he felt a calm assurance that spoke to him of his need.

As he trekked ever closer the drumbeat surrounded and directed him, passing through him, echoing in his mind and in his heart. He felt the energy of the drummer (or was there more than one?), the indecipherable message of the rhythms. Images began to form in his mind's eye, images that wrestled with the fleeting shadows that rushed past his unseeing eyes. He saw himself as a child, at his father's funeral, wondering aloud why his father had left without saying goodbye. He saw himself as a teen, arguing with his mother, challenging her authority to control his life, threatening to leave her forever.

The drums grew louder.

Wyatt saw himself in college, debating a point with a professor - with Mr. Littlefield! - about self-determination and responsibility. He saw himself with Donna, telling her goodbye, explaining that he could not commit to her the way she needed commitment, could not allow himself to be limited the way she wanted to limit him, could not love her the way she needed to be loved.

The drums grew louder and louder.

He saw Sheila, smiling, beckoning, but the faster he approached the faster she withdrew. He began to run, the unseen branches whipping against his face and body, hidden roots reaching out, trying to trip him, to throw him down into the impenetrable shadows. But he would not be thrown, would not be stopped. He knew now where he must go, he knew what he must do.

In the distance a large amorphous shade loomed menacingly. But rather than turn aside, he found himself drawn to the nebulous form, ready to confront, to embrace it. The drum beat synchronized with his heartbeat and they moved as one, pounding, sounding, attracted and repelled, driven and withheld. More clearly than possible he saw the shape slowly edging into focus. Saw the jungle part and the clearing open before him. He saw it all.

And then he saw the hut.

*****

The cry was brief but shattering.

"That's Wyatt!" Sheila said, grabbing Malcolm's arm reflexively.

The old man nodded slowly, his expression a mix of confusion and fear. "It do sound like him."

"We've got to go to him. He may be hurt!"

She started to race down the darkened pathway, but she quickly realized that Malcolm could not match her pace. She ran back to exhort him, to grab him by the hand and drag him if necessary. But it was no use. Malcolm had already struggled too hard and too long under the sweltering African sun. He was near exhaustion and could not move any faster.

"Go on ahead," he said. "I be coming along by an' by. You go find that man o' your."

Part of her wanted to argue that she couldn't leave him alone. But there was something much more powerful than mere conscience that committed her to action.

"I'll be back for you as soon as I find Wyatt," she said. She bent down and kissed him on the cheek. "Just stay on the path. We'll find you."

"I be here," he said. "Now go - go!"

Without waiting for a second invitation she took off running as fast as her legs would carry her. In the near-total darkness there was no way to see everything in the path, but she did not hesitate. Somehow it didn't matter. She felt as if she were enclosed in a protective cocoon, a projection of sheer energy that cleared her path and gave strength to her exhausted legs. She ran with an abandonment that she hadn't trusted since her childhood. Since before the divorce, before the arguments and mistrust. Since before they had stopped being a family. Since before her father had left.

She found her legs churning to the pounding rhythm of the drumbeat, a steady, driving rhythm that crept into her body and pulsed through her limbs. It surrounded her, engulfed her, overwhelmed her. She saw faces racing out of the darkness, faces from her past, from her present. Some faces she didn't recognize at all. They beckoned her, guided her, protected her. She felt the breeze rush past her face, whipping sweat-drenched hair back and forth, back and forth across her shoulders, but the reality of the moment blurred. It was as if she was not really there, gliding in slow motion through a dreamlike trance.

The rhythm yanked her off the path and yet she continued pell-mell through the green-black shadows of the living jungle, untouched, unbothered. The drumbeat grew louder, stronger, faster. It felt like her chest would burst open from the pounding of her heart and the rasping gasp of her breathing. But she did not slow her pace. He must be near now.

Suddenly she felt moonlight on her face. She had broken free from the grasp of the jungle and found herself out in the open, crossing a broad grassy plain. And then she realized. It was The Plain. From the dream. And she was both in the dream and separate from it, conscious of her actions and yet outside of them, watching as if a spectator to her own reality. She wanted to stop, to think, to change the course of the dream if she could, but the drum wouldn't let her. It drew her along, commanding her to come nearer. And she obeyed.

She ran with the drum, to the drum. There was nothing else, nothing but the drum, beating incessantly, calling, demanding, directing. It filled the air, filled the ground, filled her to overflowing. And so she ran with all her might, sprinting through the unknown blackness to answer the call. The call of the drums. There was nothing else.

In an instant of revelation she threw open her eyes and slid to a panting stop. The drums had stopped. The surrounding jungle was silent. And she stood before an all too familiar thatched-roof hut, a red ceramic figure at the entrance bidding her enter.

*****

Malcolm heard the drums stop from a little over a half-mile away. He stood silently still and reached out to the jungle with all his senses. He touched nothing.

"I don' mine tellin' you, I don' like this much," he muttered to himself. "But I guess I can' stop now..."

He adjusted his backpack and hefted his walking stick to chest level with both hands. As he walked he started whistling a strange, almost eerie tune that he quickly realized he didn't know. He thought to try again, but his mouth was too dry. And the night was too quiet.

In fact, for the first time since they'd come there the silence of the jungle was complete: no animal cries, no buzzing insects, no rustling leaves, nothing. Just as the pounding drum had filled the air with its rhythms, its absence seemed to have drained all sound from his surroundings. The hushed blackness hung upon Malcolm like death and he struggled to overcome its stifling closeness. He felt his years pulling him down, calling to him to heed their promise of unending rest. But he did not listen. He had come too far and believed too much. And beyond everything else, he would not leave his two companions. Oh, they were strange enough, all right. Not at all like him. But they had shared the dream and come with him to Africa. He would not leave them until their journey was complete. And so he tottered forward, his muscles aching, the emptiness in his stomach echoed in his arms and legs. Each step required a force of will that was nearly beyond him. It had all become so unreal, so nightmarish. For just a moment he wondered if he were the dream.

Then he heard the beat once more. The same rhythm, the same tone, the same sense of insistence. But it did not come from the far distance. Nor even from close by. It came from within him, from the living, pumping drumbeat of his own heart. And it gave him strength; it gave him hope.

Stepping off the path like a novice pushing off on an expert slope, the old man moved into the jungle without trepidation. He knew now why he had come, knew what he must do. He walked more quickly, his legs moving almost of their own accord. The passage through the dense undergrowth seemed to reveal itself with each step, an unthinking revelation that he did not challenge, did not examine. It was part of the gift, and he accepted it completely.

He was aware of his movement and yet somehow independent of it. The image of a flowing river slid through his mind as he was directed, drawn through the jungle, pulled along in a flood of memories, hopes and dreams. Breaking free of the overhanging trees he basked in the bright moonlight; in his mind he saw the sun rising on a distant beach long ago. A numbness of muscle and bone, an overload of sensory input, deadened his senses to the exhaustion, hunger, thirst and anticipation that consumed him. It would not be long now. The end of the trail was near.

Ahead something glimmered in the silvery light, a structure, surrounded by others of the same design. He rushed forward to convince himself that it was, indeed, the hut he had seen so many times in his sleep. And in that moment he rushed into The Dream.

The red ceramic figure signaled his arrival even as his feet slowed of their own accord and turned, unhurried at last, into the doorway. Taking a deep breath, nearly rigid from the overwhelming mix of hope and dread, he stepped inside.

Wyatt and Sheila sat off to one side, wide-eyed. Directly across from them, a masked figure stood expectantly, hands poised above his drums, waiting. No sooner did the old man step into the swirling currents of smoke that enveloped them than the figure began the drumbeat anew, its pounding rhythms ever more urgent, more demanding. The wisps of smoke tumbled and whirled in a chaotic dance of release, a dance that commanded attention. They stared blankly into the whirling brew, lost in a maelstrom of colors, shapes and images. Although they could not know it, each saw a completely different tableau, one that emerged out of and fed into their own wants and needs

At first Malcolm saw nothing but the smoke itself; something in its movement, its seeming aliveness, kept him riveted to every nuance of its constantly changing patterns. And then, gradually, as when the rising sun burns away the early morning fog, there emerged a flood of...memories? There was a moment from the home of his youth, his mother standing over him as her words flayed his hopes until he shut her out and dreamed of escape to a better place; at school, where a teacher renewed the assault on his youthful spirit, unwilling to accept deviation, unwilling to recognize an inner self waiting to spring forth; the whites-only fountain where he was going to damn well drink whenever he damn well wanted, landing him behind bars for the first of many such visits, where he met Matthew, teaching the inherent equality of all people and the need for Negros to believe in themselves; until the night when those drunken white boys wouldn't leave well-enough alone and Sophie tried to pull him away, crying for him not to sacrifice himself, but the die was cast and the fists flew out of years of frustration and the police came again - how often they seemed to intrude upon the stream of his existence - and of course it had been his fault and the judge wouldn't listen to Sophie's words in his defense, defending him, defending her world, defending what was right in a world where right was white, and then he was locked away again where hatred could have easily boiled up and overwhelmed who he was, but the brother spoke of Africa and the heritage he never knew and all these years that truth lay deep in his heart, hidden, waiting, while he walked the highways seeking another truth, a homegrown, individual, life-sown truth that would fit him like a glove and bring unity to a shattered soul that needed unity like the dry earth needs the rains that come from a heaven without bitterness, without blame, with only the shining light of God's own sun, shining on all men equally no matter who they are or what color their skin and then he felt the light of God's love caress his face and those rains falling down from the heavens above with the cool, cleansing power of their righteous truth.

From across the hut Wyatt and Sheila saw the old man, currents of smoke enveloping him, bathed in an aura of light, his face upturned to the heavens, tears pouring down his cheeks. Sheila tried to call out to him, to scramble to her feet to hold him, but the light sought her out and pinned her to the spot.

   And in the naked light she saw, thousands of people, maybe more, swaying to a pounding beat, crazed by the summer heat, potted, besotted and united by a sound that carried them to a place where nothing hurt and everything was possible, at an age and a time when life was beautiful and tomorrow brought only the answers to whispered prayers made as falling stars crashed across the heavens to bring love and happiness to a young woman who, though comfortable in her life, was perfectly miserable in her heart without the love she'd dreamed of – eternal, encompassing, uncompromising, love like she'd never known until suddenly there he was, saying all the right things, pledging his devotion; but all dreams must end: the doctor confirmed her suspicions and the dream became not a nightmare but worse: mundane; she said, 'I do', not 'I will', but 'I do', leaving tomorrow to take care of itself, which, of course, it never does; the baby, still and silent at birth, unneeding of care, unneedful of parents, who then, unneedful of each other, became strangers in sadness, shattering the fragile bonds of teenage dreams, leaving only the scars and the mistrust, the absence of belief that sent him – all of them – away, no matter how sincere, no matter how strong their love, until at last she was truly alone, living in internal exile, separated from herself and her dreams, moving through life as if it were an obstacle course with all joy and trust to be avoided, all happiness suspect, all lovers to be discarded before the pain could come again, the terrible, aching, burning pain that lives on, and on, and on until… the dream lived once more, a sharing without words, a commitment out of time, a rebirth beyond her power to deny in the warm glow of his love and the influence of his smile. Wyatt felt her hand touch his and he squeezed it tenderly

The smoke seemed to grow thicker by the moment; from Wyatt's position at the periphery of the hut both Malcolm and Sheila seemed to slowly dematerialize as the young traveler was drawn into the swirling maelstrom of memory and emotion by the pounding rhythms of the drums. At first he felt disconnected from the experience, even while he was swept along by the ever-shifting currents. But then, it was as if the music and the pulse somehow seeped into his body and then he was there, back as a child, as his mother tried to explain where his daddy had gone, to soothe the hurt and ease the fears of a small boy who couldn't understand, couldn't accept her 'forever gone', who wanted explanations, reassurances, and rejected both as quickly as they came, hoping against hope that if he did not accept the truth, it would not be so, that if he did not acknowledge the absence, it would end, if he did not mourn, there would be no reason to mourn, but despite his best efforts the empty seat at the table remained empty and the empty space in his heart grew larger and larger with each passing year, until by his teens his heart had been swallowed whole, had disappeared into the black sorrow of his unending grief, and not even the blandishments of Deby - he could see her coiffed red hair and the soft pink sweater so amply filled by such tempting curves as she leaned against him at his locker - could illuminate the shadows within; and so he turned to books, the rational world of philosophy, and spent long hours angled in those stiff-backed wooden chairs, reading everything he could get his hands on, and migrating, slowly, imperceptibly, toward the Kant and Confucius and Aquinas and Sartre and Kierkegaard tomes, giving him a world view that extended so far beyond that of his peers that it effectively built a wall between them, and then he was truly alone, his father gone, his mother and friends unable to appreciate, let alone understand what he was thinking, and nothing to draw him out of the world of ideas that swirled through his searching mind and led him through six years of college and onto the road, looking for adventure, or whatever came his way, until gradually he began to realize that philosophy was only real in the living of it, and for the first time in years he lived his life in the world of people and things instead of books and thoughts, a world that brought him first Malcolm, then The Dream and now Sheila, the one constant in the unending swirl, the north star that guided and directed him. He saw her face materialize in the roiling streams of smoke and smiled. It was several seconds later that he realized she was real, just inches away, and smiling back. He leaned forward and kissed her

In that moment the pounding rhythm of the drums stopped abruptly.

A gentle breeze swept through the hut and gradually dissipated the smoke. In the dim light of a single torch the three travelers found themselves facing the masked demon of their dreams. Their hearts raced, but before they could say or do anything, it reached up, grabbed the carved and painted mask they all knew all too well and pulled it away in a casual, almost dismissive gesture. The sweat-streaked face of their guide emerged from the last straggling wisps of smoke. His intense eyes seemed to burn like blazing embers.

"You have confronted the shades of your past," he said, his deep voice reverberating in their bodies as well as their minds. "Now you must confront the reality of now. I wish you well." He nodded to them in a half bow and walked out the door.

The three companions sat there in stunned inaction, barely able to blink. Sheila regained her composure first.

"Wait! Walli!" she called out, struggling to her feet. Her voice broke the trancelike stare of her companions, who followed her out the door. There they found themselves staring into the empty night, with no sign of the guide to be found anywhere.

"Walli!" Sheila called again, but her voice was swallowed by the black expanse of jungle.

"He gone," Malcolm said.

"What do you mean, 'he's gone'?" Wyatt asked testily. "You don't think he'd just leave us here, in the middle of nowhere, do you?"

"I don' thinks nothin'. He done it."

"He's right, Wyatt," Sheila said. "Walli's gone."

"How do you know that? Did he say something? Leave a note?" The sarcasm was tinged with fear.

"I can feel it. I just know."

Wyatt took a deep breath and let it out slowly. Now that he'd allowed himself to feel, he knew it too. "So it's just us."

"Looks that way."

He nodded numbly. "Okay. What now?"

For a moment no one said a word. Wyatt felt as if he was coming down off of acid. The stars seemed brighter than normal; he could hear every sound in the surrounding jungle. He felt incredibly alive, despite the circumstances. Despite everything.

"I don't know 'bout you two, but I's feelin' damn tired. I think I's gonna lay me down and get some sleep," Malcolm suddenly announced. "Maybe tomorrow we can figure things out. After a good night sleep. See you in the mornin'." The old man ducked into a nearby hut.

"Wait – Malcolm!" Wyatt turned back to Sheila. "We're stuck here in the middle of the jungle, after that incredible experience, and he's going to bed?!" Wyatt asked in amazement.

"And so are we," Sheila said assuredly, taking him by the arm.

"You're tired? How can you be tired?! I feel like exploding!"

"Good," Sheila said as she guided him into the familiar hut.

Wyatt couldn't see her smirk, but he knew it was there. He didn't argue any further.

CHAPTER TWENTY-TWO

Morning did not come early. The sun was already high above the treetops by the time they stumbled out of their huts. They found baskets of fruit and juice just outside their doorways, but there was no sign of who brought them.

"Does it really matter?" Wyatt asked as he dove into the basket with complete abandon. It didn't.

It wasn't until their initial hunger and thirst had been satisfied that Malcolm casually broached their shared problem.

"You two have the dream again too?"

Sheila smiled sadly and shrugged. "Hey - we tried. Maybe there's more to this trip than what we've experienced so far."

"Not for me. I feel like I got more than I came for, dream or no dream," Wyatt said, turning to Sheila and putting his arm around her shoulders. "We're heading back to Lagos and getting on a plane out of here as fast as we can. Just like in the dream."

Malcolm looked up, his eyes wide. "Like in da' dream? What dream?"

"THE dream. What other dream would I be talking about?"

"That weren't my dream," the old man said.

"You didn't see our masked buddy point the way down the path toward the highway?" Wyatt asked, his voice beginning to show the realization that was awakening in him.

"Yeh. I seen that."

"Me too," Sheila said. "And then we came into the small village where everyone was waiting for us to start the ceremony."

"What ceremony?" Wyatt asked.

"I jus' hops in a truck and goes back to Oshogbo."

"You get off in Oshogbo in your dream?" Wyatt asked. The excitement in his voice was growing.

"'Course. Not you?"

"No! Sheila and I go to the airport and get the hell out of Dodge."

"After the ceremony."

"What ceremony?"

"You didn't see the ceremony?" Sheila asked. Her voice suddenly wary, even frightened.

"No, I didn't see any damn ceremony! What ceremony?"

"It gone!" Malcolm suddenly shouted aloud, sending a small flock of brightly colored birds scattering into flight. "That goddamn, good fo' nuthin' dream is gone!"

For the first time it really hit them. Wyatt grabbed Sheila, who grabbed Malcolm, and the three travelers whirled around and around in a giddy children's dance of release. Wyatt broke into song and Sheila followed as if rehearsed.

"Ding dong, the Dream is gone!"

"Which old dream?"

"The wicked dream!"

"Ding dong, the wicked dream is gone!"

Malcolm pulled back and eyed the two singers suspiciously. "What you two been drinkin'?" he asked.

"Nothing, nothing at all!" Sheila said, giving him a big hug.

"Don't you know the Wizard of Oz?" Wyatt asked.

"No, don' know as I ever met the man. But one thing I do know, and that's that white folks are straaaange."

Wyatt and Sheila laughed and hugged each other in sheer delight. When they finally pulled apart, the laughter had subsided. They stared into each other's eyes, standing perfectly still as if any movement might shatter the dreamlike quality of the moment.

"I've found my dream," Wyatt said softly.

"If this is a dream, I don't want to wake up." Sheila said, stretching up on tip-toes as Wyatt leaned down and kissed her.

"Whoo-ee!" Malcolm said. "Dis be gettin' sappier than As da Worl' Turn. I think it be time to get outta here and get on with it!"

There was no disagreement. The three travelers packed up their meager belongings and set off once again, following the path as they had seen it in their dreams. But just a short way along the trail Wyatt could not resist the urge to look back one more time on the village scene he had witnessed so many times in his dreams. To his amazement, it was nowhere to be seen. The jungle seemed to have engulfed it completely.

"That's weird," he said aloud.

"What is?" Sheila asked.

"Where the heck is the village? Shouldn't we still be able to see it from here?"

Sheila and Malcolm came back to where Wyatt stood and looked back along the trail.

"You'd kind of think so, huh?"

"It's like it just evaporated."

"Prob'ly just the angle. This jungle's some pretty thick shit," Malcolm said.

"We're only a hundred yards away at most," Wyatt argued. "It should be there."

"Maybe it went when the dream did," Sheila said.

Wyatt rolled his eyes and smiled. "What, like Brigadoon?"

"Could be."

"Come on, Sheila. Now you're starting to sound like Malcolm."

"She could do worst," the old man said.

"Well, I'm going to go check it out." Wyatt started back toward the village, but Sheila grabbed his arm.

"Let it go, Wyatt," she said. "Just chalk it up to one of those little unexplained mysteries of life."

"But..."

"Was it in yo' dream?" Malcolm asked. "You wanna chance gettin' that damn dream back?"

Wyatt tilted his head, thinking. "You know, maybe it doesn't matter what happened, or didn't happen to the village. Why don't we just get the hell out of here."

"Good decision," Sheila said, kissing him on the cheek.

"I'm learning..."

As the sun climbed high overhead they continued on their way. Just as they had all dreamed, the path snaked its way through the jungle, carrying them north and west under the thick green canopy. They moved slowly, for even with the night's rest and all the fruit they'd inhaled for breakfast, all three, but particularly Malcolm, were near exhaustion. It was an uneventful trip until mid-day when they saw a thinning of the trees ahead, a scene that reminded them of the surroundings in which they'd found the village of their dream.

Soft drums and the tinkling of what might have been bells drifted on the minimal breeze.

"This is it!" Sheila said excitedly.

"This is what?" Wyatt asked.

"The ceremony! This is it!"

She pushed past him and hurried on ahead, caught up in the wonder of seeing her dream coming true.

"I guess we're going to a ceremony," Wyatt said.

"Hope it ain't no shrinkin' of heads, or some such voodoo shit," the old man said.

"That'd be nice," Wyatt agreed, with just a hint of concern. They walked as quickly as they could in Sheila's wake.

As they got closer, the music became increasingly clear to them. As opposed to the pounding rhythms of the previous night, these drums were subtle, relaxed, almost inviting. There were bells, or chimes, and a recorder-like instrument that carried a lovely, melodic tune. They also heard the murmuring of a fairly large crowd, a situation that did little to ease the duo's anxieties. As they came into the clearing they saw Sheila standing next to a large palm tree, looking off to her right. Following her gaze they saw at least a hundred villagers, all clothed in their most colorful finery, standing in a half-circle around a young man and woman and an older man who appeared to be some sort of official. The villagers acknowledged their arrival by ignoring them. Wyatt sidled up to Sheila.

"Is this how you saw it?" he whispered in her ear.

"N...not really," she stammered. Something in her voice made him turn toward her. He was amazed to see tears in her eyes.

"What are you crying about?" he asked.

"It's not us!" she whispered.

"What's not us?"

"It's not us getting married!" she insisted.

Wyatt stood open-mouthed for a second. "No, no you're right there," he finally recovered. "Were you expecting it to be?"

"In my dream - I saw us...with all the African clothes."

"In this village?"

"Well, I saw the village. And then I saw us. But...I don't know!"

She turned and fled back down the path, just as a man and a woman from the village wedding party approached to greet them.

"Sorry. Wrong wedding," he said as he rushed past them, following close on Sheila's heels.

"White peoples," Malcolm added, twirling his index finger next to his temple to illustrate. The two villagers looked to each other in confusion as the old man shuffled after his two companions.

It wasn't long, less than an hour, before they came to the highway, a two-lane, mostly-paved road that ran due north and south. Where they emerged from the jungle was, as all three had seen in their dreams, a spot on the road where travelers from the various villages congregated to catch a ride with the buses, vans and trucks that plied their trade along the route. And as such, it wasn't long at all before they spotted a dented and rusting yellow mini-van with the young conductor hanging out the sliding door yelling "Oshogbo!" By now seasoned Nigerian travelers, the trio pushed and shoved their way into position in the line and managed to grab three seats back to the city of the Shrine without getting into a major fracas with the other would-be riders.

Once again it was hot, overcrowded and bumpy, but somehow it didn't seem half as bad as the last time. This time their thoughts were focused on the future, and in the case of

Sheila and Wyatt, on each other. In fact, it seemed like no time at all before they rolled into the familiar concrete block city and disembarked to find a van to Lagos. Luck or fate was with them, for in minutes they'd located a van with just three seats remaining. Sheila and Wyatt hopped aboard and turned to help Malcolm scramble into the last empty seat. But when they turned to offer a hand, the old man didn't step forward.

"Come on, Malcolm! You know these guys - they won't wait!" Wyatt called out to him.

The old man smiled wistfully. "I ain't comin'," he said.

"What? Malcolm, you don't know when the next van will come with empty seats. You could be stuck here for hours!" Sheila said.

"I knows that," the old man said softly. "But it don' matter. I ain' comin' - not today, not tomorrow. Maybe not ever."

"What?"

"This is *my* dream," he said. "This is my place. Fo' the firs' time in...I don' know how long, I feels at home. I feels good. And I don't feels like leavin'."

"But Malcolm, what are you going to do for money?"

"And food, and a place to stay?"

"I' get by. I always does."

"Come on now, Malcolm. I know this dream stuff is some really amazing shit, but...live here?" Wyatt asked.

"Dis is my home. I knows that now."

"But...

Just then the last seat was filled by a grotesquely overweight woman wrapped from head to toe in spectacularly colorful hand-dyed cloth. The van literally sagged to the right.

"Malcolm!" Sheila called out. Ignoring the revving engine, she jumped out of her seat and gave the old man a big hug and a kiss. Wyatt slid out behind her, the conductor yelling wildly in his strange language, and shook the old man's hand.

"You take care of yourself," he said, fighting back a sudden lump in his throat.

"You too," Malcolm said. He glanced over at Sheila, who wiped away a tear. "I thinks you'll do all right."

Wyatt dug into his pocket and pulled out the last of their money. He handed it to the old man. "Here. This should hold you for a little while."

The old man didn't look down, but took the money and slipped it into his pocket. "Thanks, man. Don' take any wooden naira."

Just then the young conductor, his patience at an end, literally grabbed Wyatt and Sheila by the shoulders and dragged them back into the van.

"Goodbye, Malcolm!" Sheila called out as the van labored away from the dusty turn-out.

"The Dream lives!" Wyatt yelled

The last they saw as the van sped away down the highway was the old man, surrounded by local villagers, waving slowly.

*****

Wyatt and Sheila didn't speak much during the long trip back to Lagos, each feeling the loss of their companion more than they had expected. Then too, each was lost in thoughts of where they had been, what they had seen, and what it all might mean. The roar of the engine and the howl of the wind made it difficult to hear, and so they were silent.

It was nearly nightfall by the time they arrived in Lagos. The van stopped at the big bus stop out near the airport, aswarm with people headed every which way; they were prepared to hop out and make their way out to the islands however they could, but to their surprise and relief the conductor signaled for them to stay put as the van started up again and continued on through the mainland, across the third mainland bridge, and cruised on into Ikoyi, arriving just at sunset. With their last five naira they even persuaded the driver to drop them in front of the Ikoyi Hotel, a landmark Wyatt remembered from their previous visit.

From there it was less than a mile to their ultimate destination. When they got to the wrought-iron gate they told the guard who they hoped to see, and he buzzed the home on the intercom.

"Sheila and White here to see you, sir," the guard intoned.

"That's 'Wyatt'," the young man corrected.

"Yes?" the guard said, ignoring him completely.

In just minutes the familiar figure of the RSO came strolling out to the gate.

"Well, well, well. So, you're still both alive, huh? What happened to Malcolm?"

"He decided to stay up in Oshogbo," Wyatt said.

"You mean permanently?" Wolf was visibly shocked.

"Looks that way," Sheila said. "Says he's found himself."

"Sounds like he's lost his mind. And what about you two - going to make Lagos your home?"

"Not a chance in the world," Wyatt said. "In fact, as soon as we can make some reservations we're headed back home."

"What's the matter - didn't find your dream world?"

"We found it, all right," Sheila said. "But inside, not outside."

"Oh?" the RSO asked, his eyebrows knit in consternation. "What exactly does that mean?"

"Let's just say we're glad we came," Sheila said.

"If you say so. Where you staying?"

"Nowhere yet," Wyatt explained. "We just got in this minute."

"Yeh? Well the Ikoyi Hotel's not bad. Close by and cheap."

"I think we saw it on the way in," Wyatt stalled.

Sheila was more to the point. "Actually, we're a little short on money..."

"William Wolf! You bring those two kids in here right this minute!" a familiar voice ordered over the intercom.

"Sounds like you've been invited to spend the night," the RSO said with a sheepish grin.

"We don't want to impose," Sheila began. Wyatt rolled his eyes.

"Apparently there's a difference of opinion on that score," Wolf said. "Anyway, it doesn't matter. The Missus has ruled. Come on - let's get in before some malaria-ridden mosquito decides to feast on the two of you."

The gate swung open and the two travelers followed their host through the compound to the familiar two-story townhouse. Mrs. Wolf was waiting for them at the door.

"You don't know how glad I am to see you two again," she began as they came through the garden gate and up the front walk. "I've been worried sick that something was going to happen to you. Where's Malcolm? Isn't he with you?"

"He decided to stay in Oshogbo."

"What? Why?"

And so they explained the whole incredible trip, sipping soda and beer and munching on stale Lays potato chips while waiting for the cook to finish with the dinner preparations. Both Wolfs interrupted frequently at first with questions and comments, but as the story unfolded they sat in complete silence, dumbfounded.

"You know that all this sounds completely wack-o," the RSO said when they'd finished. "You two haven't been smoking any of that Oshogbo Gold, have you?"

But Sheila and Wyatt defended their tale with such earnest passion that neither of their hosts took exception. They didn't believe them exactly, but they didn't question their story any further. As the conversation lagged, Bill arranged for them to speak with a travel agent who made reservations for their flight back to the States.

By the time dinner was finished and they'd polished off a couple of after dinner liqueurs, Wyatt and Sheila were in no condition to continue the conversation. One look at their drooping eyelids and nodding heads gave Lynn Wolf all the justification she needed to order them up to the guest bedroom. They didn't resist.

"We're sorry to be such lame guests," Wyatt said. "But we've had a pretty tiring past few days."

"That, is an understatement," Lynn said, guiding the two by their shoulders up the stairs.

"What time do you want to get up in the morning?" Bill called after them.

"How about three or four in the afternoon?" Wyatt's drowsy voice answered from the top of the staircase. He was only half-joking.

"How about we just let you sleep until you wake up," Wolf said. "You're booked on the 8 o'clock B.A. flight, right?"

"That's right."

"Well, I'll have our travel office reconfirm the two of you in the morning. And you should get out to the airport no later than 6. You've seen how things function out there - to use the term generously."

"Okay. Thanks," a voice croaked back. Wolf wasn't sure if it was Wyatt or Sheila.

The RSO straightened up the living room until his wife came back down from putting her charges to bed. He followed as she went straight into the kitchen to clean up.

"Pretty incredible story, huh?" he asked as handed her some glasses to load into the dishwasher.

"Pretty incredible," she agreed. "Only thing is, I believe them."

"You believe all that crap about visions and drums and all that?"

"I know it sounds impossible, but somehow I think they're telling the truth. There's something about the two of them...something different from when they were here before."

The RSO laughed and shook his head.

"What? You don't believe them?" his wife asked.

"Actually, I noticed the same thing. I thought I was going nuts."

Lynn slipped her arm around his waist. "Well that's been happening for years now. You can't blame that one on them."

"No? Then that only leaves you..."

They looked into each other's eyes with the unspoken communication of long-time partners and kissed.

"I think that's the end of cleanup for tonight," Wolf said, leading his wife by the hand to the stairway. "The maid can get the rest in the morning."

And she did.

CHAPTER TWENTY-THREE

True to their word, Wyatt and Sheila slept straight through the morning. Their sleep, unburdened by the recurring Dream, was for the first time in months completely restful. It was close to one in the afternoon when they finally got up, and close to two by the time they'd eaten breakfast. Tipped by the maid to their stirrings, Lynn called soon after they came downstairs and reiterated her offer of the run of the house.

After breakfast Wyatt and Sheila ventured outside for a short walk, but they did not go out beyond the compound gate. They both felt that they'd been impossibly lucky to have survived their many brushes with disaster and didn't want to press their luck with departure so close at hand. They chatted with the guard for a while, staring out through the gate bars at the seemingly gentile suburban life that passed slowly by, explaining what had transpired over the past several days. To their surprise, he wasn't surprised.

"African magic very strong," he said. "Change your life."

"That's for sure," Wyatt said fervently. The guard nodded absently.

They exchanged a few other pleasantries with the bored gatekeeper and then took a stroll around the enclosure, checking out the gardens that a few ambitious embassy families had nourished - with the help of a local gardener - and marveling at the unusual flora and fauna. As the afternoon shadows grew longer a huge fruit bat crisscrossed the tops of the banana trees before deciding that it was too early for dining; it disappeared back into the blue-gray sky.

Before long it was time to pack for the trip home. Perhaps a few minutes earlier than was necessary they went back into the townhouse and stuffed their meager belongings into their now well-worn packs and deposited everything next to the front door. Bill Wolf had explained that he'd come pick them up at five in an armored embassy van to take them out to the airport.

"Just a precaution," he'd reassured them.

"Right," was Wyatt's only comment.

At five of five the gate creaked open and the heavy rumble of the lightly armored van announced their hosts' arrival. Lynn Wolf led her husband into the townhouse.

"All set?" she asked as soon as she stepped through the door.

"Ready as we'll ever be, I guess," Sheila said, depositing the dishes from a last-minute snack into the kitchen.

"And that's very ready," Wyatt added.

"I bet you are. Let's get you out to the airport then."

The two travelers said goodbye to the Wolf's maid and marched out to the waiting car. Somehow it seemed reassuring to get into the huge white vehicle, even if it did stand out among the tiny Euro-cars and motorbikes like a sore thumb. When the small talk of how everyone's day had gone stalled just minutes into the drive, the RSO tried to liven things up by explaining how just a few months earlier a vehicle identical to that one had been attacked in a go-slow, the passengers robbed and slashed on their way to the airport.

"Just trying to cheer us up?" Wyatt asked.

"Oh Bill, you always do this," Lynn chastised.

"Nothing to worry about. I wasn't with that trip," Wolf said cheerfully.

"Reassuring," Wyatt whispered to Sheila.

The Wolfs continued a stream of embassy reception chatter as they drove, varied enough to keep up interest, but light enough not to require thought. Wyatt and Sheila mostly listened, chipping in with the occasional grunt or exclamation as called for.

As the vehicle wound its way out of the run-down gentility of the residential islands, moved through the abject poverty and concrete block sameness of the inner city, and then headed out across the technologically impressive but already pot-holed and disintegrating Mainland Bridge, Sheila found herself moved by a completely unexpected surge of emotion. At a break in the Wolfs' tag-team monologue Wyatt commented on her silent attentiveness to the passing cityscape.

"You're awfully quiet," he said. "What are you so deep in thought about?"

She looked back at him, a wan smile on her lips. "You're going to think I'm crazy."

"That's a given," he said. "So?"

"In a way, I'm going to miss this place."

Wyatt shook his head as if to clear his ears. "They can't stop her from leaving by reason of insanity, can they?" he asked Wolf.

"Hell, if that was a reason for stopping travelers, half the embassy staff would never leave this place."

"I'm serious," Sheila insisted. "I know there's a lot that's awful here, with all the poverty, and the crowding..."

"And the con artists, and the sixty-seven flavors of insect borne diseases," Wyatt added.

"But despite all that, there's something here. An energy. A spirit, maybe."

"The ghost of honesty past?"

She gave him a look of pure disappointment. His wise-ass smile shriveled and disappeared.

"Of real life. Not the polished and deodorized fakeness of modern existence. These people have to scratch so hard to survive, I think they understand what life really is better than we do."

There was an awkward silence before Lynn spoke up.

"I don't think I've ever heard anyone put it quite like that before," she said. "But now that you have, I think you have a point."

"I don't know," the RSO said. "It's awfully hard to see the flowers for the thorns."

"But they're there!" Sheila said. "You can't help but feel it. Even here in Lagos. Although I'd have to admit that it's a lot easier to get the real sense of the place outside this awful city."

Wyatt sighed. "You know, I must be losing it. I think I understand what you're getting at."

"Sounds like love to me," Lynn said.

"Is that what it is?" Sheila asked, her tone suddenly much softer.

"That, or temporary insanity."

Lynn didn't look around fast enough to see what prompted Wyatt's groan of pain.

Light banter carried the foursome the rest of the way through heavy late-afternoon traffic to Murtala Mohammad Airport. All the street vendors, the beggars, the bizarre driving, all the characteristic trademarks of Lagos which had seemed so alien and threatening, now seemed merely insane. Even the go-slows were less egregious than some of the no-goes they'd seen before. It was as if Lagos was putting on its best face for their departure, or perhaps they had just acclimated to the different pace of life. At least from the safety of their armored vehicle.

Unfortunately, the airport was no different than when they'd arrived. A fist fight broke out the moment they pulled up at the departure terminal as two completely unofficial porters jockeyed for position to have first dibs at purloining their luggage. More accurately, an almost-fight ensued, as the two young men squared off, yelled at each other, feinted two or three times and then noticed that a third porter had sneaked in while they jawed at each other and was wheeling the luggage into the terminal. They made as if to pursue and harass their dishonorable brethren, but one look from the RSO quickly sent them back to their carts muttering in pidgin.

Wolf lent his fame and the embassy's prestige to the task of checking his two guests in at the airline counter, managing to browbeat the airport manager into upgrading their seats to business class. Then it was off to customs and immigration, where Wyatt was caught completely unawares with a demand for $20 per person in departure tax.

"Uh, you couldn't loan us a few bucks, could you?" he asked Wolf, his sheepish look an honest expression of his embarrassment.

"I think that could be arranged," the teddy-bearish Wolf said, reaching into his pocket. "What do you need - ten?"

Wyatt shook his head.

"Twenty?"

Wyatt silently signaled no once again.

"Okay, I give. Two Thousand? A Maserati and a home on the Riviera? What do you need?!"

"We're broke," Sheila said. "We gave our last money to Malcolm. Didn't think we'd need it."

"Here, here's fifty," the RSO said, handing her the money. "Send me a check when you can."

"Oh thank you," Sheila said, hugging the blushing Wolf around the neck.

"Hey, that's my money too, you know," Lynn said.

Wyatt gave her a kiss on the cheek. "Not bad," she said. "We can negotiate the interest payments at a later date."

"Better have a lawyer with you," Bill said. Lynn eyed him with a glare fit to kill.

"I'm sure it'll be worth it, whatever it is," Wyatt said. "So, where to next?"

"For you it's straight over there to the right and straight on out to the gate. For us, it's hasta la bye-bye."

"You're not coming to the gate?" Sheila asked.

"The Nigerians won't let us. They're afraid we'll compromise their air-tight security. Besides, I think you can make it all by yourselves at this point. Just keep your hands on your wallets, passports and tickets at all times and don't let your luggage out of your sight."

"Bill! You're going to scare them!" Lynn complained.

"Better that than have to lend them enough money for another ticket. So, bon voyage, write when the spirit moves you, and pray for us."

Everyone exchanged hugs and handshakes. With a last wave goodbye the two young travelers passed through the final customs gate and headed down the semi-modern terminal walkway toward their gate. Just fifty yards or so along their path they came to a double doorway with a long collapsible card table sitting alongside. As they approached, the man and woman behind the table looked up with a bored indifference that Wyatt and Sheila had already come to expect from Nigerian public officials.☐

"Just here to wish us bon voyage?" Wyatt whispered.

Sheila was already digging for her tickets and passport. "Somehow I don't think so."

The man, dressed in civilian clothes that looked as if they'd been slept in, raised his hand when they were still a few steps away.

"Your tickets and boarding pass," he said officiously.

Sheila and Wyatt complied immediately and handed the ticket folders to the man, who handed them to the woman. She opened them up, glanced inside and then closed them again. Instead of passing them back, however, she held them in her hand and looked up at the two anxious passengers-to-be. And then she smiled.

'Uh oh,' Wyatt thought. 'Now we're really in trouble.'

"Something for dinner?" the woman asked, implicitly linking the return of their tickets to a contribution to her dinner fund.

Acting instinctively, and angrily, Wyatt reached down, grabbed their tickets from the stunned woman, and then with a voice as sweet as pounded yam pie said, "No thank you. We've already eaten."

Sheila would have been left standing at the doorway with her mouth hanging open if Wyatt had not grabbed her by the arm and dragged her along with him.

As it was, a few seconds later when the duo turned the corner toward the security check they chanced a quick glance back toward the folding table, where both ticket inspectors where staring after them with a look as if they'd been struck between the eyes with a two by four.

"I can't believe you did that!" Sheila squealed excitedly.

"I've made my last involuntary contribution to these people," he said, not breaking stride. "They can find their own dinner money."

But almost before he'd gotten the words out of his mouth another airport employee, also un-uniformed, raised his hand to direct them to another folding table.

"Your luggage, please," the man said civilly.

"What is this? Luggage tag examination?" Wyatt asked.

"Security," the man said evenly. They handed him the bags. Quickly, and surprisingly thoroughly, the man went through the two packs looking for who knew what; closing them carefully, he handed them back to the two travelers.

"Thank you. You can go through the detectors now. Please put the packs on the conveyer belt." He smiled and then jotted something on a piece of paper.

"Is that all?" Wyatt asked.

"Yes. You may go now."

Wyatt reached into his pocket and pulled out a dollar bill. He handed it to the surprised official.

"Thank you," Wyatt said

The official looked puzzled. "That is not necessary," he said.

"I know," Wyatt retorted. "That's why I'm giving it to you."

The man shrugged, looked around surreptitiously, and took the tip. "Thank you. Have a good flight."

"We will," Wyatt said. "By the way, you're doing a great job."

They crossed to the conveyers and put their packs flat on the belt as directed. Then they walked through the large metal detector door frames. On the other side of the detectors a man with a small hand-held device asked Wyatt to raise his hands while he efficiently swept his clothing for any proscribed possessions; a young woman did the same to Sheila. Then they were allowed to take their packs off the conveyer.

"Maybe we've been too hard on these people," Sheila said softly as she threw her pack over one shoulder.

"Maybe," Wyatt said. "Then again..." He nodded toward the x-ray screen next to the conveyer. A uniformed man sat there, seemingly staring at the screen, but it wasn't illuminated.

"Makes me feel safer already," Sheila said.

Since the traffic had been much lighter than anticipated they'd arrived well over an hour early and were among the first to get to the gate for their flight. At the entry to the waiting lounge another security person swept their bodies and searched their belongings again before they were allowed to enter. They settled down in the typical, impossibly uncomfortable injection-molded plastic seats that were probably designed by some famous Scandinavian and had no doubt been featured in the Museum of Modern Art in New York, and were reading some magazines they'd borrowed from the Wolfs, when a small commotion at the lounge entrance caught their attention. They looked up to see a regal-looking African man in a richly textured gold African costume sweep into the lounge accompanied by three lovely young women, all dressed similarly.

Sheila was about to ask Wyatt what sort of eminence this person might be when the entourage swept across the lounge and stopped right in front of them. The man pressed his hands together in front of him, bowed, and then opened his palms, face up. The three women, standing just behind him, all in a row, emulated his greeting. But it wasn't until the man actually opened his mouth that they realized who he was.□

"Jus' wanted to say goodbye," the regal African said.

"Malcolm!" Sheila screamed. Several security people glanced briefly at the odd assemblage, nearly roused to consciousness by the noise.

Wyatt stood and eyed his old companion appraisingly. Not only was he beautifully clothed, but he'd shaved, someone had cut his hair, and he seemed a good ten years younger than when they'd last seen him.

"What is all this?" Wyatt asked.

"You look fantastic!" Sheila bubbled.

"Jus' like in the dream," the not so old man said. "I seen it, and now here it be."

Malcolm explained that when he left them at the Oshogbo bus stop he'd had no idea of what he was going to do next. But while he was standing there, feeling a bit lost, a young girl, no more than eight, had suddenly appeared out of nowhere and asked him to follow her.

"Didn' have nothin' better to do," he said with a smile. "So I went with her."

She led him through the streets and back alleys of Oshogbo, taking him at last to a large, reddish-brown, African rococo mud building that stood apart from a poor neighborhood at the outskirts of the city.

"I was thinkin' it was some kind of brothel," the old man said with a wicked grin. "But it was sumthin' even better."

As it turned out, it was a temple, a place of meditation and spiritual healing of a group calling itself African Consciousness.

"These here three lovely sister they clean me up," Malcolm explained further, "shave my scraggly ol' beard, cut my hair, even gives me a bath. Might say they take care of all my needs." Wyatt was tempted to ask the extent of those needs, but he held his tongue. His thoughts were not so easily silenced. *'Maybe that's why he looks so young,'* he mused, surreptitiously eyeing the three beaming maidens.

Sheila's questions were more pertinent. "Who runs the temple, Malcolm? What exactly do they do there?" There was a sense of almost motherly concern in her voice.

"Well," Malcolm began, searching for the words, when one of the young women stepped forward to bail him out.

"African Consciousness is a union of like-thinking men and women who wish to foster the inherent, forgotten, powerful consciousness of native Africans," she said in a clipped English accent.

"Wherever they may now reside," another added.

"It is not run by any one person," the third contributed. "But by the Council of Ten - an elected council, may I add."

The polished presentation surprised Wyatt and Sheila, and their shock must have registered on their faces.

"Pretty damn slick, ain't they?" the old man said.

"Pretty slick indeed," Wyatt mused. "Do you have...religious ceremonies?" he asked.

"Not as you might think of them," the first young woman answered. "We meditate, we discuss, but mostly we educate and help our brothers and sisters to first survive, then succeed, and finally transcend. The program is based on the teachings of Ree Walli Mustafa."

Wyatt's eyelids flew open like cheap window shades.

He turned to Sheila, who turned back to him at exactly the same moment. "Walli!" they said in unison.

"This is really too weird," Wyatt said, shaking his head.

"Definitely strange," Sheila said.

"When you 'sperience someone else's reality, it be strange," Malcolm said.

"You're really getting into this, aren't you?" Wyatt asked.

"It is getting into him," the first of the young women said.

Wyatt and Sheila looked at each other with a shake of the head.

Just then the mass of passengers waiting to board the flight began to scurry from their seats toward the gate.

"Do you think this means something?" Sheila asked, grabbing the strap to her backpack.

"It mean it time to say goodbye," Malcolm said.

Sheila looked questioningly into his eyes. "You sure you want to stay here?" she asked.

"You kidding?" Wyatt said looking at the old man's three attractive young companions. "I'm wondering why I'm leaving."

Sheila grabbed an earlobe.

"Ow! Just kidding, just kidding!" Wyatt said, throwing up his hands in surrender.

"You better be," Sheila said, her mock growl fully believable.

"I am where I got to be," Malcolm interrupted. "I knows that as sure as I knows anything."

"Well, good luck to you, old friend," Wyatt said, shaking his hand. "What a long, strange trip it's been."

"It ain't over yet."

"No, I suppose not."

Sheila looked as if she might cry as she threw her arms around the old man's shoulders and gave him a big hug. "We're going to miss you," she said.

"And I gonna miss you'all too. Now go on and get goin' before you misses yo' plane."

She gave him a big kiss on the cheek and then turned to the three young women. "You take good care of him, you hear?"

"He is our brother come back to us. He will be venerated," the most outgoing of the three said. "We wish you a safe journey."

By this time the line had begun to disappear down the boarding ramp and there wasn't anything left to say.

"Will you write?" Sheila called back to the old man, as Wyatt led her by the arm toward the gate.

Malcolm waved and smiled, committing to nothing.

By the time they got to the plane most everyone had already boarded. There was one Nigerian engaged in a furious discussion with the flight crew just outside the door, but the two Americans nonchalantly slipped around the rowdy scene to make their way to their seats. A blandly pleasant attendant pointed out the section of the 747 where they would be sitting, but declined to show them to their seats, opting instead to linger by the door to catch the last of the verbal fisticuffs.

When they got to their seats they found a Nigerian couple, dashing in their national costumes, already seated and completely unwilling to consider that they might have made a mistake. An attendant, who managed to tear herself away from the still-ongoing debate with the would-be passenger at the door, came over to see what was causing the discussion and immediately chose to transcend, rather than solve, the entire problem.

"Come with me; we'll find you some seats," she directed Wyatt and Sheila.

"But, these are our seats!" Wyatt protested, looking back longingly at the bulk-head Bill Wolf had so cleverly reserved.

The attendant did not even hesitate. With no other avenue open to them, the American duo followed her through the entire length of the crowded business section.

"Where is she going, the rest room?" Wyatt asked after moving through what seemed like a football field full of occupied seats.

But when the attendant finally stopped, she indicated with a regal sweep of her hand that two huge, fluffy, footrest-outfitted first class seats were at their command. "For your trouble," she announced with a wink.

Sheila was speechless - almost. "Thanks," she managed to mumble as the attendant swept back into the body of the plane to deal with some minor dilemma. Wyatt glanced down at the seats and then back at Sheila.

"Nice bathroom," he said.

"I feel like Queen for a Day."

Wyatt bowed and ushered Sheila into her seat. "Your Highness - after you."

It took a while for the argument at the door of the plane to be settled, and then a while for the attendants to get all the carry-on luggage stowed, and then another while to demonstrate the safety features of the plane to 300 equally inattentive passengers, but finally, about 45 minutes late, the plane taxied away from the gate and out toward the runway. Wyatt had settled down into his seat, headphones on, music cranked loud enough that Sheila was moved to ask him to turn it down. The pilot cut into the program to welcome everyone and spew a litany of altitudes, speeds and times that everyone ignored as thoroughly as the safety info. The music had just come back on when a tug on his arm roused Wyatt from his music-induced stupor. Sheila was motioning for him to remove the headphones.

"What's up?" he asked, obliging her.

"I just remembered," she said excitedly, "there weren't any huts!"

Wyatt looked at her closely. "I'd say there's been some serious brain damage here."

"In my dream! Of the wedding?"

A flicker of understanding lit up his eyes.

"There weren't any huts! Just African costumes, so I assumed it was the village. But it can be anywhere - like back home!"

Wyatt couldn't believe what he was hearing. "You want African costumes at our wedding?"

"That's what the dream says."

Wyatt shook his head and sighed. "Well far be it for me to contravene the dream. African costumes it is. Anything else?

She took his hand. "Have I told you lately that I love you?"

"Not in the past five minutes."

"Well I do."

"Glad to hear it. Wouldn't want to think I was the only one who'd gone off the deep end."

They kissed as the plane bounced along the pot-holed taxiway. When they pulled apart they smiled silly lovesick smiles.

"Let me know when you want to remind me again," Wyatt finally said, kissing her again quickly before slipping the headphones back on.

Sheila ran her fingers idly through his hair as she stared out the window at the scenery rolling by. It didn't seem possible that they were really going to leave.

Suddenly Wyatt felt her tugging at his arm again, shouting something he couldn't quite understand. Prepared to be vexed, he pulled off the headset.

"Look! Look! It's him!"

"It's who?" he asked, leaning across her body to follow her pointing finger out the window.

There, on the rooftop of the airport terminal, standing all alone, he saw a familiar white-robed figure, his gown whipping in the hot evening breeze.

"I don't believe it!" he said.

Sheila waved frantically at the distant figure, but he either didn't see or chose not to respond. Until, that is, the plane had come to a stop on the runway and the jet engines began to roar for take-off. Then, in a single, practiced, elegant move, the figure pressed his two palms together, bowed and then opened them in front of him. At that precise moment the plane lurched forward and raced down the runway, leaving the terminal far behind. Sheila stretched her neck to look back as long as possible, but in seconds he, and the terminal were long gone.

As they soared into the air, the plane banked sharply and the terminal came once again into view. But there was no white-robed figure visible on the roof, or anywhere else.

"It was him. I know it," Sheila said softly.

"I wouldn't be surprised. Nothing about this trip surprises me anymore," Wyatt said, slipping the headphones back on.

He was, in fact, amazed, but he decided it was time to get back into his own reality and let the magical reality of the past few days go its own way. He flipped the tuning dial and found a channel playing some evocative African music that reminded him immediately of the village and Malcolm and the guide and the dream. Part of him was tempted to just flip the dial, change the channel, rid himself of the memory. But part of him was held mesmerized, and he listened as rhythmic drums swept into the music, calling out to him.

Just then the attendant came down the aisle. Wyatt reached out and grabbed her arm.

"Do you know where I could get this music?" he asked. "I'd like to buy a CD."

A curious look crept across the attendant's face. "Oh? On what channel?"

Wyatt bent down and inspected the dial. "Channel...13."

The surprise changed to skepticism. "We don't have any music on Channel 13," she said bluntly. "That must be your own music."

She didn't wait to hear more, and, in truth, Wyatt didn't know what else to say. And so he eased back in his seat, cranked up the volume, and reached out for Sheila's hand. He took it gently in his own, so involved in the music, his eyes closed, his head bobbing to the rhythm, that he didn't see her loving smile in return.

Wyatt knew where the music came from, but he didn't care. It was good music, and he hoped it would be with them always.